Emma Lee-Potter spent ten years as a journalist on the *Evening Standard, Sunday Express* and *Today*. She is now a freelance magazine writer and lives in Oxfordshire with her husband and two children. She is the author of *Hard Copy* and *Moving On*, also published by Piatkus Books.

Also by Emma Lee-Potter

Hard Copy
Moving On

Taking Sides

Emma Lee-Potter

PIATKUS

✦ Visit the Piatkus website! ✦

Piatkus publishes a wide range of exciting fiction and
non-fiction, including books on health, mind body & spirit,
sex, self-help, cookery, biography and the paranormal.

If you want to:

- read descriptions of our popular titles
- buy our books over the internet
- take advantage of our special offers
- enter our monthly competition
- learn more about your favourite Piatkus authors

visit our website at:

www.piatkus.co.uk

Copyright © 2002 by Emma Lee-Potter

First published in Great Britain in 2002 by
Judy Piatkus (Publishers) Ltd
5 Windmill Street, London W1T 2JA
email: info@piatkus.co.uk

This edition published 2002

The moral right of the author has been asserted

A catalogue record for this book is available from the British Library

ISBN 0 7499 3309 7

Set in Palatino by Palimpsest Book Production Limited,
Polmont, Stirlingshire

Printed and bound in Great Britain by
Mackays of Chatham Ltd, Chatham, Kent

With very special thanks to everyone at Piatkus, especially Judy Piatkus, Gillian Green and Jana Sommerlad, and to my agent Jane Judd, for all their encouragement and support. Thank you, too, to my friends Susan Desmond, Susie Wessely, Angela Dowson, Sam Pritchard and Alex Lester – I'd never have finished the book without them. And as always, a huge hug for Adam, Lottie and Ned for putting up with me while I wrote it.

For my mother

Chapter One

A shiver ran down Juliette's spine as she slammed the door of her clapped-out Golf. Her body felt like ice, though whether this was due to the autumnal chill that hung in the air, or apprehension about the day ahead, she wasn't entirely sure.

'Come on Mummy,' shouted a cheery voice from the back seat. 'We haven't got all day, y'know.'

Glancing in the rear view mirror, Juliette grinned. Freddie was just six years old, yet he could always be relied upon to lighten the atmosphere. She only had to look at his mop of untidy chestnut hair and his broad smile and her heart turned over with love.

'Right Freddie-boy,' she yelled, turning the key in the ignition. 'Let's hit the road.'

For one excruciating moment there was silence. Neither of them, not even Freddie, uttered a word. Bloody hell, groaned Juliette. This was all she needed. Today was Freddie's first day at his new school and *her* first day in her new job. She had to be at the *Evening Eagle* in Bowater for nine.

Juliette wrenched the key from the ignition. She took a deep breath, counted to ten, then tried it again. And again. Fourth time round, the car spluttered feebly into action and Juliette and Freddie both shouted 'hooray' in unison.

If she hadn't been so pressed for time – and terrified that the car was going to die on her – Juliette might have enjoyed the drive more. The tiny whitewashed cottage that had been home for the past eleven days stood halfway up a wooded valley, a mile outside the tiny village of Newdale. It was the end house in a long terrace and you could walk straight out of the garden gate and onto the fells. On a clear day, Juliette could stand in the kitchen and make out the tiny matchstick figures of walkers striding along the top of Miston Moor.

It was so different from the busy South London street that she and Freddie had left behind. Down there, the pavements were covered in dog shit and litter, there was a constant roar of traffic and they'd had no view to speak of. In any case, the crime rate was so high that Juliette had had to get security bars fixed across all the ground floor windows in a bid to keep the burglars out. It hadn't worked, of course. When the house was broken into for the third time in as many months and her brand new company car got vandalised by a bunch of petty thieves she'd gone ballistic. She'd declared that enough was enough. She was through with London.

Call her stupid, but she'd blithely assumed that Joe would be in total agreement. She'd lost count of the numerous times that her husband had come storming through the door shouting that London was the pits and what the hell were they doing there. A couple of years back he'd even got as far as applying for an announcer's job on a tiny TV station in North Wales. To be fair, it was Juliette who had chickened out that time. Freddie had just started primary school, and she had only been features editor on the *Daily News* for a couple of months. It was the biggest break of her entire career, she'd told Joe, and she was sorry, but she wasn't moving.

Two years on, however, Juliette's attachment to her job

had waned. Running the features desk hadn't turned out to be much fun after all. It was well paid and prestigious, admittedly, but her hours were horrendous. The editor was a madman who got his kicks from throwing every feature out of the paper at six pm each night and starting all over again from scratch an hour before the paper went to press. Not only that, but Juliette had missed writing more than she ever would have imagined. The novelty of rewriting other people's copy had soon worn off and she'd grown sick and tired of commissioning freelances to cover stories she could do far better herself.

Worst of all was the effect that her new job had had on her relationship with Freddie. For two whole years she'd barely set eyes on her son during the week. Joe always dropped him off at school in the mornings because she had to leave for work so early. And Joe collected him from the childminder at the end of the day. He was usually reading Freddie his bedtime story by the time Juliette staggered grey-faced through the front door. The pair of them barely had time to exchange a couple of words before Joe had to leave for work himself. He was a DJ and presented the graveyard midnight till two am show on a middle-ranking commercial radio station.

But it wasn't until Juliette missed Freddie's sports day for the second year in succession that the shortcomings of their set-up hit home with a vengeance.

She'd meant to get there, she really had, but at the last minute one of the showbiz team had got wind of some crazy young rock star's antics at an awards ceremony. Outraged at losing out to a rival, the word was that he'd had to be forcibly restrained from beating his manager to a pulp. The editor had demanded Juliette drop everything instantly and produce a thousand words of golden prose about 'rock and the price of fame'. 'Sorry. Can't make it. Explain to Freddie,' she'd shrieked down

3

the phone at Joe and like a woman possessed had begun ringing round all her most reliable pop contacts.

The most galling part of the whole episode was that in the end the pop star had threatened 'the biggest libel action of all time' if they ran the story. And terrified of a crippling lawsuit, the *Daily News* had only carried a couple of incomprehensible paragraphs. Sitting on the tube to work the next day – her bloody company car was still at the garage being fixed – Juliette had thumbed the pages over and over again in disbelief. She'd missed Freddie's moment of triumph in the egg and spoon race. And for what? For some pathetic editor to lose his nerve and drop her feature in favour of a load of right-wing twaddle about bringing back military service.

That was in June and now here she was, three months on, embarking on a completely new life. In the process, she'd thrown up her house, her Fleet Street salary, and the thing that was really bugging her, maybe her marriage.

It was a fraction past eight-thirty by the time Juliette braked sharply and pulled up outside Newdale County Primary School.

Considering that Newdale's main street was one of the prettiest in the area, the school was a blot on the landscape. A shabby modern building, with two tumble-down portable classrooms and a huge pile of cardboard boxes dumped in the playground, it had clearly seen better days.

The place looked deserted too, apart from a couple of middle-aged women gossiping outside the school gate. They broke off from their conversation to stare at Juliette and Freddie clambering out of the car. As Juliette met their gaze, she suddenly felt intensely aware of how ridiculously *London* she looked in her short skirt, scarlet jacket and high shoes. The two women at the gate wore jeans and waterproof anoraks and neither of them had

4

a scrap of make-up on. Juliette was pretty sure that in their eyes she must resemble an alien from another planet who'd just landed in their midst.

'Who's that snotty cow then?' asked the hard-faced Carol Barker as she watched Juliette and Freddie disappear inside the school.

'Dunno her name, but she's from down south. There's talk that her husband's left her and she and the kid have moved into Dot Ryan's cottage up at New Bank,' said Norma Gray, the older of the pair.

'Poor old cow,' murmured Carol. Dot Ryan had lived at New Bank for fifty years. They both knew she'd still be there now if it wasn't for her arthritis and her gammy knee.

'Where's Dot ended up?' said Carol.

'I heard that the social have gone and shoved her in some old folks' home in Bowater,' said Norma. 'It'll kill her being stuck in town. She's Newdale born and bred.'

'Not like Snotty Face over there,' said Carol. 'She looks a right soft southerner, doesn't she? I bet she's never set foot outside Knightsbridge.'

The pair of them chuckled conspiratorially. They chatted outside the school virtually every morning during term-time. Carol was the school caretaker and finished her cleaning shift at eight-thirty. Norma was on her way in to do the school dinners. She had been the school cook for longer than she cared to remember, ever since her own children had been pupils there. Dawn and Ritchie were long gone now. Dawn had married a farmer and moved a couple of miles up the valley, while Ritchie . . . Norma's face clouded over. No. She couldn't face thinking about Ritchie. She didn't have a clue what she was going to do about him.

Norma was a good sort. She'd always prided herself on cooking a hearty home-made lunch for the youngsters who attended the school. But when the neighbouring schools at Wath End and Bowden had shut down a few years back, the Newdale school roll had swelled from thirty to ninety. And much to Norma's disgust, from that moment on, the school dinners had been delivered to Newdale in a van each morning, pre-packed in tin foil. All Norma had to do was warm the food through and dish it up to the children. To add insult to injury, it was nothing like the wholesome hot pot and Cumberland sausage that she'd favoured. These days it was all pizzas and hamburgers, chicken nuggets and oven-ready chips. No wonder half the children looked so skinny and under-nourished.

Inside the school, Juliette and Freddie were trying to find a teacher. As they clattered hand in hand down the bare corridor, peeping into each of the classes in turn, Juliette wondered why the place was so silent. It was the first day of term – she would have expected it to be bustling with activity. What the hell was she going to do if she'd cocked the date up? Take Freddie with her to the *Eagle*, she supposed. That would go down fantastically well with her new boss.

At the end of the corridor was a door marked 'Staff Only'. Juliette paid no attention to this and walked straight in.

There was a sharp intake of breath at her unscheduled entrance from the four women poring over a sheaf of papers on the table.

'I'm terribly sorry but we're in the middle of a staff meeting,' said the oldest of them, jumping to her feet. 'It's not your fault – you're obviously new – but children aren't allowed into school until eight-forty-five. Unless there's an emergency of course.'

Juliette gazed back at her with interest. Presumably this tall, gangly woman with round spectacles, dangly earrings and slightly hippyish-looking clothes must be Mrs Gyngell, the head teacher. They'd spoken at length on the telephone and the woman had been helpful and warm. Now her tone seemed icier than Siberia.

'I'm afraid I didn't know,' apologised Juliette, summoning up all her charm. 'It's Freddie's first day here and I terribly wanted to get him settled before I go off to work.'

She smiled awkwardly before adding: 'He's only six and he doesn't know a soul in Newdale.'

All at once Mrs Gyngell seemed visibly to relax.

'Of course,' she murmured. 'Poor little fellow. It's not your fault, is it? He's in your class, Joanna, isn't he? Can you see to him?'

A slim young woman in black trousers and a bright pink cardigan edged with velvet ribbon got up from her chair and walked over to Freddie.

'I'm Mrs Booth,' she said, crouching down to Freddie's level so she could address him directly. 'Come along Freddie. Let's go and have a look at Class Two together, shall we? The walls are very bare at the moment but we're going to paint lots of great pictures to fill all that space. I'm sure you like painting, don't you?'

Freddie looked doubtful. He didn't mind some things about school – like football, PE and playing musical instruments (the louder the better) – but he loathed anything that remotely resembled work. Yuk. It made him feel sick to even think about it.

As she sped along the dual carriageway at eighty mph, Juliette couldn't get Freddie's lost-looking face out of her mind. Poor little boy. She'd been so convinced that she was doing the right thing getting him out of London and into the country. But now she wasn't so sure. And it was obvious he was missing Joe like mad . . .

Oh God, Joe. She banged her fist against her head in irritation. How could she have forgotten? It was his first morning at Radio Wave. His brand new job. The big break he'd been dreaming of for so long.

Juliette fiddled cackhandedly with the radio dial, trying to find Radio Wave with one hand while she steered with the other. The Lake District was all very well, she thought, but these bloody hills made the radio reception dire.

After struggling for several seconds, a muffled but very familiar voice boomed out of the car radio.

'. . . and this one's for my son Freddie. It's my first day on the breakfast show and his first day at his new school. We're both new boys. So, Freddie, keep your pecker up, son, and we'll talk later. Here's Van Morrison . . .'

At the sound of 'Precious Time' blaring out of the speakers, a lump formed in Juliette's throat. Joe didn't often mention anything personal on his shows these days. But 'Precious Time' was Freddie's favourite record ever. She'd lost count of the number of times she'd walked up the garden path in London to hear Van the Man's distinctive voice blasting out of the house. It was sometimes so loud that the neighbours used to hammer on the party wall in protest. She'd then stumble inside the house to find Freddie and Joe – completely oblivious to the racket they were making – jiving away on the sofa together.

And now she and Freddie were up here and Joe was down there. What was she thinking of? She'd fallen in love with the countryside around Newdale years ago after being sent to write a holiday piece about the northern Lakes. When the idea of getting out of grimy old London had first occurred to her, she'd been thinking of somewhere unadventurous like Kent or Gloucestershire. But then she'd spotted an ad for a cottage for rent in

Newdale in one of the Sunday papers and it had seemed meant. Now they were actually here however, it seemed mad and irresponsible.

And the big drawback of course was that Joe had gone and put his foot down. Refused to come. Said that he'd been waiting for the chance of his own breakfast show on a national station for his entire career and that he couldn't possibly turn it down now.

That row had been their most vitriolic in seven years of marriage. She shuddered even to think of it.

'It was fine when it was *me* who wanted to leave London and you didn't,' Joe had yelled, jabbing his finger in the air at her. 'You were desperate to take that crap features job on the *Daily News*. Remember? You never gave what me and Freddie wanted a second thought then.'

Juliette had exploded at this last accusation.

'Don't you dare bring Freddie into this,' she'd stormed. 'I only want what's best for him. It's taken me a bit of time to come round, I know, but I don't want him to grow up in London. I don't want him cooped up in a city all day long. I don't want him watching videos all day long and swapping Pokémon cards and dodging drug dealers at the school gates. I want him to be out in the fresh air. Walking and riding and making dens in the woods. We can't possibly give him that here.'

Joe's face had visibly softened at this. But he still wouldn't back down.

'If that's the way you feel, why don't we move to some-where like, oh, I don't know, Epsom? Or Guildford?'

'The suburbs, you mean,' sneered Juliette.

'All right then, you go up north,' said Joe a bit more gently. 'You and Freddie move up there. And I'll come at weekends.'

Juliette's eyes had widened in shock at this suggestion.

Did he want a separation or something? Had he found somebody else?

As if he could read her mind, Joe had taken her face in his hands and kissed her on the lips.

'It won't affect anything, you'll see,' he whispered. 'Loads of people live apart in the week and it works fine. Surely you can see that I've got to give this new show a go? I'll regret it for the rest of my life if I don't. I can always come and join you both in a few months time if it doesn't work out.'

And somehow, God knows why, Juliette had gone along with the idea. Before she knew it, she'd handed in her notice at the *News*, let the house and found a job on the *Evening Eagle* in Bowater. Joe had never once asked her to reconsider and although Freddie's lip had trembled at the prospect of only seeing his dad at weekends for the time being, he'd perked up at Juliette's promise that he might be able to have a puppy.

Listening to Joe burbling away on the radio now, Juliette felt oddly detached from him. He was good. He was very good. There was no doubt about that. He was bright and funny – and amazingly, he sounded like he didn't have a care in the world. You'd never imagine he was a man with a wife and child living three hundred miles away and a marriage teetering on the brink of survival.

Chapter Two

''Ere, where the 'ell do you think *you're* going?'

Striding through the shabby entrance hall of the *Eagle*, Juliette stopped dead in her tracks and turned to see who was bellowing at her.

Her eyes met those of a short, thickset man of indeterminate age, wearing a navy blue security guard's uniform and peaked cap. He seemed to have appeared from nowhere.

'I'm sorry, what did you . . . ?' she began.

'You haven't signed in at reception,' said the man. 'We don't just let anyone walk in off the street, y'know.'

Juliette pulled herself up to her full five feet five inches. With her heels to give her extra height, she towered over him.

'I think you'll find that I'm the new feature writer,' she said. Her tone was more imperious than she intended. 'And the editor's expecting me.'

'Makes no difference to me if you're the King of China,' said the man good-naturedly. 'You'll still have to sign in.'

'What?' said Juliette. 'Every morning?'

'That's right. Every morning. I like to keep tabs on people. I'm Stubby, by the way.'

Juliette groaned and followed Stubby back to reception. All she wanted to do was come in to work, do her job and get back home to Freddie again as fast as possible. No fuss. No hassle. Plain and simple.

She signed her name with a flourish and made a dash for the stairs before Stubby could collar her for anything else.

Sitting behind the desk, Stubby studied the fancy-looking scrawl with interest. 'Juliette Ward,' he read. 'Chief feature writer.' Chief feature writer indeed. The way things were going upstairs, he'd give her six months at the very most.

The *Evening Eagle* newsroom was on the first floor, overlooking the cattle market. Pausing in the doorway, Juliette breathed a sigh of relief when she saw it. Here, at least, she was on familiar territory. The *Eagle* newsroom was a lot smaller than she was used to, it was true, but the layout and the desks and the frantic, slightly deranged atmosphere were pretty much the same. And after the hostile glances she'd got in Newdale this morning, it felt like coming home.

She threaded her way through the maze of desks towards the editor's glass cubicle office. What was it about editors? They always had offices like goldfish bowls. Most of the time they kept their blinds *open* so everyone could see exactly what they were doing. And on the rare occasions when they were *drawn*, it was a dead giveaway that something was up.

As she approached Geoff Lake's door, one difference between the *Eagle* and the *Daily News* struck her forcibly. At the *News* she'd never managed to get past the editor's guard-like secretary without an advance appointment. Here, she knocked softly on the wide-open door and was beckoned in by Geoff Lake himself.

Juliette had met Geoff once before, at her interview. He was an ex-Fleet Street man himself and she'd taken an instant liking to his decisive, no-nonsense approach.

In turn, he had clearly been impressed by her cuttings file.

'There's no question that we'd welcome someone of your experience on to the staff with open arms,' he'd told her. 'What's more at issue is exactly what you'd like to do for us.'

Juliette had dropped her guard, confiding how desperate she was to move Freddie out of London and how much she missed writing. They'd struck a deal within five minutes. Juliette would get the new title of chief feature writer, a salary less than half she'd been paid in London ('. . . and I'll be pushing the boat out to give you that' said Geoff) and, he was making no promises, but he'd try and swing a four-day week. It was this last factor that made Juliette's mind up. A four-day week would mean she'd see far more of Freddie. And the pressure on the *Eagle* would be non-existent after the grief she'd had to put up with on the *News*.

'Juliette,' said Geoff now, running his hands through his greying hair. 'You're here at last. Look, I'm afraid I've got a bit of a crisis on. Management stuff and all that. I'm going to have to hand you straight over to Alex Davis.'

Juliette looked blank. Who the hell was Alex Davis when he was at home?

A distracted expression crossed Geoff's face.

'Alex is our features editor,' he muttered quickly. 'Your new boss. He's been here for donkey's years. Don't cross him, will you?'

Juliette wasn't sure whether he was joking or not.

Freddie stood alone in the corner of the Newdale playground and stared forlornly at the other children. He'd never felt so miserable in his life.

True to her word, Mrs Booth *had* taken him under his wing. After assembly, she'd stood him at the front of the class and introduced him to the other children. He'd felt like a prize exhibit at the zoo. She'd praised him to the skies when he read a boring book about farm animals aloud to her and had held his hand firmly at playtime.

Then suddenly everything had gone wrong. A large boy with a spiteful grin and a shock of black hair had punched a smaller boy to the ground – for no apparent reason. The smaller boy had gashed his head and since she was the only teacher on playground duty Mrs Booth had dropped everything, including Freddie's hand, and rushed to the boy's aid.

Walking round and round the playground on his own, Freddie tried to look as though he was having a great time. He'd asked a couple of boys from his class if he could join in their game of Power Rangers but they'd said no and turned their backs. A group of older girls playing with a skipping rope had demanded to know where he came from. He explained he'd just moved to Newdale from London and they burst into peals of laughter.

'You don't half speak funny,' said one of them.

'Are you a poof or are you posh?' said another girl, shrieking with hilarity. She was wearing a crop top and pedal pushers and had sparkly nail varnish on her fingers. She looked, thought Freddie, staring down at his own grey trousers and sensible lace-ups, as if she was going to a party.

Freddie hated his mum for doing this to him. Why had she gone and made them move away from London in the first place? It was horrible leaving all his friends. And worst of all, it was horrible leaving his dad. He hated the thought of only seeing him at weekends. Why had she done it? They'd been happy the way they were. And Daddy was the fun one, the one who always took him swimming and roller blading and helped with his Meccano and things. Mummy was the boring one who made him eat up his greens and went on at him for not cleaning his teeth properly.

Just as Freddie thought playtime was never going to end, one of the other teachers came out and rang a heavy iron bell. The children dutifully lined up in their classes (Freddie was elbowed to the back of the Class Two queue) and filed back inside the school.

One playtime down, thought Freddie morosely. Only another two to go.

'You're late,' snapped Alex Davis as soon as the editor was out of view. 'I'd have thought you'd have made more of an effort on your first day. Or don't they care about something as mundane as timekeeping in London?'

Juliette stared at him, aghast. Perhaps she was impossibly naïve but she'd been expecting something more along the lines of 'great to have you on the team,' or 'it's about time we hired someone of your calibre'.

Tempted though she was to say something tart back, she restrained herself. Better not go wading in on her first day.

'I'm sorry,' she said quietly. 'I had a few teething problems. It won't happen again.'

'It had better hadn't,' grunted Alex, sifting through a pile of papers on his desk. 'Ah, here's the one I'm looking for. I take it you're up to speed on Denim Heart?'

'Denim Heart?' repeated Juliette. What was he on about?

Alex Davis glared at her. Juliette noticed that he had bags under his watery-blue eyes and that his hands were shaking ever so slightly. He looked like a man at the end of his tether. Why this should be, Juliette couldn't possibly imagine. Running a features department in the wilds of Cumbria must be an absolute doddle.

'Geoff's told me that you come very highly regarded by the *Daily News*,' said Alex Davis. His voice was cold.

'It cuts no ice with me. And I'd have expected you to have done a bit of research at the very least on your new patch.'

Once again, Juliette steeled herself not to yell at him. Bloody patronising bastard.

'Denim Heart,' he continued, 'is one of the best-known companies in the area. It's a mail-order business on the outskirts of Bowater employing around three hundred people. I can't believe you've never heard of it. I thought most women were into lipstick and fancy soap.'

Juliette stared at him. She'd never met anyone so openly hostile in her entire life.

'Of course I know Denim Heart,' she said smoothly. It rang a vague bell somewhere in the recesses of her brain. 'What's the story?'

Alex Davis picked up a folder from his desk and handed it to her.

'It's all in here,' he grunted. 'Tim Dawner – he's the boss, but I'm sure you must know that – has won this year's Enterpreneur of the Year award. It's embargoed till tomorrow but we want you to do an in-depth profile of him to run alongside the news piece. Don't be dazzled by his charm, though. The *Eagle* quite likes him – it's good to have someone as high profile as him around – but there are rumours flying about that Denim Heart isn't quite as successful as he'd have us believe.'

Intrigued, Juliette opened the folder. A photograph of a stunningly good-looking man in his mid-thirties, with fair hair and a raffish smile, stared back at her. If Tim Dawner was as talented as he was good-looking, then he must be dynamite.

Driving west out of Bowater on the Newdale road, Juliette reflected on the muted reception she'd received at the *Eagle*. Geoff Lake had been so eager for her to join the staff when they first met. So why had he been so harassed today that he could barely string two words together? And what on earth she could have done to get up Alex Davis's nose, she couldn't imagine.

She'd been hoping for an easy ride on her first day, perhaps a tour round the office followed by a civilised lunch with Geoff. She couldn't have got it more wrong – although the way things had turned out, she simply felt grateful to have escaped the office and her poisonous new boss.

Tim Dawner's picture didn't do him justice. If anything, he was even more gorgeous in person. Tall, slim and athletic-looking, he was wearing a beautifully cut charcoal suit and an azure tie that matched his eyes.

'Juliette,' he said warmly as she was shown into his office. It was a vast, airy room lined with modern abstracts and with a breathtaking view of the hills. 'How delightful to meet you. Tracey, could you bring us both some coffee?'

Tim Dawner's secretary was quite clearly besotted by her boss. A young girl in her early twenties, she gazed adoringly at him, almost tripping over her feet in her eagerness to do as he asked.

Juliette bit the inside of her cheek to stop herself giggling. If this was the effect he had on his female staff, it was a wonder that anyone ever got any work done at all.

Tim Dawner, however, seemed completely oblivious to all this. Leading Juliette to a matching pair of black leather sofas in the window, he gestured to her to sit down. Then he collapsed on to the sofa facing her.

'You're new, aren't you?' he said suddenly. 'We haven't met before.'

'Mmmm,' said Juliette, concentrating on getting her tiny tape recorder to work. She didn't want to give

Alex Davis any more excuses for snide remarks. 'Yep. I've just moved up from London. I used to be on the *Daily News.*'

'Good paper,' murmured Tim Dawner with a lazy smile. 'I know a couple of reporters who work on it. Bit of an odd move for you though, isn't it? Won't Bowater be rather dull after London?'

'I don't see why,' said Juliette briskly. It seemed to have escaped Tim Dawner's notice that she was here to ask *him* questions, not the other way round.

Tim Dawner must have sensed her irritation because he cut the small talk and sprawled back against the sofa.

'Let's get down to business,' he said, unknotting his tie and chucking it to one side. 'God, that's better. I hate those things. Now come on, fire away. Ask me anything you like.'

Juliette chuckled at this.

'That's music to an interviewer's ears. I don't think anyone's ever said that to me before. I don't believe a word of it, mind you.'

'Try me,' said Tim, his voice casual.

'OK. You started Denim Heart eight years ago. Right?'

'Yeah,' said Tim. 'With my partner, Helen Brown. She concentrates on the day to day running of the business. I'm the one in charge of strategy. Plus I make all the financial decisions.'

'When you say partner,' asked Juliette, 'do you mean that you're partners in the business sense? Or in private too?'

'I'm glad to see you're taking me at my word,' he laughed. 'Let's cut the business crap. Get down to the nitty-gritty. Yeah. Helen and I are an item. Well, sort of. Things aren't always sweetness and light between us – but that's what comes of muddling up your love life with

18

your business. Don't go on about that too much though, will you? Whatever happens in our private lives, we're joined at the hip work-wise. We always will be. We've been through far too much together to fall out now.'

Tim Dawner glanced at the wedding ring on Juliette's finger.

'I see *you're* married,' he murmured.

'I'm the one asking the questions. Remember?'

Tim laughed good-naturedly and they carried on with the interview.

After an hour Juliette reckoned that she'd got plenty and drew things to a close. Tim Dawner could have been a bit more forthcoming about certain aspects of Denim Heart, like its exact turnover and expansion plans, but she knew she had enough to make a good piece.

'Thank you, Mr Dawner,' she said, holding out her hand. 'You've been very helpful.'

'It's been a pleasure,' said Tim Dawner, hanging on to it for a few seconds longer than necessary. 'Call me Tim though, won't you? I always think people must be talking to my father when they call me Mr Dawner.'

'Put your chairs on the tables, then collect your things and go,' Mrs Booth told her class, thankful that the long and trying first day of term had finally come to an end. It always took the children a few days to settle down after the long summer break. This lot had been fidgeting and messing about all day.

Freddie watched the other children in his class flip their chairs over and plonk them on top of the desks. Once he'd got the hang of what they were doing, he laboriously copied them. All the same, he reflected, it seemed a very odd thing to do. At his old school, the teacher had always ended the day by reading them a story. Then she led them into the playground herself to reunite them with their parents. Here at Newdale, the children were allowed to race out by themselves, a noisy throng chattering and yelling and screaming.

Freddie dutifully packed his things into his Action Man rucksack and followed the other children outside. Crossing his fingers inside his tightly clenched fists, he scoured the faces of the grown-ups milling around in the playground. His mum had promised that if there was any way she could get off work early and meet him, then she would. Please, please let her be there.

A hand tapped him sharply on the shoulder. He whirled around to see a sharp-faced woman with brown curly hair and a bright blue cagoule.

'Hello, Frederick,' she said in a no-nonsense sort of way.

'Hello,' said Freddie, his voice flat with disappointment. No one nice ever called him Frederick. The woman was Mrs Taylor, his new childminder. She lived a few hundred yards along from them at New Bank and looked after several Newdale children every day after school. Freddie felt like crying. Mummy clearly hadn't made it after all.

'Come on, let's go and find the others,' said Mrs Taylor briskly. 'I've got four of you to sort out today.'

Dragging his feet, Freddie followed Mrs Taylor out of the school gate. The three other children she was minding, a boy of about four and two older girls, ignored Freddie and chattered away merrily to each other.

'Where's your car?' asked Freddie. His legs ached with tiredness from all that walking around the playground.

'Get away with you,' laughed Mrs Taylor. 'You're living in the country now. We always walk home from school. It's only a mile or so. Do you the world of good, get some colour into those pale city cheeks of yours. Come on, you soppy ha'porth.'

By the time he stumbled through the door of Mrs Taylor's cottage, Freddie could barely put one foot in front of the other. It had begun to rain and he could feel the trickle of cold water down the back of his shirt. The others didn't even seem to have noticed.

Much to Freddie's relief, Mrs Taylor marched straight into the sitting room and switched on the TV. Instantly, the screen was filled with a *Pokémon* cartoon. The older girls protested feebly but *Pokémon* stayed on.

For the first time in the entire day, Freddie felt that he was on familiar territory. He forgot his troubles, snuggled into the corner of one of Mrs Taylor's comfy armchairs and was swiftly engrossed in the adventures of Pikachu and Ash.

Chapter Three

It felt like the middle of the night when the first of Joe Ward's two alarms went off.

Joe poked his hand out from beneath his duvet and banged it irritably. He glanced at the illuminated clock face and groaned. Bloody hell. *Four am*. Of course it seemed like the middle of the night. It *was* the middle of the bloody night.

He fought against the lure of ten minutes more sleep, knowing that if he succumbed he'd be lost. He'd never get in on time. He sat up and cautiously swung his legs out of bed, then jumped with fright when the second – and louder – alarm sounded. He'd gone to bed stone cold sober at eight pm but God, he felt awful now. He must have aged twenty years in the two weeks he'd been doing the breakfast show. The hours were a complete killer.

Joe made himself a cup of industrial strength tea, picked yesterday's heap of clothes off the floor and hurriedly pulled them on. At least working in radio meant that his appearance didn't matter. He couldn't imagine what breakfast telly must be like. The thought of being bright and breezy *and* looking a million dollars at this time in the morning . . . Well, it simply couldn't be done. Not by him, anyway.

Wandering into the sitting room, he cast his eyes over the floor. He hadn't heard Willy come in but his pal had clearly had quite a night of it. Empty beer cans were strewn all over the carpet and the remains of a couple of dodgy-looking Indian takeaways had been dumped in the bin in the corner. Joe gingerly moved a pair of Willy's jeans off the sofa and sat down to drink his tea.

On the dot of four-thirty am the doorbell rang. Joe swore out loud and ran for it. Willy would go apeshit if Steve, the cabbie generally used by Radio Wave, woke him up again. He'd only just forgiven Joe for last week's episode when the idiot driver had leaned on the buzzer at dawn and carried on ringing till Joe answered it.

Willy – or Wild Willy Brown to give him his working title – was Joe's new landlord. He and Joe went way back, to the days when they were both trying to scratch a living in scruffy nightclubs in and around south London. They'd broken into local radio at around the same time and now they'd both been signed up by Radio Wave. The crucial difference was that while Joe had bagged the prestigious six to nine am breakfast slot, Willy's show went out between ten pm and midnight. But then again, Willy, who – when he wasn't having his sleep interrupted – was one of the most laid-back men Joe had ever met, didn't seem to care. 'They'll make you play S Club 7 and boy-bands all morning, man,' he'd laughed. 'At least I'll get to choose a few decent tracks.'

Joe had been deeply touched by Willy's offer of a roof over his head when Jules and Freddie moved north. Out of all his friends, Willy was the last person he'd have expected to help him out of a hole. Willy was in his mid-thirties yet he'd remained resolutely single. Whereas Joe had spent the past few years planning his work around Juliette and Freddie, Willy had been as free as the air. From what Joe picked up on the grapevine, Willy was out clubbing every night. As for his love life, Joe didn't have a clue. Women buzzed around Willy like bees round a honey pot, but in all the time they'd been mates Joe had never known him to have a steady girlfriend. According to Willy, life was a long and happy succession of one-night stands.

Despite Willy's kind-hearted offer, the prospect of moving into his flat had worried Joe a lot. For a start he didn't want to ruin their friendship. *Neither* did he want to cramp Willy's style. And *then* there was the problem of their hours. On the face of it, the pair of them were utterly incompatible. Joe had to be up at four am and get to bed early, while Willy could sleep all day, arrive for work at around nine pm and then party till the early hours. A couple of times already the pair of them had collided on the doorstep at four in the morning – Joe dashing out to work rubbing the sleep from his eyes, a half-cut Willy staggering in after a heavy night.

Climbing into the back of Steve's decrepit Ford Cortina, Joe brushed a pile of crisp crumbs onto the floor with the back of his hand. That done, he closed his eyes and attempted to concentrate on the show ahead.

After a long conversation with Jules on the phone last night about the teething problems Freddie was having settling into school, he'd gone to bed far later than he'd intended. And he hadn't given this morning's programme nearly enough thought. As a rule, Joe tried to keep his show as unstructured as possible. It was cluttered up enough as it was, with news bulletins and weather forecasts, racing tips and traffic reports. He didn't like his input to be too rigid, preferring to fly by the seat of his pants. Nevertheless, he usually scribbled a few ideas on the back of an old envelope. He never referred to this much, but he liked to have it in front of him all the same. Just in case. Just in case the unthinkable happened and his mind went blank and he couldn't think of anything to say.

'Terrible morning, mate,' mumbled Steve out of the corner of his mouth. 'Been pissing with rain all night. *And* they've gone and closed Vauxhall Bridge.'

Joe groaned inwardly. Why didn't the man ever take the hint and belt up? He didn't give a shit about Steve's route. Just so long as they got there on time and in one piece.

'Mmmm,' murmured Joe.

'Wotcha gonna talk about this morning, then?'

'Dunno,' answered Joe.

'Heard an ace joke last night in the pub. Wanna hear it?'

'Go on,' said Joe wearily, all too aware that he was going to hear it anyway.

The one bonus of arriving for work at the unearthly hour of five in the morning was that there was rarely any traffic on the road. Radio Wave had taken over the top two floors of a swanky new building in the West End so the journey from Willy's mansion flat in Battersea took fifteen minutes at the very most.

Joe shut his mind to Steve's burbling and wrote a few random words on the back of an old restaurant bill he'd found in his pocket. Rain. Boiled eggs. Tracing paper. Man United. Then he started doodling Freddie's name and drew a huge heart around it. God, he missed him. What the hell were they doing living apart?

'Virtuoso stuff this morning,' remarked Joe's producer Annie Smith as Joe pressed a key to play his final jingle of the morning.

A chorus of sopranos singing the name Joe Ward over and over again blasted across the airwaves, making Joe chuckle for the millionth time. He'd had his own jingle for years on other radio stations and they were always ghastly. But this one, it had to be said, was particularly

25

gruesome. And the thought of a load of girls turning up to a recording studio simply to record his name over and over again at the tops of their voices never failed to make him laugh.

'Thanks,' he said, switching his microphone off and dumping his headphones on the desk. 'It went pretty smoothly, didn't it? Well, apart from that stupid news-reader reading yesterday's news at the top of the eight o'clock bulletin.'

'Yep, that was a bit of a disaster,' admitted Annie with a grimace. 'And Dermot's so dim that he didn't even realise. I had to slide a copy of today's news underneath his nose before he grasped what I was on about.'

'Has anyone upstairs said anything yet?' asked Joe. He stood up and pulled on his battered leather jacket.

'You bet they have. And Dermot's definitely for the chop this time, I'm afraid. I can't protect him this time.'

The huge number of cock-ups Dermot Brady had made in the two short weeks they'd been on air ran through both their minds. Forgetting to switch his mike on. Missing out items. Making an utterly unsuitable joke immediately after he'd broadcast the untimely death of a soap star. The list seemed endless.

'It's silly, really,' said Annie. 'I know he's worse than useless but I still can't help feeling sorry for him. *And* he's got a wife and two young kids to support.'

Joe stared at her, surprised at her concern. In the fortnight that they'd been working on the breakfast show together Annie had struck him as being as tough as old boots. She was about thirty-five, a tall woman with long legs she kept covered up in jeans and auburn hair caught back in a clip. She was a consummate professional, with a brisk no-nonsense manner and a deep sexy voice that made Joe wonder whether she'd ever tried broadcasting herself.

26

'D'you fancy a coffee round the corner?' he asked suddenly. He usually spent a couple of hours after the show catching up with letters and running through the play-list for the following day but that could all wait. The thought of escaping the claustrophobic confines of Radio Wave for half an hour or so was oddly appealing.

Annie looked doubtful.

'I've got loads to do,' she began. 'Giving Dermot a bollocking for a start. Oh, what the hell. Go on. Twist my arm. It's about time we discussed how it's all going, isn't it? And I've got a couple of new ideas I want to run past you.'

Strolling into Café Firenze, the stylish Italian coffee bar on the corner of the street, it struck Joe that he knew next to nothing about his new producer. So far their conversations had been restricted to the thorny issues of which version of 'American Pie' to play, Don McLean's or Madonna's, and whether they should invite listeners to phone in during the programme. Annie seemed to actively discourage talking about anything personal. He had no idea where she lived, whether she had a partner (Joe had already noted she didn't wear a wedding ring) or where she'd worked before.

They ordered a couple of lattes and sat down by the window. The morning rush was over and apart from the two of them and a man in a business suit lolling against the counter trying to chat up the checkout girl, the place was empty.

'It still feels odd finishing work just as everyone else is starting theirs, doesn't it?' remarked Joe. He didn't know why, but he felt a bit awkward with Annie.

'I know what you mean,' said Annie, stirring her coffee thoughtfully. 'When you're on air you're in a different world. Completely detached from real life. Actually, that's what I like about it.'

'Where were you before?'

'What? You mean where did I work?' asked Annie.

'Yep,' said Joe.

Annie smoothed a stray hair away from her face and took a sip of her coffee before answering his question.

'Oh, I've worked all over the place,' she said finally. 'In fact, tell me a radio station I haven't worked on. I'm a right old tart. How about you?'

Joe got the distinct impression that Annie didn't want to discuss it any further so he didn't pursue it.

'Speak for yourself,' he laughed. 'I'm definitely not a right old tart. In fact I'm a happily married man. Have been for years.'

'Is your wife in the same business?'

'Sort of,' said Joe. 'Jules has always been pretty career minded. She used to be features editor of the *Daily News*. Only now she's gone off her rocker and buggered off to the Lake District. She's got this bee in her bonnet about getting Freddie – our son, I mean – away from London and all its wicked ways, and bringing him up in the country. We've let our house and she's rented a cottage in the middle of bloody nowhere. They both sound bored out of their skulls whenever I speak to them but she won't admit it. Mad, isn't it?'

Joe looked so morose that Annie leaned across the table and squeezed his hand reassuringly.

'That must be tough,' she said softly.

'It is,' said Joe, thinking that this must be the understatement of the year.

'How old is Freddie?'

'Six,' said Joe. 'You got kids?'

Annie shook her head.

'No, I haven't,' she said. 'Now, I don't know about layabout DJs like you, but I've got a hell of a lot of work to do. You coming?'

28

Chapter Four

Freddie clung desperately to Juliette's legs, pleading with her not to make him go to school.

'*Please, Mummy, please,*' he begged. 'I feel sick. I've got a sore throat and my ear hurts. I won't get in your way, I promise. Please. I'll do anything. Please let me stay with you. *Please, please let me.*'

Juliette pulled away from Freddie and crouched down low to take a better look at his face. She was in the middle of writing a two-page piece on shoplifting for the *Eagle*. Alex Davis wanted her to include some profiles of real-life shoplifters and he'd called her late last night to tell her about a couple of cases coming up at Bowater magistrates court this morning. She was due there in less than forty-five minutes. There was simply no way she could take Freddie to court with her.

Not for the first time, Juliette wished that Joe was around to help. On the rare occasions that Freddie had been ill in London, it was Joe who'd stayed at home with him. Now she had no one to call on. Gill Taylor, the childminder, was such a frosty old cow – she didn't want to ask any favours from her. No, Freddie would simply have to toughen up and get on with it.

She laid her hand on his forehead just to check. It didn't feel particularly hot. The possibility that Freddie was trying all this on to avoid school crossed her mind.

She must have a word with his teacher soon. Freddie had been at Newdale for a fortnight now yet he showed no sign of settling down. Every night he regaled her with horror stories of how everyone laughed at his London accent and no one would play with him.

When she was going to find the time to see Mrs Booth she couldn't imagine. In the mornings Freddie's teacher was up to her eyes with photocopying and hearing children read and in the afternoons Juliette was busy trying to meet her deadline for the following day's paper. Geoff Lake's promise of a four-day week still hadn't materialised either.

'Come on, darling,' soothed Juliette. 'It's Friday, remember? Just get through today and we'll talk about everything tonight, I promise you. I'll do a special tea as well, if you like.'

Freddie's eyes lit up.

'At McDonald's?' he said excitedly.

'No, of course not at McDonald's,' said Juliette, trying her best not to let her irritation show. 'There isn't one around here for fifty miles.'

The light in Freddie's eyes instantly died away.

'This is a stupid place,' he said, sticking his lower lip out sulkily. 'I *hate* living here. In London we could walk to McDonald's whenever we liked. Everything was better there. *And* Daddy was there.'

Juliette forced herself not to lose her temper.

'Look darling, I haven't got time for all this now. You know how much Daddy loves you and he'll be here tomorrow, remember? It always takes a bit of time to get used to living somewhere different. But you just wait. In a few months time, you'll have forgotten all about silly old London. Now, what special treat can I get you for tea? Chicken nuggets? Burgers?'

'None of them,' wailed Freddie, stomping off in a huff. 'I hate all of it.'

Juliette watched her small son march down the school path, a solitary figure carrying a rucksack almost as big as himself on his back. Oh God. What the hell had she done dragging him up here?

'Is everything all right?' asked a woman whom Juliette had spotted earlier with two sweet-looking girls in blonde bunches. She was wearing a scruffy old tracksuit and had a kind, care-worn sort of face.

Juliette rolled her eyes.

'Oh just the usual morning sort of thing – you know what it's like.'

She glanced down at her watch.

'Oh my God. I'm sorry. I must dash. I'm going to be *so* late for work.'

Fi Nicholson stared as Juliette leapt into her car and roared off down the lane. She felt oddly envious at the thought of being late for work. Now that the girls were all at school, she had nothing more exciting than washing up the breakfast things to look forward to.

In fact Fi was being typically hard on herself. When she and Dai, her husband, had first met in London, he'd been a medical student struggling on a minuscule grant. She was a graphic designer for an advertising agency and thanks to a couple of inspired campaigns for a major restaurant chain, she'd been coining it in. They'd married within three months and Lily, their eldest daughter, was born a couple of years later. Fi had fallen so desperately in love with her baby that she'd found herself unable to leave her for a second. She'd given up work without a backward glance.

Soon afterwards, Dai had got his first GP's post in a practice in Cumbria and that had pretty much been that. They'd moved up north when Lily was one. Now – Fi couldn't quite get her head round it – Lily was eleven, a thoughtful academic girl who'd just started secondary school in Bowater. And Fi's two younger daughters, Lizzie and Molly, were seven and four. *Seven and four.* She could hardly believe it. They still seemed like babies to her, although Molly had started primary school this term.

Fi knew that now she had the time, she should take up her painting again. But two weeks into the school term, all she seemed to have done was sit at home and wonder where the years had gone.

'Good morning, Fi,' said Louise Newman, bustling out of the school gate. Lost in her own thoughts, Fi looked up with a start and smiled absent-mindedly. Perhaps she should take Louise's lead and fill her spare time with school activities and good works.

Like the Nicholsons, Louise and Tom Newman were originally from London. But there the resemblance ended. Fi and Louise were like chalk and cheese. Louise came from Barnes and seemed hell-bent on trying to turn Newdale into a mini version of the smart London suburb. She was forever arranging coffee mornings and, although she'd only lived in the village for a year, she was already a leading light in Newdale Primary's parents' group.

'Have you seen the league tables in *The Times* this morning?' she demanded.

'No,' said Fi. 'I can't say I have.'

Dai had left for work at the crack of dawn and it had been all she could do to get the girls dressed and fed, see Lily onto the school bus and drive the others down to Newdale for nine.

'Oh honestly,' said Louise, clicking her tongue in irritation. 'I know some of the other parents are absolutely hopeless but I thought that you of all people would have a look at them. Anyway, I'm organising an emergency meeting of the parents' group for tonight. I hope you'll be there.'

'No, I'm afraid I won't,' said Fi. 'Dai's on call. But what's so urgent that it can't wait till the next meeting? We've got one in a couple of weeks time, haven't we?'

'Newdale's dropped thirty places in the county tables,' said Louise. She sounded so shocked that at first Fi thought someone must have died.

'We've got to do something before it gets any worse,' Louise went on. 'Tom and I would never have dreamed of sending the boys here if it hadn't performed so well in last year's tables. It's terribly upsetting.'

Fi stared at her. Sometimes Louise Newman seemed to be living on another planet. She never got her knickers in a twist over anything important.

'Oh for goodness sake,' said Fi briskly. 'Lily was in the year that sat their Key Stage 2 tests last summer and she did absolutely fine. Most of them did. If you want to get in a lather about something then you should be concentrating on the terrible state that Class Two's Portakabin is in. The roof is leaking like mad now. Why don't you call an emergency meeting about that? It's high time the council got its act together and did something.'

Louise glared at Fi. Both her boys had progressed beyond Class Two so she wasn't particularly concerned about the Portakabin. And anyway, league tables were *far* more important than a bit of damp.

'Oh well, if you're not bothered, I'll have to look elsewhere for moral support,' she said. 'Although I must say, I am rather surprised at your *laissez-faire* attitude.'

In her present mood, Fi was tempted to tell Louise where to go. But loath to get into a slanging match, she bit her tongue. Inside, however, she was seething. Her earlier intentions about going straight home and getting out her easel had completely evaporated.

* * *

Juliette gazed intently at the defendant. There was something familiar about her, but she couldn't put her finger on what it was. Poor woman. Judging by her lowered head and half-whispered answers, Norma Gray had never been before a magistrate's court in her life.

Norma, it transpired, was pleading guilty to walking out of Bowater's main supermarket with half a pound of butter and a pint of full cream milk stuffed inside her coat. Having failed to get anything sensible out of her, the store detective had called the police. They'd duly charged her with shoplifting.

The chairman of the magistrates gently asked Norma whether she had a job. Norma murmured something inaudible and he prompted her again.

'Dinner lady,' whispered Norma, staring down at the floor.

'And where do you live?'

'5 Top Row, Wath End,' mumbled Norma.

The Crown Prosecution Service solicitor rose to his feet to outline the facts of the case. Juliette noted down all the details, her pen flying over her notebook at top speed.

Then Norma's own solicitor, a young woman in a sober grey suit and high-necked white blouse, got up to give the magistrates some background about her client.

'Mrs Gray, I'm sure you will realise, is a woman of impeccable character,' she told the bench. 'She has never been in trouble before. She is deeply ashamed to find herself standing in front of you now. She realises full well that there is no excuse for her actions.

'On the day in question, however, she was under enormous strain. She simply had no idea what she was doing. Mrs Gray's husband died last year after a long battle against leukaemia. Not only has she had to come to terms with this tragic loss, but earlier this year her daughter suffered a miscarriage late in her first pregnancy. My client was desperately worried, too, about her son, who at the age of twenty-four, is unable to find a job.

'Mrs Gray picked up the milk and butter fully intending to pay for the items at the checkout. The next thing she knew, so she says, she was on the pavement outside being apprehended by a store detective . . .'

Juliette glanced across at Mrs Gray again. Compared to this woman's problems, her own suddenly seemed trivial.

The three magistrates conferred for a few minutes. As they were doing this, Juliette saw that Norma Gray was gripping the seat in front of her so tightly that the whites of her knuckles showed.

Finally the chairman cleared his throat.

'Mrs Gray, we understand that you have experienced some difficulties over the past few months,' he said. 'We have also taken into account the fact that this is your first offence, and the regret that you have expressed. We have therefore decided to give you a conditional discharge . . .'

This was clearly a huge relief for Norma Gray. A sob rose in her throat and she clutched the seat in front even more fiercely than before. She'd been terrified the magistrates were going to fine her. Things were tight enough as it was; she couldn't imagine how on earth she would ever have paid it.

Juliette was halfway home when she suddenly remembered her promise of a special tea to Freddie. She banged her hands on the steering wheel in frustration. Bugger it. The only shops in Newdale were a tiny post office that opened twice a week and a tea-room that had had its shutters drawn ever since they'd arrived. Despite Freddie's insistence that nothing but McDonald's would do, she turned the car round and headed back in the direction of Bowater.

When she got to the supermarket, it was packed to bursting with Friday night shoppers. Bowater only had one proper supermarket and even that, Juliette reckoned, wasn't much cop. You couldn't get dolcelatte or decent olive oil and the only pasta it sold was spaghetti. Determined to keep her word to Freddie, however, she grabbed a shopping trolley and dashed towards the frozen food aisle. As she stuffed oven-ready chips, chicken nuggets, milk shakes and chocolate ice cream into her trolley, she smiled to herself. The nearest McDonald's might be miles away – but she was hot on improvisation.

The checkout queues snaked right down every aisle. Juliette cursed to herself. She'd promised to pick Freddie up from the childminder's at four today. It was going to be well after five at this rate.

'I'd never have put you down as a junk food addict,' said a male voice behind her. 'I thought you'd be more of a sun-dried tomatoes and organic yoghurt kind of girl . . .'

Juliette swung round in annoyance.

'Why don't you mind your own bloody b . . .'

Her words died away in her throat. The man perusing her shopping trolley with such amusement was Tim Dawner, the Denim Heart boss she'd interviewed two weeks earlier.

'Oh, I'm s-s-sorry,' she stuttered, blushing scarlet. 'I didn't mean to be rude. I didn't realise it was you.'

Tim Dawner smiled engagingly.

'Serves me right for being so nosey, doesn't it?' he said. 'This place is so horrendously busy that looking at the contents of other people's trolleys is the only way to pass the time.'

Laughing, Juliette peered into *his* trolley. It was stuffed full with bottles of beer, wine, vodka and gin.

'You're either an alcoholic or planning a party,' she said.

'I'm pleased to say that it's the latter,' said Tim. 'We've just had a record sales month so I'm throwing a bash for the sales and marketing team. D'you want to come?'

'What?' said Juliette. 'To write about it? I don't think I'd get it in the paper.'

Tim rolled his eyes in mock horror.

'Don't you ever think about anything else but work? Of course not to write about it. For fun.'

'When is it?'

'Tomorrow night,' said Tim. 'Eight pm. In my office. Try and make it, won't you?'

Mrs Taylor's face looked like thunder when she came to the door. It was nearly five-thirty, an hour and a half after Juliette had promised to collect Freddie.

'Mummy,' shrieked Freddie, diving past Gill Taylor and into Juliette's arms. 'I've been waiting for you for ages and ages. I thought you'd forgotten about me.'

'I'd never do that, sweetheart,' murmured Juliette, hugging him back. 'I just got . . .'

'Can I have a word?' asked Gill Taylor. Juliette could tell from the expression on her face that it wasn't something that could wait.

'Run and get in the car will you, sweetheart,' she whispered to Freddie. 'I won't be a moment.'

Juliette turned to Gill Taylor.

'What's happened? Has there been a problem at school?'

Gill Taylor stared at Juliette, the hostility in her eyes unmistakable.

'Mrs Ward,' she said coldly. 'You may have assumed that it was perfectly all right to behave like this in

37

London but I can assure you that it most certainly is not acceptable up here. If you tell me that you are going to pick your son up at four pm then I expect you here on the dot. It isn't fair on me – and it isn't fair on Frederick either. Poor little lad. He was terrified that something had happened to you.'

Juliette's eyes filled with tears but she brushed them away angrily. She couldn't bear the thought of Freddie being upset because of her.

'I'm so sorry,' she said quietly. 'I'll make sure it never happens again.'

Gill Taylor pursed her lips.

'You're right – it won't be happening again,' she said, her voice sour. 'And that's because I won't be collecting Frederick from school any longer. From now on you'll have to make other arrangements.'

Chapter Five

The following morning Freddie was up at dawn. Lying in bed next door, Juliette heard him pad down the stairs and assumed that he'd gone to switch on children's TV. A few minutes later, however, he pushed open her bedroom door and crawled into bed with her.

'What time is it?' she groaned, not wanting to wake up properly.

'Half past seven,' said Freddie brightly, tugging most of the duvet off Juliette and over himself. 'When's Daddy arriving?'

'I told you last night. It's a very long drive. I shouldn't think he'll be here till lunchtime. Why don't you go and put a video on?'

In her exhausted state, Juliette was vaguely aware of Freddie wriggling out of bed and disappearing downstairs again. She pulled the duvet back over herself – she'd just snatch another half-hour's sleep before fixing them both some breakfast.

When she finally woke up again it was well after nine. Sunlight streamed through the flimsy curtains and she could hear the murmur of voices below. Juliette smiled to herself. Freddie must still be watching his video. She pulled an old jumper over her pyjamas and tiptoed downstairs.

On pushing open the kitchen door, she gasped with

shock. There, sitting at the table, bold as brass, eating fresh croissants and strawberry jam with Freddie, was Joe.

'Oh my God,' she said. 'When did you get here?'

Joe leapt up from the table and crossed the room to wrap her in his arms. For some reason, she didn't quite know why, Juliette felt inextricably shy. She gently disentangled herself from his embrace. They'd been married for what? Seven years? And yet within the space of two short weeks Joe had somehow turned into a stranger.

It wasn't that he didn't look good. He did. He was wearing an old Guernsey jumper and faded jeans that Juliette herself had bought for him what seemed like a lifetime ago. He just looked – well, different.

Sensing her coolness, Joe shrugged his shoulders and sat down again.

'Mummy, look what Daddy's brought me,' shouted Freddie.

Juliette smiled, relieved that Freddie's exuberance had broken the tension between her and Joe.

'What, darling?'

'Look. A Game Boy. I've been wanting one for ages and ages.'

Freddie jumped to his feet, excitedly brandishing a mini scarlet computer in her direction.

'*And* a game,' he shouted. 'Look. Wacky Races. The one I saw on telly.'

'That's lovely, darling,' she murmured to Freddie, who'd now switched his present on and was trying to work out how to play it. Meanwhile Juliette turned towards Joe, her exasperation plain to see.

'You should have asked me first,' she mouthed at him over Freddie's head. 'I'll never get him off the bloody thing now.'

40

Ignoring her anger, Joe shifted his chair closer to his son and bent his head over the Game Boy.

'Come on, Freddie, let's have a look at the instructions. You'll be a champion in no time.'

Juliette and Joe barely spoke more than two words to each other for the rest of the morning. At lunchtime Joe silently packed up a picnic and took an ecstatic Freddie off on a bike ride. As she watched them go, Freddie wobbling down the lane in a shiny black bike helmet that made him look like a worker ant, and Joe riding protectively behind him, Juliette felt a lump in her throat. Freddie had only learned to ride a two-wheeler a few months ago and it had been his passion for cycling that had first put the idea of moving into her head. There'd been nowhere for him to ride his bike in London. Their pocket-handkerchief garden was too small to swing a cat and riding in the road outside was unthinkable.

It was ironic that they'd been living in the country for more than a fortnight now and Juliette still hadn't got round to getting the bikes out. Yet Joe had only been in the house for two minutes and he'd instantly made Freddie's day by mending two punctures and suggesting a bike ride.

It was nearly four by the time they got back. Freddie had rosy cheeks and his eyes glowed with the excitement of it all as he burst through the door.

'We rode for miles and miles, Mummy, and I didn't fall off once,' he yelled at the top of his voice. 'We picked some blackberries and we bumped into Lizzie Nicholson and her sister and they've invited me to tea next week. Can I go?'

Gathering him into her arms, Juliette hugged him tight, marvelling once again at the smoothness of his skin.

41

'Calm down, will you? Yes, of course you can go,' she whispered into his neck. 'Is Lizzie in your class?'

'Yes,' said Freddie. 'Only she's just had her birthday and I'm not seven till March, am I?'

Juliette looked up and saw Joe coming in through the back door. A shiver of pleasure ran down her spine, only to be dashed by Joe's coolness towards her.

'Freddie and I are going to have a go at making some blackberry crumble with these,' he said, plonking a bulging paper bag next to the sink.

'I've tried some already and they're yummy,' said Freddie. His mouth, Juliette noticed fondly, was stained purple with blackberry juice. 'Do you want one, Mummy?'

'If Daddy gives me a kiss first,' said Juliette shyly. She felt slightly guilty for involving Freddie like this but she was desperate all of a sudden to break the ice between them.

'Go on Daddy,' implored Freddie.

Forced into a show of affection, Joe gave Juliette a chaste kiss on the cheek. It wasn't quite what she'd been hoping for but it would have to do for the time being. Perhaps their marriage was a bit like Joe's cooking, she thought, as she watched her husband slop the crumble mixture on top of the cooked blackberries. It needed a bit more care and attention before it turned out quite right.

By the time Freddie was in bed and they'd both had a couple of glasses of wine, Joe's frostiness began to thaw a little.

'I'm really enjoying the new show,' she said, opening another bottle of Chardonnay and sloshing it into their glasses.

'I thought you preferred Radio Four in the mornings,' said Joe, his voice neutral.

'Not any more,' said Juliette. 'Me and Freddie always

listen to you. Every day. Without fail. And he loves it when you mention him. It gives us both a real lift.'

A hint of a smile crossed Joe's lips.

'I'm glad,' he said softly.

They both stared at each other, similar thoughts running through their minds. They'd been married for so long – how come they felt so awkward with each other now?

'What are the people at Radio Wave like?'

'How's the new job going?'

They both started to speak at the same time. Juliette laughed nervously. The pair of them were behaving like they'd only just been introduced, each trying desperately to make polite conversation.

'You go first,' said Juliette.

'No, you,' said Joe.

Juliette proceeded to tell him about the strange atmosphere at the *Eagle* and Alex Davis's antipathy towards her. She told him about Tim Dawner and Denim Heart and the shoplifting piece that she'd written for that day's paper.

'Oh but this is all so trivial compared to Freddie,' she said, banging her fist on her knee in frustration. 'We should be talking about him.'

For a second Joe looked desperately sad.

'I miss him so much,' he murmured. 'I can't tell you how much I miss him. Just being with him today, cycling and cooking and knocking a football around the garden brought it all home to me.'

Juliette swallowed hard. Joe had said nothing about missing *her*. Only Freddie.

'Well, if that's the way you feel, why don't you do something about it?' she said. Her voice was perhaps sharper than she'd intended.

'What do you mean?' asked Joe, regarding her dangerously.

'It's simple. If you miss him so much, why don't you come and live up here with us?'

'There's another option,' said Joe. 'You and Freddie could come back to London. We could move back into the house and carry on where we left off. How about it, Jules? It would be so much better. For *all* of us.'

Juliette glared at him.

'Oh, that would suit you very well, wouldn't it? But what about us? What about me and Freddie? We both love it up here. And anyway, we can't go back – we've let the house for a year.'

'That's not what Freddie's told me,' said Joe quietly.

Juliette sat bolt upright at this, a million thoughts running through her head all at once.

'What are you saying? What has Freddie told you?'

Joe stared dispassionately at Juliette. She didn't have a conventionally beautiful face – her eyes were set too far apart and she had a dimple in her chin – but he could still see the Jules he'd fallen in love with all those years ago. He wished, though, that she could be more laid back, that she wouldn't fly off the handle quite so often.

'Keep your hair on, Jules. He told me that he wished we were still living together as a proper family. In London.'

'Freddie wouldn't say that. He loves it here.'

'Correction,' said Joe. His voice sounded harsh. 'Freddie does *not* love it here. You may love it here. Freddie doesn't.'

'He loves living in the country,' said Juliette, refusing to give ground. 'He loves having a proper garden to play in and somewhere safe to ride his bike.'

'And how often have you taken him out on his bike?' said Joe accusingly.

Juliette inspected the intricate daisy pattern on her skirt closely. It reminded her of the daisy chains she used to make as a child.

44

'You know I haven't taken him out yet. But that's only because there hasn't been time – what with moving and settling into the house and Freddie starting his new school.'

'And does he like his new school?' asked Joe. It was obvious from his voice that he knew the answer to this too.

'He's had a few teething problems, I agree. But he's starting to settle down. And he's been asked out to tea next week.'

'Yes, I was there when Lizzie asked him,' said Joe acidly. 'And how about his new childminder? Does he like her?'

'No,' said Juliette. 'For God's sake, stop playing games, Joe. You know that's gone belly up. I've got to find another one.'

'So who's going to care for him after school until you do?'

Disconcerted by Joe's intense cross-examination, Juliette finally snapped.

'Stop going on at me, all right? I'll sort it. Watch my lips. *I'll sort it.*'

'Fine,' said Joe. 'But when exactly, Jules? My God, he's only six. He's been dragged from one end of the country to the other. He's been looked after by a new childminder he loathes and he hates his new school. Get real, will you?'

'Oh yes,' said Juliette. 'I'll get real while you swan around London doing what the hell you want. And if me and Freddie are very lucky, you might just find time in your busy schedule to pop in and see us once in a while. We're dying of gratitude.'

'Oh for God's sake, Jules,' said Joe. 'You knew how it would be. It was *you* who wanted to bring Freddie up here in the first place. I told you that Radio Wave was a big break for me – but would you listen? Would you hell. You didn't give a damn about me or what I wanted. You just went full steam ahead. As per usual. And now it's all gone wrong and you haven't got the guts to admit it.'

Juliette glared at him.

'I can't bloody stand this interrogation any more,' she snapped. 'I'm off to bed. You can sleep on the bottom of Freddie's bunk bed. It's all made up.'

When Juliette awoke the next morning the house seemed ominously quiet. She lay there for a few minutes, unable to summon up the strength to drag herself out of bed. She'd been half expecting, half-hoping, that Joe would creep in next to her last night. Then they could have made up their petty squabbles in the best way possible and things would have been fine again. But he'd stayed put in Freddie's bunk bed – and Juliette had been so disappointed that she'd barely slept a wink.

When she peered round the door of Freddie's room, she was horrified to find that both beds were empty. There was no one downstairs either, just two empty mugs and the remains of two bowls of porridge on the table.

A slither of panic ran down the back of Juliette's spine. Surely Joe couldn't have taken Freddie back to London. He'd never do that. He just wouldn't.

Her heart pounding like an express train, Juliette ran out into the front garden in her nightdress. As luck would have it, the first person she saw was old Mr Spratton from next door. As usual, he was weeding his vegetable patch, his primary joy in life since his wife died earlier in the year. His eyes looked as if they were about to pop out of their sockets at the sight of Juliette, hair awry, legs bare and half her buttons undone.

'Mr Spratton, Mr Spratton, have you seen Freddie?' she

demanded urgently. 'Have you seen Freddie at all this morning?'

Mr Spratton stared at her as if she was some wild creature. He'd lived in this sleepy backwater of Newdale for all his seventy-seven years and he'd certainly never seen a woman running around in this state before.

'Aye, of course I have,' he spluttered when he'd got hold of his senses. 'The boy went out cycling with – is it his dad? – about an hour ago. He loves that bike of his, doesn't he?'

Mr Spratton managed to get his words out without looking directly at Juliette. He didn't know what the rest of the village was going to say when they heard about this. The shame of it. He'd never live it down.

'Look, is that them there now?'

The old man swung his gardening trowel in the air and pointed at a man and a child in the distance, cycling slowly up the lane.

'Oh yes, thank goodness.'

Beside herself with relief, Juliette leaned over the garden wall and planted a huge kiss on old Mr Spratton's cheek. Flushing scarlet with embarrassment, he wiped his brow with a large white handkerchief. No one had kissed him since Mabel died. You didn't do that sort of thing round here. This woman was clearly quite mad. Quite mad.

Chapter Six

'It's eight o'clock and this is Joe Ward on Radio Wave. *The best way* to start your day. Ain't that right, son?'

Freddie was sitting in the kitchen stuffing rice crispies into his mouth at the rate of knots. At his father's words he jumped off his chair, flung his arms in the air and shouted 'hooray'. A mouthful of cereal promptly spewed out all over the floor.

'Come on, Freddie,' said Juliette, dropping to her feet to wipe up the gooey mess. 'You don't need to go all silly every time Daddy mentions your name. Do you?'

Seated back on his chair, Freddie looked up and beamed at her.

'But it's so exciting, isn't it? Has Daddy ever talked about you on the radio?'

Juliette thought back to the early days with Joe. They'd met at a press conference to launch a new radio station down in the West Country. She'd been working as a news reporter for the local paper and he'd just been signed up as the station's lunchtime DJ. Joe had asked her out there and then. For the first few weeks of his new show he'd mentioned the 'gorgeous new lady in my life' so often on his programme that Juliette had become quite blasé about it. Her friends had teased her mercilessly but deep down she'd thought it terribly romantic. Now she was older and wiser, she knew better. With three hours of live radio to fill every afternoon, Joe had simply used everything – including his new girlfriend – at his disposal.

'Yes, he has,' Juliette told Freddie now. 'Quite a long time ago. Before you were born.'

'It's nice, isn't it?' said Freddie, beaming up at her.

'Yes, sweetheart. It is. Now go and brush your teeth, will you? We've both got a busy day ahead of us.'

Buoyed up by Joe's mention of him on the breakfast show, Freddie got cracking with cleaning his teeth, tying his shoelaces and finding his coat. This meant that for the first time in days, they weren't late. Juliette even had time to accompany Freddie into his class, rather than drop him and dash like she usually did.

As they strolled down the school path, Juliette slowly became aware of a frosty atmosphere descending on them. She was used to a bit of whispering and nudging – you expected that when you were new to a place. But this was different. Today some of the other parents were shooting openly hostile glances at her.

Even Freddie noticed that something strange was going on. He called out a cheery 'hello' to Mrs Bailey, the school secretary and was shocked to see her pointedly turn her back and hurry into school.

'Why didn't she say hello?' asked Freddie in a miserable voice. 'I thought she was one of the nice ones. She gave me a Liquorice Allsort at playtime last week.'

Juliette squeezed Freddie's shoulders comfortingly. Bloody woman, she thought. It didn't take much to say hello to a six-year-old trying desperately hard to find his feet at a new school.

'She probably just got out of bed the wrong side,' she told Freddie, who promptly burst into fits of giggles.

'I couldn't get out of bed the wrong side, could I, Mummy?' he said. 'Because my bunk bed's pushed up against the wall.'

49

'That's right, sweetheart,' smiled Juliette, pleased to see him cheering up. 'You're always jolly in the mornings, aren't you?'

They clambered up the steps of Class Two's Portakabin and Juliette popped her head around the door. It didn't exactly look inviting, she thought, remembering with fondness the cosy place filled with colourful artwork that had been Freddie's last classroom. This one looked cold and austere, and – she sniffed the air suspiciously – it smelled damp. Mrs Booth was deep in conversation with another parent, so Juliette kissed Freddie on the forehead, reminded him that come what may she'd be picking him up from school today and legged it back to the car.

'Mornin' Jules,' shouted Stubby the security guard.

Dashing through reception, Juliette grinned back at him and waved. Joe was the only person who'd ever called her Jules before. Now for some reason Stubby seemed to have hit on the nickname too.

After his initial scepticism towards Juliette, Stubby had come to the conclusion that she was a good egg. He'd grown used to getting the cold shoulder from snooty feature writers who didn't deem him important enough to talk to. But Juliette, it emerged, was different. She always said good morning, always thanked him profusely when he held the door open for her and – shock, horror – had even bought him a carton of coffee from the café round the corner once. That had cracked it for Stubby big time. No one had ever done anything like that before.

Unlike the news reporters, who arrived at the *Eagle* at seven to churn out stories for the first edition, feature writers worked a day ahead and didn't have to start work till nine. Even so, Juliette was always the last of the four feature writers to arrive. By the time Juliette hurried through the newsroom most people usually had their heads down. But this morning the entire features department was huddled together in deep conversation. Juliette could even hear Alex Davis laughing, which, considering that his face generally looked like thunder, was astonishing in itself.

'What's going on?' she said, pushing her way through the throng. 'Have I missed something exciting?'

Cara Bell, a young feature writer who'd just been promoted from her reporting job, giggled and pointed at Juliette's desk.

Juliette gasped out loud. Lying on top of her desk was the biggest bouquet of flowers she'd ever seen. White roses, lilac, lily of the valley and stocks – it looked, and smelled, absolutely divine.

Her heart leapt. Joe must have got back to London, regretted his heartless behaviour and decided to do something spectacular. Wow. She couldn't quite believe it. He was usually more of the whoops-forgot-the-anniversary-better-buy-chocs-from-the-garage sort of man.

Lost in thought, she suddenly realised that the whole newsroom seemed to be watching her reaction intently.

'Come on you lot – d'you mind?' she said. 'Haven't you got any work to be getting on with?'

Juliette took the little white envelope attached to the flowers and tore it open. When she saw the message, however, her heart plummeted with disappointment. She couldn't make sense of what she was reading.

'*Juliette*,' said the card in big bold letters. '*You missed a great party. Some other time perhaps? Tim.*'

From her desk directly opposite, Cara observed Juliette's reaction.

'You look as if you've lost a tenner and found 10p,' she said.

'Too right I have,' murmured Juliette. 'The flowers . . . they're . . . they're not exactly from who I expected.'

'They're pretty stunning all the same,' said Cara, thinking that she'd give her eye-teeth for a bunch like that.

'What?' said Juliette. 'Oh yes, they are, aren't they?'

'You're having a bit of a morning, aren't you,' said Cara sympathetically.

'Am I?'

Mystified as to what on earth Cara was hinting at, Juliette looked at the writer inquiringly.

'Come on. Spit it out. What else has been going on?'

'You know the feature on shoplifting that you had in Saturday's paper?'

Juliette nodded wearily. It seemed like a hundred years since she'd written that piece. She knew she'd checked everything in meticulous detail, but judging by the look on Cara's face, someone must have made a fuss.

'Has there been a complaint or something?'

'I'm afraid there have been quite a few of them,' said Cara. 'I got in at eight-fifteen and the phone's been ringing non-stop.'

Juliette wracked her brains. She couldn't think of anything particularly contentious about the feature. The main body of the piece had comprised a general look at the rise in shoplifting in the region, complete with facts, figures and an interview with a shopkeeper who claimed theft was costing him so much that he was in danger of going out of business. Then she'd written two short case histories of women who'd been caught shoplifting. One was an eighteen-year-old who'd pilfered lipsticks and nail varnish from the chemist. The other was Norma Gray, the middle-aged woman whose case had been up before Bowater Magistrates Court.

At that moment Juliette's telephone rang and she picked it up.

'Is that Juliette Ward?' said an angry-sounding voice.

For a second Juliette was tempted to pretend to be someone else entirely but honesty prevailed.

'Yes. Can I help you?'

'How could you do such a thing to my mum?' wailed the woman on the other end of the line. '*How could you?*'

'I'm sorry,' began Juliette, 'but I'm not entirely sure what you're talking about. What am I supposed to have done to your mum?'

Juliette's words seemed only to incense the woman further.

'You bloody reporters, you're all the same. Writing your poisonous little articles and then pleading innocence when you've ripped people's lives to pieces. My mum had to go through all this when our Ritchie got sent down. But I never thought *you'd* put the boot into her too. After everything she's been through.'

Bewildered by this tirade, Juliette took a deep breath and tried to stay calm.

'Look, Miss, Mrs . . . I don't even know your name. Who am I speaking to?'

'Mrs Lewis. Dawn Lewis. Mrs Lewis to you.'

'Thank you, Mrs Lewis,' said Juliette. 'Right. Now I desperately want to sort all this out but I honestly don't know what on earth you're talking about. What am I supposed to have done? Can you tell me? I can't help if you don't tell me, can I?'

Another sob was clearly audible from the other end. Juliette feared that Dawn Lewis was in such a state that it was going to be impossible to make head or tail of what she was so upset about.

'Your article on shoplifting,' said Dawn Lewis finally. 'One of the women you wrote about was . . . is my mother. She's had so much to cope with over the past

53

few months – my dad dying, me losing the baby and Ritchie . . . oh, I can't face talking about Ritchie. Anyway, she's been in such a state that one day she goes and picks up a couple of things in the supermarket and walks out without paying for them. She didn't have any idea what she was doing. But she went to court on Friday and thank God, got a conditional discharge. But just when she thinks that everything is over and she can start getting on with her life you have to come along and write about it. Hardly anyone knew about it before but now it's all over the village. She can hardly hold her head up in the street. You could have written about anyone – why did you have to go and choose her?'

Juliette pushed the bouquet of flowers to the side of her desk – the smell of them sickened her all of a sudden – and opened her notebook.

'Is your mum Norma Gray?'

'Of course she's Norma Gray,' snapped Dawn Lewis. 'I'd have thought that was pretty obvious. She cooks your lad's dinner every day, doesn't she?'

The mention of Freddie pulled Juliette up short. Alarm bells began ringing in her head. What did Freddie have to do with any of this?

'What do you mean?'

'I mean my mum cooks your lad's dinner every day. She's the dinner lady at Newdale. Don't play silly buggers with me. You know she is. That's what makes what you've done so much worse.'

It was like a light going on inside Juliette's head. In a flash everything fell into place. She remembered thinking that Norma Gray looked vaguely familiar in court. And Norma had actually told the magistrates that she was a dinner lady. She just hadn't said where. It certainly explained why virtually everyone had cut her and Freddie dead at school this morning. They must have thought she'd picked out Norma Gray for her feature on purpose.

'Oh my God,' said Juliette, banging the palm of her hand against her forehead. 'I had no idea. No bloody idea.'

'It's all very well for you to say that now,' said Dawn, her voice sharp. 'The damage is done. My mum's never going to be able to hold her head up again. She's so ashamed about what's happened that she even called in sick today. She's convinced the school is going to sack her.'

'They can't do that,' said Juliette, aghast.

'Can't they?' retorted Dawn. 'You just watch them. They've been threatening to get rid of her for years. You don't know the half of it. This is just the sort of excuse they've been waiting for.'

Juliette's mind was spinning. She'd been hoping for an easy ride today. She had an interview with the chairman of the local TV station later in the week to prepare for. With that out of the way she'd planned to leave the office at three to meet Freddie.

'Look,' she said firmly. 'You may find this hard to believe – I can scarcely believe it myself – but I honestly didn't have a clue who your mum was. I'd never have used her as one of my case histories if I'd known she was the dinner lady at Newdale . . .'

Juliette broke off, wondering what on earth she could do to sort this mess out.

'Can I come and see you? I'm sure if we put our heads together we could think of something that might help. They can't give her the sack for something as trivial as this. Are you around this morning?'

Dawn Lewis's voice sounded hard.

'I'm always around,' she said stonily. 'You always are when you're married to a farmer.'

'Oh, I didn't realise,' said Juliette. How the hell was she supposed to know? 'Give me some instructions on how to get there and I'll be with you in an hour.'

Alex Davis looked sceptical when Juliette told him something big was brewing and that she had to talk to a contact. She certainly wasn't going to admit that a load of readers had gone ballistic over her shoplifting piece.

'What do you mean, "something big"?' he demanded gruffly. 'Will it make a splash?'

Juliette tried to backtrack a little.

'Well, not that big exactly. But something that could be big in the future. I'll explain more when I get back to the office. Please? You're always going on about how crucial it is to build up my own contacts. I've got to start somewhere.'

Chapter Seven

Twenty minutes later, Juliette was heading out towards Hillthwaite, the isolated hamlet where Dawn Lewis lived. As she drove through Newdale and on past the school, she couldn't help wondering what Freddie was up to right now. She gripped the steering wheel tightly. God, she hoped none of the teachers had said anything to him about Norma Gray. They wouldn't take out their exasperation on him, surely? And more to the point, what was going to happen about the children's lunch today? If the school cook didn't turn up for work, who was going to prepare it for them?

Once she was out of Newdale, the road to Hillthwaite narrowed into a single track that snaked sharply along the west side of the fell. Glancing down the steep incline to her left, Juliette prayed she wouldn't meet anything coming the other way. The view across the wooded valley to the lake beyond was simply breathtaking but she didn't fancy the thought of a milk tanker thundering down the hill towards her.

After three weeks of living in Newdale, Juliette felt more of a townie than ever. It wasn't simply her clothes that set her apart, or her frustration at not being able to pop down to a shop on the corner for a pint of milk. No, she simply didn't understand the way things worked up here. Last night's *Eagle* had carried a story about children's ignorance of country ways. Admittedly, even Juliette had been stunned to read that loads of city kids had never encountered real sheep and didn't realise that bacon came from pigs. But at the same time it struck her forcibly that there were still so many things about the countryside that she hadn't got to grips with herself. She couldn't imagine, for instance, *how* people like Dawn Lewis and her husband survived up here in the winter. The Hillthwaite road seemed treacherous enough now. What on earth must it be like in the middle of winter when it was cut off by snow?

Juliette was so deep in thought that she was barely aware of what happened next. One moment the road was clear. The next a beaten up old Escort was roaring round the hairpin bend towards her. Juliette jammed her foot on the brake in panic. The car shuddered to a halt and then stalled. Juliette was so stunned that she burst into tears of shock.

A few seconds passed before she could bring herself to check what had happened to the other car. To her astonishment, it was only about six feet away from her bumper, the driver gesticulating wildly at her from his seat. She looked behind her and saw that there was a passing place just a few yards back. Overcome with relief, she started the car again, reversed carefully into the lay-by and waited for the Escort to drive on.

As it drew close to her, she glanced across at the driver, expecting a wave of the hand or a mouthed 'sorry' for driving like a maniac. The car slowed down all right, but instead of giving a contrite wave, the young driver wound down his window, flicked a V-sign at her and, his face contorted with hate, yelled 'you fucking bitch'.

Unnerved by just how close she'd come to plunging down the side of the fell, Juliette sat in the lay-by shaking uncontrollably. It was another fifteen minutes or so before she felt composed enough to drive on.

She was still trembling when she eventually pulled up in the yard at Hillthwaite Farm. Actually, she wasn't a hundred per cent confident that it *was* Hillthwaite Farm. There was no house sign and the place looked barely habitable, a complete dump. The burnt-out remains of two cars lay in a heap in one corner of the farmyard while dozens of sheets of rusting corrugated iron were piled high against the far wall. To add to the air of desolation, two terrifying-looking dogs, both chained up thank God, immediately began barking their heads off at her.

Juliette wasn't sure what to do. She half-hoped that the barking might bring someone scurrying out of the house, but it didn't.

This is ridiculous, she told herself sternly, pull yourself together. In her ten years as a journalist she'd been in far scarier places than this, everything from drug dens to prisons. She got out of the car and walked briskly towards the farmhouse door. Her actions seemed to incense the dogs even more. They charged forwards as far as their chains would allow them, still barking maniacally. Juliette was just wondering whether it might be wise to leg it back to the car when the door opened and a vastly overweight woman in her early thirties ventured out.

'Buster, Dragon – what the hell d'yer think yer playing at?' she yelled. 'Put a sock in it will you?'

Juliette reckoned she sounded as fierce as the dogs. If this was Dawn Lewis, she didn't fancy getting on the wrong side of her. Juliette swallowed hard. Come to think of it, she already *was* on the wrong side of her.

'Er, Mrs Lewis?' said Juliette in a timid voice that sounded completely alien to her.

'Who wants to know?' said the woman.

'Er, me. I'm Juliette Ward. From the *Eagle*. And . . .'

The woman looked Juliette up and down, clearly noting the impractical high-heeled shoes and short skirt. She herself was wearing a shapeless, rather grubby red tracksuit and filthy trainers.

Juliette clocked her scornful gaze and immediately wished that she'd nipped back home to change into jeans and wellies. When was she ever going to learn?

'So you are, are you?' said the woman.

'Yep,' said Juliette. 'And are you . . . ?'

Suddenly the woman's voice softened. She looked unbearably weary.

'Aye, I'm Dawn,' she said. 'Yer'd better come inside.'

Juliette followed Dawn into the house. The dogs, she was relieved to see, remained outside and eventually ceased barking.

'Want a brew?' said Dawn, leading Juliette down a dark dingy hall and into an even dingier kitchen.

'Mmmm,' said Juliette, thinking that she'd run a mile rather than let anything pass her lips in this house. 'That would be great.'

'Amy,' bellowed Dawn down the hallway. 'I'm just brewing up. D'you want one?'

From the far reaches of the house, Juliette heard a young girl's voice call back. 'No thanks, ta. I've just had one.'

'Is that your daughter?' asked Juliette, keen to keep things as pleasant and polite as possible.

Dawn's face instantly clouded over.

'No, she's not,' she said curtly. 'I haven't got any kids. Not yet, anyway.'

Realising that she'd said more than she'd intended, Dawn clamped a chubby hand over her mouth.

'I didn't say nothing, right?' she said in a desperate sort of air.

Juliette waved her hand in compliance.

'Don't worry,' she said, completely mystified as to what was going on. 'You didn't say anything. Truly.'

Once Dawn had made two large mugs of steaming hot tea, she beckoned to Juliette to follow her.

'Come on,' she said. 'We'll go into the parlour. I've lit the fire in there.'

Dawn led Juliette back along the hallway and into the small parlour at the front of the house. It was a pretty room, old-fashioned and cosy with a faded sofa, two armchairs and a wondrous view of the valley. Dawn lowered her vast bulk onto the sofa and motioned to Juliette to sit in the armchair next to the window.

'Oh, that's better,' she groaned. 'I've been on my feet all morning and I've still got Morton's dinner to see to. Morton – he's my husband.'

Juliette stared long and hard at her. If she wasn't so overweight, she thought, Dawn Lewis would actually be quite pretty. She had a lovely clear complexion and long dark hair drawn up in a bun.

'I'm so sorry to have upset you and your family,' began Juliette.

Dawn gave a bitter laugh.

'So what's new?' she said grimly 'We're used to it in this house.'

'Honestly, if I'd realised who your mum was I'd never have mentioned her in my piece,' said Juliette.

Dawn shrugged her shoulders.

'So what are yer going to do about it?'

The truth was, thought Juliette, there wasn't a lot she *could* do about it. The article had been used in the paper two days ago, most of Newdale had probably seen it and even if the education authority hadn't heard about the shoplifting incident before, they sure as hell would have by now.

'You said something on the phone about the council wanting to get rid of your mum for years,' said Juliette. 'What's all that about?'

An anxious look crossed Dawn's face.

'I don't remember saying that,' she said quickly.

Juliette leaned forward in her chair and cupped her face in her hands.

'Look, Dawn. I know I'm a journalist but I promise you that anything we talk about today won't go any further than these four walls. Unless you want it to, of course. I'm new here and I haven't a clue about anything but I really would like to help. Truly I would.'

Dawn took a huge slurp of tea – Juliette still hadn't touched hers – and swallowed it noisily. It sounded a bit like water sloshing down a large plughole.

'How do I know if I can trust you or not?' she said.

'You just can, that's all,' said Juliette fiercely. She wasn't sure how she could convince Dawn Lewis of this. As a breed, journalists weren't exactly renowned for keeping their mouths shut.

'Well, what do you suggest then? How can you stop them getting rid of Mum?'

Juliette sat back in her chair again and considered the matter.

'Suppose you tell me everything,' she said. 'Come on, Dawn. What exactly has the education authority said to your mum in the past?'

Once Dawn Lewis started talking, she didn't draw breath for half an hour. It seemed a relief to her to be getting things off her chest – things she'd clearly never told a soul before.

'Everything started going wrong after my dad died,' mumbled Dawn.

'How long ago's that?' prodded Juliette.

'Just over a year back,' said Dawn, 'though it seems

like yesterday. He and Mum were never right together – Dad was always a bit of a sod to her – but Mum went to pieces when he died.'

Juliette nodded sympathetically.

'I've heard a lot of people say that before,' she said. 'You'd have thought that unhappy couples wouldn't be so badly affected when one of them dies, wouldn't you? But it's not like that, is it? It's as if they start grieving for the missed opportunities, the things they wished they'd said. And then all of a sudden it's too late.'

Dawn nodded wordlessly. Juliette suddenly realised that tears were spilling down her cheeks. She moved forward to try and comfort her but Dawn waved her away.

'I'm all right, really I am. It's just . . . it's just that when I start talking about things it makes me cry. Not that I let anyone see. Not usually, anyhow.'

She pulled a large wodge of tissues out of her track suit pocket and blew her nose loudly.

'Now, where was I? Oh yes, Dad dying. When he died it was only Mum and me at the funeral. Ritchie couldn't come because he was . . .'

Dawn stopped abruptly again, reluctant to say what was uppermost in her mind.

'Go on,' said Juliette. '*Why* couldn't Ritchie come?'

'He couldn't come because he was inside,' cried Dawn with an angry sob. 'He's a complete no-hoper, only Mum's too blind to see it. She thinks the sun shines out of his backside. He's never done a day's work in his life. He just has to go whining to Mum and she gives him whatever he wants. That's why she never has two pennies to rub together for herself.'

'Why was he inside?' asked Juliette.

'He got three years for beating up a couple of teenagers outside a nightclub in Bowater. From what I've heard

63

since, these poor lads hadn't done anything to him. It was completely unprovoked. It always is with Ritchie. One lad asked the time and he went berserk. It was the drink that did it. He can't take his drink.'

'Is he out now?'

Dawn's eyes glazed over, as if she was miles away.

'You what? Oh yeah, he's out now. Came out quite a few months back.'

'Where's he living?' said Juliette.

'With Mum, of course,' sighed Dawn. 'Only now she's pretty skint so he's forever up here trying to scrounge off me. To pay for his drink and his drugs and whatever else it is that he gets up to.'

A thought suddenly occurred to Juliette.

'He wasn't up here this morning was he? Driving a red Escort?'

Dawn nodded her head wearily.

'Aye, that's him,' she said. 'Come across him, did you?'

'He nearly ran me off the road,' said Juliette. 'He came round one of those really sharp bends at about seventy mph. He could have killed us both, the way he was driving.'

Dawn didn't look in the least surprised. Incidents like this were normal occurrences where Ritchie was concerned.

'Yeah, well,' she said. 'That's what he's like.'

At that moment, the parlour door was pushed open and a washed-out looking young girl of about thirteen or fourteen peered in.

'I'm not feeling very well, Dawn,' she began, before realising that Dawn wasn't on her own.

The girl flushed scarlet and disappeared down the hall muttering: 'I'm sorry. I'm sorry. I thought it was safe to come down.'

Unable to comprehend what she had just seen, Juliette stared at Dawn. She was so aghast that for a few seconds she couldn't bring herself to utter a word. This girl couldn't be more than fourteen at the very most, she just couldn't be. She was small and skinny, with stick-like arms and legs – all of which served to make the distinctive swell of her stomach even more shocking. She must be at least six months pregnant, maybe more.

Juliette stared questioningly at Dawn. There was no messing about with something like this.

'Who is she?' she said bluntly.

Once again, a sob caught in Dawn's throat.

'You won't tell anyone, will you?' she said. 'You mustn't. You really mustn't.'

'I won't tell anyone at work, if that's what you mean,' muttered Juliette. 'But just look at her. She needs help. Who is she?'

Dawn wrung her hands helplessly in her lap.

'Amy Barker,' she said in a half-whisper. 'Carol's daughter.'

'What?' said Juliette. 'Carol Barker? The caretaker at the school?'

Dawn nodded without speaking.

'And how old is she?'

'Fourteen next month,' mumbled Dawn.

'And why is she here?'

Juliette knew she was barraging Dawn with questions but she couldn't stop herself.

Dawn sighed heavily.

'It just seemed like the obvious thing to do,' she said finally. 'Carol knows that I'm at home all the time so I can keep an eye on Amy. Poor little thing. She was adamant she wasn't going to get rid of it – and you know how people in the village talk. Up here we're on our own, well away from the nosey parkers. There's enough of them in Newdale.'

'And who's the father?'

Dawn glanced away, reluctant to look Juliette in the eye.

'Dunno,' she said, staring down at her trainers. 'Amy won't tell us.'

Juliette wasn't sure she believed this, but she left it alone and ploughed on.

'Has she seen the doctor?'

On surer ground once more, Dawn looked up and smiled wanly.

'Yes,' she said. 'I take her to her ante-natal appointments every month. And social services know about her too. I wouldn't let Amy take any risks with her health, you can be sure of that. You may not agree with all this, but we're not irresponsible people, you know.'

Relieved to hear this, Juliette sat back in her armchair and reflected on what she'd just heard. What a mess. With Amy Barker to worry about, the shoplifting article in the *Eagle* must have been the last straw as far as Dawn was concerned.

'Look,' she said. 'You've got an awful lot on your plate, Dawn. I know you probably don't trust me – but I promise I won't mention any of this to the paper. I absolutely give you my word.'

Juliette paused for a moment. 'Will you do me a favour though?'

Dawn looked wary.

'Like what?' she said, a trace of aggression detectable in her tone.

'Will you let me come up and see you both sometimes? Just so I know that Amy's all right and you're coping. For my own peace of mind.'

'All right,' said Dawn grudgingly. 'But I don't want any interfering, right? Is that agreed?'

'Agreed,' said Juliette. 'Oh, and there's one other thing.'

'What's that?'

'I don't know what the education authority has said before, but you just let me know if they start any funny business about your mum's job. A story in the *Eagle* about a heartless council threatening to sack an impoverished widow who's given her whole life to Newdale School should soon bring them to their senses.'

Chapter Eight

Joe was feeling pretty pleased with himself. His show had been on air for a month, and letters, faxes and e-mails were rolling in, nearly all of them favourable. Advertising revenue was going up steadily and even the sour-faced bosses upstairs seemed happy with his performance.

No, the only part of his life that was a complete disaster was him and Jules. When he rang to speak to Freddie – as he did each night without fail – Juliette made no attempt to hide her hostility. And the fact that he'd failed to get up north for two weekends on the trot now had made things a million times worse. Freddie had seemed fine about it, especially when Joe bunged a couple of new games for his Game Boy in the post. But Jules was completely intransigent. Her reaction had been unequivocal, even when he explained he had no choice in the matter – Radio Wave had ordered him to attend a brainstorming session one weekend and a promotional tour the next. 'Get your priorities right for a change, will you?' she'd bellowed, then slammed the phone down on him.

The oddest thing about his new life was finishing work at nine am. Sometimes he and Annie met informally after the show to discuss how it had all gone and decide the following day's running order. But once that was out of the way, he was as free as the air. He'd joined a swanky squash club in the City and although he'd always steered clear of showbiz parties and press launches in the past, he'd now started turning up to a few of them. At least it was a way of passing the time.

'Honestly, Joe, you'd go to the opening of a paper bag these days,' chuckled Bob Carter, his sound engineer, after Joe had regaled him with a few choice titbits of showbiz gossip. 'I thought you were more of a pipe and slippers man yourself.'

Joe laughed. But Bob had struck a nerve. He *was* a different person to the old Joe, the Joe who'd hurried home to Jules and Freddie every night.

Today he was having lunch with Daniel White, his new agent. This was another recent development. For years Joe had never bothered with one, figuring that he was perfectly capable of sorting out pay and conditions for himself. But everything had snowballed at Radio Wave. Suddenly all the red tops wanted to do interviews with him, a couple of stores had asked him to make personal appearances and a TV station had broached the subject of him hosting a daytime quiz show. Joe fully appreciated that this had only a fifty-fifty chance of coming off but having Daniel White to act for him looked far more professional. He didn't have the time to deal with everything himself any more. Far better to stick to what he was good at.

Striding into the Ritz's elegant restaurant, Joe had to pinch himself to make sure all this was really happening. He was used to negotiating a couple of quid extra for a show over a pint at the pub. If he'd ever dreamed he'd be discussing telly offers over lunch at the Ritz he'd have laughed his head off.

'Joe,' said the urbane Daniel White, standing up to greet him. 'How delightful to see you.'

'And you,' murmured Joe. He'd made a big effort to

wear a suit and tie, rather than his usual jeans and T-shirt, but he felt hopelessly scruffy alongside Daniel. Regarded as one of the sharpest agents in the business, Daniel White prided himself on his appearance. A tall, elegant man of around forty, today he was wearing a beautifully cut navy Paul Smith suit, pale pink tie and brogues that were so highly polished Joe could see his reflection in them.

Daniel ordered them each a glass of champagne and insisted that they study the menu properly before getting down to business.

'Show's going splendidly, Joe,' remarked Daniel when they'd finally ordered.

Joe grinned. He knew perfectly well that Daniel was more of a Radio Three man himself. It was ironic that this highly cultured man had ended up representing DJs, down market comedians and game show hosts. Yet professional to the core, he always monitored his clients' performances as closely as he could bear.

'Glad you're enjoying it. Just say the word and I'll play you a request if you like. What do you fancy? Coldplay or Westlife?'

Daniel shuddered inwardly. He couldn't think of anything worse.

'Don't worry,' said Joe. 'I was only joking.'

Daniel's face remained impassive. Joe didn't know him well enough to appreciate that he didn't have much of a sense of humour.

'Very kind of you, I'm sure,' murmured Daniel. 'Now, I asked you to lunch so that we could take a look at your career in the longer term. Plan our strategy if you like.'

Joe took another sip of his ice-cold champagne. He'd never given his long-term career much thought, still less planned a strategy. After all, playing records, interspersed with a little chat, wasn't exactly rocket science.

'Er, what exactly did you have in mind?'

Daniel sat back in his chair and regarded his newest client keenly. Joe Ward definitely had potential, there was no doubt about that. He was bright and funny and yes, he had the kind of easy charm that went down well with the punters. He was good-looking in a moth-eaten sort of way too – Daniel made a mental note to send him along to a decent tailor. His hair, mid-blonde and curling over his collar, was perhaps a touch too long but given that he worked in the music industry, that wasn't really a problem.

'We need to raise your profile,' he said finally. 'The Radio Wave breakfast show is a good start but it's not enough. No, we've got to get you into TV, there's no doubt about that. It's where the money is these days. And if we smarten you up a little around the edges we'll do it, I'm sure.'

Joe stared back at Daniel. He didn't like the sound of the smartening up bit at all. And for God's sake, this was him in his best suit, *on a good day*. Daniel would have a heart attack if he could see him at five am on a normal day, in a pair of ancient jeans, T-shirt that had run in the wash and yesterday's stubble.

'The *Mirror* definitely wants to do an interview with you and the *Daily News* is interested too. That'll all help. And can I make another suggestion?'

'Go ahead,' said Joe good-naturedly.

'You need to get out and about more,' said Daniel.

'Sorry?' said Joe. Daniel made him sound like a sad housebound git.

'The best way to get you better known is for you to go to everything you can – showbiz parties, film premieres, first nights. You name it, I want you to be there.'

'I already go to quite a lot of them.'

'Not enough,' said Daniel, his voice firm. 'We want to

get people talking about you. And the best way to do that is to get you into the gossip columns. Make a beeline for some of the It-girls at parties – that's one way. You could even try that old trick of lifting pretty girls off the ground and hurling them over your shoulder. It would do your image the world of good. Make you look a little daring. A bit unpredictable.'

'You must be joking,' said Joe. Turning up to a few parties was one thing but he drew the line at bloody acrobatics.

'Oh well, it was just a thought,' said Daniel hastily. 'But I'm sure you get my drift. Now, what else is there? Oh yes, you need to make sure that you're in top condition. I'm not saying you're flabby exactly but TV puts pounds on you. You need to stay off the beer and start working out every day. Do you belong to a gym?'

'Er, I've just joined a squash club,' mumbled Joe. 'Smart's. In the City.'

'And how often do you play?' asked Daniel.

Joe cast his mind back over the past week. He'd fixed up one game, only to cancel it when he got wind of a drinking session with a bunch of old DJ pals. The longest amount of time he'd spent at Smart's to date, come to think of it, was in the bar.

'Oh, it varies,' he said vaguely, hoping to throw Daniel off the scent.

Daniel, however, was like a dog with a bone. He refused to drop the subject, even when the waiter brought their first courses to the table.

'Blimey,' said Joe, eyeing the stunning goat's cheese soufflé in front of him. 'It's a work of art.'

'Never mind that,' said Daniel, spooning carrot and ginger soup into his mouth. He even did that elegantly, thought Joe.

'Now,' continued Daniel, 'I think that we should set

up an exercise regime for you. What time do you finish the programme?'

'Nine,' said Joe, slightly miffed that his agent professed to listen to the show, yet didn't know when it ended.

'Right,' said Daniel, in a voice that brooked no argument. 'I want you at the squash club by ten every morning. If you have a daily session there you'll get rid of the flab in no time.'

'I reckon I'm fine as I am. It's not as if I'm grossly overweight.'

'No, you're not,' agreed Daniel. 'But it's a sad fact that in this game it matters how you look. When did you last go to the dentist by the way? Have you ever thought of having your front teeth capped?'

By the end of lunch Daniel had persuaded a reluctant Joe to embark on an intensive grooming and styling campaign. The only thing Joe had firmly drawn the line at was Daniel's suggestion that he should think about trying a pair of sky blue contact lenses.

'They'd really bring out the blondeness of your hair,' said Daniel. 'Perhaps you should consider having a few highlights too, come to think of it.'

Midway through lifting a petit four to his mouth, Joe stared at Daniel uncomprehendingly.

'No way,' he said, so shocked that he dropped most of the chocolate delicacy onto the pristine white tablecloth. 'Absolutely no way. I know you are trying to do your best for me but I'm a DJ, Daniel. *A DJ*. Not a bloody supermodel.'

As Joe wandered off down Piccadilly – Daniel had stepped smartly into a cab – he found himself missing Juliette for the first time in ages. If she'd been in London he would have rushed straight round to her office to tell her all about Daniel White's preposterous ideas. She'd have found the whole thing as hilarious as he did.

Sitting in the back of his taxi, Daniel White mused over his meeting with Joe. The man definitely had potential, he thought as the cab whizzed round Hyde Park Corner. There was no doubt about that. And he quite liked Joe's point-blank refusal to highlight his hair or try coloured contact lenses. It showed character – and there was precious little of that knocking around the TV business these days.

Chapter Nine

Juliette stamped her feet impatiently on the platform at Bowater station. It was the first day of November and winter had set in with a vengeance. The cottage was so freezing that Freddie had crept into her bed for five nights in a row complaining that he was cold.

But cold apart, life in the north was definitely looking up. Juliette had been getting a reasonable show in the paper and Freddie seemed a tiny bit happier at school too. He'd had a whale of a time at Lizzie Nicholson's house and Juliette had invited the little girl back to tea at the weekend. She still hadn't managed to find another childminder to meet Freddie from school but Fi Nicholson had helped her out a couple of times and now her mum was coming to hold the fort for a few days.

At that moment the inter-city train from Euston thundered into the station, blowing a gust of ice-cold air in its wake. Juliette's heart started hammering wildly. She told herself not to be so ridiculous – this was her mum she was meeting, not the Prime Minister – but she couldn't help feeling on edge.

Juliette's relationship with her mother had always been rocky, even at the best of times. She couldn't put her finger on why – they just seemed to rub each other up the wrong way. Freddie adored her though. And while Maura Stanley had never bothered much with her own children, she was perfectly happy to get down on her knees and play silly games with her grandson.

Her mother was one of the last people to emerge from the packed train. When she did, an immaculate figure in an emerald green suit, coral silk scarf and black knee-length boots, Juliette walked briskly to greet her.

Perhaps she imagined it but she was pretty sure that her mother hesitated for a split-second before returning her hug. But there again, Maura Stanley had never been one for hugs and kisses. Even now it was always Juliette who had to grab hold of her mother, never the other way round.

'You look fantastic, Mum,' said Juliette, stepping back to take a proper look at her.

'Thank you, dear,' said Maura, patting her perfectly-coiffed hair with satisfaction. 'I believe in taking good care of myself, you know that. Have you come straight from the office? You don't look as smart as you used to in London.'

Thanks Mum, thought Juliette. You always know how to make a girl feel a million dollars.

'Yep,' she replied. 'It's my lunch-hour anyway and I've sort of wangled the afternoon off.'

'That's nice, dear,' said Maura, only half-listening. She pulled the collar of her jacket more tightly round her neck. 'I don't know how you stand this chill. It must be several degrees colder up here than it is in Eastbourne.'

In fact Juliette had lied through her teeth to Alex Davis, claiming that she was working on something that could turn out to be big and she had to meet a vital contact. Alex was looking even more tired and drawn these days – no one had a clue what was bugging him – and amazingly he hadn't questioned her further.

'Come on, I'll carry your bags. The car's just outside.'

As Juliette lugged her mother's leather vanity case and

two matching suitcases – God only knows what she'd packed in them – along the platform, she wondered whether this visit was such a terrific idea after all. Her mum had only been here for five minutes and she was already irritating the hell out of her.

On the drive back to Newdale the two of them made polite conversation. Maura asked about Freddie and how he was getting on at his new school and in turn Juliette inquired about Gerald, her stepfather of five years.

Throughout all this Juliette felt as if she was stepping on eggshells. She avoided mentioning David, Gerald's own son, because he was like a red rag to a bull where Maura was concerned. 'A money-grabbing oily little toad' had been one of her mother's more polite descriptions for him. And she didn't inquire about Johnnie, her older brother, because he'd just started a two-year contract in Chicago and Maura always burst into tears when anyone reminded her how far away he was.

Looking back, Juliette was well aware that Johnnie had always been her mother's favourite. Whatever *she* did was wrong as far as her mother was concerned. Even when she'd rung to explain about them moving north and Joe commuting up to see them at weekends – what a joke that had turned out to be – her mother had tut-tutted sharply. 'He'll leave you, you know,' she'd said. 'If you move a good three hundred miles away he'll find someone else. That's how men are.' Juliette had clenched her fingers tight inside her fists to stop herself saying something she might regret. Then she'd taken a deep breath and neatly changed the subject.

Juliette wasn't entirely sure where things had gone wrong between her and her mother. Admittedly, as a child she'd always gravitated towards her father, Denys, who was unpredictable and full of fun. He was the one who'd suggest going off camping on the spur of the moment. Or would arrive home with a huge cuddly lion he'd spotted in Hamleys on the way home from work and simply couldn't resist. He adored people dropping in for a drink – if he'd had things his way he'd have held open house all weekend. 'The more the merrier' was his attitude.

What had drawn her parents together in the first place remained a mystery. While Denys, a sports writer on a Sunday newspaper, was slapdash and exuberant, Maura was fastidious, organised and wouldn't dream of stepping out of the house without full make-up. She hated mess and chaos and was forever on at Denys to clear his things up. When Juliette was about nine, he'd decamped from the house altogether at weekends and spent most Saturdays and Sundays in the small shed at the bottom of the garden, along with his books and papers, Nat King Cole records and favourite malt whisky. Juliette sneaked down there as often as she could – that is when Maura wasn't ferrying her to the ballet and riding lessons she insisted on. And it was there that Juliette had found her father lying on the floor one Saturday morning, writhing in agony. He'd suffered a massive heart attack – and died on his way to hospital. Juliette was just thirteen.

'Is this it then?'

Deep in her own thoughts, Juliette glanced across at her mother.

'Yep,' she said, pulling up outside the row of white-washed cottages. 'This is it.'

She noticed Mr Spratton's net curtains twitch a fraction and although this would have irritated the hell out of her only a few weeks back, now it made her smile.

'What do you think? It's pretty, isn't it?'

Maura's face was a picture. Not only had her skin turned puce but her mouth kept opening and closing like some half-crazed goldfish. Juliette had no idea what her mother had been expecting – a rambling farmhouse with hens clucking by the door perhaps, or a Georgian rectory – but certainly not this humble row of farm workers' cottages.

'Er, y-yes, dear,' stammered Maura. 'If you say so. I had been expecting something a little larger, I must admit.'

At least, thought Juliette, her mother no longer had the power to get to her. In her twenties, she would have snapped back with something acerbic and paid for it later. Now, however, she smiled beatifically and walked round to the boot to lift out her mother's luggage.

'Come on,' she said. 'I'll show you up to your room. Me and Freddie spent all of Sunday decorating it for you.'

An hour later, after Maura had had a cup of tea and a lie-down, they drove down to Newdale to collect Freddie from school.

'He does like it here, doesn't he?' said Maura as they stood together at the school gate.

'He loves it, Mum,' said Juliette quickly. 'You know how mad he is on outdoor things. It was the best thing we ever did, moving up here.'

Maura glanced at her daughter. She couldn't put her finger on it exactly, but something seemed wrong.

'Good,' she said. 'Oh look, the children have started coming out. What a shame they don't wear uniform. I can't wait to see dear little Freddie. He must have grown such a lot since the summer.'

Freddie was always one of the last to emerge from Class Two's grotty Portakabin. Juliette wasn't sure why, but it seemed to take him far longer than anyone else to find his coat and reading folder and retrieve his lunch box from the shelf. After Freddie's graphic descriptions of mashed potato with black bits in and gristly mince, Juliette had succumbed and let him start taking a packed lunch to school.

Now Juliette frowned. He was later than ever coming out today. She wondered what was keeping him.

'I'll just go and see if I can . . .'

Her words stuck in her throat as Freddie suddenly appeared at the top of the steps, a small vulnerable figure with his coat done up all wrong and tears streaming down his face. In an instant, she'd completely forgotten her mother. She dashed across the playground, desperate to scoop him up in her arms and cuddle him.

'Darling,' she cried when she got to him. 'What on earth's the matter?'

'Craig Barker hit me,' he sobbed into her shoulder.

'What? Just now?'

'Y-y-yes,' howled Freddie.

'But why did he do that?'

'He said I'm a southern nancy boy and I should go back where I belong. He's always saying it.'

Beside herself with fury, Juliette stood up.

'Come on, darling,' she said firmly. 'We're going to see Mrs Booth. No one's allowed to talk to you like that and get away with it. Not if I can help it.'

At this, Freddie grew hysterical.

'No, you can't, Mummy. You can't. If he finds out I told on him he'll pick on me even more. Please Mummy. Please don't. Please.'

Acutely aware that her mother was watching all this, Juliette took hold of Freddie's hand and led him through the playground. It crossed her mind that she was probably handling things all wrong but she dashed such thoughts from her head.

'All right, darling,' she said. 'I won't talk to Mrs Booth today. But you've got to promise me that if anyone ever hits you again or calls you rude names you'll tell me. I mean it. Straight away. And I *will* go to Mrs Booth or Mrs Gyngell next time, I promise you.'

When Freddie spotted Maura waiting for him at the gate, his eyes lit up.

'Granny, I forgot you were coming,' he screeched and ran straight into her arms.

Freddie was so exhausted by the events of the day that he dozed off after his bath and didn't protest when Juliette insisted on tucking him up in bed soon after seven.

'Phew, that's a first,' she told her mother as she sank thankfully into an armchair in the sitting room. 'Most nights I have to cajole him for about half an hour before I can get him upstairs.'

Sitting opposite her with a stiff gin and tonic in her hand, Maura regarded her daughter keenly.

'He's missing Joe terribly, isn't he?'

Juliette stared at her mother.

'What do you mean? Has he said something to you?'

'Only that he isn't quite sure when he's going to see his dad again,' said Maura.

Juliette sighed wearily.

'He knows that Joe's coming up this weekend,' she said. 'I've told him a million times.'

'Yes, you have,' agreed Maura. 'But Joe's promised to be here for the past two weekends, hasn't he? And then at the last minute he hasn't turned up. You two have got to sort yourselves out, Juliette. Because it's not fair on Freddie if you don't. It's obvious that he's in a complete muddle about what's going on. He's only six and he doesn't understand any of this.'

Juliette could feel her blood rising. She couldn't believe that her mother had the gall to sit there and lecture *her* about being a good parent.

'And was there anything else you needed to get off your chest before I cook supper?' she asked.

'Well yes, as a matter of fact, there is,' said Maura, ignoring Juliette's sarcasm. 'I hate to interfere, you know I do, but it's quite obvious that you and Freddie aren't coping up here. From what Freddie's said, he doesn't have a clue who's going to be meeting him from school each day. And he told me that you forgot to make his packed lunch twice last week so he had to ask his teacher for a school lunch.'

Juliette took a sharp intake of breath at this. Freddie hadn't mentioned anything to her, although if she was honest, work had been chaotic and making Freddie's lunch could easily have slipped her mind.

At that moment the phone rang. Grateful for a chance to escape her mother's lecture and calm down for a bit, Juliette ran into the hall to answer it.

'Hello,' she said, conscious that her voice sounded flat and subdued.

'Juliette, is that you? It's Alex. From work.'

'Hi there. Is there a problem? I'll be filing my fell rescue piece tomorrow if that's what you're worried about. I've just got a couple more people I need to talk to in the morning.'

Alex gave a humourless laugh.

'No, I'm not worried about that. Look, it's Tim Dawner.'

The mention of Tim Dawner's name sent a shiver down the back of Juliette's neck. She'd sent him a polite note a couple of weeks back thanking him for the amazing flowers but she hadn't heard a thing in return. She'd felt relieved in a way.

'What about him?' she demanded.

'I'm still at my desk rewriting Cara's latest joke of a piece – why the hell Geoff Lake moved her over to features I don't know – and Dawner's just rung asking for you,' said Alex. 'Says there's something important brewing and he's prepared to give you the exclusive.

He sounds in a bit of a state actually. He wants you to go down to the Denim Heart office now.'

'*Now*?' repeated Juliette. 'But it's nearly eight o'clock.'

'Thank you, Juliette, I can tell the time,' said Alex curtly. 'Look, can you just get on with it? Geoff popped his head round the door an hour ago moaning that we haven't got a splash for tomorrow's paper. So you never know, you could have it in the bag. Oh, and another thing . . .'

'What's that?'

'Tongues are wagging round the whole of Bowater about the mess Denim Heart's in. So use your head, won't you? Don't let Tim Dawner tell you everything's all fine and dandy when it's not. That's not the story we're after.'

Chapter Ten

Driving towards Bowater in the dark, Juliette dipped her headlights as another car approached. Thank God her mother was staying. It would have been impossible to drop everything at a second's notice otherwise. She'd momentarily shoved her mother's harsh words about Freddie to the back of her mind. Now wasn't the right time to think about all that. It was important to get the Tim Dawner interview out of the way first.

When she arrived at the Denim Heart office about twenty minutes later, she drew up alongside the only other car in the car park, a sleek red Morgan, and strode straight to the front door. The instant she touched the handle, a battery of security lights snapped on, illuminating the forecourt and half-blinding her in the process. Seconds later, the loudest alarm she'd ever heard in her life erupted out of nowhere.

Terrified by the commotion, Juliette was tempted to leg it straight back to the car and get the hell out of this place. But before she could do anything, Tim Dawner suddenly charged out of the door at top speed and threw his arms around her.

'Don't panic,' he yelled into her ear, trying desperately to make himself heard over the alarm. 'The police will be here in a second so we'll sort it. Then we can get on with our chat. At least I know the new security system is up to the job now.'

Juliette caught his eye and grinned.

'All I did was park my car and walk to the front door,' she said. 'It's like a scene out of *The Bill* round here.'

'I'm sorry,' said Tim, his eyes warm. 'We were burgled a few months back so I had to get everything tightened up.'

'That's the understatement of the year,' murmured Juliette as a police car, lights flashing and siren blazing, raced into the car park. Two absurdly young-looking coppers jumped out.

'Everything all right, Mr Dawner?' said the first one.

'It is now,' said Tim, his voice smooth and charming. 'I'm so sorry to have brought you rushing out for nothing on a bitterly cold night. One of the managers must have thought I'd left for the evening and switched the alarm system on. This is Juliette Ward by the way. From the *Eagle*. She's doing an interview with me.'

'Sure she is,' whispered the second policeman under his breath, noting the way Tim Dawner's arm was casually draped around Juliette's shoulders. 'Don't let us get in your way now, will you, Mr Dawner? You've obviously got a lot more important things to be seeing to.'

'Bloody cheek,' muttered Juliette as she disentangled herself from Tim Dawner's arm and followed him inside the building.

'What was that?' asked Tim, flashing her a heart-stopping smile.

'Oh nothing,' said Juliette. 'Do you often work this late?'

'Only every night. It's not as if I've got much else to do.'

85

'My heart bleeds for you,' joked Juliette, though privately she couldn't help wondering what his girlfriend thought of his working habits.

Tim Dawner led her through a maze of dark corridors and into the office where she'd interviewed him a couple of months earlier. It looked completely different at night. Now it resembled something out of *Homes and Gardens* rather than a place of work. Thick velvet curtains the colour of clotted cream had been drawn across the windows and the vast room was lit by a couple of brass lamps. She couldn't help noticing too that there was a bottle of champagne in an ice bucket on the table, and two elegant long-stemmed glasses.

'Look,' said Juliette, not quite sure what to make of all this. 'Alex Davis said that you had a story for the *Eagle*. He'll go stark raving bonkers if I don't turn up with one so can we get on with it?'

Tim laughed at the agitated expression on her face.

'For goodness sake, Juliette, sit down and relax, will you? Of course I've got a story for you. Why would I ask you here otherwise?'

This last question hung in the air for a few seconds. Then Tim threw back his head and roared with laughter again.

'There's no need to be so bloody suspicious, Jules,' he chuckled. 'I asked for you because you're the only decent journalist in the place. I need someone who knows what they're doing. Not some teenager straight out of college.'

'Flattery will get you absolutely everywhere,' smiled Juliette, noting the way he too had called her Jules. 'And yes, I suppose you're right. I'm not usually the type to blow my own trumpet – but most of the others wouldn't spot a story if it came up and whacked them in the face.'

'My point exactly,' murmured Tim. 'Now, before we get down to business, can I pour you a glass of champagne?'

'Just half a glass,' said Juliette. 'What are you celebrating?'

For a brief moment, Tim looked despondent.

'I'm not,' he said, deftly popping the cork into his hand. 'Not celebrating, I mean. Drowning my sorrows more like.'

Juliette pulled a notebook and pen out of her bag.

'Right,' she said firmly. 'You'd better tell me what's going on at Denim Heart.'

'Oh, I love it when you get all masterful,' said Tim.

'Come on,' insisted Juliette. 'What's going on here?'

Tim took a long slurp of champagne and slumped down on to the leather sofa opposite Juliette. He looked shattered. There were dark shadows under his eyes and she was pretty sure he'd lost weight since they'd bumped into each other at the supermarket.

'Where do I bloody start?' he said, a trace of bitterness clear in his voice.

'How about the beginning?' prompted Juliette gently. 'Come on, Tim. I haven't got all night.'

'Shame,' murmured Tim, his eyes humorous once more. Then noticing her stern expression, he plonked his feet on the low table in front of him, folded his arms and began to talk.

'Bowater's a small place,' he said. 'It's pretty obvious that everyone's gossiping about Denim Heart. Spreading it around that we're in trouble, that we might go to the wall. I expect you've heard all that, haven't you?'

Juliette stared at him. She'd been so wrapped up in Freddie and her own work for the last few weeks that apart from Alex's remark on the phone she'd heard nothing of the kind. Mind you, even if Madonna herself had just snapped up a house in Bowater, it was pretty doubtful that she'd know about it.

'Well, you know,' she said, hedging her bets. 'A bit.'

'It's complete bollocks,' he said, angrily thumping the sofa beside him. 'Why does everyone bad-mouth you when you're successful? Why are they so eaten up with jealousy? Why do they want to knock you off your perch? After everything I've done for this bloody place. Created loads of jobs. Set up youth training schemes. No one would have bloody heard of Bowater if it weren't for me. And this is all the thanks I get.'

Juliette stopped writing in her notebook and looked across at him again.

'Look Tim, could you just stop the ranting and raving and calm down? What exactly is going on at Denim Heart? That's what I need to know.'

It was a few seconds before Tim replied and when he did, his voice sounded exhausted.

'The main problem right now is the *Chronicle*. The bloody, bloody *Chronicle*. Most of their readers are women – they pride themselves on that – and they've been fascinated by Denim Heart since we started. In the beginning it was all fluffy lifestyle stuff. In other words, completely harmless. You know the sort of thing – beauty pieces, nice little profiles of me and Helen at home, features about us running a successful make-up business in the back of beyond . . . Any time they were doing a piece on successful entrepreneurs under forty, I'd be one of the first people they'd call.'

'Not Helen?' inquired Juliette.

'I told you before. Helen's always been in the background. It's my company. *My* concept. *My* creation.'

'Fine,' said Juliette. Questions about the balance of power at Denim Heart clearly grated with him, so she tried to steer him back to his quarrel with the *Chronicle*.

'And so what's the *Chronicle* done to upset you now? I'd have thought it was water off a duck's back to you.'

'Oh God, don't remind me,' said Tim. He ran his fingers agitatedly through his hair. 'Look, I told you that up until the beginning of the year they were all over me like a rash. They couldn't get enough of Denim Heart. Right? Then for some reason – I haven't a clue why – they bloody turned against me. First it was knocking stories about our products. Then they ran a piece slamming our delivery times. Said we promise to deliver inside forty-eight hours and never do. And then to cap it all, they told me a couple of hours ago that they're running a story tomorrow saying that we're on the verge of bankruptcy.'

'And are you?' asked Juliette calmly, cutting straight through Tim's histrionics.

'What?' screeched Tim, jumping to his feet. 'I can't believe you bloody well said that. I thought you were on my side. Of course we're bloody not. That's the whole point. Come with me and I'll show you.'

Juliette was on the point of saying that she wasn't on anyone's side. But before she could utter a word Tim grabbed hold of her hand and pulled her towards the door.

If anyone else had done this, Juliette would have resisted like the plague. But for some reason, she didn't feel in the least threatened by Tim Dawner. This was only their third encounter and yet she felt more at ease with him than with anyone else she'd met in a long time. In fact he was the only person in Bowater who seemed remotely on the same wavelength as her.

Still clutching her hand like grim death, Tim marched her down another long corridor, through a pair of bright blue double doors and straight on to the factory floor. Juliette's eyes widened in shock as she gazed around the huge, cavernous area. She couldn't believe what she was seeing. Slipping her hand out of Tim's, she wandered along the workbenches to take a closer look. The factory was equipped with all the latest technology all right – computerised packing, lifting equipment, you name it – but it was a complete shambles. Every work surface was piled high with cosmetics, shampoos and every conceivable kind of beauty product. There were packing cases everywhere and yard upon yard of paper spewed forth from the fax machines in the corner.

'There,' said Tim, waving his hand with a flourish. 'Does this look like a company that's on the verge of going bankrupt?'

Juliette remained speechless for a few seconds. She couldn't think what on earth to say. She didn't have a clue what a company on the verge of bankruptcy looked like – but even if Denim Heart was healthily in the black it badly needed a good spring clean.

'Er, I'm not sure,' she said lamely.

'Just take a butchers at this then.' Tim wrenched a wad of paper from the fax machine. 'These are just some of the faxed orders we've received over the last few hours. Look at them. They're coming in from all over the world.'

He ran his eye down the orders.

'I reckon there must be a couple of grand's worth there. Now do you think you're looking at a company that's going down the plug hole? Mmmm? Do you?'

'Why the hell are you asking *me*?' said Juliette. 'I haven't the faintest idea about business. But come on Tim, you've got to give me a better line than that. It's all very well us running a story saying "Tim Dawner denies claims that Denim Heart is going under . . ." That's what you *would* say, isn't it? Can't you come up with something a bit more juicy?'

'Juicy, eh?' muttered Tim. 'Well, how about this for

starters? Helen's only gone and bloody walked on me out after eight years. From now on I'm going to be running the business on my own.'

Juliette gaped at him. She'd never met Helen Brown but this was the last thing she'd expected. From what Tim had told her during their first meeting, she'd got the impression they were bound together for life.

'What brought all this on? Can I use it in the paper?'

'Yep,' said Tim. 'Just so long as you make it quite clear that the *Chronicle*'s got its wires completely up its arse. Denim Heart is on the up and Helen's going to rue the day she quit. It's all her bloody fault that our delivery times slipped in the first place. I had an idea that she'd taken her eye off the ball a few weeks back but I just didn't have the heart to have it out with her. Serves me right for being so soft. I felt I had to protect her, and look where that's bloody got me. But now she's gone, there'll be no looking back. You just watch, Jules. You're the first person to know this but Denim Heart is really going places now.'

It was another hour before Juliette was happy with the information she'd gleaned from Tim. The way he told it, his relationship with Helen would have petered out years ago if they hadn't been tied together by the business. Helen was a couple of years older than Tim and she'd been desperate for them to have children together. Sadly, it had never happened.

'I don't know why I'm telling you all this,' said Tim at one point. 'I don't usually like talking about personal things. It's your fault. You're too easy to talk to.'

Juliette's sole misgiving about the story was that she'd only heard Tim's side of things. Experience told her that Helen's own version would be completely different.

'What's Helen like?' Juliette was curious to know more

about the woman who'd been such a crucial part of Tim's life.

Tim stared at her, an expression of stupefaction on his face.

'She's changed a lot since we first met,' he said finally. 'She's a lot harder, a lot more ruthless than she used to be. Sometimes I think . . .'

He faltered for a moment before adding: 'No, I can't. It's not fair on Helen to discuss her behind her back.'

'Can I talk to her then?' said Juliette urgently. 'At least to get things from her point of view. It's only fair.'

Once again, a look of amazement crossed Tim's face. It clearly hadn't struck him that Juliette might suggest this.

'Oh no,' he said hurriedly. 'I'm afraid not. No. No. It's impossible. She told me she was going abroad to think things over.'

'Where's she gone? Surely I can contact her wherever she is?'

'I don't know where she is,' said Tim quickly. 'She wouldn't tell me. Just said she was going somewhere hot to sort her head out. We haven't even started to discuss all the financial implications of all this, you know. It's going to take quite a bit of untangling, that's for sure.'

'Have you got her mobile number?'

'She hasn't got one,' said Tim. 'Well, she did have, but she threw it at me when she left. I've still got it in my drawer. I'm really sorry, Juliette, but I can't help you.'

By the time Juliette climbed back into her car, it was just after ten pm. The time had flown by. She couldn't believe she'd been talking to Tim Dawner for nearly two hours. A wave of guilt about her mother washed over her. Maura would never let her forget being left to babysit on the first night of her stay.

'Mum?' she mumbled hesitantly into her mobile when her mother finally answered the phone.

'Juliette. Where on earth are you? I've been worried sick. What's taken you all this time?'

'Is Freddie all right?'

'He's fine,' said Maura. 'Hasn't stirred since you left.'

'I'm so sorry, Mum. I feel dreadful for abandoning you when you've only just arrived. Have you had any supper?'

'There wasn't much to have, dear, was there?' said Maura. 'But I made myself a sandwich, so don't worry.'

Juliette groaned inwardly. No matter what she did, her mother always made her feel in the wrong.

'I'm afraid I've got another favour to ask you,' she said in a hurried voice.

'What's that, dear?'

'Just say if it's completely out of the question and I'll come straight back. But I really ought to go and write this story in the office. It's a bit of a tricky one and they want it for tomorrow's front page. If I do it now then it means I can still take Freddie to school myself in the morning. Otherwise I'll have to leave at the crack of dawn. Would you mind terribly?'

There was a stunned silence at the other end of the phone.

'What? You're saying you need to go to work? *Now*? At ten o'clock at night?'

In fact Maura wasn't quite the innocent she sounded. She knew perfectly well that working on a newspaper meant unsociable hours. She'd been married to a sports reporter for nearly twenty years after all – she understood that it came with the territory.

'Yep, Mum,' said Juliette. 'I really do. Is that all right with you?'

'Well, I suppose it'll have to be, won't it?' said Maura tartly. 'But we're going to have to talk about all this, Juliette. You can't go gadding about when you've got a little boy to look after. It's not fair on Freddie. We both know that.'

Inside Juliette was seething. Her mother made her feel like a teenager begging to be allowed to stay out late. She was well aware, however, that this wasn't the moment to have a blazing row with Maura. Especially when her mother was doing her a favour.

'No, you're right, Mum,' she said. 'It isn't. Don't wait up for me though, will you? I'll see you in the morning.'

Juliette slid her work pass through the security lock. Instantly the front door slid open. She half expected to see Stubby slumbering at the reception desk but it was empty. Even the conscientious Stubby had gone home.

When she walked into the newsroom on the first floor, the place was virtually deserted. Deserted, that is, apart from her boss. Alex Davis was still poring over his computer screen, an Anglepoise lamp illuminating the top of his balding head.

'I didn't expect to find you still here,' she said as she dumped her stuff on her desk. 'Do you work this late every night?'

Alex glanced up from what he was doing. He looked, it struck Juliette, slightly on the defensive.

'Sometimes, yes,' he said gruffly. 'Especially now Geoff's increased the number of features pages. And it's much easier to get things done once the rabble has disappeared off to the pub. It's quiet and you don't get interrupted by the phone all the time.'

'Doesn't your wife mind?' asked Juliette casually as she logged on to her computer and scrolled through her e-mails. There was a message to ring Dawn Lewis – just sod's law that she'd rung on the one afternoon she was out of the office.

Juliette stared across at Alex. He was hardly the life and soul of the party at the best of times, but tonight he seemed more withdrawn than usual. As well as completely ignoring her question, he hadn't even bothered to ask how the Tim Dawner interview had gone.

'Are you sure you're all right, Alex?' she asked. 'You don't seem quite yourself.'

Alex stared back at her, a vacant expression on his face. For a moment he looked as though he was miles away. Then suddenly he seemed to pull himself together.

'Mind your own bloody business, will you?' he snapped. 'And what the bloody hell did you get out of Denim Heart?'

Juliette ignored his ill temper and proceeded to outline, quietly and calmly, what Tim Dawner had told her.

'It's a bit of a tricky one,' she said, 'because Helen Brown isn't around to give her side of things. What do you think? Can we still use the story?'

Alex thought hard for a moment.

'I don't see why not,' he said finally. 'Just so long as we've done everything we possibly can to get a reaction from Helen Brown. I'll get a reporter down to the house first thing to double-check she isn't there, and another to the Denim Heart office. And you'll have to write it pretty carefully.'

'No problem,' said Juliette. 'I've got so much stuff from Tim Dawner that it'll write itself.'

It took Juliette an hour to complete the story, and sure enough it was pretty straightforward. When she'd finished, she sent a copy over to Alex to read. He nodded approvingly as he scanned through the piece.

Denim Heart boss Tim Dawner last night condemned rumours that his Bowater-based make-up business is in financial trouble as 'scandalous and wicked.'

*The dynamic entrepreneur also revealed exclusively to
the Eagle that he has split with his long-time partner and
girlfriend Helen Brown. He will run the company alone
from now on.*

*'It is very sad but Helen wanted to move on,' said
Mr Dawner, 35. 'Every single one of my three hundred
employees, however, can rest assured that, contrary to
spiteful reports in the London media, the business is in
fine shape. Judging by our order book, we look set to
have a record Christmas. And I have many exciting new
ventures planned for next year . . .'*

'Yes, you've got it about right,' said Alex when he got
to the end of the story. 'Thank God for a decent splash.
Geoff was worrying that we'd have a blank space on the
front page tomorrow. He'll be made up when he comes
in first thing. D'you fancy a drink?'

Taken aback by this suggestion – especially after Alex
had been so rude – Juliette glanced at her watch. It was
well after eleven.

'What, now?'

Alex looked slightly embarrassed.

'Oh, I know it's late, but the King's Head round the
corner is always open after hours. I reckon that we could
both do with one. Yes?'

'Go on, then,' said Juliette. She was pretty sure that her
mother would have gone to bed by now and she might as
well take advantage of the luxury of having a babysitter
for a change. 'You've twisted my arm.'

The King's Head turned out to be a complete dive. It
was tiny, with threadbare carpets, rickety wooden tables
and a landlord who spent most of his time chatting to
punters on the wrong side of the bar. For all that, Juliette
felt completely at home. It reminded her of the tatty old
pubs the *Daily News* reporters had haunted when she first

arrived in Fleet Street. Now the majority of newspapers had decamped to the far reaches of Docklands all the hacks she knew had either turned teetotal or chose to drink in chic wine bars they wouldn't have been seen dead in back in the old days.

To Juliette's astonishment, Alex downed three scotches in quick succession.

'It's all right,' said Alex, stumbling across to the bar to order another. 'I only live round the corner. I'll be walking home.'

Nursing a mineral water, Juliette was puzzled. She could have sworn that he lived in Burndale, a pretty lakeside village about five miles the other side of Newdale.

'But I thought you . . .'

Alex turned to look at her, dull-eyed.

All of a sudden it struck Juliette how shabby and unkempt he looked these days. No one was going to be at their best at this time of night, especially after a long shift at work and three scotches on the trot, but this was different. When she'd first met Alex, he'd hardly been supermodel material but he'd always appeared neat and tidy and *clean*. Right now, with his face unshaven and wearing a crumpled shirt and grubby tweed jacket, he looked as if he'd been sleeping rough for a few nights.

'You thought what?'

'I thought you lived out of town,' she said lamely.

'Well, you thought wrong,' grunted Alex, polishing off his fourth scotch in one go. 'Now, I don't know about you, but I'd better be making tracks. I'll see you in the morning.'

The first thing that Juliette heard as she tiptoed into the house was Freddie crying. The sound wrenched straight through her, just like when he was a baby and he'd woken desperate with hunger.

She dashed up the stairs three at a time, almost falling over her feet in her desperation to get to her son.

When she burst into his room, however, Freddie was sitting on her mother's knee. Maura was tenderly rocking him and stroking his forehead.

'It's all right, darling,' she whispered softly. 'It's all right. It doesn't matter. Everything will be fine in the morning.'

At that moment, Maura looked up and her eyes met Juliette's.

'He wet the bed,' she mouthed softly so that Freddie wouldn't hear. 'I've changed his pyjamas and the sheets and I think he'll drop off to sleep again in a moment.'

Juliette knelt down on the floor next to them, her mind working overtime. Freddie had never wet the bed in his life. He'd been dry at night since the age of three. Poor little boy. What the hell was going on?

Chapter Eleven

Tim Dawner read Juliette's piece in the *Evening Eagle* over and over again. The paper had splashed her story across the front page under the headline *TIM FIGHTS ON ALONE*. She'd also written a short – and, he was gratified to see, highly flattering – profile of him on page three.

The *Chronicle* story, however, was a different matter altogether. Tim had been so incensed when he read it first thing that he'd hurled it to the other side of the room in a blind rage. The pages of the downmarket tabloid had scattered all over the place but he couldn't be bothered to pick them up. When Tracey, his young secretary, had tottered in on her new six-inch heels to ask if he'd like a cup of coffee, she'd gone flying. He groaned at the thought. A damages claim from an employee with a broken ankle was all he needed right now.

After gathering the pages together, Tim steeled himself to skim through the *Chronicle* piece once more. In fact, he admitted to himself on second reading, it could have been a lot worse. At least the story was tucked away in the *Chronicle*'s business section and the paper's lawyer had clearly toned it down. Instead of coming straight out and saying that Denim Heart was on the verge of going bust, the piece had an unnamed source hinting darkly at problems and claiming that the business might have to seek outside investment in order to survive.

At that moment one of the three phones on Tim's desk rang. He snatched it up quickly, still hoping that it might be Helen ringing to say she was sorry for leaving him in the lurch and she was coming back.

'Mr Dawner?' said a female voice on the other end of the line. She sounded very posh, and very young.

'Who wants him?' growled Tim.

'It's Natasha, from Rollercoaster PR,' said the posh voice. 'We've had virtually every paper in London requesting an interview with you.'

'Why?' demanded Tim.

'Do you mean "why do they want to interview you?" or "why should you do it"?' asked Natasha. She sounded flustered.

'I mean why are they all so desperate for an interview now? What angle are they looking for? You've had the nouse to find *that* out, surely?'

There was a long pause at the end of the phone, and the sound of papers being shuffled frantically.

'I'm sorry,' said Natasha, 'I've only just started working here and I haven't quite . . . Ah, here it is. A paper called the *Evening Eagle* has carried a story saying that you've split up with your girlfriend and that in future you'll be running Denim Heart by yourself. Do you know the paper? Have you spoken to them?'

Tim closed his eyes. Helen had frequently warned him that using a fancy PR company more than three hundred miles away was simply throwing money down the drain. Why the hell hadn't he listened to her?

'Of course I bloody know it,' he bellowed down the phone. 'It's the local evening paper up here. Call yourself a bloody PR? *You* should bloody well know it too.'

'I'm sorry, Mr Dawner. I didn't realise . . .'

Suddenly the strain of the past few weeks caught up with Tim and he completely flipped.

'I've been paying your company tens of thousands of pounds every year for the last three years. And for what? For some slip of a girl to ring me up halfway through the day and tell me things that I already bloody know. If you'd been doing your job properly I wouldn't have to put up with this crap from the *Chronicle* either. Tell your bloody boss that I'm terminating my contract with Rollercoaster. With immediate effect.'

Tim slammed the phone down and put his head in his hands. Everything was falling apart around his ears.

Juliette woke up in a blind panic. After her late night drink with Alex and the shock of finding that Freddie had wet his bed, she'd been tossing and turning all night. Not only that, but she'd forgotten to put the alarm on and overslept by an hour and a half.

'Oh my God,' she screeched when she opened her eyes and saw that it was already eight-thirty. '*Freddie. Mum.* Are you awake?'

They clearly weren't because the house was silent and still. After a few seconds however, Freddie stumbled bleary-eyed into her bedroom in his Action Man pyjamas. Then the spare room door opened and her mother appeared wearing an immaculate silk dressing gown. She looked like something out of a Noel Coward play.

'Quick, Freddie, we're terribly late. Quick, quick, quick. Can you be dressed in five minutes? And don't forget to put on a clean vest, will you? I'll make you some toast and you can eat it in the car on the way to school.'

Juliette felt the icy blast of her mother's disapproval down the back of her neck. She'd been so determined to show how well she and Freddie were coping – and instead she kept showing Maura that everything was a mess. Oversleeping was simply the last straw.

'You don't mind meeting Freddie from school today,

do you Mum?' asked Juliette. 'I've asked Fi Nicholson from four doors down to give you a lift there and back. She'll ring the doorbell for you at twenty past three.'

'It's not a question of whether I mind or not, is it, dear?' said Maura tartly. 'But of course I'll meet him. It'll be a pleasure. Now, it's all right if I take a bath, isn't it?'

If she'd had an easier relationship with her mother, Juliette might have felt able to explain that she had to be in the car in ten minutes – and that it would help a lot if she could use the bathroom first. But she nodded wordlessly and began pulling yesterday's clothes back on again. She'd treat herself to a long hot soak when she got home tonight.

By the time Juliette stopped the car outside school, it was a few seconds after nine and the bell had already gone.

'Come on, Freddie,' she said, getting out of the car to give him a hug. 'Get cracking. If you race, you'll be in your classroom by the time Mrs Booth calls your name in the register. It's lucky your name starts with a W and not an A, isn't it?'

To Juliette's surprise, instead of hugging her back and running off down the path, Freddie's face crumpled and he burst into tears.

'Darling, what on earth's the matter?' she said, scooping him into her arms. 'This isn't like you. You used to love school. What is it? What's making you unhappy?'

Freddie could hardly speak through his tears. He was sobbing so hard that it took him three attempts to get his words out.

'You've . . . you've forgotten to make my lunch again,' he wept, as though it was the end of the world.

Juliette banged her hand hard against her forehead.

He was right. In her panic to get out of the house, Freddie's lunch had completely slipped her mind. He was the most important person in the world and she'd let him down. Again.

Things didn't improve as the day went on. Alex Davis went ballistic when she arrived at the office an hour late. For once in her life, however, she wasn't bothered. She knew she'd got her priorities right. She'd dashed home, cobbled together a chocolate spread sandwich, a bag of crisps and a strawberry yoghurt (with her mother droning on in the background about the importance of a nutritious lunch) and then dropped it all off at school on her way into work. Freddie's dazzling smile when she pushed open the Portakabin door with his lunch box in her hand had been worth a million bollockings.

'Don't worry, he's been in a foul mood all morning,' whispered Cara Bell from the desk opposite.

'Why?' Juliette whispered back.

'No one knows for sure,' said Cara, drumming long purple fingernails on her keyboard. 'People are saying that the last set of circulation figures show sales have dropped by five per cent and Geoff Lake's blaming Alex. But some of the snappers reckon that Alex's marriage is in trouble. They've seen him drinking in the King's Head at night. One of them has it on good authority that he's left his wife and moved back into town.'

Juliette didn't say anything, though lots of things about Alex's recent behaviour suddenly made more sense.

'God, I don't know why *any* of us bother with it,' she said, logging on to her computer. 'Marriage, I mean. It's a bloody nightmare.'

Cara, who wasn't interested right now but assumed

she'd meet Mr Right one day and live happily ever after, wondered what had brought all this on.

'I thought yours was rock solid,' she said. 'I mean I know you're living at opposite ends of the country but that's the impression you always give.'

'What?' said Juliette, wishing she'd kept her mouth shut. 'Oh yep. Rock solid. Definitely. Love's young dream, in fact.'

Something about her face made Cara realise that it might be unwise to pursue the thorny subject of marriage with Juliette right now. Juliette was usually the first to see the funny side of things in the office. But now she looked desperately unhappy – as though nothing in her life was coming up to scratch.

At that moment their conversation ended abruptly. Alex bellowed at Cara to pull her finger out and get on with some work for a change.

'And you,' he bawled at Juliette. 'You can come here now.'

Privately wondering what she had done to deserve being treated like a schoolgirl – she'd bloody provided the splash this morning for goodness sake *and* gone for a drink with him last night – Juliette shrugged off her irritation. She threaded her way between the other feature writers' desks to Alex Davis.

'Here you are,' he said aggressively, shoving a folder in her direction. 'A group of villagers are fighting plans to build an out of town supermarket at Grasdale. Fascinating stuff. I'm sure it's worthy of your stunning talents. It's got your name written all over it.'

Seething, Juliette grabbed the bundle of papers and stomped out of the newsroom in search of the coffee machine. She couldn't believe her career had come to this. Three months ago, she'd been features editor of the *Daily News*. She'd been the person in charge of drawing up the features schedule, allocating interviews with everyone from the Prime Minister right through to Robbie Williams. And now what? She'd been reduced to covering stories about whiney villagers. Maybe her mum was right. Maybe she and Freddie *should* admit defeat and slink back to London with their tails between their legs.

Something within her, though, made her rebel at the very thought. It was pig-headed of her, but she couldn't bear to acknowledge that she'd been wrong. Especially not to her mother. And especially not to Joe. She was going to *make* this work if it was the last thing she did.

Juliette was standing in the middle of a muddy field, listening to the woes of the Grasdale Says No Group, when her mobile trilled its irritating tune.

'If the council let this go ahead, our lives will be made a misery,' said Adam Elliott, the group leader, an earnest man in a brown cagoule. 'It hardly bears thinking about. It will cause noise, extra traffic, dirt, dust . . .'

Juliette felt sorely tempted to ignore the call and switch her phone off. The trouble was, there was always the risk that the call had something to do with Freddie. Perhaps he was ill or in trouble – they were the first things that always leapt into her mind.

'I'm sorry, can you just hang on a minute?' she said, interrupting Adam Elliott in full flow. 'Hello, Juliette Ward.'

There was a long silence at the other end. Juliette gazed over the valley where the supermarket was planned. She couldn't believe the council was even contemplating this. Mile upon mile of fields and hedgerows stretched before her, with the snow-capped fells rising majestically in the distance. It was one of the most beautiful rural landscapes she'd ever seen. The council should be bloody shot.

'Hello?' said Juliette again. 'Is anyone there? Come on. Speak to me.'

She was about to give up and stuff the phone back in her pocket when a nervous voice said: 'I'm sorry to bother you but it's, it's . . . Norma Gray.'

Stunned that Norma should suddenly make contact out of the blue, Juliette edged away from the action group for a little more privacy.

'Norma, it's good to hear from you,' she said, trying to set Norma at ease. 'Is everything all right? Are you ringing about your job? Has someone threatened you with the sack?'

'Oh, I don't care about my job,' Norma said quickly. 'Well, I do. But no, it's nothing to do with that. No, it's Dawn, and Amy . . . Poor little Amy.'

A picture of the doll-like Amy Barker, dwarfed by her huge stomach, flashed through Juliette's head. The girl had been six months pregnant weeks ago – she must be getting near her time now.

'What's happened?' whispered Juliette urgently. 'Where is she?'

'We need your help,' said Norma. 'We need you now. Amy's started her contractions . . . doubled up in agony she is. Dawn's called the ambulance and it's on its way but Amy's hysterical. It's a month early and she's terrified that when the baby's born it'll be taken away from her. I'm up here with them and Dawn says you're the sort of person who'll know how all these official things work. Can you do something?'

Juliette glanced across at Adam Elliott and his motley crew. When a girl of fourteen was in desperate straits and on the brink of giving birth, the supermarket somehow didn't seem quite so important.

'Don't worry,' she told Norma, trying to sound as calm and confident as she could. 'I'll meet you at the hospital. Is it Bowater General?'

'Yes,' said Norma tearfully. 'You'll do all you can, won't you, Mrs Ward? Please say you will.'

'Of course I will,' said Juliette. 'But I'm sure there's nothing to worry about, Norma. If Amy can show she's able to care for her baby, then they're certain to let her keep it. Will you tell her that? You've got to try and get her to calm down. It can't be good for the baby if she's got herself worked up like this.'

Within half an hour Juliette drove into the hospital car park at top speed. Adam Elliott hadn't been too impressed when she'd told him that there was an emergency and that she had to go. But still. That was his hard luck. She couldn't ignore Norma's plea for help. She'd never forgive herself if anything happened to Amy and her baby.

As she locked the car and ran towards the grim-looking maternity unit next to Casualty, it struck her suddenly how *involved* with people she'd become up here. Without even realising it, she seemed to have been drawn into the fabric of life in Bowater – in a way she'd never been in London. First Tim Dawner and his problems, now Amy Barker. She hadn't ever intended it to happen; it had simply crept up on her without her even realising it.

107

Chapter Twelve

Joe stretched his arms out lazily. The week had flown by and it was Friday already. There was no doubt about it, he thought, chucking a press release in the bin, being a DJ certainly beat doing a proper job for a living. He was having the time of his life.

The only cloud on the horizon was the long drive north that lay ahead of him. After three weeks away from Freddie, he couldn't wait to throw his arms around his son again. He couldn't say the same about Jules. She'd sounded pricklier than ever on the phone.

'Superb show again, Joe,' said Annie, appearing behind him. Turning his head, Joe did a double take when he saw his producer. Bloody hell. She looked absolutely gorgeous. She'd let her long auburn hair flow loose for once and instead of her usual jeans and sweatshirt was wearing tight leather trousers and a tiny mauve cardigan.

'Thanks, sweetheart,' said Joe appreciatively. He knew Annie well enough now to realise that she was straight as a die. She never said anything she didn't mean. 'The show flew past today. Why is it that some days talking on air is like wading through treacle? And other days you simply can't fit in everything you want to say?'

Annie caught his eye and laughed.

'Don't ask me. You're the pro round here.'

'Stop it,' said Joe good-humouredly. 'I can't take all these compliments. You're making me blush.'

Without even stopping to think what he was doing, he leapt to his feet and threw his arms around her. For a split second, they both stared at each other, surprised to have found themselves in such close proximity in the middle of the studio. Joe had barely been within a foot of a woman since Jules left London. But standing this near to Annie – breathing in her distinctive scent and feeling the softness of her cheek next to his – made him realise how much he craved physical contact.

For her part too, Annie was overcome with confusion. She'd been telling herself sternly for weeks now that there was nothing special about Joe. He was undeniably good-looking. And funny. And good at his job. But nothing special. Nothing to write home about. Not really.

At that moment, Bob Carter, the breakfast show sound engineer, popped his head around the door to announce that he was off home for the weekend. The sense of intimacy between them evaporated into thin air.

'I'd better be on my way too,' said Joe. His voice sounded slightly unnatural. 'I've got to be up north by teatime.'

'Yep, I've got next week's running order to sort out,' said Annie. She avoided looking him in the eye.

'I don't suppose you've got time for a coffee today then, have you?' said Joe. He was reluctant to leave with this awkwardness hanging over them.

'Sorry. No. Too much to do,' said Annie in an oddly staccato tone.

'OK. I'll see you first thing Monday morning.'

'Right. See you then.'

Aware though he was of an inexplicable shift in their relationship, Joe refused to dwell on it. He picked up his stuff, along with a couple of *Thunderbirds* videos he'd been sent, and set off back to Willy's flat.

When he reached Willy's front door, however, he was struck by a terrible sense of foreboding. Everything had seemed perfectly normal when he'd left at four-thirty am. Willy's door had been shut so he'd assumed that his flatmate had been out on the tiles as usual last night and was safely tucked up in bed. But now the door to the flat was hanging off its hinges and Joe could see half of Willy's belongings scattered down the hallway. Pictures had been ripped up, china smashed and Willy's prized sculpture of a naked man lay in pieces on the carpet.

Without even considering the wisdom of his actions, Joe ran into the flat, flinging all the doors open as he charged through the place like a madman. Every room, including his own, had been trashed but Joe didn't have time to worry about that.

'Will,' he roared, and then more desperately. 'WILLY.'

There was no response. Fearing the worst by now, fearing that Willy had been beaten up by burglars and left for dead, Joe burst into his friend's room. The bed looked as though it had been slept in but there was no sign of Willy. All of a sudden though, Joe was aware of the sound of moaning coming from Willy's tiny en-suite bathroom. Realising that the room had been locked from the outside and the key left in the lock, he wrenched it open. He nearly tripped over in his haste to get inside.

For a few seconds, Joe stood there, unable to comprehend what he was seeing.

Willy lay on the floor, with a gag in his mouth and his arms and legs bound together. He was only wearing a pair of thin pyjama bottoms and crying out in pain.

'Oh my God, Will, what happened? Who did this to you?'

Joe threw himself onto the floor and began struggling

to undo the narrow strips of sheeting that had been used to bind his friend. When eventually he managed to work them loose and Willy sat up, he was so relieved he threw his arms round him.

Willy looked terrible – white-faced and shocked – and far older than his thirty-five years. He had a nasty-looking gash down the side of his face and his chest was badly bruised.

'What the hell happened?' asked Joe again. While he was waiting for an answer he shoved the sheeting under the cold tap and began to bathe Willy's gaping wound.

All the time he was doing this, Willy stared glassy-eyed back at him.

'Come on, Willy. You're in shock but you've got to tell me. I'm going to call the police.'

This finally prompted a response from Willy, although not the one Joe had been expecting. Willy grabbed hold of Joe's hand and stared at him, his agitation plain.

'No, Joe. No. No. Please don't. There's no need. I'm fine, man. Really I am. I've had a bit of a fright but I'll have a beer and then I'll be right as rain. I'm working tonight anyway. That'll sort me out. Best thing for me.'

Joe was bewildered by Willy's reaction.

'For God's sake,' he bawled. 'You've been beaten up, trussed up like a chicken, the flat's been trashed – of course I'm going to bloody phone the cops. D'you have any idea who did this to you?'

Willy went silent again. But in a flash of understanding, like a light switching on inside his brain, the truth began to dawn on Joe.

'You do, don't you? You know who it was.'

Willy nodded. He looked sad and desperately weary, as though he was on the verge of breaking down altogether.

'I've done something so stupid, man,' he moaned. 'So stupid. I can't believe how stupid I've been.'

111

'What?' shouted Joe. 'What have you done? Drink, drugs, women? Come on, it can't be so bad that you're afraid to tell me. We're mates, aren't we? Always have been, always will be.'

Willy closed his eyes, as though he was trying to blank everything out. Joe was having none of it.

'Willy, tell me,' he yelled again. When there was still no response, he began shaking his friend in a desperate attempt to get him to talk.

'Right, that's it,' said Joe, getting to his feet. 'I'm ringing the cops *right now*.'

This finally prompted a reaction.

'OK man, OK,' mumbled Willy. 'Give me a break and I'll tell you.'

'I'm listening,' said Joe grimly.

'It's none of those things you said,' said Willy, his voice so quiet that Joe had to strain forward to hear what he was saying.

'So it's not drink or drugs. Thank God for that. It's not women trouble. So what else is there?'

'A man,' muttered Willy in a half-whisper. 'It's a man.'

Joe stared at him, incomprehension written all over his face.

'What do you mean?' he said. 'Some crazed listener or something? There are so many nutters out there. Who was it?'

Willy laughed humourlessly.

'God, man. For someone who's supposed to be on the ball you aren't half dumb sometimes. I said a man, didn't I? A lover. Someone I screwed.'

Joe's jaw dropped.

'You're joking,' he mumbled. 'You mean you're gay? When did all this happen? I had no idea. You've had so many girlfriends over the years. Stunners, most of them. I can't believe it. You're having me on.'

Willy gazed at him morosely.

'I've always been gay, Joe,' he said softly. 'I mean, I never shot my mouth off about it – it was my business, no one else's – but I assumed that all my best mates knew. I assumed *you* knew.'

It struck Joe that a lot of things about Willy made sense all of a sudden. The fact that he adored women but never appeared to have a steady girlfriend. His mysterious one-night stands. His love of clubbing into the early hours.

'You're not bothered by it, are you?' asked Willy. He tentatively touched the cut on his cheek with his hand and grimaced in pain. 'Tell me if you are and . . .'

'And what? Don't be ridiculous, Will. Of course I'm not bothered. I wouldn't care if you turned pink with purple spots. We're mates, you know that. No, I'm just worried about that cut down the side of your face. We've got to get you to hospital. And quickly. Surely you can see that?'

All the colour had drained out of Willy's face by now. He was clearly exhausted by the morning's traumatic events.

'OK,' he said wearily. 'But Evan took my car keys. You'll have to call me a minicab.'

'I'll call us both a cab,' said Joe his voice firm. 'You're not going to hospital on your own. You're not going anywhere on your own. Is that clear?'

As they sat by the front door waiting for Kwik Cabs to arrive from Clapham Junction, Willy told him a little more about the events leading up to his attack.

'I met Evan at a club in Soho last week. He's an art student, only nineteen and so beautiful. God he's beautiful. He takes your breath away. We were good together.'

'Oh yeah?' said Joe. 'So good together that he goes and beats the living daylights out of you?'

'He didn't mean to do that,' said Willy hurriedly.

'No? Those kind of blokes are all the same. Give them a wide berth next time, will you?'

'Look,' said Willy. 'I know I've been a fool but I thought me and Evan . . . I thought we were right together. Anyway, he came down to Radio Wave last night after the show and we went to Flashman's – that new gay club on the river. We had a few drinks and then he started dancing with this other guy. It was provocative stuff, tongues down each other's throats and all that. Then they disappeared for a while and it was pretty clear what they were up to. I was so upset I couldn't bear to watch. I came back here at about five and tried to get my head down for some kip. It was about six when the doorbell started ringing. It went on and on, like someone was leaning against the doorbell. I ignored it at first but it was doing my head in. When I got to the door, it was him, Evan. He went ballistic. Demanded to know why I'd left without him. Who did I think I was? He was shouting and swearing and throwing stuff around. I was half asleep and before I really knew what was happening he'd got this knife out and sliced my face open.'

'Then knocked you to the ground and tied you up in a truss,' murmured Joe. 'He's a nice guy, all right. Bloody hell, Will. He could have killed you.'

By the time the minicab dropped them outside the casualty department at All Saints' Hospital, it was getting on for eleven and the shock of what had happened was finally beginning to dawn on Willy. He started shivering uncontrollably.

'You won't leave me here, will you?' whispered Willy as Joe took his arm and guided him towards the reception area. He sounded like a small child.

'Of course I won't,' said Joe, trying to sound reassuring. He was all too aware that he should be halfway to

Cumbria by now. But he couldn't simply abandon Willy
– surely Freddie and Jules would understand that?

It was a good three hours before a pretty young
registrar took a look at Willy's face and decided that
the wound was so deep that it needed stitches.

'We'll be able to do it later this afternoon,' she said.
'We'll keep you in overnight and with luck you'll be
able to go home tomorrow. Have you got anyone to look
after you?'

'I'm, I'm not sure,' stuttered Willy.

'Yes he has,' said Joe firmly. 'Me.'

Chapter Thirteen

Amy Barker lay huddled on the hospital bed. She looked terrified. She'd been crying for so long that she was completely exhausted. Her face was red and blotchy with tears and everything around her seemed blurred. Her contractions were coming thick and fast now and the midwife kept urging her to 'remember her breathing exercises'.

Gripping the teenager's tiny hand in her own more substantial one, Dawn Lewis felt every bit as scared as Amy.

'Come on, love, you can do it,' she whispered as Amy's face contorted with agony once more. 'Keep on trying. Don't give up. You're nearly there.'

'It hurts, Dawn, it hurts,' panted Amy, her face wet with sweat. 'Help me. I don't know what to do.'

'Just listen to the midwife, love,' said Dawn. She'd never felt so helpless in her life. She tenderly wiped the young girl's face with a damp flannel. 'If you listen to her, she'll tell you exactly when to push. Now come on. I know that you can do it. Just think about the baby and you'll be fine.'

Amy smiled wanly back at her. Then the next contraction swept through her and she cried out again.

'D'you want your mum in here?' asked Dawn. 'Or mine? They've been though all this themselves. They might be able to help you more than me.'

Amy tightened her hold on Dawn's hand and shook her head vehemently.

'No,' she moaned. 'I don't want none of them. I just want you. You won't leave me, Dawn, will you? Please say you won't.'

'Of course I won't, you silly girl,' murmured Dawn. 'I'm not going anywhere till that baby's born.'

Outside the maternity suite, Norma, still dressed in the white cooking overalls she wore for work, was pacing anxiously up and down the corridor like an expectant father. She'd never known time pass so slowly. If only Carol, Amy's mum, would get here soon. And where on earth was Juliette Ward? They were going to need her by the looks of it.

At that moment the door at the end of the corridor opened and Juliette shot through it like a sprinter doing the one hundred metres.

'Any news?' she panted.

Norma shook her head.

'No. Our Dawn's in there with her. Amy's certain it's Dawn she wants. I don't know why because Dawn knows as much about labour as I do about car mechanics.'

'It's understandable,' said Juliette, sinking down on to a bench along the side of the wall. 'I mean, Dawn's the one who's been with her all the way through and they're very close, aren't they?'

Norma nodded.

'They are that,' she said. 'I think Amy's told her everything.'

Juliette looked at Norma questioningly.

'Who the father is, you mean?'

'Maybe,' said Norma, her voice quiet. 'I'm not sure. But Dawn wouldn't tell me. Said she couldn't break Amy's confidence. Said it wouldn't be fair on the girl.'

Juliette stared at Norma. She couldn't put her finger on

117

it but she got the distinct impression that Norma wasn't being straight with her.

'Is there something you're not telling me, Norma?' she said. 'I think you've got a pretty good idea who the father is yourself, haven't you?'

Norma stared at the wall, not saying anything, and then down at Juliette's feet, which were still filthy from her visit to Grasdale.

'Why are your shoes so muddy?' she asked out of the blue. It was clear she considered the subject of the father of Amy's baby closed.

It was another hour before the door of the maternity suite finally opened and a dishevelled Dawn stumbled out. Juliette thought she looked more down at heel than ever in her usual moth-eaten tracksuit and trainers. Her hair hung limply down her back and she was carrying a scruffy duffel bag over her shoulder. But despite all this, Dawn's eyes shone with happiness and relief.

'Mum,' she cried, throwing her arms around Norma. 'It's a girl. Amy's had a little girl. Six pounds, four ounces, with loads of dark hair. Just like . . .'

She stopped abruptly and stared into space.

Norma was in floods of tears. She was so overcome that she couldn't say anything at all, just clutched hold of her daughter.

'And they're both all right, aren't they?' she said when she'd finally recovered herself enough to speak.

Dawn nodded.

'They're grand, Mum,' she said. 'Well, Amy's exhausted of course, poor little mite, but they're grand. The doctors are just doing a few tests and then they'll take both of them up to the ward. They say we can go up too if we like.'

Witnessing all this, Juliette felt awkward and out of place. This was a private occasion and she shouldn't be

118

intruding on it. She wasn't even sure why Norma had rung her in the first place. After all, she barely knew Amy, and apart from giving a bit of moral support, there was nothing much she could do to help.

'If you don't mind, I'd better be off,' she murmured softly to Norma and Dawn. 'Give lots of congratulations to Amy, won't you?'

Hearing this, Dawn spun round and clasped Juliette to her ample chest.

'Don't go,' she pleaded. 'Amy's terrified that someone's going to take the baby away. And if anyone knows how the system works, it's you. You will stay for a while, won't you? Please? Just for a bit? For Amy's sake?'

Juliette shrugged her shoulders. She didn't have much choice.

'Of course I will,' she said. 'If it's all right with Amy. But I'm sure that if Amy wants to keep the baby she'll be able to.'

The three of them made their way up to the maternity ward on the next floor. On the spur of the moment Juliette told the others to go on ahead and stopped off at the hospital flower shop to buy Amy a huge bunch of tulips and roses. Poor girl, she thought. She didn't have a clue what lay in front of her. Juliette had found looking after a tiny baby tough with Joe beside her and a reasonable wage coming in. Dawn and Norma were well meaning enough but she couldn't imagine how on earth fourteen-year-old Amy was going to fend for herself and the baby.

Juliette was in the middle of paying for the flowers when her phone rang. She fumbled in her bag to find it and then wedged it between her ear and her shoulder.

'Hello,' she said. As she spoke she noticed a huge picture of a mobile on the wall opposite with a thick red cross drawn through it. The florist was looking daggers at her.

'Jules? It's me. Joe. Are you all right to talk?'

'Sort of,' said Juliette, hurriedly gathering the bouquet into her arms and walking as fast as possible towards the hospital exit. She didn't want her mobile to be responsible for making the hospital's computer systems crash.

'Where are you?' he asked. 'It sounds like Piccadilly station wherever it is.'

'Bowater General,' said Juliette. 'Well, I'm outside the Accident and Emergency bit now.'

Three hundred miles away, Joe's mind ran riot.

'What the hell's going on, Jules?' he yelled down the phone. 'Has something happened? Is Freddie all right? Tell me. I need to know.'

'Calm down, Joe,' said Juliette. 'Freddie's fine. And so am I. A friend of mine – well, she's a sort of friend – has just had a baby and so I've come to see her.'

'Thank God,' said Joe, his relief clearly discernible. 'You had me worried for a second.'

'I'm glad you care,' said Juliette sharply.

A wave of irritation swept through Joe.

'Oh come on, Jules. Don't give me a hard time. You know I care.'

'So you're not ringing to tell me that something's come up and you won't be able to make it this afternoon? That's great. You'll be halfway up the M6 by now, I take it.'

There was a long silence at the other end of the line. For a moment Juliette thought they'd been cut off. Then Joe let rip at her.

'Will you stop being such a bloody cow?' he bellowed. 'There's nothing more I want in the whole world than to see Freddie. I miss him so much that it hurts.'

'So what's stopping you this time?' demanded Juliette.

'What excuse have you got hidden up your sleeve for him today?'

Once again there was silence while Joe struggled to keep his temper.

'It's Willy,' he said finally. 'The flat's been broken into and he's been badly beaten up. He's had twenty stitches and they're keeping him in overnight. But someone's got to collect him from hospital in the morning. I've managed to get hold of his parents and I'm going to drop him off at their house in Birmingham on the way up north tomorrow. If I'm lucky I should be with you by about six.'

Listening to all this, Juliette felt a pang of guilt. Joe sounded badly shaken.

'Look, Joe, I don't see why it has to be you sorting him out but I'm sorry. Give Willy my love, won't you?'

When Juliette reached the ward, she found Amy in a curtained-off cubicle at the end of the room. Norma and Dawn were taking it in turns to hold Amy's baby.

'Ooh, you're absolutely gorgeous, aren't you?' cooed Norma. 'And there's something so familiar about you. It's like you've been around for ever and ever.'

Norma passed the baby to an awe-struck Dawn to hold. Considering that Dawn didn't have any children of her own, she seemed remarkably at ease with the baby, cooing gently and stroking her soft, downy cheek.

Throughout all this, Amy lay in bed with her eyes closed, oblivious to everything. Her face looked grey with tiredness. She was clearly exhausted by the labour she'd just been through.

'Poor lamb,' said Norma gently. 'She's only a baby herself really, isn't she? She'll have to wake up soon, mind, because the baby'll need feeding.'

121

'Oh, I can do that, Mum,' said Dawn quickly. 'Let Amy get some rest.'

Norma stared in astonishment at her.

'Don't be silly, love,' she retorted. 'Amy'll be feeding the baby herself. And I know how much you want to help but there are limits, aren't there?'

'No, Mum, you don't get it,' said Dawn. 'Amy's already decided. The baby's going on the bottle. It's what she wants. She told me.'

'Well, it wasn't like that in my day,' said Norma, pursing her lips in disapproval. 'It'd be so much better for the baby if she could feed her herself, build up her immune systems and such like. I think me and Amy will have to have a little chat about all this.'

Dawn looked at her mother imploringly.

'Not now, Mum. All right? Not when Amy needs her rest. Wait a bit longer, won't you? Till she's good and ready.'

Juliette remained silent during this exchange. Privately she couldn't help being a little taken aback by the reactions of both women. Both by Norma's passionate support for breastfeeding and by Dawn's determination to take charge.

At that moment a midwife in a starched blue and white checked uniform bustled up and moved them all to one side.

'Now, can we have Baby?' she asked Dawn briskly.

For a split second Dawn looked reluctant to let go of the tiny bundle in her arms. Then she thought better of it and obediently handed her over to the midwife.

'Come on, Amy,' said the midwife softly. 'I'm Marie. I'm here to help you get sorted out. It's time your baby had a feed.'

Amy opened her eyes and, realising where she was, quickly shut them tight again.

'Come along, Amy. There's nothing to be frightened of. Wake up. I'm not going to rush you. We'll take it slowly. I'll show you what to do.'

This time Amy opened her eyes and sat up cautiously. Marie placed the baby expertly into her arms and then sat down on the bed next to her.

'She's beautiful, isn't she,' said Marie. 'Have you thought of a name for her yet?'

'Billie,' whispered Amy, her voice barely audible.

'Katherine,' interjected Dawn.

Marie turned and glared at Dawn.

'Are you Amy's mum?' she asked.

'No. I'm a friend. A close friend. I've been looking after Amy all through her . . .'

Marie smiled at Dawn.

'Look, I know this is all very hard and you only want the best for Amy, and er, Billie . . . But I think it's best if you leave the two of us to get sorted out. Why don't you all go and find a coffee and come back later? Give us an hour or so, will you?'

Norma took Dawn by the arm and led her out of the ward. Juliette picked up her bag and followed a little way behind.

When she caught up with them, however, she was astonished to see that Dawn was crying.

'What the matter?' asked Juliette. 'There's nothing to worry about, you know. The baby's fine. Amy's fine. And as long as Amy wants to keep the baby and can show that she can look after her properly it's very unlikely that social services would try to take her away.'

Dawn began sobbing even harder at this. Norma, at a loss as to what to do, put her arm round her daughter and urged her to pull herself together.

'It's been an emotional day all round, love, hasn't it?' she added. 'All these months of looking after little Amy by yourself – it's taken it out of you, love. I can see that now. Look, why don't we go and collect some of Amy's things? The ambulance left the house in such a hurry that she's hardly got anything with her.'

Juliette glanced at her watch. It was half past four. If she got a move on, she'd just about have time to take the pair of them up to Hillthwaite and then drive them back to the hospital.

'It's Friday, it's ten and it's the Wild Willy Brown show,' said Joe, trying to put as much oomph into his delivery as he could muster. Which in the current circumstances wasn't an awful lot.

Once he'd pressed the button on the computerised play-out system and Willy's first track was in full swing, Joe cast his eye down the running order. No wonder Willy had poured such scorn on the tedious Britney Spears and S Club 7 records Joe had to play on the breakfast show. Willy's stuff was so weird that even a pro like Joe hadn't heard of half of it.

Joe couldn't help feeling a twinge of envy. It was true that his own listening figures were about ten times Willy's but at least Willy had a free hand with his show. Joe's slot was so cluttered up with sensible weather summaries and traffic reports that it didn't leave much scope for creativity. The list he was holding now made him realise how much he missed the fun of discovering new bands for himself.

As the dying bars of the first number died away, Joe leaned towards the mike once more.

'If anyone out there's wondering why Wild Willy doesn't sound quite himself tonight . . .' he said, '. . . it's because he isn't quite himself. I'm Joe Ward, DJ on the Radio Wave breakfast show, and Willy's one of my closest friends. I've stayed up late tonight because Willy sadly can't be here. He won't thank me for saying this but he's lying in a lonely hospital bed right now. So if you're listening, Willy, we love you and we want you back on the air the moment you're fit and well enough.'

Once he'd got the stuff about Willy off his chest, Joe sat back and enjoyed the rest of the show. Two hours flew by and before he knew it he was winding the whole thing up.

'Thanks mate,' said Willy's producer, giving him a slap on the back. 'Don't know how we would have managed at such short notice without you.'

Like Willy, Joe had known Steve Fairbrother for years. Steve had been a DJ himself for a while but had suffered chronic stage fright at live gigs and moved into production.

'No problem,' said Joe. 'I quite enjoyed it in fact. Especially the chance to play some decent records for a change.'

Steve laughed.

'I thought the boy-bands weren't quite you somehow,' he said. 'But from what I hear, the powers that be have got great plans for you. Reckon you've got star quality and all that jazz. We'll be bragging we know you soon.'

Joe shrugged his shoulders.

'Can't quite see it myself, but still. Anyway, what's happening with Willy's show next week? He's pretty shaken. I should think he'll be off for a few more days yet.'

'Not sure,' said Steve. 'You know what the men in suits are like. They operate on a need to know basis. Certainly don't tell minions like me anything. You visiting Willy in the morning?'

'Yep,' said Joe. 'And if the doctors let him out I'll give him a lift up to his old man's house. Willy's been so good to me over the past few months it's the least I can do.'

Chapter Fourteen

Maura Stanley was in a filthy temper by the time Juliette staggered through the door. Admittedly, it was well after seven pm, a good two hours after she had promised to be home from work, but all that yo-yoing back and forth to the hospital had taken longer than she'd anticipated.

Freddie had been playing Maura up and she was at the end of her tether. He'd refused to eat the shepherd's pie she'd made as a special treat for his tea and then gone into a sulk when she wouldn't let him watch *Rugrats* on TV.

'Mummy always lets me see it,' he'd grumbled in a whiny voice.

'Well, I'm not Mummy,' said Maura briskly. 'I'm Granny and I want us to sit down and do a nice jigsaw together.'

'Don't like jigsaws,' Freddie had said, sticking his bottom lip out in resentment.

'How about a game of Scrabble then?' said Maura, casting her eye down the pile of games on the kitchen dresser.

'Don't like Scrabble.'

And so it had gone on. Freddie had turned his nose up at everything she suggested, from drawing through to baking.

'Everything OK?' Juliette asked breezily as she whirled through the kitchen door. 'Where's Freddie?'

126

'In his room,' said Maura, her voice stony.

Juliette did a double take at this.

'What do you mean? You know he doesn't go to bed till eight. Is he feeling poorly or something? You should have rung me, Mum.'

'No dear, he's not poorly. He's fine but he's been behaving so appallingly that I sent him up to his room.'

Juliette stared at her mother in amazement.

'What on earth . . . ? How long has he been up there for?'

Maura glanced at her watch.

'About forty minutes, I should think,' she said.

Juliette let out a sigh of aggravation and dashed upstairs.

When she hurried into Freddie's room, she felt like bursting into tears herself. Freddie lay face down on the bed with his head buried in his pillow. He was sobbing inconsolably. Juliette sat on the bed next to him and proceeded to stroke his back gently.

'Darling,' she said. 'What's the matter?'

It was half a minute or so before Freddie could get his words out.

'G-G-Granny got cross with me,' he wept.

'I know,' said Juliette softly. 'But I'm sure she didn't mean it.'

'She did,' cried Freddie. 'She did mean it. She called me a naughty spoiled boy.'

'There, there,' soothed Juliette. 'She loves you very much. You know that. All grown-ups get cross sometimes.'

'Granny never has before. I didn't like it. She scared me.'

A wave of anger against her mother swept through Juliette. She knew only too well how Freddie felt. She'd experienced her mother's wrath often enough to know how chilling it could be. Especially when you were only six and didn't understand what you'd done wrong.

Juliette didn't bother to go back downstairs. She gave Freddie a bath and then helped him into his pyjamas. It wasn't until she'd read him a story and tucked him into bed with all his favourite teddies that she ventured back to the kitchen to face her mother.

Maura was standing at the kitchen sink, washing up the tea things. Juliette could tell from the set of her shoulders that she was livid.

'Mum?' she said hesitantly, then felt furious with herself for sounding like a wimp.

'What?' said Maura. She didn't turn round, just continued to scrub furiously.

'Don't worry about doing that – I can put it all in the dishwasher,' said Juliette. 'Will you come and sit down? We need to talk.'

'All right,' said Maura, removing Juliette's bright yellow rubber gloves from her hands and putting her wedding ring back on. Her voice was grudging.

The two women sat facing each other at the long pine table. Juliette studied the grain of the wood intently. She couldn't think how to broach the subject at first, then everything came out in a rush.

'I know you mean well, Mum, and you've really helped me out of a hole this week . . .' she began.

'But what?' said Maura coldly.

Juliette stared at her mother.

'What do you mean?'

'You were going to say ". . . but it's not working out".'

'I wasn't,' said Juliette. 'Well, maybe I was. It's just that we're so different, Mum. We go about everything so differently. I mean, I know you don't approve of the way Joe and I are living at the moment but you've got to let us get on with it. And that goes for Freddie too. I let him

128

do things you wouldn't have allowed me and Johnnie to do in a million years, like watch TV in the afternoon and stay up late . . . But he's my son. You can't dictate what I do any more. You just can't.'

Maura sighed.

'I haven't got the least interest in dictating what you do,' she said stiffly. 'You and Johnnie are adults now. You can do precisely as you please. But don't forget, Juliette, that I didn't ask if I could come and stay. It was you who rang me last week and pleaded for help. I was doing you a favour, remember, not the other way round.'

'I know that, Mum. And it was very kind of you.'

'What time's Joe arriving?' asked Maura, changing the subject.

Juliette's heart sank. Joe's change of plan would be yet another excuse for her mother to give her a lecture.

'Something came up at the last moment. He won't be here till tea-time tomorrow.'

Juliette fully expected her mother to mutter something about letting Freddie down again but much to her surprise, Maura didn't comment. She got up from the table, put the rubber gloves back on and resumed the washing-up.

'I think it would be best if the three of you had some time on your own as a family,' she said after a few seconds had passed. 'Gerald rang just before you got back. We've been asked out to lunch at the golf club on Sunday and he suggested I catch the train home tomorrow. Could you drop me at the station in the morning?'

'But don't you want to see Joe?' asked Juliette. Her brain was in a flat spin. She'd assumed her mum would stay for a couple of weeks. Who the hell was going to collect Freddie from school now? Everything was falling apart at the seams.

*   *   *

'And now we have a major exclusive for your delectation,' trilled Sally Shaw, Radio Wave's Saturday afternoon presenter. She was young, inexperienced and in Joe's view at least, complete crap. 'Britney Spears' new single. And you know what? It's going to be absolutely mega . . .'

Joe groaned out loud and snapped the car radio off. Major exclusive indeed. What was Silly Sally on about? He'd been playing the new Britney Spears single all week. They all had. In fact, if he had to listen to it one more time today he would go completely potty.

The ensuing silence made a pleasant change. Living and working in London, especially for a mainstream radio station, he was surrounded by tinny pop music blaring out wherever he went. He couldn't even whizz round to the corner shop for a pint of milk without having to listen to something from the Top Ten. He adored music, especially jazz and blues, but some of the stuff Radio Wave made him play was more like assault and battery on the ears.

Driving north past the Lancaster turn-off, Joe felt relieved to be out of London. Picking Willy up from hospital had been terrible, far more traumatic than he'd envisaged. It had been fine to start with. Apart from the dressing plastered to the side of his face, Willy had seemed in pretty good shape – and grateful to be in one piece. But everything had gone downhill rapidly after he was discharged.

'I can't thank you enough, man,' Willy had murmured softly as they walked out of the ward together. 'If it hadn't been for you I'd still be lying comatose on that bathroom floor now. The cops came down to question me first thing and that's what they said too. That I owe my life to you.'

'Come on, Willy,' said Joe. He felt a bit embarrassed.

'That's completely over the top. And anyway, you'd have done exactly the same for me. I keep telling you – that's what friends are for.'

As the pair of them sauntered slowly across the marble-floored reception area and through the swing doors leading on to the street, they both stopped dead in their tracks.

There, waiting at the bottom of the steps, was what could only be described as an army of reporters and photographers. The instant Willy and Joe emerged, the picture men swung into action, snapping away furiously at them from all angles.

'Hey, hang on a minute, guys,' said Joe, putting his hand up in a fruitless attempt to stop them. 'What's going on? What do you think you're doing?'

The photographers took no notice. They continued snapping for two or three minutes more. Meanwhile, Joe and Willy stood rooted to the spot, completely bemused by what was going on.

'How does it feel to be a hero, Joe?' a young woman reporter piped up once the snappers had calmed down a little.

Joe stared at her, completely mystified.

'What the hell are you on about?' he muttered. 'I'm no hero.'

'Well, you are now,' said the young woman. 'The coppers say you saved Wild Willy Brown's life. That's good enough for us.'

For once in his life, Joe was completely lost for words.

'Who told you about Willy?' he asked when he'd recovered himself enough to speak.

'You told the whole bloody nation last night,' chuckled an older reporter wearing a stained beige raincoat. 'Remember? On Willy's show?'

Joe rolled his eyes. Of course he had. Sitting in the

intimacy of the Radio Wave studio, he'd relayed the news that Willy was in hospital. Why hadn't he kept his bloody mouth shut?

'I'm so sorry, Will,' Joe whispered under his breath. 'Me and my big mouth.'

'Any idea who did this to you, Willy?' shouted another reporter. 'There's a rumour doing the rounds that it was your ex-boyfriend. Is that true? Which one was it exactly?'

Willy's face looked so pale and drawn by now that he looked as if he might faint. Glancing anxiously at his friend, Joe put his arm round him and led him down to the pavement below. The reporters and photographers pressed even closer, asking more and more questions.

'When did you come out, Willy?'

'Have you told your family?'

'When are you back on air?'

'Take no notice, Will,' Joe whispered. 'Forget about them. It must be a quiet news day or something. The story's a one-day wonder. They'll have forgotten all about it by tomorrow.'

The pair of them were now in the midst of the throng. Willy clung on to Joe's arm like grim death.

'Look, guys,' tried Joe again. 'Give it a rest, will you? I need to get Willy home so he can put his feet up and recuperate.'

But the hacks refused to let up.

'Just give us your version of what happened, Willy,' said a burly reporter Joe vaguely recognised from a *Daily News* Christmas party he'd gone to with Jules. 'In your own words. Come on, it won't hurt.'

As Willy shrank even further behind him, Joe finally saw red.

'Will you all just fuck off?' he bellowed at them. 'Can't you see Willy's sick? He doesn't need all this aggro.'

'Ooh, temper temper,' chuckled the *Daily News* guy.

At this, Joe completely lost it. Letting go of Willy, he punched the reporter smack in the jaw. The man staggered back in agony, clutching his face. He tottered forward again to hit Joe, then seeing Joe's livid face, clearly thought better of it.

The snappers, meanwhile, were going crazy, shooting roll after roll of film. They were so eager to capture the fight in its full glory that they ignored Willy altogether.

'You haven't heard the last of this, pal,' grunted the *Daily News* reporter. 'You'll be hearing from our lawyers on Monday.'

Shaken to the core by what he'd just done, Joe grabbed hold of Willy once more and led him through the crowd. Willy was so stunned by all the commotion that he didn't utter a word. Joe cursed himself for being so stupid. He hadn't helped anyone, least of all Willy, by losing his rag.

When they'd finally made it back to Joe's car, two streets away, Willy sank grey-faced into the passenger seat and slept all the way to Birmingham. Joe, however, couldn't stop agonising about what he'd done. He hadn't lost his temper like that in years – what on earth had come over him? And worst of all, if he hadn't waded in with his fists, the tabloids would probably have reported the story as a straightforward break-in. It would have been done and dusted in a couple of paragraphs. But now Joe had gone and guaranteed them both blanket coverage in all the Sundays. And Willy was such a private man – he would be aghast if they started digging up all the gory details about his love life. It could set his recovery back by weeks.

Joe dropped Willy off at his parents' house in a quiet, tree-lined Edgbaston street and continued his drive north. After the turmoil of the last twenty-four hours he was glad to be getting away from everything. He couldn't wait to be with Freddie either. He'd missed holding his son so much – it was like a physical ache.

It was dark by the time he finally drew into Newdale and Joe's heart was hammering fit to burst. He suddenly realised that he'd been so taken up with worrying about Freddie and Willy that he hadn't given Jules a second's thought. But as he drove up the hill towards New Bank, he felt nervous about seeing her again.

Don't be ridiculous, he told himself sternly. She's your bloody wife. You can't feel nervous.

As he parked the car outside the cottage, the front door burst open. A small figure shot out like a bullet and before Joe even had a chance to get out of the car Freddie hurled himself into his arms.

'Daddy, Daddy, where have you been?' screeched Freddie, beside himself with excitement. 'I've been waiting all day. You've taken ages.'

Joe hugged Freddie tight.

'I can't believe how much you've grown, sweetheart,' he murmured. 'What's Mummy been feeding you?'

A puzzled look crossed the little boy's face as he considered this question.

'Carrots, broccoli, fish fingers . . .' began Freddie. 'Beans on toast, Ready Brek . . .'

It was true, thought Joe with a smile. In the three weeks he'd been away, Freddie had shot up. Joe reckoned he was easily a couple of inches taller. Not only that, but his face somehow looked older and wiser. Bloody hell, he reflected, if he and Jules didn't get their act together soon, Freddie would be eighteen and leaving home before they knew it.

Joe followed the ecstatic Freddie into the cottage, remembering to lower his head as he stepped through the door. Once inside, he felt suffused with a sense of warmth and light. A fire blazed in the sitting room and all the lamps were on. Jules herself was hovering at the end of the hall. He was pleased to see that she looked as apprehensive as he felt.

Without giving himself time to even think about it, Joe went straight up to her and put his arms around her. She felt warm and wholesome and he could smell the faint scent of the Jo Malone perfume he'd given her for her birthday back in the spring.

'I've missed you, Jules,' he murmured into her neck as she – he was sure he wasn't imagining it – hugged him back.

Suddenly he felt a tug on his jumper. He looked down to see Freddie grinning up at him.

'I've managed to get on to the next level of that Game Boy game you gave me,' said Freddie proudly. 'Shall I show you, Daddy?'

Juliette beamed at them both.

'You're in the middle of your tea, darling,' she smiled. 'If you eat all your pasta up I'm sure Daddy would love to see afterwards. D'you want a cup of tea, Joe? Or something stronger?'

Joe followed Freddie and Juliette into the kitchen. Once again, it struck him forcibly that this place was how a real home should be. Willy's flat was comfortable enough but it was a bit minimalist for Joe's liking and when all was said and done he was only camping there. He'd made no effort whatsoever to personalise his room. He'd barely even unpacked his stuff. Apart from his clothes, CD player and a photograph of Freddie propped by his bed, the rest of his possessions still lay in the cardboard boxes he'd brought them in.

But Jules had made a huge impression on this place. She'd painted the kitchen bright yellow since his last visit and filled the old dresser with her vast collection of spongeware. He'd often teased her that they could invite fifty people for tea and still have plenty of cups to go round. She'd stuck lots of Freddie's artistic creations on the wall and filled a jug with the longiflorum lilies that she'd always loved.

As Freddie tucked into his pasta – glancing up every now and again to check that he wasn't dreaming and his dad was really there at last – Joe sipped his beer and began to relax.

'How's Willy?' asked Juliette. 'Is he back home with his parents now?'

'Yep,' answered Joe. He didn't want to go into too much detail in front of Freddie, especially not about the fight. 'He's still a bit shaken but the doctors reckon he'll be back at work in a week or so.'

'A couple of the Sunday papers rang earlier on,' said Juliette. 'They were going on and on about you being a hero. They wanted to do pictures of you with me and Freddie.'

Joe groaned and put his head in his hands.

'Bloody hell, don't remind me. I hope you told them where to get off. Willy doesn't want any fuss. Nor do I for that matter.'

Juliette grinned at Joe.

'Course I told them. The last thing I want is a horde of snappers stampeding through the house when you're supposed to be spending time with Freddie. I think they were a bit surprised though. Thought you'd love the publicity and all that. The *Sunday Sentinel* were so desperate that they even asked *me* to write a piece on what it's like being married to a hero.'

'What's a hero?' asked Freddie.

'It's someone who helps rescue other people from danger,' said Juliette.

136

'Like Scott Tracey on *Thunderbirds*?' said Freddie, pushing his empty pasta bowl away.

'Exactly,' laughed Joe. 'Did they say anything else by the way?'

'Like what?' said Juliette.

Joe shrugged his shoulders.

'Oh nothing much. Now, Freddie, where's that game you were going to show me?'

As Joe took charge of Freddie, bathing him and building a Lego model upstairs with him, Juliette thought it felt like old times. If she really put her mind to it she could almost convince herself that they were a normal family after all. But then again, she wasn't entirely sure what a normal family was any more.

Chapter Fifteen

When he woke up, Joe couldn't work out where the hell he was. He wasn't in the narrow spare bed at Willy's flat, that was for sure. He yawned lazily and stretched out his arms and legs.

'Ouch, that hurt,' muttered Juliette indignantly. Still half-asleep, she turned on to her side, yanking most of the crumpled floral duvet over her as she did so.

Joe opened his eyes wide in shock. Bloody hell. He and Juliette were in bed together. *They'd actually slept in the same bed together.* What's more, he thought, casting his mind over the events of last night, they had even made love. And it had been bloody brilliant.

The door opened a crack and Freddie peeped in.

'Ssssh,' whispered Joe, putting his finger to his lips. 'I'm getting up. Let's not wake Mummy.'

Feeling slightly regretful, Joe eased himself out of bed and grabbed his clothes off the floor on the way out through the door. Freddie was waiting for him on the landing and they crept downstairs together.

After a mug of black coffee for Joe and a bowl of Shreddies for Freddie, Joe asked his son what he'd like to do next.

'Go on a bike ride, Daddy, pleeeease,' shrieked Freddie with excitement.

'But it's only eight o' clock in the morning,' said Joe.

'Please, Daddy, please. Mummy's always promising to take me out on my bike but she never does. And Granny didn't either when she was here.'

Joe had forgotten about Maura's visit. Last week Juliette had warned him that his mother-in-law would be staying for the weekend and instructed him to be polite. He wondered why she wasn't there.

'When did Granny go?' he asked Freddie.

'Yesterday,' replied Freddie. 'And I was glad.'

Joe glanced at his son. He was fully aware that Jules had rarely seen eye to eye with her mum but as far as he knew Maura had always been delightful to Freddie.

'Why's that?'

''Cos she said I was naughty,' said Freddie. 'But I'm not, am I?'

'Course you're not,' said Joe, ruffling his son's chestnut hair. 'Grown-ups talk a load of rubbish sometimes, don't they?'

All the same, as they cycled along the lane in the direction of Miston Moor, Joe found himself wondering how well Freddie was really settling in up here. There was obviously something worrying him, something he couldn't quite put his finger on. He seemed a little more anxious than he'd ever been in London, a little more on his guard.

When they reached the path snaking up to the summit of Miston Moor they both got off their bikes and sat on the grass.

'Guess what I've brought in my rucksack,' said Joe, heaving it off his back.

Freddie's eyes lit up underneath his bike helmet.

'Biscuits?' he said hopefully.

'What sort?'

'Custard creams?'

'How did you know?' asked Joe, offering him one from the top of the packet.

'Just did,' said Freddie, munching away happily.

Joe gazed at the stunning landscape that lay in front of them. The fields stretched for miles, green and lush even at this time of year, with the fells soaring behind. It was as far removed from grotty old London as you could possibly get. Joe cursed inwardly. In a few hours time he'd be back in the smoke and grime and all this would seem like a figment of his imagination.

'D'you like living up here, Freddie?' he asked suddenly.

'Sometimes,' said the little boy, chomping through his third custard cream.

'When do you like it best?'

'When you're here and we're all together,' said Freddie without hesitating. He glanced up at his father and then his words came out all in a rush. 'Why can't you be here all the time? I think I might like it all the time then.'

Joe's face fell. He didn't know what to say.

'Maybe that'll happen one day. I don't know. It's just that Mummy and me, we've got to work to pay for things like shoes and bikes and things. And my job's in London and hers is up here. So what can we do?'

Freddie stared at his father. The answer, as far as he was concerned, was quite simple.

'You could get a job up here, Daddy. That would sort it out, wouldn't it?'

Joe tried a different tack with him.

'Do you remember when you said you liked living up here sometimes?'

Freddie nodded solemnly.

'Well, what don't you like about it? Apart from me not being here all the time, I mean.'

Freddie wrenched a fistful of grass from the soil and gazed at it intently.

'School,' he said. His voice was so quiet that Joe had to lean forward to catch what he was saying.

'Why don't you like school?' said Joe softly.

Freddie stared into space. He didn't reply.

'What don't you like about school, Freddie?' repeated Joe. 'What's wrong with it? Is it the teacher? The lessons? The other kids?'

For a moment Freddie looked as though he was about to say something. Then he thought better of it and shrugged his shoulders aimlessly.

'Dunno. It's just boring.'

On the ride back to the house, Joe couldn't get Freddie's comments out of his mind. He'd refused pointblank to tell Joe any more, just stared down at the ground and said that things were fine really. But Joe knew they weren't.

The two of them parked their bikes in the front garden and wandered into the house. Yet again, Joe felt apprehensive about seeing Jules. The trouble was that she was like Jekyll and Hyde these days. He never knew if she was going to welcome him with open arms or give him the cold shoulder treatment.

'Is that you, Freddie?' yelled Juliette from the kitchen as they piled into the hall. 'Can you pop next door to Mr Spratton's? He wants you to help him dig up some potatoes for lunch.'

Freddie looked questioningly at Joe. He usually liked helping old Mr Spratton in the garden but he was reluctant to leave his father's side.

'Go on, son,' said Joe. He knew from the tone of Jules's voice that something had happened. 'It won't take long and I'm not leaving till tea-time. We'll have plenty of time to play football together this afternoon.'

Freddie grabbed his wellies from the hall and scampered off. Meanwhile, Joe sauntered into the kitchen.

The instant he saw the tight-lipped expression on

Jules's face he knew that last night's intimacy was well and truly over.

She was sitting at the kitchen table in a scruffy old dressing gown with a huge pile of Sunday papers laid out in front of her.

'What the hell did you think you were playing at?' she railed when she saw him. She thrust the front page of the *Sunday Sentinel* at him. 'As if we haven't got enough on our plate. You didn't have to go and beat Mike Baker to a pulp. What were you thinking of?'

Joe glared coldly at her.

'Have you quite finished?'

'No, I bloody haven't,' stormed Juliette. 'There's plenty more I want to say to you.'

'Don't you think you ought to find out exactly what happened first?' said Joe, his voice icy. 'Listen to my version of events perhaps? Before you take sides?'

'What else do I need to know – it's all down here in black and white,' shouted Juliette. 'Mike Baker – who, you may have forgotten, I used to work with – asks a perfectly straightforward question about Willy's injuries. And instead of giving him a civil answer you knock him out cold. Look at those bruises.'

'I did not knock him out cold,' said Joe. He was seething with anger. What's more, glancing at the picture of Mike Baker, he reckoned the reporter's glorious shiner owed more than a little to a touch of make-up. 'Is that what it says in that penny rag? No way did I knock him out. Look, Jules, you know me better than anyone. Well, I thought you did. Would I hit someone for no reason at all?'

Juliette stared at him.

'I'm not sure – I don't think so,' she said quietly.

'Thank you,' said Joe. He sat down opposite Juliette and began leafing through the other red tops. He was

142

on the front page of every single one of them. *'DJ JOE KOs TABLOID HACK'* screeched the *Sunday Sentinel's* headline while the *Sunday Mirror* had splashed with *'RADIO STAR IN STREET BRAWL'*.

'Oh God,' he murmured, putting his head in his hands.

'My sentiments exactly,' said Juliette. 'I can't believe you've been quite so stupid.'

Joe struggled to keep his temper.

'Well, what would you do if a friend of yours got beaten up? Hmm? What would you do if they were set on by a pack of snappers when they'd only just been discharged from hospital? Willy was completely terrified and all that lot could do was bombard him with questions about being gay and whether his family knows or not. You don't need to tell me that I shouldn't have hit the guy – I know I shouldn't. But they drove me completely crazy.'

'It says here that he's going to press charges,' said Juliette.

'Oh God, that's all I need.'

They were still glaring at each other when Freddie raced into the kitchen carrying a bag filled with potatoes.

'Look Daddy, look Mummy,' he yelled. 'Look how many I've got. Can we cook them for lunch?'

Joe was halfway down the M6 when he remembered that to cap it all he'd completely forgotten to talk to Jules about what Freddie had said about school. He'd been so caught up in the row about him socking Mike Baker in the jaw that everything else had disappeared from his mind.

At that moment his mobile rang.

'Hello,' he yelled crossly into the tiny microphone dangling from his mirror.

'Joe?' said a vaguely familiar voice at the other end of the line. The man sounded smooth and cultured. It couldn't possibly be a reporter.

'Yep,' said Joe.

'Where are you?'

'Just gone past Sandbach services on the M6. Look, who is this?'

'It's Daniel,' said the man, clearly irritated that Joe had failed to recognise his voice. 'Daniel White. Your agent?'

'Oh God, Daniel, sorry. I've been on another planet all day.'

'I can't say I'm surprised,' said Daniel, his voice cool. 'Look, Joe, I know I told you we needed to raise your profile but what on earth were you thinking of? I'm trying to convince the TV bosses that you're ideal for family shows. At the end of last week I was pretty confident that Primetime were about to ask you to audition for their new daytime quiz. I know I told you to get out and about a bit more but they're not going to touch someone who goes wading into street brawls. It's completely the wrong image. You must see that.'

'I suppose so,' said Joe, his voice weary. He knew he ought to feel devastated at Daniel's words but he was too tired to care.

'Are you all right, Joe? Is there something that you're not telling me?'

'Like what, exactly?'

Daniel wasn't entirely sure. But after twenty years of dealing with people in showbiz he knew from bitter experience that something was bothering Joe.

'Come on Joe, if I'm going to represent you, you've got to trust me. When we met I had you down as a regular kind of chap – a fun guy with a top-flight radio show and ambitions to move into TV. Then this morning I open up the Sundays to find that you're living with a gay guy, you've got an appalling temper and you've just beaten the living daylights out of one of the best-known reporters in the business. Now do you see what I mean about telling me things?'

Joe tightened his hold on the steering wheel. He steeled himself not to fly off the handle.

'Are you insinuating what I think you're insinuating?' he bellowed into the microphone.

'For goodness sake, Joe, calm down,' said Daniel quietly. 'Look at this from my point of view. I'm not insinuating anything. Why should I? We're on the same side. I'm just trying to sell you as the kind of chap who'd make a great job of hosting Primetime's new game show. I want you to raise your profile by showing your face at showbiz parties and having a laugh. *What I don't want* is for you to be going round getting into fights. The public doesn't like it and it certainly doesn't go down well with the TV bosses. Is that understood?'

'So you're not giving me the elbow then?'

'No, I'm not,' said Daniel. 'Not for now, anyway. But this is your last chance. One more spot of bother and then, I'm sorry, but I won't be in a position to represent you any more. Do I make myself clear?'

'Crystal,' murmured Joe.

'Oh, and Joe?'

'What?'

'Get yourself a decent lawyer, won't you? Just in case.'

Chapter Sixteen

Tim Dawner woke with a start just after six am on Monday morning. Ouch, his head hurt – thanks to the half bottle of whisky he'd downed the night before. His mouth was dry and his legs felt like blocks of concrete. Although sleeping on the sofa in his office had seemed like a good idea at midnight, when he'd finally finished poring over the figures, he'd barely got any kip at all. The sofa had proved cold, hard, lonely and uncomfortable.

As he gradually came to, it dawned on him that the packers on the shop floor would be arriving for work in less than an hour. He bloody well didn't want to bump into any of them in this state. Picking up the papers strewn all over the floor, he grabbed his flying jacket and dashed out to the car. He was due at the bank later this morning so a bath, shave and smart clothes were essential. The bank manager was a nice enough old buffer but he was hardly likely to extend Denim Heart's overdraft facility if he turned up looking like a down and out.

Three hours later Tim strode purposefully into the bank in Bowater High Street. Clad in a dark business suit, ice-blue Jermyn Street shirt and sober tie, he now looked every inch the dynamic young businessman. Think positive, he told himself. If you can't persuade George Darnley to up the overdraft to three million, then you should get out of business right here and now and go and run a sweet shop.

'I've got an appointment with Mr Darnley at nine,' he told the young woman at the counter.

'And you are . . . ?' she asked, blushing bright scarlet. She knew perfectly well who the gorgeous man standing in front of her was. Everyone in Bowater did.

'Tim Dawner,' he said breezily. 'I'll go straight in, shall I?'

'Er, no,' said the woman. 'I'm afraid you can't.'

'Oh?' said Tim, slightly surprised. The bank usually laid out the red carpet for him. 'Running late, is he?'

'Not exactly, no. I'm afraid Mr Darnley was, er, has, er . . . Mr Darnley has taken early retirement. That is, he doesn't work here any more.'

A shiver of alarm ran down Tim's spine. Mr Darnley's relaxed approach to banking and abhorrence of detail had been the main reasons why Denim Heart had continued to bank in Bowater. Helen had frequently urged him to move to a bigger, more international outfit but Tim had steadfastly refused.

Sure enough, Tim's very worst fears were realised when the solid oak door of Mr Darnley's office opened and a serious-looking, bespectacled man in his mid-forties stepped out.

'Mr Dawner,' he said, striding towards Tim with his hand outstretched. 'How charming to meet you at last. I'm Keith Birch. Your new bank manager. Come along in. We've got a heck of a lot to get through.'

There followed two of the most uncomfortable hours of Tim's life. Where George Darnley had been easy going and impressionable (he'd loved hearing Tim namedrop about famous Denim Heart customers), Keith Birch dourly went through the new business plan with a fine tooth-comb.

'I see from your records that you've had a one million pound overdraft in place for the past two years,' said Keith Birch, peering over his gold-rimmed glasses disapprovingly. Tim felt like a naughty schoolboy who'd been hauled up in front of the headmaster.

'Yes, that's right,' said Tim, trying to sound suitably humble. 'We built a brand-new state of the art factory a couple of years ago. We hoped to have been in a position to pay the loan off by now but business has been a little tougher than we envisaged. Our sales are very healthy, really they are. But I have to admit that we haven't got our overheads down as quickly as we would have liked.'

'I see,' said Keith Birch with a frown. 'And your management team, I take it, is you and Miss Brown. Anyone else?'

Tim cleared his throat nervously. What was all this about? George Darnley hadn't given a damn whether Denim Heart even had a management team, let alone who was in it.

'No.'

Keith Birch sat back in his seat and regarded the man in front of him keenly. It was perfectly obvious that things weren't quite as straightforward as Tim Dawner implied.

'You have asked for an increase of your overdraft facility to three million pounds,' he said thoughtfully. 'That's a lot of money. If, and I mean if, the bank agrees to extend it, we are going to need more than simply your word that you can repay it at any time we ask for it. A lot more. An awful lot more. We shall need Miss Brown's agreement, for a start, as well as a number of guarantees.'

'What sort of guarantees?' asked Tim.

Keith Birch ran through the list of conditions the bank had in mind.

'Oh, and one other thing,' he said. 'I've consulted

my colleagues at our regional office in Manchester and they've decided to put Denim Heart into Corporate Recovery.'

'And what's that exactly?' asked Tim. 'It sounds more like medicine than business.'

'It is in a way,' said Keith Birch. 'I'm sorry but it means that your account is no longer this branch's responsibility. Our Corporate Recovery department is a specialist team that looks after companies with problems. And Denim Heart most certainly has problems. I'm sure you appreciate that.'

By the time Tim stumbled out of the bank, white-faced with shock, he had agreed to let the Corporate Recovery people trawl through Denim Heart's most intimate affairs. He hadn't had much choice.

Tim was so appalled by Keith Birch's unyielding approach to Denim Heart that he couldn't face heading straight back to the office. Instead he found himself wandering aimlessly down Bowater High Street. Monday was market day and the town was heaving with shoppers, most of them bundled up in heavy overcoats to ward out the November cold. Twice Tim was forced to step off the pavement and into the road to avoid the hustle and bustle of the crowd.

What the hell was he doing in this backwater? For years he and Helen had congratulated themselves on their vision. While most of their business contemporaries had set up shop in London, they'd opted for the Lake District, where rents and wages were half the price. By installing sophisticated new technology systems they'd been able to compete with companies all over the world. And if he was honest with himself, he'd loved being a big fish in a small pond. He loved the fact that Denim Heart was the biggest employer in the area and everyone knew who he was.

But right now he didn't feel quite so clever. Helen had packed her bags and walked out, business was way down and to cap the lot he had a hawkish new bank manager scrutinising his every move. If he wasn't careful he risked losing everything he'd ever achieved.

Keen to delay his return to the office for as long as possible, he stepped into Giovanni's coffee house on the corner of the market square. Giovanni's family had lived in Bowater for three generations but his café still looked out of place in the old-fashioned Cumbrian town. Light and elegant, with circular steel tables, matching chairs and a long narrow kitchen at the back, it was like something straight out of Milan. And Giovanni's coffee and home-made ice cream were second to none.

'What can I get for you, Mr Dawner?' asked Giovanni, scrupulously polite as always. He looked immaculate in his habitual long white apron and dark shirt.

'Espresso please, Giovanni. The café's a bit slack for market day, isn't it? This place is usually heaving.'

'You should have seen it half an hour ago,' chuckled Giovanni. 'We were so full you wouldn't have even got in through the door. They've all had their fry-ups and disappeared off to the sheep auction now. But we'll be getting the lunchtime crowd in soon.'

As he spoke, the door opened and two women came in, chattering nineteen to the dozen. The younger one had a mass of dark curly hair and was wearing an extraordinary fur-trimmed mini-skirt and psychedelic Doc Martins – not exactly your typical Bowater out-fit. The older one wore a more restrained navy suit and beige knee-length boots. Tim smiled at her. It was Juliette Ward.

'Slacking again, Jules?' he commented with a grin. 'I'm amazed you lot ever get the paper out at all.'

'Look who's talking,' said Juliette, unwinding a cream

wool scarf from around her neck and pulling off her jacket.

'Touché,' said Tim. 'Why don't you both come and join me?'

Juliette raised her eyebrows at Cara.

'What do you think, Cara? Is that OK with you?'

Cara Bell, the *Eagle*'s junior feature writer, nodded vigorously. She'd been dying to meet Tim Dawner in the flesh ever since he'd sent Juliette those amazing flowers.

'As long as I won't be playing gooseberry,' she giggled.

'Don't be ridiculous,' snapped Juliette. 'Don't take any notice of her, Tim. This is Cara Bell, by the way. She's supposed to be a feature writer but she's really the office joker.'

'Sure,' said Tim. He wasn't particularly interested in what Cara was. 'How are things with you, anyway?'

'Oh, stressful as usual,' muttered Juliette. 'You know how it is.'

'Anything I can do?' murmured Tim.

Cara stared wide-eyed at Tim. She'd never met anyone like him in Bowater. This guy was so smooth he'd give Pierce Brosnan a run for his money. And the way he was gazing at Juliette . . . she couldn't wait to tell everyone back in the office.

'Domestic stuff mainly,' said Juliette. 'I won't bore you with the grisly details.' She ran her fingers distractedly through her shoulder-length hair.

'Well, at least let me buy you a coffee then.'

Once again, Cara noticed that the Denim Heart boss was unable to take his eyes off Juliette. It suddenly occurred to her that she might be a little surplus to requirements.

'On second thoughts I'll leave you two to it,' she said, standing up. 'I've got to collect my dry cleaning and if I don't finish that planning committee profile Alex is going to have my guts for garters. We lead such a glamorous life on the *Eagle*, don't we?'

As she whirled back through the door Tim looked questioningly at Juliette.

'Was it something I said?'

'I should think she wants to hot-foot it back to the office to spread a bit of gossip around,' said Juliette. She felt irritated by Cara's abrupt departure – especially as it had been Cara who'd suggested popping into Giovanni's in the first place and not her. Up to her eyes writing her tedious supermarket feature, Juliette had only agreed in the first place because Cara wanted to ask her advice about something.

'What's there to gossip about?' said Tim.

'Oh nothing,' said Juliette quickly. 'Anyway, what about that coffee you promised me? I haven't got much time.'

After ordering another coffee, Tim swung round to face Juliette once more. He held her gaze just a fraction too long. Feeling uncomfortable, she glanced away.

'So how's everything going at Denim Heart? Have you heard from Helen yet?'

A look of irritation flashed across Tim's face. He didn't want to talk about Helen. Especially not right now.

'Oh, she's sunning herself on some beach in the Caribbean,' he said dismissively. 'And yeah, we're managing fine at Denim Heart without her. Hasn't made much difference in fact, her going off like that.'

At that moment, Giovanni placed a large cup of frothing coffee in front of Juliette. She took a long sip before turning her attention back to Tim.

'Mmmm, this is exactly what I needed. Any stories for me then?'

Tim laughed.

'Oh, so you only want me for one thing, do you? You journalists are all the same. I might have known.'

Tim pretended to look downcast and Juliette found herself laughing despite herself.

'That's better,' said Tim softly. 'You look much prettier when you laugh. Now Jules, how about telling me what's wrong?'

Juliette seldom confided in anyone. Certainly not in her mother or close friends – and the way things were with Joe right now, rarely in him either. But all of a sudden, and without having the least intention of doing so, she found herself pouring all her troubles out to Tim.

'Everything's gone wrong since we moved up here,' she said.

'Everything?' queried Tim.

'Everything,' repeated Juliette firmly. 'Things are pretty terrible with Joe. Rock bottom more like. I haven't had anything decent in the *Eagle* for days, not since that Denim Heart splash. But none of that matters really because it's Freddie I'm worried about. He's only six and he's so vulnerable . . .'

To her horror, Juliette dissolved into tears. She immediately grabbed the napkin from beneath her coffee cup and began wiping her eyes.

'I'm sorry,' she said, embarrassed that Tim Dawner should see her in this state.

Tim gazed tenderly at her. Seeing Juliette like this made him forget his own troubles.

'Don't be,' he said, putting his hand over hers. 'We're mates, aren't we? And if you can't talk to a mate, who can you talk to?'

'It's not exactly professional though, is it?' snuffled Juliette into her napkin. 'I should be firing pertinent questions about Denim Heart at you. Not blubbing about my own problems. Anyway, I really must go.'

Tim took a card out of his jacket pocket and scribbled a number on it.

'Here's my mobile number,' he said, sliding it over the table. 'Just remember, Jules – you can ring me any time. *Any time at all. Day or night.*'

Back in the office, Cara was busy regaling some of the other *Eagle* hacks about Juliette and Tim.

'I don't *think* there's anything going on between them – well, not yet anyway – but you should have seen the way he kept looking at her. He could hardly take her eyes off her.'

'She definitely hasn't been quite herself recently, has she?' reflected George Anderson, one of the features subs. George led such a boring life – at home as well as work – that gossip was the only thing that kept him going. 'She's barely been here at all for the past week or so. And I know that it's really pissing Alex Davis off the way she keeps doing her disappearing act halfway through the day. You don't think . . .'

'That she's been nipping off to see Tim Dawner?' said Cara, finishing his sentence for him. 'Surely not . . . She's married, with a kid . . .'

'I wonder whether I should mention anything to Alex,' said George thoughtfully. He liked stirring it. 'I mean, I'm pretty sure he wouldn't want her writing stories about Denim Heart if she was, you know, *involved* with the boss. You can't take sides when you work for a paper. Everyone knows that.'

'I didn't say she *was* involved exactly,' hissed Cara. 'Just that she *might* be. Maybe it would be better to leave things the way they are for now. She's all right, is Juliette. Best not to interfere.'

It was at precisely that moment that Juliette wandered back on to the editorial floor. The other feature writers and subs instantly melted away, though Cara couldn't help noticing that Juliette's eyes were puffy and red, as though she'd been crying.

'Are you OK?' whispered Cara as Juliette slumped on to her chair.

'What?' said Juliette distractedly. She logged on to her computer and scrolled through her e-mails.

'I asked if you were all right. You look a bit upset.'

Staring at her screen, Juliette's face turned pale. The last message was marked timdawner@denimheart.com. It had been sent just a couple of minutes earlier.

'*Jules,*' said the e-mail. '*I hate seeing you so sad. Can we have dinner soon? T.*'

Without thinking what she was doing, Juliette pressed the delete button. What had she been thinking of pouring her heart out to Tim like that? She certainly didn't need any more complications in her life right now.

Chapter Seventeen

Freddie was having the time of his life. After an ace weekend with his dad, he'd been dreading coming back to horrible old school on Monday. But so far, so good. Better than that, in fact. Today everything had gone swimmingly. He hadn't stumbled over a single word when he'd read his Biff and Chip book aloud to Mrs Booth and she'd been so impressed that afterwards she'd praised him in front of the whole class. Then later on, a couple of footballers from Bowater United had turned up to give Class Two a coaching lesson. And much to everyone's surprise, including his own, Freddie had proved a natural. He'd even scored a goal.

'Well done, lad,' bellowed Darren Goodison approvingly from the other side of the pitch. 'There's some real talent there. You'll have to get your dad to bring you along to one of our Sunday morning sessions at the club.'

Freddie had beamed with pride. He only wished his dad had been there to witness his triumph.

But there was no doubt in his mind about the best thing that had happened. It was that Craig Barker hadn't turned up for school.

'Craig?' Mrs Booth had called, peering over the top of the register at Class Two. 'Craig? Has anyone seen Craig Barker this morning?'

Freddie had glanced down at his lap and crossed his fingers on both hands. Please don't let Craig be here today. Please, please, please. Please let him be very ill and off school till Christmas.

Freddie hadn't admitted this to anybody, but Craig Barker made his life a misery. He'd been making it a misery since Freddie's second day at Newdale.

Craig was Carol Barker's youngest child. It wasn't that he was a strapping lad, far from it. He was the oldest in the class – he'd been seven on 1 September – but he was a small, wiry boy with round glasses taped up at the side with sticking plaster and a crew cut. He looked as though he wouldn't dare say boo to a goose.

But Craig's appearance, as Freddie had learned to his cost, was deceptive. He was the youngest child of four and as tough as old boots. He'd picked on Freddie from the start for being a newcomer, punching and kicking him in the playground whenever the teachers' backs were turned. He taunted him for 'talking posh' and was forever nicking his belongings. Freddie had lost count of all the things Craig had taken – his new felt tips, a woolly hat, two pairs of gloves and a Lego model he'd brought in especially to show Mrs Booth.

Freddie wasn't sure why he hadn't told anyone about Craig Barker. Well, he hadn't told his mum because she was always too busy to listen. And he hadn't mentioned it to his granny because she probably would have said that it was his fault for being soft. But he couldn't think why he hadn't said anything to his dad. There had been a moment on a bike ride when he'd been on the verge of telling him but he'd changed his mind at the last minute. He'd been having the time of his life with his dad and he hadn't wanted to spoil a single second of it by mentioning horrible old Craig.

At the end of school, Mrs Booth presented Freddie

with a Postman Pat sticker for working so hard during the day.

'Just make sure you keep this up, Freddie,' she said, smiling at him.

Freddie beamed back proudly and even though he absolutely hated Postman Pat, stuck the sticker on his jumper. Thank goodness Craig wasn't there to witness it. He would have teased him like mad.

When the bell went Freddie raced into the playground. Juliette had promised faithfully that she would be there to meet him and he couldn't wait to tell her about the day's triumphs. By the time he got to the school gate, though, his pace had slowed to a dawdle. There were loads of mums and childminders waiting there – but Juliette wasn't one of them.

'Freddie,' a cheery voice behind him called. 'Come and wait with us.'

Freddie turned to see who was talking to him. When he realised that it was Fi Nicholson, Lizzie and Molly's mum, he smiled wanly and shuffled over to her, dragging his rucksack behind him.

'Mummy promised that she'd be here to meet me,' he said in a whiny voice.

'And she will be,' said Fi soothingly, stroking the top of his hair. 'She rang just as I was setting off to say that she was on her way and could I wait with you.'

'Thanks,' said Freddie grumpily.

'How come you're out of school so quickly? You must have got a move on. I can't see any sign of Lizzie and Molly yet. They're such slow coaches.'

Fi knew full well that it usually took Freddie an age to get his stuff together. She'd often noticed him wandering desultorily out of the Portakabin a good ten minutes after the other children in the class. Lizzie and Molly were frequently in the car and fastening their seat belts by the time Freddie appeared. Perhaps he'd rushed out extra-fast today because Juliette was meeting him.

At that moment Juliette's tatty Golf screeched to a halt outside the school. She double-parked next to Louise Newman's flashy four-wheel drive and jumped out.

'Sweetheart,' she cried, wrapping Freddie in her arms. 'I'm so sorry I'm late. Can you forgive me?'

'I s'pose so,' Freddie mumbled into her coat. 'It didn't matter *too* much. Lizzie's mum looked after me.'

'Thanks so much, Fi,' said Juliette. 'I owe you one.'

'Don't mention it,' laughed Fi. 'Any time. Actually, I've been meaning to have a word with you for a while. About meeting Freddie I mean. D'you fancy popping round for a cup of tea?'

'What, now?'

'Why not?' said Fi. 'Freddie could play with the girls and we could have a chat. Or have you got something else on?'

Juliette smiled to herself. If only Fi knew. Her life outside work was deadly dull. In fact the most exciting thing she had on most nights was a supermarket curry for one in front of the telly.

'I'd love to,' she said. 'Shall we see you there?'

As she turned to leave, Norma Gray hurried through the gate. The collar of her anorak was turned up to keep out the biting wind and she seemed anxious not to catch anyone's eye.

'Hang on a minute, Freddie,' said Juliette. 'I must have a word with Norma.'

Juliette ran after Norma, who was rushing along the pavement.

'Norma,' she said, catching her by the arm. 'I've been meaning to ring you but I've been up to my eyes at work. How's Amy getting on with the baby? Are they out of hospital yet?'

Norma stared at Juliette blankly. There was a look of defeat in her eyes.

'I think she and the bairn are coming out tomorrow,' she said in a weary voice.

'Have you and Dawn been visiting them everyday?'

'No, we haven't,' snapped Norma. 'Now, I know you mean well but if you don't mind, I've got a bus to catch. My Ritchie'll go mad if his tea isn't ready when he gets in.'

Puzzled by Norma's gruff manner, Juliette kept hold of her arm.

'Has something happened, Norma? You and Dawn were over the moon about the baby on Friday. What's happened to change everything?'

Tears welled up in Norma's eyes. She tried to speak but she was so choked that it was a few seconds before she could get her words out.

'I can't really talk about it here, love,' she whispered. 'It's Dawn. I had no idea all this was going through her mind but over the months she's somehow gone and got the idea that Amy was going to let her have the baby. Bring her up, like. Dawn and her husband Morton, they've been trying to start a family for ages, only nothing's happened. Not since the miscarriage. She's so desperate for a littl'un and, I don't know, she went and got the wrong end of the stick about Amy's bairn.'

As Norma spoke, Dawn's bizarre behaviour at the hospital began to make a bit more sense. She'd been so proprietorial about the baby. So insistent that the little girl was going to be bottle-fed. So surprised when Amy announced she was going to call her Billie and not Katherine. It was obviously because she'd convinced herself that the baby was rightfully hers.

'Norma,' sighed Juliette. 'I'm so sorry. I had no idea. No idea at all.'

'No, none of us had,' murmured Norma.

'So where are Amy and the baby going to live?'

'They're going back to Amy's mum's. Heaven knows Carol's got enough on her plate but Amy and the bairn are going home to her. Now, if you don't mind, love, I'd better be getting on.'

Shaken by what Norma had told her, Juliette called out to Freddie to get in the car. He'd been playing tag in the playground with Louise Newman's two boys and ran up looking flushed and out of breath.

'Come here, you,' she said, grabbing hold of him. 'I need to give you a big, big hug.'

At that moment, Louise Newman charged through the school gate looking absolutely livid. She'd rushed into school to try and organise a meeting about the parents' group's latest fund-raising campaign only to find that the teachers were in a staff meeting and didn't have time to talk to her.

'Well thanks very much,' she protested when she saw that her car was parked in by Juliette's shabby Golf. 'For God's sake. Just because you can't be bothered to get here on time doesn't mean you have to be anti-social to the rest of us.'

'All right, keep your hair on,' muttered Juliette, taking Freddie by the hand. 'Come on, sweetheart. Let's get out of the cross lady's way.'

Ten minutes later, sitting in Fi Nicholson's warm kitchen – Freddie had scampered off to play with the girls – she told Fi about Louise losing her temper.

'Honestly, that woman,' seethed Fi. 'She's completely off her trolley. The parents' group was doing absolutely fine before she arrived on the scene. We raised enough money to help buy a few library books *and* paid for the children's summer outing every year. But no. That wasn't good enough for la-di-da Louise. She had to go one better and set about raising enough for a blooming adventure playground. She's so insensitive. She doesn't realise that people round here hardly have two pennies to rub together. Some of the farming families find it tough enough putting food on the table, let alone paying for Louise's fancy schemes.'

'I suppose *I* ought to start helping a bit,' said Juliette thoughtfully. She'd been feeling guilty for a while about her lack of involvement at the school. She knew that Fi went in every week to hear children read and some of the other mums were helping to make costumes for the nativity play.

'Well, if you can stand Louise bossing you about, then that would be absolutely great,' said Fi. 'And it would be nice to have another sane voice at parents' group meetings.'

Juliette took another sip of her tea and looked around her. Fi's kitchen was huge, with a long dining table at one end and an old-fashioned cream Rayburn pumping out heat at the other. Fi had strung a washing line across the middle of the room, on which she'd pegged her children's latest works of art. For the first time since she'd arrived in the north, Juliette felt at home.

'Are you happy living up here?' Fi asked suddenly.

'Why do you ask?' said Juliette, startled by her bluntness.

'Oh, I don't know. It just seems quite tough on you, that's all. Moving up here from London, working full-time, looking after Freddie on your own most of the week . . . All that.'

'I can't complain,' said Juliette, putting her mug down on Fi's flower-sprigged tablecloth.

'Why not?' said Fi. 'I do. All the time.'

Juliette laughed. She was starting to like Fi more and more.

'No, I mean the reason that *I* can't complain is because moving up here was all my idea in the first place. Joe was against it and Freddie hated the idea of living apart from his dad in the week. But I railroaded them both into it. I was sick of the traffic and the fumes and the noise in London. We'd been burgled three times and the car used to get broken into just about every other night . . . So I had the bright idea that if we moved right away everything would be so much better. Only . . .'

Juliette's words trailed away as she reflected on what she'd done.

'Only it isn't,' said Fi, finishing her sentence for her. 'It's cold and damp and unfriendly. The countryside is stunning but most of the time it's shrouded in mist and you can't even see it. You have to drive five miles to get a pint of milk and no one's ever heard of wild rice or mascarpone.'

Juliette's eyes widened in astonishment.

'How did you know?' she asked.

Fi threw back her head and laughed.

'Because we did exactly the same. Me and Dai, we've lived here for more than ten years now and the whole of Newdale still treats us as jumped-up newcomers.'

'They don't just treat me as a newcomer,' said Juliette. 'More like a creature from another planet.'

'Even at work?'

'Even at work. More so, in fact. The younger ones can't understand why on earth I should want to leave a good job in London to come and work for the *Eagle*. And the older ones are so paranoid that I'll think they're amateurish and useless that most of them barely even speak to me.'

'That good, eh?' murmured Fi.

'Yep. That good. I can't imagine what I was thinking of when I took the job.'

'Is there *anyone* you get on with?'

Juliette groaned out loud.

'Oh, I'm making it sound worse than it is. The office isn't quite that bad. The editor's a bit tense at the moment – I think management's giving him a hard time about the dire circulation figures – but he's OK.'

Fi regarded Juliette keenly.

'Tell me to mind my own business if you like but meeting Freddie from school seems tricky for you,' she said.

'You're right there,' said Juliette. 'I mean, the mornings are fine, and I can sometimes wangle things in the afternoons, but not that often.'

'Would it help if I met him and brought him back here? He could have tea with the girls and you could pick him up when you'd finished work.'

Juliette could hardly believe what she was hearing. For a minute she was tempted to leap to her feet and throw her arms around Fi.

'Are you sure?'

'I'm quite, quite sure,' said Fi.

'But there's one condition,' said Juliette. 'You must let me pay you the going rate. I mean, I know we're friends, but I'd feel like I was taking advantage otherwise.'

Fi laughed merrily.

'Well, if that makes you happier, fine. But remember that I'll be meeting the girls anyway and cooking their tea. Bunging an extra couple of sausages in the oven for Freddie is hardly going to be that arduous, is it? Anyway, he's such a sweetie that it'll be a pleasure.'

By the time they got home, Juliette felt more cheerful than she had for ages. She'd told Freddie about Fi's offer and he'd jumped up and down with excitement.

'I really like going to Lizzie and Molly's house, Mummy,' he said. 'And now I'll be going everyday, won't I?'

Stumbling into the kitchen, Juliette snapped the light

164

on and groaned at the chaos in front of her. She'd been in such a rush first thing that she hadn't got round to clearing up the breakfast things. There were two bowls of congealed Weetabix on the table, toast crumbs scattered everywhere and two mugs of half-drunk tea. A heap of washing she'd meant to put in the machine before she left the house lay all over the floor and the radio was still blaring because she'd forgotten to switch it off.

Juliette started to laugh. Now that her mother had gone the house was back to being a slum again. The mess would have appalled Maura, but to tell the truth, Juliette didn't care. It was simply a relief to have the house back to herself once more.

Chapter Eighteen

There was no doubt about it, thought Joe, his show had gone appallingly this morning. With the Mike Baker brawl hanging over him – and Daniel White on his case too – he'd wanted to give it all he'd got. Prove how good he was at his job.

But he'd been crap. Just when it really mattered, he'd gone and given one of the most lacklustre performances of his entire career. Instead of entertaining the listeners with a string of sparkling, witty anecdotes about his life and times, he'd stumbled through the show like an amateur overcome with stage fright. Even Annie, who was usually quick to praise him, had found it difficult to look him in the eye today.

Joe left the studio quickly and – just in case there were any hacks hanging around the Radio Wave entrance to quiz him about the rumpus with Willy – disappeared down the back stairs. He made straight for his usual coffee bar on the corner. He needed to mull over the thorny question of how he was going to rescue his career from the doldrums. The way he was going he'd be back where he started before he knew it. Doing the graveyard shift on some grotty local station in the back of beyond.

'Mind if I join you?' said a familiar voice.

Joe looked up from the latte he'd been staring gloomily

into for the last fifteen minutes and saw Annie standing there. She had a concerned look on her face.

'Nope,' he said. 'If you're sure you don't mind being seen with someone whose career is going down the tubes.'

Much to Joe's surprise, Annie threw back her head and laughed. Her laughter was so infectious that he couldn't help joining in.

'God, you are in a bad way, aren't you? I always thought you were different from the other DJs. All those prima donnas who spend their time poring over listening figures and taking themselves just a tiny bit too seriously. Seems I was wrong.'

'Leave it out, Annie, will you?' said Joe, serious again. 'One way and another I've gone and made a complete ass of myself. It's hardly surprising that I'm feeling a bit sorry for myself this morning.'

Annie sat down opposite him and flicked her long ponytail over her shoulder.

'Look Joe, it's not the . . .' she began.

'If you're going to tell me that it's not the end of the world I'll bloody murder you,' seethed Joe.

Annie put her hands in the air.

'Sorry I spoke. Look Joe, I only wanted to help. Maybe it's best if I leave you to it.'

As she got up to go, Joe seized Annie's hand without thinking.

'Don't go,' he said softly. 'I could really do with someone to talk to. Please stay. *I'd like you to.*'

Annie stared at him. For the first time since they'd begun working together, Joe seemed strangely vulnerable – like a small boy who'd done something stupid and didn't know how to redeem himself.

'All right,' she said. She sank on to the chair once more. 'If that's what you want I'll stay.'

Joe and Annie ended up spending the whole morning in the café. It wasn't as if they didn't have anything else to do. Annie was supposed to be planning the following week's running order while Joe had fixed up a game of squash at Smart's as part of his new fitness regime. But they were so deep in conversation that they lost all track of time. Joe told Annie about his shambles of a marriage and how much he missed Freddie. And Annie suddenly started talking about how terrified she was that she'd end up never having children.

'Have you got any plans for lunch?' said Joe.

'Sandwich at my desk, I should think. I lead a pretty glamorous life, don't I?'

Joe thought for a moment. He'd been invited to a drinks party at the Savoy to launch a new charity record. He hadn't been at all keen on going but Daniel White had told him to show his face. And he certainly didn't want to antagonise his agent any more right now.

'D'you fancy going to a charity do at the Savoy?'

'I'm hardly dressed for it,' said Annie.

Joe glanced at her. She was wearing narrow-cut black trousers and a pink waist-length jacket over a plain white T-shirt. The effect was understated but stylish.

'You look utterly gorgeous,' he said.

'So do you,' whispered Annie, her voice so soft that Joe couldn't be sure that he'd heard her properly.

Strangely, when they got there, it was Joe who felt out of place. The Lancaster Room was filled with people from the record industry that he vaguely recognised and a host of B-list celebrities. Waiters in immaculate white aprons glided unobtrusively between the guests serving glasses of champagne from polished silver trays, while the charity PRs endeavoured to introduce people to each other. The boy-band that had made the record was larking around in the corner.

'They look about twelve,' he chuckled to Annie. 'Hardly out of short trousers.'

Joe had assumed that Annie wouldn't know anyone but he couldn't have been more wrong. She was soon pounced on by a couple of executives from a rival radio station.

'Annie,' said the older one, a good-looking man of about fifty, with a shock of white hair. 'How good to see you. Have you seen sense and changed your mind about joining us yet? I keep saying that we could really do with someone of your talent. Can I introduce you to our new MD?'

Away from their usual habitat, Joe was beginning to see Annie through different eyes. At Radio Wave, she always seemed like part of the furniture. But here she was far more at home than he was. She appeared to be on first name terms with all the top brass.

It also struck him forcibly how stunning she was. Not in a flashy, obvious sort of way – no, it was more than that. It was her style and her personality that singled her out from the crowd. You somehow knew that Annie was someone you could trust implicitly. Someone who would never let you down.

'You've done all right for yourself, haven't you?' said the man standing next to him. He gestured in Annie's direction and elbowed him in the ribs.

Joe very nearly choked on the canapé he was eating.

'What did you just say?' he demanded. He must be getting paranoid in his old age. The man couldn't possibly mean what he thought he meant.

'Your bird,' said the stranger. He was a burly man in his mid-thirties, wearing an expensive wool suit that was a couple of sizes too small for him. 'She's a bit of all right, isn't she?'

Incensed both by the fact that the man assumed Annie

169

was his 'bird', *and* by the derogatory way in which he'd referred to her, Joe struggled not to lose his temper.

'Two things, pal,' he said, his voice menacing. He felt like head-butting the man. 'One is that she is not my "bird," as you so charmingly put it. And two, she . . .'

Before he could elaborate, Annie appeared by his side once more.

'Larry,' she said smoothly, shaking the stranger by the hand. 'It's ages since we last met. Have you and Joe been properly introduced? Joe, this is Larry Penman, chief reporter on the *Daily Chronicle*. And Larry, meet Joe Ward, Radio Wave's breakfast show presenter. Joe and I work together. I produce his show.'

'Sure,' said Larry, glowering at Joe. 'Thought I knew the voice.'

Chauvinist git, thought Joe.

'I'd better be off, darling,' said Larry. 'It's a bit of a slow news day so I hoped I might pick a story or two up here. Seems I was wrong.'

The same thought struck Joe and Annie.

'You don't think . . .' began Annie once he'd gone.

Joe banged his hand against his head.

'Of course,' he said. 'Of course that's why he made a beeline for me. Thought if he insinuated something about you and me I'd take a pop at him. And bob's your uncle, there's his story. *DJ goes wild again*. I can't deny it, mind you. I nearly punched him in the mouth.'

'What's got into you recently?' asked Annie. 'You're usually so laid-back. Radio Wave will be sending you on an anger management course if you don't watch out . . .'

'Don't be ridiculous,' laughed Joe. 'I'm a pussy cat. You know that.'

'I know that I've had quite enough of all this nonsense,'

said Annie, grimacing at the other guests, most of whom had had one drink too many by now. 'D'you fancy making a move?'

Not half, thought Joe.

'How about a coffee back at my flat?' he said. 'It's in Battersea. Just over the river more or less.'

He didn't know why, but all of a sudden he couldn't bear the thought of leaving her.

Annie looked surprised, as though this was the last thing she'd been expecting. To Joe it seemed like an age before she answered.

'Go on then,' she said lightly. 'I've hardly done any work all day. I might as well carry on the habit of a lifetime.'

Sitting in the cab to Battersea, the two of them barely exchanged a word. As the taxi drove down Whitehall and past Westminster Bridge, Joe gazed out of the window. What the hell did he think he was doing? Why had he invited Annie back to the flat?

On the other side of the cab, seated as far as possible from Joe, Annie was asking herself exactly the same thing.

She was undeniably attracted to Joe – she had been for weeks – but it would be a complete disaster to get involved with him. He was married, for God's sake, with a little boy. And they worked together too. She'd got involved with someone from work once before and it had all ended in tears. Typical, though, that the ill-fated liaison hadn't affected *his* career in the slightest. Indeed his friends had considered him a bit of a lad for getting away with it. No, it was her career that had collapsed in a heap – her who had been forced to leave the company and look for another job.

As the cab sped over Battersea Bridge and turned right into Prince of Wales Drive, Annie forced herself to stop dwelling on that miserable episode. The memory of it was too painful, too raw.

'You're lucky living so near the park,' she said, trying to make polite conversation.

'Yep,' said Joe. He couldn't think what else to say. 'Can you drop us on the next corner, mate? Yep. That's great.'

Annie followed Joe into the redbrick mansion block and up the steps to the fourth floor.

'It must keep you fit living here,' she said lightly.

'What?' said Joe. He turned his key in the lock. 'Oh yep, it does. There's no lift, I'm afraid.'

As he opened the door it struck him once again how odd it was being in Willy's flat without Willy. The place seemed cold and neglected. And even though he'd been living there for weeks now, Joe still felt as if he was trespassing on Willy's territory.

He led Annie into the kitchen, hoping she'd turn a blind eye to the state it was in. When it came to washing up and cleaning, he and Willy were as one. It was an unspoken agreement between them that neither of them ever washed anything up. Not until they were down to their last mug or fork and it was absolutely necessary. Willy had kept threatening to find a cleaner but he hadn't got round to it.

'Oh my God,' said Annie, eyeing up the congealed plates in the sink and the mouldy bread on the table. 'That's revolting.'

For a split second Joe had the grace to look embarrassed.

'It is rather, isn't it. Come on, if you go into the sitting room I'll bring the coffee in there. Then you won't have to see all this. It does look a bit like a scene from a horror movie, doesn't it?'

'Don't be ridiculous,' said Annie, taking off her jacket

and rolling up the sleeves of her shirt. 'Have you got some rubber gloves?'

'What the hell d'you want rubber gloves for?' quipped Joe. 'And why are you taking your clothes off? Seems a bit kinky to me.'

Annie playfully made to hit him, but Joe caught hold of her hand in mid-air. He hung on to it and pulled her close to his chest.

'This is mad,' he murmured as he wrapped his arms around her and kissed her long and hard.

Without even thinking about what she was doing, Annie kissed him back. They must have stood there for ten minutes or more, oblivious to everything but the desire to explore each other's mouths.

'Shall we go somewhere more comfortable?' said Joe.

Annie nodded wordlessly and he led her by the hand down the hall and into his bedroom. They collapsed in a heap on to Joe's narrow single bed and slowly began to discard their clothes. As they did so, it struck Annie with a jolt how Spartan the room was. Apart from a photograph of a little boy by the bed, there was nothing personal at all. No pictures on the wall, no books on the shelf, no clues whatsoever about the person who lived there.

Joe began kissing her hungrily again. He twisted a long strand of her hair around his finger, unable to believe that he was lying in bed with Annie.

'Is that your son?' Annie asked casually, as they both surfaced for air.

Immediately the spell was broken. At the mention of Freddie, Joe let go of Annie and sat bolt upright. He wrenched the photograph frame off the bedside table and stared at it. Had he gone stark raving bonkers? He was married to Jules, for God's sake. She was a pain in the arse sometimes, but he loved her. And Freddie was their son. Things had reached rock bottom with Jules, that was for sure, but going to bed with Annie wasn't going to solve anything.

'Joe, what's wrong?' said Annie, rubbing his back. 'Tell me. Please.'

Joe turned and looked at Annie longingly. God, she was beautiful. That amazing hair. That stunning face. He yearned to make love to her.

'I'm sorry, darling,' he moaned as he got up from the bed and began hurriedly to put his clothes back on again. 'I can't do this. Don't ask me why. I just can't.'

Chapter Nineteen

'You make sure you look after yourself, dear,' Marie, the hospital midwife, instructed Amy Barker. 'And if you're worried about anything to do with baby Billie, ring us at the maternity ward any time. Will you remember that? Anything at all, you just ring us.'

Marie stared hard at Amy. Some girls of fourteen – with their immaculate make-up and trendy clothes – were more like eighteen-year-olds. But if anything, Amy looked even younger than her age. She was small and slim, with a pale, anxious face and long dark hair that hung limply down her back. Dressed in jeans and a baggy tracksuit top, you'd never imagine that she'd just had a baby. God, it was going to be tough on her, thought Marie. And Amy's mum looked as if she was going to be as much use as a chocolate teapot. She just prayed that Amy would have the resilience to cope.

It was almost a week after Billie's birth and Amy was finally leaving hospital. The teenager lingered on the steps for a moment, bewildered to be in the outside world once more. Desperate, too, to delay the moment of departure for as long as possible. The maternity unit had seemed so safe somehow, like a warm cocoon. Amy had begun feeding Billie herself on the second day and it had been hard at first. She wasn't sure she'd ever master it. But Marie or one of the other midwives had been on hand constantly to offer encouragement and support. They'd shown her how to change Billie's nappy, how to wind her and give her a bath. And often, when the baby had woken in the night to be fed, they'd brought her a cup of strong, sweet tea to boost her energy and keep her spirits up. In the six days Amy had been in hospital, she'd felt as if she really belonged somewhere.

'Come on, love,' shouted Amy's mother Carol. Her voice sounded like a foghorn. 'The taxi meter's ticking. We'd better get a move on.'

Amy carefully checked that Billie was strapped into the second-hand car seat that the midwives had given her and picked it up by the thick plastic handle. She walked gingerly down the hospital steps, terrified that she might trip and drop her precious bundle.

'Thanks Marie,' she mumbled, turning to give the midwife a little wave. 'Thanks for everything.'

Inside the taxi, Carol took no notice of Amy and Billie. She slumped down in the front, leaving Amy to fumble with the car seat in the back. She was far more interested in chatting to the taxi driver than checking that her daughter and baby granddaughter were all right.

Amy felt a lump in her throat. She wished that she could have stayed in hospital.

They were halfway to Newdale when Billie started crying. Softly at first, then a loud angry bawl. Amy tried stroking her scarlet face, but it didn't do any good.

To begin with Carol took no notice but finally she couldn't stand it any longer.

'For crying out loud, Amy, can't you get her to belt up?' she snapped. 'What's the matter with her?'

'I don't know, Mum,' said Amy, the distress clear in her voice. 'I fed her just before we left, like Marie told me to. And changed her nappy. What do you think it could be?'

Carol clicked her teeth with annoyance.

'How do I bloody know? All I know is that I can't be doing with it. I hope she's not going to be one of those babies who cries all day long. My nerves won't stand for it.'

Amy felt like bursting into tears. Deep down she'd known her mum would be like this but for the past week she'd been trying to kid herself that she wouldn't. Her mum had always been too full of her own affairs to bother what her children were getting up to. She wasn't going to change the habits of a lifetime just because Amy had had a baby.

Amy suddenly yearned for Dawn. It was true that Dawn had been a bit gruff and impatient with her at times but at least she'd been kind. She'd talked to her and looked after her. And she'd *really* seemed to care, which was more than Amy could say for her mum. Dawn had been the first person to observe Amy's thickening waist and washed-out appearance and suspect that she was pregnant. And then she'd offered to take her in until the baby was born.

Those few months up at Hillthwaite had been the happiest of Amy's life. Dawn had given her the attention that had been sadly lacking in her life – and slowly Amy had begun to come out of her shell.

The second youngest of Carol's four children, Amy had never given her mum a moment's anxiety when she was little. Carol's husband John had walked out on the family for good years ago and none of them had ever seen him again. If she bumped into her dad in the street now, Amy wouldn't recognise him. And her younger brother Craig couldn't remember him at all.

It had been a constant battle for Carol to make ends meet. Whatever else you could say about Carol, that she was loud and selfish and not that interested in her kids, you couldn't say she wasn't a grafter. She'd worked as the school caretaker at Newdale for most of Amy's life, and fitted in a load of other cleaning jobs along the way. It was backbreaking work and at the end of the day she simply didn't have the energy – physical or emotional – to deal with her children and their problems.

The news that Amy was expecting a baby was the final straw as far as Carol was concerned. Her two older children, Sarah and Wayne, had both left school and found jobs in Bowater. Sarah was a packer at Denim Heart and Wayne worked for a local garage. After all the years of scrimping and saving, the pair of them were at last bringing in a wage and things seemed easier. The family no longer lived from hand to mouth. Carol even had a bit of extra cash each week to go and play bingo or meet the girls down at the pub.

Then Amy had dropped her bombshell. Or at least Dawn had dropped it on her behalf. Amy hadn't had the nerve to tell Carol herself. She'd got Dawn to do it for her. But the upside had been that Dawn said Amy could move in with her and Morton for a while. The arrangement had suited everyone so well that Carol had blithely assumed that it would continue after the baby was born.

Only it hadn't. For the life of her Carol didn't know why, but Norma had suddenly turned up out of the blue a few days ago and announced that Amy and the baby couldn't go back to Dawn's when they came out of hospital. Carol had tried to press her but Norma stood firm, refusing to elaborate. She said they just couldn't. They'd have to live at Carol's.

'Here we are,' said the cab driver as he turned off the Newdale Road and into Langdale Avenue. 'Number thirteen, did you say?'

'That's it,' said Carol, glancing along the familiar row

of terraced houses. 'We're the pebbledash one on the right. Next to the lamp-post.'

Amy gazed protectively at Billie. All that crying must have exhausted her because she'd fallen asleep in her car seat, one tiny tear still visible on her soft cheek.

'Welcome home, baby,' she whispered softly. 'Everything's going to be all right, I know it is.'

Carol paid the cabbie and hurried into the pebbledash house, leaving Amy on her own to cope with Billie. The teenager fumbled with the car seat, all fingers and thumbs as she tried to undo the clasp.

'Here, let me help you with that,' said the cab driver, seeing her struggling. 'I'm an old hand with these baby carrier things. My daughter's got two littl'uns herself – so I have to be.'

He deftly undid the seat belt and lifted the car seat out of the cab.

'Look, you take the baby,' he said, 'and I'll bring the bags in for you. You're going to need all the help you can get, sweetheart.'

The cabbie was as good as his word. Amy carried Billie into the house and he followed behind with the luggage. Not that there was much of it, mind, just a couple of carrier bags, a pack of newborn nappies and a huge teddy bear that Dawn had brought for Billie the day she was born.

'You look after yourself, love,' he said as he dumped it all in the hall. 'And here's a little something for the baby. Don't give it to your mum. You'll make sure you buy something nice for the baby, won't you?'

Amy glanced at the piece of paper he'd stuffed into her hand. It was a £10 note – twice as much as the taxi fare he'd charged Carol.

'Thank you,' she said shyly. 'I will.'

* * *

179

Dawn sat in the parlour at Hillthwaite staring out over the hills. It was nearly dusk now and the sun glowed bright orange against the dark fells. When she'd married Morton and first come to live here she'd never been able to get enough of this view. But now it barely even registered. All she could think about was the baby. And how much she'd been looking forward to bringing her back home to Hillthwaite.

'Here you are, love,' said Morton. 'I've brought you a brew.'

Dawn looked up at him and smiled wanly. Morton was a dear man, she thought. Not the sharpest knife in the box, that was true, but sweet and kind. He worked his guts out running the small farm that had been in his family for generations and never ever complained. He did it all on his own too, apart from a stockman who came and lent a hand every now and then, when Morton was especially pushed.

Dawn had never mentioned anything to him about her yearning to adopt Amy's baby and bring her up as their own. She hadn't told anyone apart from her mother – and she'd only told *her* because she'd guessed the truth. But Morton seemed to sense her sorrow and was clearly trying to do his best for her.

'You sure you're all right, love?' he said, the concern evident in his warm brown eyes.

'Course I am,' said Dawn, lifting her large frame from the armchair. 'Why wouldn't I be? Now, I'll just drink this brew while it's hot and then I'll come and make your tea. Hotpot all right for you?'

Relieved that Dawn was sounding more like her old self again, Morton beamed.

'Grand,' he nodded. 'Just grand.'

Amy lay on her bed in Langdale Avenue and stared up at

the ceiling. She'd fed Billie and now the baby was sleeping peacefully in a wicker Moses basket on the floor.

It was so strange being back in this house. So familiar, and yet so strange. She felt as if she'd aged twenty years since she was last living here. Before she'd moved up to Dawn's, she'd shared a room with Sarah, her older sister. Sarah was seventeen, and full of herself. It was she who'd insisted that they draw a line down the middle of the room to designate which half belonged to who. She'd then proceeded to fill the walls on her side with posters of Liam Gallagher. On her side, Amy had stuck pictures of Billie Piper and Britney Spears she'd torn out of magazines.

But now that Amy had Billie, Sarah refused pointblank to share with her any more.

'It's not fair,' she'd whinged to her mum. 'I need my own space.'

So the whole family had shifted round to accommodate Sarah's wishes. Amy had moved into Wayne's old bedroom, a tiny cupboard of a room next to the stairs, Craig was sleeping on a mattress in Carol's room and poor old Wayne was dossing on the sofa downstairs.

Eighteen-year-old Wayne was the sweet one in the family, thought Amy. Sarah had barely even bothered to glance at the baby when she got in from her Denim Heart shift at dinner time, let alone admire her blue eyes and rosebud mouth and say how beautiful she was, like Wayne had done.

The only thing Sarah had said was: 'Oh you're back then.' As if she'd just popped out for a bag of chips or something.

And then a bit later on she'd muttered: 'I hope your baby's not going to cry all night. I need my kip. And you won't change her nappy down here, will you? Ugh. The very thought of it makes me puke.'

Amy was touched to see that at least her mum had made a bit of an effort to sort out Wayne's room. She hadn't gone as far as painting the horrible mushroom-coloured walls but she'd cleared out all Wayne's motor-bike stuff and fetched the old Moses basket down from the attic.

Amy's eyes closed with exhaustion. The strain of the last week was finally catching up with her. She wasn't used to being woken three or four times during the night for a start. And it was only now she was home that the reality of looking after a tiny baby was beginning to dawn on her.

It was dark by the time she woke up and Billie was crying.

Disorientated for a moment as to where she was and what was happening, Amy reached out and switched the bedside lamp on.

'Oh, you poor little thing,' she said, lifting Billie out of the basket and bringing her close. At her touch, the baby instantly stopped crying.

As Amy nuzzled Billie against her breast, the bedroom door opened and Carol peeped in.

'You all right, love?' she said, her tone slightly kinder than usual. 'Mrs Frost, you know, the community midwife . . . She's come to see you and the baby. I'll bring her up here, shall I?'

A shiver of apprehension ran down Amy's spine at the mention of Mrs Frost. She'd talked to her a couple of times before she left hospital and even though the woman had been perfectly kind, she made her feel ner-vous. Amy had insisted repeatedly that she wanted to care for Billie herself. But she was still terrified that if she put a foot wrong, Mrs Frost would take her baby away.

Amy sat on the bed stroking Billie's forehead. Her heart

began beating wildly as she listened to the stomp of two pairs of feet up the narrow staircase.

'Here we are, Mrs Frost,' said Carol, showing the midwife into Amy's room. 'Can I make you a cup of tea?'

'Thank you, that would be very nice,' said Sheila Frost, welcoming the chance to talk to Amy on her own. She was a homely-looking woman of about forty-five, with a salt and pepper bob, navy-blue uniform and sensible lace-up shoes.

Sheila made her way gingerly past Billie's Moses basket and Amy's luggage, which she hadn't yet got round to unpacking, and sat down on the wooden chair in the corner. There wasn't room to swing a cat in here.

'Now, dear,' she said, her voice warm. 'How are you and Baby getting on?'

'Her name's Billie,' said Amy quickly.

Sheila smiled.

'I'm sorry, dear. I'll start again. How are you and Billie managing now you're back home?'

Amy stared at Billie and then back at the midwife. She still couldn't believe that the little girl was really hers.

'Fine,' she said eventually. 'Fine, I think.'

'And you're absolutely sure that you'll be able to cope? You're only fourteen. It's asking an awful lot of you.'

'Billie's all I ever wanted,' said Amy softly.

She couldn't help smiling as she said this. It was absolutely true. She'd always adored babies, always longed to have someone she could love and who would love her back. Not like . . . No, she wasn't even going to go there . . . Especially not now.

'And the feeding's going all right?'

'I-I think so,' said Amy.

'You know you've got to keep your strength up, particularly when you're breastfeeding. Eat regular meals and drink plenty of fluid.'

Amy nodded brightly. She tried not to think about the packet of salt and vinegar crisps and Mars Bar her mum had thrust at her at dinner time.

'Good,' said Sheila. 'And you've got everything you need? Baby clothes? Toys? Pram? Cot?'

Amy's face fell. She hadn't thought that far ahead. It had seemed easier to take the days one at a time. The notion that Billie would need a pram and toys – and a cot once she'd grown out of the Moses basket – simply hadn't occurred to her.

'Well, maybe not quite everything, no,' she said hurriedly. 'I mean, I haven't got a pram yet.'

'That's exactly where I can help,' said Sheila. 'Let's go through what you need. If your mum can't afford much then I'm sure I can ask social services to come up with something.'

'So you're not going to . . .' Amy broke off what she was saying, anxious not to put the thought into Sheila's head.

'Not going to what, dear?'

Amy bit her lip.

'Not going to keep checking up on me.'

Sheila smiled at her.

'Let's get one thing straight, dear. I'm not here to check up on you. I'm here to help you. Midwives always visit new babies at home. Till they're about ten days old. Then the health visitor takes over. It's not just you, you know. We visit every baby in the area. Now, shall we weigh her?'

When Sheila left, Amy changed Billie's nappy. Then she got herself into a comfortable position on the chair in the corner and patiently began feeding her once more.

Driving home to Wath End in the car, Sheila Frost couldn't stop thinking about young Amy Barker.

184

The midwife had been anxious about how such a young girl was going to cope with a tiny baby. But now she'd seen Amy at home and watched her with Billie, she felt a little happier. The girl wasn't a silly flibbertigibbet – like a lot of the teenage mums she came across in her job. No, she seemed sensible enough – and she clearly adored the baby. It was early days and they were both going to need a lot of support, especially when Amy resumed her schooling, but she was cautiously optimistic.

Chapter Twenty

Watching Freddie acting the part of a shepherd in the school nativity play, Juliette felt like bursting into tears. The little boy was wearing a simple cotton robe and open-toed sandals. He had a checked tea towel draped over his head, with a cord tied round it to keep it in place. Peeping out from underneath, he looked so solemn, so determined to get his few lines word perfect.

Freddie had been bitterly disappointed when she'd told him Joe couldn't make it tonight.

'*Why* can't Daddy come?' he'd screeched hysterically at her. 'I want him to. I don't care about *you* coming. I want *Daddy* to see me. Why can't you *make* him come?'

Deeply wounded by this tirade, Juliette tried to put it to the back of her mind. Freddie was only six, she kept telling herself. He was just lashing out at the nearest person – her, in other words. He didn't mean it. He really didn't.

Once Freddie had got through his bit and left the stage, Juliette glanced around the school hall. The staff had done their utmost to make it look festive, festooning multi-coloured paper chains and nativity scenes along the walls and placing a huge Christmas tree in the corner. As her eyes scoured the audience, however, it struck Juliette that she barely recognised anyone there at all. Well, apart from the teachers and Fi Nicholson. Oh, and there was Norma Gray, skulking in the corner as if she would rather be somewhere else.

At the end of the performance, once all the applause had died down, Juliette hurried round to Class Two's Portakabin to collect Freddie. Her heart sank as she opened the door and peered inside. With its harsh fluorescent strip lighting, the classroom looked as cheerless as ever. It still smelled damp too. The children, however, were in high spirits, chattering nineteen to the dozen as they changed out of their nativity costumes and back into their everyday clothes.

All of them, that is, except for Freddie. He sat on a chair in the far corner, lost in a world of his own. He was still in his shepherd's robe and had made no effort to even start getting changed.

Instantly Juliette's eyes met Mrs Booth's.

'Can I have a word?' mouthed Freddie's teacher.

Juliette made first for Freddie. Wrapping her arms tightly around him, she whispered in his ear: 'Sweetheart, you were fantastic. I was so proud.'

Freddie barely seemed to react to her words.

'I wanted Daddy to come,' he mumbled.

'He'll come next year, sweetheart,' said Juliette. 'I promise you.' If I have to bloody drag him up here kicking and screaming, she thought bitterly.

'Now come on, Freddie, you get changed and I'll have a quick chat with Mrs Booth.'

'Why?' said Freddie. 'I want to go home.'

'I just want to tell her how fantastic the nativity play was. How hard you all must have worked.'

Juliette could tell from Mrs Booth's expression that this wasn't simply a casual chat. She had something serious to say.

'Is everything all right?' said Juliette, knowing full well that it wasn't.

'Tonight probably isn't the right time or place to say

this,' said Mrs Booth, 'and it may be nothing. But I'm a little bit worried about Freddie.'

A quiver of alarm ran through Juliette.

'Why? What do you mean?' she asked, her voice urgent. 'He hasn't said anything to me.'

'Is everything all right at home? I mean, I know that Freddie hasn't been with us for very long but he doesn't seem himself. He's a bit withdrawn in class, doesn't contribute very much. Is there anything I should be aware of? Any changes?'

Juliette stared at Mrs Booth, unable to speak. She felt as if her whole world was crashing around her ears.

'It's true that Freddie's missing his dad a lot during the week,' she said finally. 'But Freddie understands all that – and Joe's up here most weekends, of course.'

'Of course,' repeated Mrs Booth, still looking serious. 'But there's nothing else that you can think of?'

Juliette racked her brains over and over again. Freddie wasn't particularly keen on school – that was for sure. But that was simply because he didn't like being cooped up in the classroom all day.

'I can't think of anything specific – apart from missing his dad, that is.'

Mrs Booth seemed relieved.

'Well, perhaps it's just a phase he's going through, perhaps he'll shake himself out of it. I'll keep a close eye on him though, make sure he's mixing with the other children at playtime all right. He's been teaming up with Craig Barker a bit, so that's a good sign. I often see them huddled in the corner of the playground together.'

Juliette's face brightened at this. Freddie hadn't mentioned Craig Barker's name to her recently – not since he said the boy hit him – but she was pleased they'd made friends with each other now.

* * *

When they got home to New Bank, Juliette poured Freddie a mug of hot chocolate and sat him on her knee.

'What did Mrs Booth say to you?' he asked abruptly.

Juliette grinned at the chocolate moustache round his mouth.

'She was telling me that you've become good friends with Craig Barker. I'm really pleased. Is he nice? Is he anything to do with Mrs Barker? The school caretaker? Would you like to invite him to tea at the weekend?'

Freddie's face clouded over. Home had always been a haven, a place where he could forget that someone as horrible as Craig Barker even existed. But now that his mum had mentioned his name, he didn't feel quite so safe.

'What do you think, sweetheart? He lives in Newdale, doesn't he? Shall I fix it with his mum?'

'No,' said Freddie in a quiet voice. 'I don't want to. Not this weekend. Because Daddy's coming, isn't he? It would spoil it having someone else here.'

Juliette kissed the top of Freddie's chestnut hair.

'Of course, sweetheart. We'll ask Craig another time.'

It was nine pm by the time Juliette got Freddie into bed. He'd been particularly clingy tonight. He'd made a huge fuss about sleeping in his own room and even when Juliette agreed he could jump into her bed he'd refused to settle down till she'd cuddled him for quarter of an hour. Finally, exhausted by the demands of school and the nativity play, his eyes had closed and he'd drifted off to sleep.

Juliette marched straight into the kitchen, poured herself a large glass of chilled white burgundy and slumped on the floor with her back to the radiator. The warmth seeped comfortingly into her back.

The more she considered what Mrs Booth had said,

189

the more she was inclined to believe that the teacher was right. Freddie wasn't himself. He wasn't himself at all. In fact he hadn't really been himself since they'd moved to Newdale.

Juliette put her head in her hands and burst into tears. The move up north was supposed to have been a new start for the three of them. And all it had done so far was pull them further apart than they'd ever been before.

At that moment the telephone rang. Juliette was so deep in thought that she nearly jumped out of her skin.

'Hello,' she said, her voice still wobbly from crying.

'Jules?' said Joe. 'What's the matter? Are you all right?'

'No. Not really.'

'Is Freddie in bed?'

'Yep,' said Juliette. She cleared her throat noisily, trying to make her voice sound more cheerful.

'Come on, Jules, What's the matter? Why are you crying?'

'I'm not,' said Juliette. 'Crying, I mean. I'm just feeling knackered and a bit sorry for myself. That's all. You know how it is. What sort of day have you had? Come on, tell me some of the gossip. That'll help me snap out of all this.'

'OK,' said Joe. 'Umm, Willy's back in the flat. The top brass have been pretty understanding about everything and he's doing his show for the first time tonight. My listening figures have gone up again. Oh, and I've just been to a do at the Groucho Club to launch a new band – and guess who I bumped into?'

'Haven't a clue,' snapped Juliette. She felt a pang of envy at the glamorous life Joe was leading. What had her own day consisted of? Interviewing the new (and very tedious) mayor of Bowater, writing a feature about a proposed new by-pass for the village of Wath End and then turning out to watch Newdale School's nativity play. She could scarcely cope with the excitement of it all.

'Do you remember Jeany Jordan, you know, that showbiz reporter on the *Daily News* who you always said was useless?'

'Yep,' said Juliette suspiciously. 'Face like an angel but zero talent.'

'Well, Primetime TV obviously reckon she's got an angel face and *bags* of talent. They've just signed her up for a showbiz slot on one of their news programmes. She says they're paying her megabucks.'

'Bully for her,' said Juliette sourly. 'She always was a double-crossing toad. I bet she's lying. Look, you *are* coming up on Friday, aren't you?'

Exasperated by Juliette's acerbic tone, Joe snapped at her.

'Of course I'm bloody coming up. I wouldn't let Freddie down, would I?'

'It has been known.'

'What is the fucking matter with you, Jules?' yelled Joe. 'I've tried being sympathetic. I've tried telling you the latest gossip stuff. But whatever I do, you just throw everything back in my face. What's your problem?'

'Oh, get off my case,' shouted Juliette. She slammed the phone down so hard that for a moment she thought she'd broken the receiver.

When it rang again a couple of seconds later, Juliette snatched it up, assuming that it was Joe once more.

'If you're bloody ringing to apologise you can go to hell,' she shrieked, then smashed the receiver back on the hook.

Two seconds later, it sounded a third time. Juliette wrenched it up in a fury, ready to let rip at Joe.

'I told you to go to hell. Are you bloody thick or something . . . ?'

'Yes, I probably am,' agreed a very calm voice at the other end of the line. 'But before you wreck my hearing for life, could you just listen for one second?'

For a moment Juliette was rendered speechless. The voice wasn't Joe's. God, she'd been yelling like a fishwife at someone who wasn't Joe.

'Who is this?' she inquired politely, praying that it was a wrong number.

'It's Tim,' said the voice. 'Tim Dawner.'

'Oh dear,' said Juliette slowly. 'Oh dear. You must think I'm completely off my rocker. Which I probably am, of course.'

'Don't give it another thought, Jules,' said Tim cheerfully. 'It's better than *EastEnders* listening to you.'

'I'm sorry,' said Juliette. 'I've had a bad day, that's all. Forget it. I didn't mean to take it out on you.'

'Well that much was obvious,' said Tim. 'Who the hell did you think I was, anyway?'

Juliette paused for a moment. Tempted though she was to rant and rave about Joe, something – a sudden rush of loyalty perhaps – stopped her. The row with Joe had been a domestic, nothing whatsoever to do with anyone else. Least of all with Tim Dawner.

'Oh forget it. How did you get my number, anyway?'

'Phone book,' said Tim.

'We're not in the phone book,' said Juliette sharply. 'Hacks never are. We always go ex-directory.'

'You promise you won't go apeshit?' said Tim.

'I haven't got the energy.'

'Promise?'

'I promise I won't go apeshit,' repeated Juliette parrot-fashion.

'OK,' said Tim. 'Cara Bell gave it to me.'

Juliette could scarcely believe she was hearing this. What the hell did Cara think she was playing at giving out her home number? Tim Dawner could be a bloody axe murderer for all she knew.

'Really?' said Juliette, her voice grim.

'Come on, Jules, you promised you wouldn't go ape-shit. I bumped into Cara in a pub in town tonight . . . She was . . . She was just doing me a favour. You won't say anything, will you?'

'Oh, I suppose not,' said Jules wearily. 'It makes me worry about who else she's been giving my number out to, that's all. I can't face being plagued at home by the nutters I write about.'

'Thanks very much, I'm sure,' chuckled Tim.

'Oh God, I didn't mean it like that. Anyway, what's so urgent that it won't wait till I'm back in the office tomorrow morning?'

It was a few seconds before Tim answered.

'I just wondered . . .' he began.

'You just wondered what?'

Tim Dawner's words came out in a rush.

'I just wondered if you'd like to have dinner with me?'

'What? Tonight?'

'Yes,' said Tim. 'Tonight. Why not?'

'I'd love to, Tim. I really would. But I can't leave my little boy. He's asleep upstairs. And it's far too late to get a babysitter.'

'Damn it,' said Tim. 'I'd completely forgotten about him.'

Juliette laughed out loud.

'Freddie would punch your lights out if he heard you say that.'

'Come on, I didn't mean it the way it sounded,' said Tim. 'It's a shame you can't make it though. Because I've got another story for you.'

Juliette's ears pricked up at this. Thanks to Alex's

tedious catalogue of stories about supermarkets, mayoral inaugurations and dog fouling, she'd had an abysmal show in the *Eagle* recently. She could really do with something to get her teeth into.

'Hang on, Tim,' she said. 'There must be a way round this. I know. Why don't you come round here instead?'

'What? To your place?'

'That's what I said. It's the perfect solution. I'll throw some pasta together and you can run the story past me. It had better be good, mind. I've had enough rubbish stories for one day, thanks.'

Tim didn't hesitate.

'Right,' he said with alacrity. 'You're on. But first you'll have to tell me where you live.'

When Juliette put the phone down, she panicked. She didn't know what to do first. Tim Dawner looked like the sort of man who lived in immaculate surroundings – a wing of a country mansion perhaps, or a stunning farmhouse halfway up the fells. She couldn't possibly let him see the squalor that she and Freddie lived in for most of the time.

It was a close call but in the end she decided that her face was the priority. She redid her make-up and brushed her hair so that it was no longer sticking up on end from lying in bed with Freddie. Then she lit the fire in the sitting room, removed the remains of Freddie's hot chocolate and hastily shoved all his books and videos under the sofa. Only when both she and the house looked presentable did she turn her attention to the pasta.

She was still rooting through the contents of the fridge – damn it, the only vegetables she could find among the detritus at the bottom were half a courgette and a mouldy red pepper – when the doorbell rang.

Flicking her hair back from her face, she took a deep

breath and walked slowly to the front door. Please Freddie, don't wake up, she thought. He'd been sleeping so fitfully when she checked on him ten minutes earlier that she was terrified he might wake up and get upset again.

A feeling of nervous anticipation swept through Juliette as she opened the door. Tim stood there looking as devastating as ever in a navy Guernsey sweater and jeans and clutching a bottle wrapped in bright pink tissue paper.

'Hi Jules,' he said softly.

Juliette's heart thumped wildly. Don't be ridiculous, she told herself. This is work, remember. It's business. Not pleasure.

'Are you going to let me in? Or are you having second thoughts about this?'

'I'm sorry,' smiled Juliette. 'I was miles away. No, come in. Of course I'm not having second thoughts. But you'd better not be winding me up. About the story I mean. I'm relying on you for tomorrow's splash.'

'Do I get a drink first?' inquired Tim. He handed the bottle to her.

'Sure,' said Juliette, leading him into the sitting room. She unwrapped the tissue paper to find a bottle of Bollinger inside.

'Wow,' she exclaimed. 'Denim Heart must be doing brilliantly.'

'Er, not exactly,' said Tim, his deep blue eyes looking inscrutable. 'If you get the bottle open I'll tell you all about it. Or do you want me to do it?'

'Absolutely not,' said Juliette. 'I'm a past master at opening champagne. It's a prerequisite when you work with a load of drunken hacks. Well, I suppose it's changed a bit now they're all on the wagon but when I first started . . .'

Juliette broke off what she was saying. What was the matter with her? Anyone would think she hadn't spoken to a soul for months the way she was gabbling.

She fetched a couple of champagne glasses from the kitchen, then opened the bottle as adeptly as she'd claimed she would.

After pouring the fizzing liquid into the two glasses, she handed one to Tim and held her own aloft.

'Cheers, she said. 'Here's to . . .'

She stopped in her tracks again. Here's to what exactly?

'Here's to us,' continued Tim. He laughingly clinked her glass and took a long sip of champagne.

'Right,' said Juliette. She wasn't certain what he was getting at. 'Let's get down to business. What have you got for me?'

'I've said before that you only want me for one thing,' said Tim in a mournful tone.

'Too right I do. Now come on. What is it?'

All of a sudden Tim looked serious.

'It's Helen again. When I told you about her before I'm afraid I didn't give you the whole story. I was a bit economical with the truth.'

'Go on,' said Juliette.

'Do you remember the story you ran in the *Eagle* about Helen walking out on me?'

'Ye-e-es,' said Juliette slowly. 'Don't tell me it was a pack of lies, Tim, please. Don't do this to me.'

A hurt expression appeared on Tim's face.

'Of course it wasn't a pack of lies, Jules. I'd never lie to you. Or anyone else for that matter. I'm pretty honourable. Surely you know that by now?'

'I'm glad to hear it,' said Juliette.

'No, it wasn't a pack of lies. But I didn't tell you everything. The truth is . . . God, this is difficult . . . No, the truth is that me and Helen . . . We didn't just split. She didn't just walk out on me. She walked out on me taking quite a bit of customers' money with her.'

Juliette stared at Tim, unable to quite believe what she'd just heard.

'How much?' she said. There was no point in avoiding the issue. She needed to know.

'A million pounds, give or take a quid or two,' mumbled Tim, staring at the ground.

'Oh my God,' said Juliette, aghast. 'But that's theft. It's fraud. Have you told the police?'

Tim didn't look up. It was as if he couldn't bear to confront the enormity of what Helen had done.

'No. I just couldn't. Surely you can see that? Helen and I were together for eight years. I know we've bust up now but I can't just pretend we were nothing to each other. At first I kept hoping that she was playing a game. Trying to give me a scare or something. That she'd walk back in with the money and tell me it was all a joke. But it's been three weeks now and I've got no fucking idea where she's gone.'

Tim's face crumpled and for one terrible moment Juliette thought he was going to break down.

'And that's not all,' he murmured.

Juliette got up from where she was sitting and went and knelt in front of him. She took his hands in hers.

'What else is there?' she said softly.

'This is completely off the record but I'm terrified that if I can't track her down there *is* a risk that Denim Heart might go under. After everything that we've worked for . . . I know she's bitter about what happened but I can't believe that she could do this.'

Juliette stared at Tim's hands. They were surprisingly small for a man of his height, she thought. Small and soft and perfectly formed.

'Tim,' she began. 'I don't know what to say. I really don't.'

'I suppose there isn't much anyone *can* say. A lot of people round here will reckon that it serves me right. You probably know that I've never exactly been flavour of the month in Bowater. They loathed me being so successful when times were hard for them.'

'You've got to work out what you want me to do, Tim,' said Juliette. 'I mean, the *Eagle* would jump at the story of Helen walking out with customers' cash. But are you sure you want us to run it?'

The moment she uttered these words, Juliette felt deeply uncomfortable. As a feature writer for the *Eagle*, she was supposed to remain impartial at all times. It was her job to report the facts – clearly, accurately and contemporaneously, as the law tutor on her journalism course had always told her. It wasn't her job to take sides. Or make judgements, come to that.

So what was she doing asking Tim Dawner whether he wanted to run the story he'd just told her? What the hell was she thinking of?

At that moment Tim looked up and caught her gaze. A quiver of excitement ran through Juliette. She quelled it sharply. It's work, she told herself yet again. For God's sake, concentrate on what he's saying.

'A report in the *Eagle* saying that Denim Heart might go bust because Helen has run off with our customers' cash would be tantamount to committing business suicide,' said Tim, thinking aloud. 'We'd never get another order if you wrote that. But I suppose you could say that there are fears that Helen might have embezzled the company out of thousands of pounds. I could give you loads of detail about her signing company cheques for her own ends.'

Juliette got up from the floor and returned to the armchair in which she'd been sitting. She picked up her notebook and pen and began to take notes.

'OK,' she said. 'I want you to run through your allegations about Helen again. I want dates, times, amounts, details. Your devastation about being betrayed by the woman you love. That's the story.'

'The woman I *used* to love,' murmured Tim, his eyes locked on Juliette's.

'Fine,' said Juliette, her voice firm. 'But I need every cough and spit, as my old news editor used to say.'

It took Tim half an hour to run through his story. After ten years in newspapers, Juliette was pretty certain that she was no longer shockable. She'd witnessed too many tragedies for that. But all the same, she was still stunned by the extent of Helen's deception.

'Are you really saying that she used a Denim Heart cheque to buy a *pied-à-terre* in Notting Hill?' she asked at one point.

'Yes,' said Tim in a quiet voice.

'And how much did it cost?'

'£320,000,' said Tim. 'It was a couple of years back so it's probably worth a hell of a lot more than that now.'

'Have you been there?' asked Juliette.

'Course not,' said Tim. 'I hate London. I avoid it altogether if I can. And anyway, I didn't even know that it existed till a couple of months back. The bank manager told me.'

By the time that Tim got to the end of Helen's spending spree, he looked completely drained. He seemed so shattered by Helen's profligacy that Juliette had to forcibly restrain herself from rushing over to give him a hug. She dug her fingernails into the palms of her hands.

'You're going to have to go to the police, you know. You can't let her get away with it. You just can't.'

'Maybe,' muttered Tim. 'Anyway, what's the gist of your story going to be? I need to know.'

Juliette flicked through the last few pages of her note-book.

'"*Denim Heart chief Tim Dawner claimed last night that his ex-partner and lover Helen Brown walked out owing the business thousands of pounds . . .*"' she began. 'Something along those lines.'

'Swindled would be a better word to use,' said Tim, his voice gruff.

'I'm sorry, Tim,' said Juliette. 'It might sound a bit tame to you but we have to tread very carefully on this one. It's important to get Helen's side of things too – so it'll just be your word against hers. Until the whole thing comes to court, of course.'

Tim was staring hard at Juliette.

'Have I given you enough detail now?' he said.

'I think so,' said Juliette. 'Although I can't guarantee that the *Eagle's* lawyer will let us use it all. Is Helen still abroad?'

'Yes, as far as I know,' said Tim. 'Why?'

'We've got to try even harder to contact her. Give her the chance to put her side. You said she was in the Caribbean before. Any idea whereabouts?'

'Oh God,' said Tim, running his hand distractedly through his hair. 'I haven't a clue. I'm not even sure she's in the Caribbean at all. She'd been talking about going somewhere hot but she could be anywhere.'

'Who else might know?' said Juliette more urgently. 'Her parents? Brothers or sisters?'

'None of them,' said Tim. 'She hasn't got any. Her parents died years ago and she's an only child.'

'OK,' said Juliette. 'I'll pass it all on to the editor.'

'Jules?' said Tim.

Juliette looked up from her notes.

'What?'

'Will you come here?'

Juliette stared at him. God, he was gorgeous, she thought. It wasn't fair that he was so gorgeous.

'I can't,' she said, knowing she wouldn't be responsible for her actions if she went near him now. It was late and they'd each drunk half a bottle of champagne. It would be fatal.

'OK,' he said lightly, getting up from his chair. 'Then I'll have to come to you.'

Juliette made a feeble effort to protest.

'No Tim, don't. I don't think that's a good idea at . . .'

Her words died in her throat as Tim pulled her to her feet. Slowly his mouth closed on hers and he was kissing her. Somewhere along the line, Juliette didn't know how or why, she realised that she was kissing him back just as passionately.

'Oh my God, Jules, I've been wanting to do that for weeks,' he groaned. 'Ever since that day you sat in my office at Denim Heart, all prim and proper, and kept asking polite questions about me being Entrepreneur of the Year. What would you have said if I had?'

For a second Juliette didn't answer. If she was honest with herself, she'd wanted it just as much as he had. She just had to look at him and her whole body felt like liquid.

'I'd have said this,' she murmured, and began kissing him again.

Juliette had no idea how long they held each other like this. It seemed no time at all before Tim was undoing the buttons of her shirt and discarding it on the floor. He began to caress her breasts so exquisitely she thought she'd died and gone to heaven.

'You are so beautiful, Jules,' he whispered. 'I want you so badly . . .'

The mood was shattered by a sudden, childish cry from above. Juliette froze. She felt as if she'd just been shot. It was Freddie. What on earth was she doing? What had come over her? What did she think she was doing standing half-naked in her sitting room with a man who wasn't her husband and Freddie crying upstairs.

'I'm sorry,' she muttered abruptly, grabbing her shirt from the floor and smoothing down her hair. 'I don't know what I was thinking of. You'll have to go.'

Chapter Twenty-one

Juliette's fingers flew over the keyboard as if some supernatural force possessed them. It was only twenty minutes before the deadline for the first edition and Geoff Lake would go crazy if she didn't make it.

She'd rung Alex Davis on his mobile late last night and related everything Tim Dawner had told her. Well, nearly everything. She couldn't bear to dwell on what had happened at the end of the evening.

'Have you done, Juliette?' asked Alex, peering over her shoulder.

'Mmmm,' muttered Juliette, still typing. 'Nearly. But you are going to get it legalled, aren't you?'

'Too bloody right, we are,' grunted Alex. 'We've brought someone in specially. It wouldn't have been *quite* so sensitive if we'd managed to track Helen Brown down and at least get her side of the story. Or if Dawner had gone to the police and she'd been charged. But the way things stand right now we've only got his word for it.'

Juliette finished typing out her last quote and read it aloud to Alex.

'*"We were so happy together, so successful," said Mr Dawner sadly. "I still can't believe she's betrayed me like this."*'

'Are you one hundred per cent sure he's telling the truth?' said Alex.

'Why?' snapped Juliette. 'D'you think he's lying?'

It was a few seconds before Alex replied.

'I don't know,' he said thoughtfully. 'There's just something about all this that doesn't quite add up, that's all.'

'I'm sure he's telling the truth,' said Juliette firmly. 'I mean, I've got to know him a bit over the last couple of months and I'm certain he's straight. For God's sake, the business is in pretty bad shape thanks to Helen. And all this is pretty humiliating for Tim. There's no way he'd go public on it if it wasn't true.'

Alex glanced sharply at Juliette. He couldn't help feeling suspicious about the way she'd sprung so instantly to Tim Dawner's defence. He made a mental note to get someone else to cover the next Denim Heart story. Something in his bones told him that Juliette wasn't quite as detached as she liked to think.

'Right,' he said. 'Have you sent it across to the editor now? He wants to go through it with the lawyer.'

Juliette pressed the 'send' button on her computer and sat back in her chair.

'Is the news desk still trying to track Helen down?' she asked.

'Yep,' said Alex. 'We've got a couple of friends' names who might be able to help. And Cara Bell is trying to trace Helen's parents. We think they might live in York.'

'Oh, they're dead,' said Juliette. 'Tim told me.'

'Really?' said Alex, a look of surprise on his face. 'I thought . . . Oh, never mind. I must have got it wrong.'

Once Alex had wandered back to his desk Juliette quickly scanned through her copy. It didn't read *too* badly, she thought, despite the speed with which it had been written. She'd tried to get the balance exactly right – conjuring up the drama of Helen owing the company money while at the same time not making it look as if Denim Heart was on its uppers.

'Wotcha Juliette,' called out Cara as she hurried across the newsroom floor to her desk.

Juliette looked up at Cara. She had to bite the insides of her cheeks hard to stop herself bursting into laughter.

'What do you think you look like?' she said. 'Did you get dressed in the dark this morning?'

Cara bore a distinct resemblance to a set of traffic lights. She was wearing a scarlet jumper, orange mini skirt – the shortest Juliette had ever seen – and leprechaun green tights.

'Why?' said Cara, plonking herself opposite Juliette. 'What's wrong?'

'I just hope Alex doesn't send you out on anything sensitive this morning,' said Juliette. 'I can't believe how much newspapers have changed. My first editor was so strict about what we wore that he once made me go home to change for wearing trousers. Said they would shock the punters.'

Cara made a face at her.

'Just shows how ancient you are, darling,' she giggled. 'How old did you say you were?'

Juliette kicked Cara playfully under the desk.

'I've got a bone to pick with you, come to think of it,' she said. 'Why the hell did you give Tim Dawner my home phone number?'

Cara looked startled.

'What do you mean?'

'Hey come on,' said Juliette. 'There's no need to play the innocent. He rang me at home last night and when I asked him how he got my number he said you gave it to him.'

'But that's crazy,' said Cara. 'I mean, I bumped into him in the King's Head and we had a quick chat but I never gave you your number. Even if he'd asked for it – which he definitely didn't – I'd never have given

205

it to him without checking with you first. You know I wouldn't.'

Juliette shrugged her shoulders in incomprehension.

'That's weird.'

'You do believe me, don't you?'

Juliette stared at Cara. She wasn't sure if she did or not.

'No worries,' she said. 'Course I do.'

When the first edition of the *Eagle* dropped at eleven-fifteen Juliette grabbed a copy from one of the newsroom messengers – a spotty youth called Striker who went puce every time she spoke to him – and rushed back to her desk to read it.

'*HELEN BETRAYED ME*' screeched the headline, while the strapline underneath declared: '*Denim Heart boss makes fraud allegation against ex-partner – exclusive report by the* Eagle's *Juliette Ward.*'

It was funny, thought Juliette, how you never got blasé about bylines. Even after ten years in the business it still gave her a glow of pride to see her name on the splash.

Juliette's story took up the whole of the front page (together with a picture of Tim looking unbearably handsome) as well as pages two and three. On page four there was a feature by Cara outlining the history of Denim Heart, from its inception to its current crisis.

Juliette had barely got to the end of reading Cara's piece – there was no doubt that her writing was slowly improving – when her phone started ringing.

'Great story, doll,' bellowed a familiar-sounding voice. 'I thought you'd moved to the frozen north to take things easy. Concentrate on being a mum, bake your own bread and all that jazz. Nice to see you haven't lost your touch.'

In an instant Juliette realised who it was – Graham

Burton, a reporter on the *Daily News*. He was better known for nicking other people's stories than for his own reporting skills, but he was such an old charmer that he always got away with it.

'Patronising git,' laughed Juliette, launching back into the old banter. 'I take it you're ringing about my front page?'

'I thought you might have gone native living up there but you're still managing to scoop the national guys. I always reckon that reporting is a bit like riding a bike. Once mastered, never forgotten. I must say though, doll, I've done a few stories about Denim Heart over the last couple of years but I never got a whiff of anything like this. It's great stuff too. Sex, business, fucking hell, you only need Dawner's ex to go off with a vicar and the story really would have everything.'

'Sure,' said Juliette dryly. 'It just took someone with real talent to crack it. Now come on, Graham, cut the bullshit. I know perfectly well that you didn't ring to go on about how wonderful I am.'

'Er no,' said Graham. 'How did you guess?'

'Let's just say that I know you too well,' said Juliette. 'What do you want?'

'I need some background stuff about this Dawner guy. Is he really as squeaky clean as he makes out? He must have some dirty linen hidden away somewhere, surely?'

Juliette thought hard. Strictly speaking, she didn't feel she could be entirely objective about Tim Dawner. It was only twelve or thirteen hours since she'd been on the verge of doing something crazy.

'I'm no psychologist, Graham, but yes, I think he probably is. I'm pretty sure he's the innocent party in all this, that's for sure.'

'What do the locals reckon to him then?' asked Graham.

Juliette felt a flash of irritation at her ex-colleague.

'Look, Graham, I know you're out for an easy life, but do you want me to spoon-feed you? Write the whole bloody story for you and file it down the line?'

'Calm down, doll, for goodness sake,' drawled Graham. 'It's not good for your blood pressure to fly off the handle like that – and it's terrible for mine. Come on, just give me the gen and I'll even put you down for a credit. I can't say fairer than that now, can I?'

Juliette sighed heavily. National newspapers frequently paid for tip-offs and background information. It felt odd to be on the receiving end for a change.

'Oh all right, Graham. But make sure you don't forget. I know what you're like. Now, don't quote me but from what I can gather and from what Tim Dawner let on, the locals can't stand the sight of him. It's a pretty close-knit farming community round here and most people are struggling to make ends meet. And I mean really struggling, not just cutting back on the beer and skittles. They think Tim Dawner's a bit flash.'

'Hmmm,' said Graham thoughtfully. 'That's more like it. And have you got any contacts for . . . What's his ex called?'

'Helen Brown,' said Juliette. 'But I can't help you there. We're trying to track her down ourselves but she seems to have gone to ground. There's talk she might be abroad.'

'You don't think there's a chance that he's bumped her off, do you?' said Graham.

Juliette burst into peals of laughter.

'God, Graham, you've been doing the job for too long. No. Definitely not. He's not the type.'

'None of them ever are,' murmured Graham. 'Stranger things have happened.'

'Is that it, then?'

'Yep doll, that's it,' said Graham. 'Oh, except for one

thing. Why the hell did that hubby of yours take a pop at Mike Baker a few weeks back? Mike's a real hard man, but it shook him up, I can tell you. I keep telling him he needs counselling.'

'Don't remind me,' groaned Juliette. 'I haven't a clue what came over him. All I know was that the pack were baiting Willy Brown and Joe lost his temper. But why are you asking? Have you heard anything?'

'Sweet FA, doll,' said Graham. 'Just curious, that's all. Oh, and by the way, I'll buy you a drink when you jack in this country nonsense and get back to the smoke. I give it six months. Six months at the outside.'

Laughing, Juliette put the phone down. Bloody cheek, she thought. But she still couldn't help liking the man. There were precious few characters left in newspapers and he was definitely one of them.

Graham's call was just the first of many that morning. Juliette spent the next couple of hours running through her story with most of the tabloids, a couple of radio stations and a local press agency. Tim Dawner, it emerged, had refused to elaborate any further on the story and everyone else at Denim Heart was sticking to 'no comment'. So the only person they could find to talk to was Juliette.

'Are you going to do any work at all today?' bellowed Alex Davis when she put the phone down at around noon.

Juliette gaped at her boss. His tone was so brusque that anyone would think she'd been slacking, not breaking a story the nationals would have given their eye-teeth for.

'What's eating him?' murmured Cara from the desk opposite, where she was struggling with yet another tedious planning feature.

'You tell me,' whispered Juliette. 'You would have thought he could at least have said thank-you. Every single hack I've spoken to has promised to give the *Eagle* a mention in their stories. What more does he want?'

At that moment, the editor, Geoff Lake appeared by her side. Juliette hadn't seen him for days – in fact she'd barely exchanged more than a few words with him since she'd started at the *Eagle*.

'Can I have a word?' he said.

'Sure,' said Juliette. 'What? Now?'

'Yes, now. In my office.'

Juliette shot a satisfied look at Cara, who gave her a thumbs-up in return. At least someone appreciated her round here.

Geoff Lake shut his office door firmly and pulled the blinds closed.

'Good show this morning, Juliette,' said Geoff, gesturing to her to sit down.

'Thanks,' said Juliette, feeling pleased with herself.

'Do you reckon Dawner's telling the truth?'

Juliette stared at Geoff. He was the third person to ask her that today.

'Yes, I do as a matter of fact,' she said, smoothing her skirt over her knees.

'Good,' said Geoff gruffly. 'But I'm afraid that's not the reason I called you in.'

'Oh?' Juliette wasn't sure why, but she felt anxious all of a sudden.

'No,' said Geoff. 'Now look, you've only been with us for what – three months? But you're probably aware that the *Eagle* isn't having an easy time of it at the present. We've got competition from all sides – local radio, TV and the free-sheets, they're all snapping at our heels. The trouble is that for a lot of people round here an evening newspaper is a luxury they can't afford . . .'

Juliette stared at Geoff. He looked exhausted, she

thought. His face was grey and he'd lost weight. She wondered when he was going to come to the point.

'What are you saying, exactly?' she asked.

Geoff had the grace to look embarrassed.

'That we can't afford you,' he said, glancing down at the boring beige carpet.

She must be mistaken, thought Juliette. Surely he couldn't have said what she thought he'd just said.

'You what?'

'Don't panic, Juliette, it's not as bad as you think.'

Juliette rolled her eyes. Geoff Lake had just informed her that the *Eagle* couldn't afford her and now he was telling her not to panic about it.

'Oh yes?' she said quizzically. 'And why's that?'

Geoff leaned forward in his chair and propped his elbows on the desk.

'Do you remember that when I took you on I told you that we were paying you a lot more than our other feature writers. Yes?'

'Yes,' agreed Juliette.

'Well, I hate to do this to you – especially when you've uprooted from the other end of the country – but I haven't got any choice. Our circulation's down and we've got to cut our overheads to survive. So you're going to have to take a salary cut of six thousand pounds. Either that, or we'll have to let you go. What do you think?'

Juliette's face went pale.

'I-I don't know what to say,' she stuttered.

'Why don't you go away and mull things over,' said Geoff. 'You can come and give me your answer tomorrow morning. But Juliette . . .'

Halfway to the door by this time, Juliette turned to look at him.

'What?' she said, her voice giving nothing away.

'Your work for the *Eagle* has been great. I hope you

can see your way to staying. And if things have picked up in a year or so's time, I'm sure we can review your salary then.'

Big deal, thought Juliette bitterly.

'I'll let you know in the morning,' she said.

Chapter Twenty-two

Juliette strode purposefully along the top of Miston Moor, deep in thought. The problem was, that humiliating as Geoff Lake's announcement was, she didn't have an awful lot of choice in the matter.

She'd burned her boats in London, chucked in her job at the *Daily News* and let the house. And anyway, even if she *could* bring herself to beg for her old job back and find another place to live in South London she couldn't bear the thought of admitting failure to Joe.

Reaching a mound of stones at the top of the grassy knoll, Juliette sat down and pulled a small flask out of her pocket. She unscrewed the cap and took a comforting sip of lukewarm coffee. Even though the sun was out, giving a stunning view across the valley to Lake Bowater and beyond, the temperature was only just above freezing. The early morning frost had barely melted at all.

She hadn't passed a soul on the walk, just a lot of black-faced lakeland sheep who'd gazed at her with fleeting interest and then carried on munching grass.

It was strange, she reflected, how the instant she'd heard Geoff's proposition, she'd been overcome with a desperate need to get out of the office and into the open air. She'd gathered her stuff together, ignoring nosey questions from Cara and abusive ones from Alex, and walked out of the office. She'd driven straight home, changed into her barely used walking gear (so much for her good intentions when she'd arrived in the north) and set off for Miston Moor.

Juliette glanced at her watch. It was two-thirty already, time she was setting off back to Newdale to meet Freddie. The school broke up for the Christmas holidays today and she'd promised she'd try her hardest to meet him. But at least the brisk climb up the hillside had given her the chance to put things into perspective, work out what she was going to do.

By the time Juliette pulled up outside the school gate, her face was still glowing from her walk. She got out of the car and joined the throng of parents waiting for their children to come rushing out of class. Even now, a good three months after they'd moved into the village, no one uttered a word to her. It was only when Fi arrived that Juliette could stop gazing into the distance, pretending that she didn't give a damn, and smile with relief at a friendly face.

'Freddie will be so pleased you're here,' said Fi warmly. She put her arm through Juliette's.

'I hope so,' said Juliette. 'I'm never quite sure what he thinks these days.'

Fi stared at Juliette.

'Are you all right? Is there something worrying you?'

'Oh, don't even start me off on that one,' grinned Juliette. 'No, really, I'm fine. Truly.'

'You would tell me if there was something wrong, wouldn't you?' said Fi. 'That's what friends are for.'

'Thanks,' murmured Juliette. 'You don't know how much that means. Really.'

As usual, most of the other children were halfway across the playground by the time Freddie appeared. He emerged from the Portakabin on his own, a bedraggled solitary figure with his shirt hanging out of his trousers and his shoes on the wrong feet. He smiled wanly from afar when he saw Juliette but nonetheless didn't make any attempt to rush.

Juliette felt like crying. Once upon a time Freddie would have torn across the playground and leapt into her arms. It was like looking at another boy now.

'Can't you stop that kid crying?' bellowed Carol Barker up the stairs at Langdale Avenue.

Overcome with weariness, Amy plucked Billie out of her Moses basket and brought the baby to her breast. Billie instantly latched on with surprising vigour for one so young and began to suck noisily.

Amy closed her eyes. Mrs Frost, the community midwife, had warned her at the outset that while breastfeeding was fantastic for the baby, it would certainly take it out of her.

'You must make sure you eat properly and drink plenty of fluid,' she'd instructed. 'And when the baby has a nap, you lie down too. You're very young, and caring for a newborn is tiring work. It's important you keep your strength up.'

Mrs Frost's advice was fine in theory, thought Amy. The trouble was that the midwife didn't have a clue what life in Langdale Avenue was really like. The rest of them were wrapped up in their own lives – they didn't have the time or the inclination to help her. Her mum was either out cleaning or off down to bingo with her friends. Wayne worked all hours. Sarah never lifted a finger to help. And Craig was only seven, poor little sod. Far from concentrating all her energies on Billie and resting when she could, Amy was left alone in the house each morning with Billie to care for and a long list of chores. Carol increasingly relied on her to do the ironing, make the beds and cook everyone's tea when they got in. It was no wonder that the teenager was permanently exhausted.

It was evening now and Carol and Craig were downstairs watching *Top of the Pops* on the telly. They'd all had fish and chips on their laps for tea because it was Friday and then Wayne and Sarah had pushed off to Bowater with their mates. Amy had felt a wave of jealousy wash over her when her brother and sister dashed out, slamming the door behind them. She couldn't ever envisage the day when she'd be off clubbing with her friends. By the time Billie was old enough for her to do that, her pals would probably be married with kids themselves. That would never happen to her, she thought miserably. No lad would touch her with a bargepole now she had a baby. And as for *him*, Billie's father, he just didn't want to know.

Tears splashed down Amy's face and dripped on to Billie's pink babygro. Amy dashed them away angrily. There was no point thinking about *him*. And no point feeling sorry for herself either. She'd made her bed, as her mum would say, and now she had to lie in it.

Amy had been feeding Billie for an hour or more by this time. She glanced at the clock on the wall to check. What was Billie playing at? She should be asleep again by now. She couldn't still be hungry.

Not for the first time, it struck Amy that maybe the baby wasn't getting enough milk. She was demanding to be fed very couple of hours these days. And far from being luscious and full, like they'd been in hospital, Amy's breasts looked more like pre-pubescent empty sacs.

Amy began to cry again. She'd done everything else wrong – and now she couldn't even produce enough milk to satisfy Billie.

* * *

Joe whistled happily to himself as he drove north. He'd had a stupendous week. Not only were his listening figures up again but Daniel White had rung this morning and told him that Primetime TV wanted him to audition for their new quiz show after all.

'I thought they'd decided my image was all wrong,' he told Daniel, then cursed himself for sounding negative. He should be far more bullish, far less self-deprecating, when he talked to his agent.

'What on earth gave you that impression?' said Daniel smoothly.

Joe had been on the point of mentioning his brawl with Mike Baker but stopped himself just in time.

'Oh nothing,' he said. 'You know how modest I am.'

'We'll beat that out of you pretty fast,' chuckled Daniel. 'Anyway, get it down in your diary. Tuesday. Two pm. Primetime studio in Docklands. Right?'

The other good thing was that Willy seemed to be back to his old self again. He'd been pretty down for the first couple of weeks back in London but now he was on cracking form. Still off the booze and avoiding the clubbing scene like the plague, he looked better than he had in years. Nowadays he spent most of his free time working out down at the gym and lunching with DJ friends, all of whom told him he looked 'disgustingly healthy'.

The only problem area in Joe's life, he reflected as he pulled into the Cherwell Valley service station on the M40 to fill up with petrol, was women. In lots of ways it was like being a teenager again. Even as a gawky sixteen-year-old he'd never managed to get the balance quite right. It was a bit like buses. You waited ages for one and then two came along at once. Likewise with women. He was either agonising because he wasn't getting enough sex or scared stiff that girlfriends would

217

discover that he was two-timing them.

He frowned. No, it wasn't like that now. Well not exactly. It was true that he'd fancied the pants off Annie and he'd nearly gone and done something completely stupid as a result. But at the end of the day it was Jules he loved. She was irritating and impossible and the most pig-headed person he'd ever known but he couldn't bear the thought of them ever breaking up.

The last couple of weeks with Annie had been excruciatingly embarrassing. Joe had dreaded facing her the morning after their near miss and he still couldn't help looking away awkwardly every time his eyes met hers. Once, much to his mortification, he'd even blushed like a schoolboy at the sight of her.

But in the end they'd got through the trickiness by concentrating all their energies on discussions about the show and making sure they were always scrupulously polite to each other. Their cosy chats at the Café Firenze had ceased altogether.

Now he couldn't wait to reach Jules and Freddie. Their set-up was unconventional, he knew that, but they were coping with it. Or at least he thought they were.

Morton Lewis was getting worried about his wife. Really worried.

It was more than a month since Amy'd had the baby and Dawn didn't seem to be managing at all. She'd barely been out of the house for a start, let alone attempted to do anything else.

Dawn's appearance had changed drastically too. She had always been large and voluptuous – and Morton had loved her that way. But over the last few weeks she'd barely eaten anything, existing solely on cups of tea and bits of toast. Now she was like a shadow of her former self – though instead of looking better for losing weight she seemed pinched and drawn.

If it hadn't been for Norma bringing up bits of shopping and hearty stews and potato pies she'd cooked, Morton didn't know how he would have managed. He was up to his eyes with looking after the farm and he simply didn't have time to take care of the housekeeping on top of everything else.

He knew that Norma was just as worried about Dawn as he was – because he'd heard raised voices in the parlour one afternoon. From what he could gather, Norma had been having a go at her daughter for not pulling herself together.

'You don't know what it's like,' Dawn had been yelling. 'It's not fair that I can't have my own.'

'Life's not fair,' Norma had shouted back. 'It's not fair on me. It's not fair on you. And it's not fair on Morton. He's a good man, Dawn. You don't want to lose him, do you?'

Morton had simply crept past the door and gone out to do the milking. He wasn't entirely sure *what* they were talking about but it sounded like women's business. Best leave it alone.

That was last week and still Dawn's spirits hadn't improved. She lay in bed till noon every day and then sat staring blankly at the TV all afternoon and evening. Often, she didn't even bother to get dressed, slopping around in an old pair of Morton's pyjamas and a scruffy tracksuit top. Ever considerate, Morton had moved into the spare bedroom so that he wouldn't wake her when he got up at five to do the milking. Sometimes, when he crept along the passage in the dark he could have sworn he heard Dawn crying. But she always denied it.

Now it was almost Christmas and Dawn showed no sign of getting better. It was time he took matters in hand, he reflected as he trudged round the fields at dusk, checking on his stock. If he didn't get Dawn some help soon, it might be too late. And then he'd never forgive himself.

Chapter Twenty-three

Tim Dawner had had a miserable week. He'd spent much of his time trekking back and forth to Manchester to talk to the bank's Corporate Recovery department. It had been a bit like being interrogated by the police. The men in suits had demanded so many facts and figures, so many profit projections and sales forecasts, that by the end of it all he'd barely known whether he was coming or going.

But for the last couple of days two young chaps from the department had themselves travelled the hundred or so miles up to Bowater. The pair of them had gone through Denim Heart's finances in meticulous detail. To add insult to injury, they'd set up camp in Tim's own office, claiming that they *had* to have somewhere private to work. Tim himself had been forced to perch in an anteroom next to Tracey, his secretary.

The whole factory was talking about the mysterious men closeted in Tim's office from eight every morning till nine or ten at night. Tim himself was so desperate to make as favourable an impression as possible that he'd been doing the same punishing hours for a change.

He still hadn't heard a word from Helen either. Even the *Eagle* story about her profligacy hadn't flushed her out.

Much as he hated to admit it, Tim felt desperately

lonely. The worst time of all was at night, when he turned the key in the lock of their isolated cottage overlooking the fells. Where once he might have found Helen preparing a delicious supper and ready to chat, now the cottage seemed cold and bleak. It was also a complete tip. Before her departure, it had always been Helen who took charge of the boring domestic details – the shopping, cooking, cleaning, washing. He'd never lifted a finger. But now that she'd gone, the place had degenerated into utter chaos. The house was filthy, the bed unmade and the curtains never drawn. For the last month Tim had existed on a diet of take-aways. In fact the only areas of his life that hadn't completely gone to pot were his clothes and his personal hygiene. Thanks to the laundry in Bowater and his insistence on two showers a day, he still looked as immaculate as ever, if a little jaded round the edges.

It was now lunchtime on Christmas Eve and the Corporate Recovery guys were preparing to set off back to Manchester.

'Have you got everything you need?' asked Tim, praying that they had. For God's sake, they must have bloody been through every document in the entire factory.

'Looks like it,' said Colin Gorman, the older, more senior chap. 'We'll be in touch again after Christmas.'

Tim's heart sank. He'd been hoping that once they'd perused the books to their heart's content, then that would be the end of the matter.

'About what, exactly?'

'About where we take it from here of course,' said Colin.

'And what will that entail, exactly?' asked Tim.

Colin Gorman sighed heavily. This was the trouble with the Corporate Recovery business. If he could just be left to get on with his job, it would be fine. Why did people like Tim Dawner always get their knickers in such a twist?

'Oh, the usual sort of thing,' said Colin.

'And what's that when it's at home?'

Colin stared at Tim. He'd met some flash gits in his time but this one took the biscuit. He knew perfectly well what the Corporate Recovery department would be telling Tim Dawner to do. Sell his showy sports car for a start. Get rid of the company flat in London. Cut the megabucks salary. Lay off some of the workforce. They were massively overstaffed.

'As I said before, we'll be in touch after Christmas,' Colin Gorman said firmly. 'Have a good one, won't you?'

Once the two men had left, Tim felt at a loose end. He and Helen had always hosted a big party at lunchtime on Christmas Eve to thank the Denim Heart staff for their efforts during the year. They'd prided themselves on choosing a new venue each time. Once they'd held the bash at the art gallery in Bowater and on another occasion they'd booked a suite in a posh hotel. Last year they'd really gone to town and taken over the magnificent oak-panelled council chamber. They'd served champagne and canapés and anyone who was anyone in Bowater had been there.

But this year it was a different story. The factory had shut down at noon and instead of donning their glad rags and setting off for the party, most of the staff had gone straight home.

They'd made no secret of their pique at being done out of their party either. Only that morning Tim had over-heard two of the packers grumbling in the corridor.

'No party, no booze, no presents,' moaned one of them. 'It's bloody great, isn't it? You work your guts out all year and get no thanks for it.'

'The only reason I joined Denim Heart was because of the Christmas do,' said another. 'And you'd have thought that they could at least have given us a gift voucher from Marks or something.'

'You've heard the rumours, haven't you?' whispered the first girl.

'What rumours?'

'Sharon in accounts says the company's in trouble. You know those blokes who've been locked in the boss's office all week?'

'What about them?'

'They're going to shut the place down. That's why they're here.'

Listening to this in Tracey's cubby-hole of an office, Tim had groaned and put his head in his hands. If that's what the girls in the factory were saying, he dreaded to imagine the gossip flying around Bowater.

It was two-thirty by the time Tim locked up the factory and climbed into his gleaming red Morgan. He didn't know what to do next. He wasn't particularly close to his parents but they'd invited him to spend Christmas with them in the Borders. He was dreading it. Dreading the false *bonhomie* and the constant inquiries about Helen. Perhaps he'd set off in the morning – he was far too pent up to drive there right now.

Tim wasn't sure why but quarter of an hour later he found himself wandering into the King's Head in the centre of Bowater.

The pub was packed with staff from nearby offices enjoying a few pre-Christmas drinks. Tim glanced dejectedly around the saloon bar. He didn't recognise anyone.

Tim ordered himself a whisky and drifted into the public bar. This was even seedier than the saloon. It was dark and smoky and there was hardly room to move.

'Hi Tim,' called a jaunty-sounding voice from the midst of the crowd.

Tim whirled round to see Cara Bell standing there. She looked quite astounding in a scarlet mini dress, white tights and Father Christmas hat. A string of multi-coloured paper chains had been slung round her neck – he wasn't sure whether by accident or design.

'Come and join us,' she yelled. Her words sounded ever so slightly slurred, but it *was* Christmas, after all. If you couldn't have a few drinks with your mates at Christmas, when could you?

'OK,' said Tim, making his way over to her and her friends. 'Thanks. I will.'

Cara made a few swift introductions. Tim didn't take in many of the names, apart from a couple of the other writers and Alex Davis, the down-at-heel looking features editor, whom he'd spoken to on the phone a few times.

'Where's Juliette?' inquired Tim, doing his best to sound casual.

Alex's eyes narrowed suspiciously.

'Why d'you want to know?'

Tim shifted from one foot to the other.

'No reason,' he said, his voice cool. 'She's done quite a few stories on Denim Heart recently so I've got to know her a bit. I would have bought her a Christmas drink if she'd been here . . .'

'Well you can buy me one instead,' giggled Cara, thrusting an empty pint glass in his direction. 'Pint of lager please. Oh, and a packet of salt and vinegar crisps while you're there.'

Grateful to escape Alex Davis's hawk-eyed stare, Tim elbowed his way through the throng to the bar. When he returned five minutes later, he was relieved to see that Alex was talking to someone else.

'Merry Christmas,' said Tim, handing Cara her pint.

'Thanks,' said Cara. 'Oh, and by the way, that reminds me. I've got a bone to pick with you.'

'Oh?' said Tim.

'Yes,' said Cara. 'Why did you tell Juliette that I gave you her home number when it wasn't true?'

Tim blinked. Cara had clearly had too much to drink. What was she on about?

'What do you mean?'

Cara glared at him.

'A couple of weeks back. You rang Juliette at home about some story or other and when she wanted to know how you got her number you said I'd given it to you. I'd never do that. Never. So come on. Why did you lie about it? Do you want to get into her knickers or something?'

An inscrutable look crossed Tim's face.

'I think I'll ignore that last remark, Cara. But as for Juliette's number, she must have got her wires crossed. I haven't got a clue what you're both going on about. Truly I haven't.'

Cara was halfway through her third pint by this point and her brain was starting to feel befuddled. Under normal circumstances she would have continued cross-examining Tim but all of a sudden she felt distinctly unwell.

'Oh no,' she groaned. Her legs started to buckle beneath her and she grabbed on to him. 'Oh no. I think I'd better . . . I think I'm going to be . . .'

It was too late. To Tim's horror, Cara was violently sick. All down the front of his best Paul Smith suit and all over his shiny black brogues. He'd never seen so much vomit in his life.

Tim was so shocked that for a few seconds he stood rooted to the spot, unable to move. A load of Cara's colleagues dashed to her side to help but he just stood there gaping at her.

Coming after everything else – Helen's betrayal, the business in meltdown, even Juliette blowing hot and cold – this was simply the last straw.

'And a very Merry Christmas to you, too,' he muttered as Cara limped white-faced into the Ladies.

After the unfortunate incident in the pub, Tim decided against going to his parents for Christmas. He couldn't face it. Far better to spend it on his own. Pretend that it was nothing special, just another day.

Back at the cottage, Tim showered over and over again, desperate to rid himself of the abhorrent smell of vomit. He'd gingerly taken off his suit, put it in a bin liner and dumped the whole thing outside the back door, ready to take to the dry cleaners after Christmas. He couldn't bear to have it anywhere near him.

When he was satisfied that he'd cleansed himself sufficiently he poured himself a glass of whisky and lay down on the sofa in the sitting room. He'd done nothing whatsoever to make the cottage look festive. There hadn't seemed much point in buying a Christmas tree or putting the pitifully few cards he'd received up when he was on his own.

At that moment the phone rang. It sounded so rarely these days that Tim nearly jumped out of his skin. The bloody thing was buried beneath a ton of debris on the floor and took him a few seconds to find. When he finally located it he snatched up the receiver.

'Hello,' he said, his voice breathless. 'Hello.'

There was silence at the other end.

Tim was on the point of putting the phone down when there was a strangled cry of rage at the other end of the line.

'Helen,' he said in a cautious tone. 'Helen. Is that you?'

'Of course it is, you bastard,' she screeched. 'You bloody bastard. You won't get away with it, you know.'

Before Tim could utter another word, Helen had crashed the phone down.

Suddenly all the frustrations of the day caught up with him. Exploding with anger, he chucked his whisky glass at the huge Inglenook fireplace. The glass shattered into smithereens, spraying a fine mist of whisky all over the cream carpet.

Bloody women, he thought. Why did they always fuck everything up?

228

Chapter Twenty-four

Sitting at the kitchen table, Juliette beamed first at Freddie, and then, a fraction more cautiously, at Joe. It was Christmas Day and the three of them were tucking into a vast lunch cooked by Juliette. Cooking wasn't exactly her forte but thanks to Fi Nicholson's foolproof instructions she reckoned she'd managed pretty well. Juliette was still convinced, however, that the person responsible for dreaming up Christmas lunch must have been a sadist. For goodness sake, she could change a tyre, mend a fuse and knock out an eight-hundred word piece on any subject under the sun – but she'd nearly buckled under the strain of keeping the turkey, roast potatoes, sprouts, parsnips and carrots hot at the same time. And as for gravy, forget it. She'd bought a carton of consommé from the supermarket and decanted it into a jug. Luckily, neither Joe nor Freddie had commented.

Much to Juliette's delight, Freddie had eaten everything on his plate with gusto. It helped to confirm her view that he was back to his old self again. Since the end of term he'd been sparky, energetic and full of fun – a different child from the morose, sad-eyed boy of the last few months.

Juliette had spent every second of the week running up to Christmas with Freddie. She'd gone into Geoff Lake's office the day after the editor dropped his bombshell and agreed to accept his humiliating new terms. On two conditions. That he gave her the four-day week he'd originally promised. And that he let her take two weeks off over the Christmas holidays.

She'd been expecting a row but to her amazement, he'd acquiesced straight away.

'Course you can, Juliette,' he'd said, plainly relieved that she'd agreed to the deal. 'You've worked your socks off since you got here. It'll do you good to spend time with your boy. Recharge your batteries and all that. We'll see you in the New Year.'

Once upon a time Juliette would have been stumped for ideas about how to entertain Freddie. The most imaginative jaunts she'd come up with in London were endless trips round Dulwich Park (she knew every tree in the entire park) and visits to the cinema.

But in Cumbria it was different. The two of them had been teeming with ideas. They'd painted and made Christmas decorations, taken winter picnics up to Miston Moor and even visited Father Christmas at Bowater's one and only department store.

Joe hadn't arrived in Newdale till late on Christmas Eve. First he'd had to show his face at the Radio Wave DJs' Christmas lunch (a rowdy affair where so much food got chucked about that the restaurateur had banned the lot of them from ever crossing the threshold again). Then he'd had a meeting with Daniel White, who wanted to update him on progress at Primetime TV. No final decision had been made yet, but Daniel assured him that the quiz show producers had been impressed by his first audition and things were looking hopeful.

By the time Joe stumbled through the door at New Bank, it was nearly midnight. But there was a light glowing downstairs and when he walked into the sitting room he found Juliette sitting on the floor surrounded by piles of tiny toys – cars, marbles, books and story cassettes – wrapping paper and tape.

'Ssssh,' she whispered, putting her finger to her lips. 'I'm doing Freddie's stocking. D'you want to help?'

'Course I do,' whispered Joe, sinking on to his hands and knees. 'I wouldn't miss this for the world. And I've got a few little things too, so Freddie's going to have a bumper stocking.'

They worked together in companionable silence, Juliette doing most of the wrapping and Joe stuffing the presents into the long scarlet stocking Freddie had had since he was a baby. When they'd finished, Juliette got to her feet and stretched her arms wearily.

'Oh God, I've just seen the time,' she exclaimed, looking at the old-fashioned station clock on the wall.

'Midnight,' murmured Joe.

'It's Christmas,' said Juliette. 'Let's make it a really happy one this year, Joe. Suspend hostilities. What do you think?'

Joe stood up and opened his arms wide.

'Come here, Jules,' he said.

He didn't have to ask twice. In an instant Juliette was in his arms.

'Mmmm,' said Joe as his arms tightened around her. 'This feels nice. We should do it more often.'

'You reckon?' said Juliette teasingly.

'Mmmm, I reckon,' said Joe, kissing her long and hard. 'Shall we go upstairs?'

'Yes please,' said Juliette. 'If you go up I'll join you in a second. I've just got to make it look as if Father Christmas and his reindeer have eaten up the mince pies and carrots that Freddie left out for them. There was enough to feed a whole zoo.'

'Make sure you don't forget this,' laughed Joe, picking up Freddie's stocking.

'Wouldn't that be awful? Freddie would be heart-broken. God, it would scar him for life.'

Halfway out of the door, Joe turned to look at Juliette once more.

'All right if I sleep in our bed? With you, I mean?'

Juliette stared at Joe. A shiver of longing ran through her. How could she have ever thought that she didn't love him?

'There'll be trouble if you don't,' she said.

Juliette tore round the house at top speed, sorting out Father Christmas's feast and re-hanging Freddie's stocking at the end of his bed. In the bathroom she cleaned her teeth meticulously, sprayed a tiny bit of scent behind her ears and then took all her clothes off.

When she crept naked into the bedroom, it was shrouded in darkness. Smiling to herself, she tiptoed across the room and slipped silently into bed.

'Joe?' she whispered, snuggling up close to him. 'Joe?'

There was no answer, just the sound of quiet, rhythmical breathing. Juliette could have wept with disappointment. Joe was asleep.

'That's bloody great,' she swore out loud. 'Just bloody great.

She turned furiously on to her side and closed her eyes. All she could think of, though, was making love with Joe.

A few seconds later, however, a hand began slowly to caress her breasts. Juliette groaned with pleasure. She must be dreaming.

'Surely you didn't think I'd fall asleep wanting you like this did you?' murmured Joe through the darkness. 'Feel how much I want you, Jules. Come on. Feel.'

The night had been perfect, thought Juliette. It hadn't even seemed to matter that they'd only managed three or four hours sleep before Freddie came charging into their bedroom with his stocking. Juliette had gazed sleepily at her watch. It was five thirty-five. She'd been tempted to send him back to bed till seven but Joe would hear none of it.

Now, at lunch, Joe lifted his glass of champagne in the air and grinned at Juliette and Freddie.

'I think we should all have a toast, don't you?' he said.

'And me,' said Freddie, holding up his glass of fizzy orange.

'When have we ever left you out, darling?' laughed Juliette. 'Right, what are we going to toast?'

'We need three,' said Joe. 'First, here's to the chef – for cooking such a delicious lunch.'

Joe and Freddie clinked glasses, Freddie so enthusiastically that fizzy orange spilled over the top of his glass and on to the table.

'To the chef,' they both chorused.

'Second, here's to the three of us,' said Joe. 'I know it sounds a bit corny, but to my fantastic family. To family life.'

'To family life,' trilled Juliette and Freddie.

'And what's the third, Daddy?' shrieked Freddie with excitement.

Joe smiled at his son's exuberance. But he never got the chance to propose the third toast because the phone interrupted him in mid-flow.

'Whoever can that be?' he asked crossly, getting up from his chair.

Juliette couldn't help laughing.

'How on earth am I supposed to know?' she chuckled. 'Maybe it's your mum ringing to wish us all Happy Christmas.'

'Or yours,' said Joe.

'Definitely not,' said Juliette. 'She's like clockwork.

Never rings before six – whatever day of the year it is.'

Joe picked up the telephone.

'Hello,' he said. 'Who? Oh, right. I'll just go and get her.'

'Who is it?' mouthed Juliette at Joe.

'Some bloke called Tim Dawner,' said Joe in a loud whisper. He shrugged his shoulders. 'Says it's something to do with work. Bit odd to ring on Christmas Day though, isn't it?'

Hearing Tim Dawner's name. Juliette's blood ran cold. He was the last person in the world she wanted to talk to right now.

'I'll run and take it upstairs. I don't want to spoil lunch. Can you put the receiver down for me?'

'Fine,' said Joe coolly. Inside, however, he was fuming. Why was Juliette being so coy? There was something about all this that didn't add up.

'Do *you* know a chap called Tim Dawner?' he asked Freddie. It was unfair of him to ask a six-year-old, he knew, but he couldn't help it.

'I don't think so, Daddy. Why?'

'Oh it doesn't matter. Come on, are you going to help me clear up? I'll wash the saucepans and you can dry.'

Upstairs, Juliette was having great difficulty understanding what Tim was on about. She dreaded him mentioning what had happened between them but he was so drunk that he could barely string two words together. The only thing that she could make out for sure was that Helen had been in touch.

'I need to talk . . .' he mumbled incoherently over and over again. 'I need to talk to you. About Helen. You're the only one, Jules. The only one who . . .'

'Stop it,' she hissed, trying to keep her voice down. 'Just stop it, will you? Can't you get it into your brain

234

that I can't talk now? I've got Joe and Freddie down-stairs. We're in the middle of Christmas lunch. I can't talk now.'

'Oh Jules. You're the only one who understands. Will you come? Please say you'll . . .'

Juliette was on the point of losing her temper.

'NO I CAN'T,' she said firmly. 'NOT NOW. Do you understand? I'll ring you next week. OK?'

By the time she got back downstairs the mood had changed. Joe was doing the washing-up and something about the brisk way he was scrubbing the pots and pans told her that the intimacy of the last few hours had completely evaporated. Freddie was glued to a *Pokémon* video and when she tried to prise him away to look at his presents he protested loudly.

So much for the toast to family life, she thought bitterly.

Joe stayed in Newdale until tea-time on Boxing Day. He spent most of the day fixing Freddie's bike and helping to build a huge K'nex model Freddie's godmother had given him for Christmas.

Juliette left the pair of them to it. She'd tried to talk to Joe, tried to get back to the way they'd been before Tim Dawner's phone call. But Joe refused to give an inch. He made it perfectly plain that he didn't want to talk – not about them, not about the prospect of him getting the Primetime quiz show, not even about how Willy was doing. Finally, she gave up, and by the time he began throwing his stuff into a suitcase she couldn't wait for him to leave.

The same, however, couldn't be said of Freddie. When Joe gave him a huge hug and promised to come back the following weekend, Freddie burst into tears and clung to his dad as if he never wanted to let go.

'Hey little guy, this isn't like you,' murmured Joe into Freddie's neck. 'What's all this about?'

'Why do you have to go, Daddy? I don't want you to. Please say you'll stay.'

Joe looked at his watch. He was back on the breakfast show in the morning and he was desperate for a good night's sleep. But he couldn't refuse Freddie.

'Look, let's make a deal,' he said. 'I'll do your bath, then read you a bedtime story and say night-night. I won't go till you're fast asleep. Is that a deal?'

'Deal,' said Freddie, striking Joe's hand in agreement.

Joe couldn't help noticing that even though his son was smiling, his eyes had lost their sparkle.

Chapter Twenty-five

The Christmas holidays were almost over. Juliette wasn't sure who felt sadder about it, her or Freddie. It was obvious from the way Freddie was slinking round the house with his tail between his legs that he dreaded the prospect of going back to school the next day. And she was equally appalled by the thought of returning to the *Eagle*.

She hadn't had any contact with anyone from the *Eagle* since the week before Christmas – well, apart from Cara, who'd popped round on New Year's Day.

Juliette grinned at the thought of Cara's monumental hangover. Whereas Juliette had been perfectly happy to see the New Year in on her own with the telly and a bottle of champagne for company (Joe was otherwise engaged, presenting Radio Wave's New Year's Eve special), Cara had spent the night on a pub crawl round Bowater with her mates.

The young writer had been nursing the worst headache of her life when she arrived at Juliette's at eight on New Year's Day.

'Oh my God, I feel like shit,' she moaned as she stumbled into the hall.

'You look like shit,' said Juliette, glancing at Cara's pasty white face. Cara undoubtedly had a style all of her own – sometimes it worked, sometimes it didn't –

but right now she'd lost it. She was wearing an old pair of what looked like her dad's pyjama bottoms and a moth-eaten sweatshirt. Her hair was unbrushed and sticking up all over the place and, unheard of for Cara, she hadn't bothered to put any make-up on.

'You don't look in a fit state to be out,' said Juliette, then couldn't help chuckling at how she sounded. 'Bloody hell, I sound like your mum, don't I?'

'Don't worry about it,' said Cara. She kissed Juliette on both cheeks. 'Happy New Year, anyway.'

Juliette offered her a glass of wine but Cara groaned at the very mention of alcohol.

'Ugh,' she said. 'I'm never going to let a drop of that evil stuff pass my lips again. Will you be my witness on that?'

'Course I will,' said Juliette. 'I don't believe a single word of it though. You'll be back in the pub by this time tomorrow night.'

Juliette handed Cara some Alka Seltzer and got her to lie down on the sofa in the sitting room. Then, instead of giving Juliette the low-down on all the scintillating *Eagle* gossip, Cara had immediately fallen asleep. When she was still dead to the world at eleven, Juliette had rung her parents to tell them Cara was staying at her place for the night. Then she'd slipped a pillow beneath Cara's head, put some blankets over her and let her sleep it off till morning. The next day, Cara had bounced up right as rain and announced she was off to the King's Head for lunch.

Now, on the last day of the holidays, Juliette had had a brainwave. She'd been racking her brains about how to prepare Freddie for going back to school. Suddenly it came to her. She grabbed hold of the phone book and scanned through the pages for the entry she was looking for. There, she'd found it. Perfect.

Half an hour later, she and Freddie were whizzing

down the hill to Newdale on their bikes. Juliette, anxious about Freddie being out on the open road, made him go first, constantly urging him to stay close to the kerb and not wobble into the middle of the road.

When they got to the primary school, Freddie stopped. Juliette could see that underneath his bike helmet he was getting anxious.

'Where are we going now, Mummy?' he asked.

'Don't panic,' smiled Juliette. 'We're not going into school. Not today, anyway. Now, come on. We've got to get cracking. It's the third turning on the left.'

The pair of them cycled past the school and turned left into Langdale Avenue.

Juliette was shocked at the dilapidated row of terraced houses that confronted them. She'd never been down here before. Even after four months, the Lake District was a constant source of surprise. Some of it was so wealthy – country mansions with vast rhododendron bushes and lakeside views, homely farmhouses that doubled up as bed and breakfasts during the tourist season. But streets like this were a world apart. Langdale Avenue, with its grey brick, satellite dishes and front doors opening straight on to the street, looked like something out of a gritty industrial landscape.

'Where are we going?' demanded Freddie once more.

'Number thirteen,' said Juliette. 'And don't worry about it, sweetheart. I think you'll be pleased.'

When they reached number thirteen, they propped their bikes outside the house and Juliette chained them together. Old habits died hard, she thought. You couldn't be too careful, not even up here.

Juliette rang the doorbell. She couldn't wait to see Freddie's face when he realised whose house this was. It was a bit like *Through the Keyhole*. She wondered how long it would take him to guess who lived here.

It seemed an age before they heard the sound of angry shouting and footsteps rushing down the stairs. When the door opened, a teenage girl was standing there in bare feet, with a small baby in her arms.

'Amy,' exclaimed Juliette. 'I had a feeling this must be where you were living. Oh, and hasn't Billie grown? Can we come in? This is my son Freddie by the way.'

'I s'pose,' said Amy. She opened the door a little wider to let them in.

Feeling shy, Freddie hung back a little. He had no idea what his mum was up to.

Amy Barker led them into a tiny sitting room, crowded with armchairs. The room was dominated by a huge TV – some daytime cookery show was blaring out at top volume.

The three of them sat down. Within a few seconds though, Freddie had climbed on to Juliette's knee.

'It's nice to see you after all this time,' said Amy in a quiet voice. 'I don't get many visitors.'

Juliette felt a rush of guilt. She'd meant to come and visit Amy and the baby, really she had. But somehow she'd never got round to it. She'd been so absorbed in her own problems that she'd forgotten all about poor Amy.

'Not even Dawn?' she said.

''Specially not her,' mumbled Amy. 'I don't know what I've done wrong. She never comes.'

'Amy, you haven't done anything wrong,' said Juliette, wanting desperately to reassure her. 'She's probably a bit busy on the farm, that's all.'

'Maybe,' shrugged Amy. It was clear she didn't believe a word of this.

'Billie's a beautiful baby,' said Juliette. She meant it too. Billie was sweet, with rosy cheeks and a mop of black hair. 'How old is she now?'

'Six weeks,' said Amy.

'Is she good? Well, I don't mean good. Babies can't be bad, can they? I mean is she easy to look after? Are you coping all right?'

'I s'pose,' mumbled Amy into Billie's hair.

'And it must be great living with your mum again. I bet she helps a lot, doesn't she?'

Amy didn't answer, just stared at the floor.

Juliette tried to think what else to say. There was something odd about this set-up. She couldn't put her finger on it exactly, but something wasn't right. Amy's appearance, for a start. You wouldn't expect a new mum to look a million dollars, definitely not, but Amy looked simply dreadful. She was wearing a shapeless old T-shirt and joggers, her hair was lank and clearly hadn't been washed for days and she had huge purply-grey bags underneath her eyes.

'Does Billie keep you awake a lot at night?' she asked.

'Oh no,' murmured Amy. 'She's pretty good, especially now she's on the bottle. I feed her at eleven and then she usually lasts through till seven.'

Amy's reply made Juliette even more suspicious. If Billie was sleeping right through the night, why did Amy look so knackered? What was she doing to look so knackered?

'Where's the rest of the family?' said Juliette. 'All out?'

'Most of them, yeah. Mum's out cleaning – she always is – and our Wayne and Sarah are at work. Our Craig's just run out the back – he's a right bugger – but he'll be off to school tomorrow.'

Up until this moment, Freddie had been sitting on Juliette's lap, bored stiff. He was still none the wiser as to why his mum had brought him here, but he wished she'd get a move on.

At the mention of the name Craig, however, his whole

body went rigid. Who was this Craig person she was talking about? It couldn't be the boy he hated most in the entire world. It couldn't be. It just couldn't be.

Freddie was so appalled by the very thought of this that he missed the next bit of what Juliette was saying.

'. . . I know. In fact that's another reason why we popped round. Mrs Booth – you know, the boys' teacher – told me that Freddie and Craig spend a lot of time together at school. So I was wondering if Craig would like to come to tea today? Freddie would love it. We could drop him back in the car if that would make things easier.'

Amy didn't answer. She was clearly miles away.

'Would Craig like to come to tea with Freddie this afternoon?' repeated Juliette, more forceful this time.

'You what?' said Amy, her voice monotone. It took her a couple of seconds to take in what Juliette had asked. 'Oh right. But it's no good me fixing things without him knowing. He won't have it. He's a right tricky bastard. I'll have to go out the back and ask him. Can you hold Billie for a sec?'

Freddie jumped off his mum's knee and Juliette took the baby in her arms. Holding her, Juliette suddenly felt a wave of nostalgia flood through her. It had been so long since she'd held a baby that she'd forgotten what it was like.

'You're gorgeous, aren't you?' she whispered, stroking Billie's soft downy cheek. 'Absolutely gorgeous.'

All of a sudden she heard the sound of sobbing at her feet. She looked down, her heart beating wildly. Freddie was slumped on the grubby oatmeal carpet, crying his eyes out.

'Darling,' she said urgently. 'What on earth's the matter? Is it because you don't like me holding the baby? Come on, *you* can sit on my lap too.'

Juliette switched Billie to her other arm and pulled the still weeping Freddie on to her knee.

'You don't need to be jealous, you know,' she murmured. 'I'm only holding Billie while Amy looks for Craig . . .'

At the sound of his tormentor's name, Freddie became even more agitated.

'I don't want . . .' he began, but he was so choked up that he couldn't finish his sentence.

'What don't you want?' said Juliette, gently prompting him.

Freddie took a deep breath to try and get the words out.

'I don't want Craig Barker to come to my house,' he said with a sob. 'He's horrible. I hate him. He hits me all the time and I don't want him to come to tea. I'll . . . I'll run away if you invite him.'

Juliette was so shocked by Freddie's outburst that she was momentarily lost for words. If it hadn't been for the fact that she had Billie in her arms she would have grabbed Freddie and left the Barkers' house there and then.

'Sweetheart,' she said, when she was able to think straight. 'Why didn't you tell me before? Mrs Booth said you and Craig were always together so I thought . . .'

At this, Freddie gave another huge sob.

'Well, you shouldn't have,' he wept. 'The only reason we're always together is because he makes me. He gets hold of my arm and pulls me and makes me go and hide behind the dustbins. And then he punches me . . .'

Juliette's anguish on Freddie's behalf had now begun to turn to fury. Fury both at herself and at the school. For God's sake, she'd been so wrapped up in her own affairs that she'd been completely blind to what was happening to Freddie. It was terrible to think that he'd been battling this all by himself. What made it even worse was that she'd written a massive three-part series on bullying just a couple of months back. And all the time it had been happening to her own son.

At that moment, Amy reappeared. Behind her followed a small stick-like boy with wire-rimmed glasses and a savage crew-cut. He was wearing a grubby white T-shirt with the word 'KISS' emblazoned across the front in black letters and some red jogging trousers. He had a runny nose and he looked in dire need of a square meal.

Juliette gaped at the boy. In her mind she'd been imagining a big fat bully and yet the boy standing in front of her didn't look capable of having the skin off a rice pudding.

Her view changed, however, when Craig saw Freddie sitting on Juliette's knee.

'What'ya doing in our house, you big booby?' he jeered. 'Come to tell on me, have ya? Well, it's no use ya telling. I didn't do nothing.'

At these words, Freddie's face went pale. But Juliette was having none of it.

'We're here to see your sister, not you,' she said firmly. 'From what I've heard, you haven't got any friends. And judging by the way you treat Freddie, I can't say I'm at all surprised.'

Craig looked stunned. He opened his mouth to say something smart back, but seeing the steely expression on Juliette's face, promptly shut it again.

Juliette paid no attention to him. She handed Billie back to Amy and caught hold of her hand.

'I'm sorry, Amy, we can't stop. Not now. But I do want to talk to you properly. I'll come and see you once your brother's back at school.'

* * *

When the door slammed behind Juliette and Freddie, Amy turned on Craig in rage.

'Have you been up to your old tricks again?' she stormed.

Baby Billie was so shocked by Amy's shouting that she began to cry. But still Amy didn't let up on Craig.

'What made you go and pick on that poor little kid? After all the warnings you've had? Our Mum will go bananas when she finds out. And then you'll be for it. You know you will.'

Craig's upper lip trembled as Amy vented her anger on him. Far from the hard man he craved to be, he'd suddenly turned into the small, frightened boy that he really was.

'Don't tell her, Amy,' he whined. 'Please don't tell our Mum. I didn't mean to hurt him – just show him who's boss, that's all. You lot all boss me so why shouldn't I boss that nancy boy? But I won't do it again, I promise. Please don't tell our Mum. I'll do anything. Honest I will.'

Chapter Twenty-six

Juliette lay awake for most of the night, agonising how best to deal with Craig Barker. She'd tried ringing Joe to ask him what he thought but there was no reply from Willy's flat. And for some mysterious reason, Joe's mobile was switched off too.

At seven-thirty am Juliette dragged herself out of bed and tiptoed into Freddie's room to wake him. She smiled at the sight of him curled up beneath his duvet with so many teddies and Beanie Babies tucked beside him that he barely had room to move.

'Come on sweetheart,' she whispered softly. 'Time to wake up. You've got school today.'

Freddie groaned and put his head under his pillow.

'Don't want to,' he mumbled. 'I hate it.'

Juliette leaned over the bunk bed and lifted the pillow away.

'Look, sweetheart, I know you've been having a horrible time. But I'm going to talk to Mrs Booth and we'll sort it. I promise. All right?'

All of a sudden, Freddie sat up with a beam on his face. Juliette stared at him. She couldn't put her finger on it exactly, but there was something different about him.

'Look, Mummy, look,' he shrieked. 'My first tooth. It's come out. I've wobbled it and wobbled it and it's come out at last.'

Juliette grabbed hold of him and gave him a huge hug. Children were so funny. One moment Freddie's world was collapsing around his ears. And now, just because he'd pulled his first tooth out, he was on top of the world again.

'I wonder how much I'll get for it?' he murmured.

Juliette looked puzzled.

'You're not going to sell it, are you? I shouldn't think anyone at school would want it.'

'Course not, silly,' said Freddie with a toothy grin. 'Don't you know anything? If you leave your tooth under your pillow when you go to bed, the fairies come and take it and leave you some money. Lizzie Nicholson told me.'

'How much money?' asked Juliette, keen for a little guidance on the matter.

'Lizzie says she got a pound,' giggled Freddie, jumping out of bed.

'What?' said Juliette, aghast. 'It used to be ten pence in my day.'

Freddie was so cock-a-hoop at what had happened that he couldn't stop beaming. He devoured a huge bowlful of Frosted Shreddies in double quick time and even had room for a piece of toast and strawberry jam.

By the time they got to school he wasn't in quite such a bullish mood. He brightened up, however, at the prospect of showing Mrs Booth his tooth, which he'd carefully wrapped in a piece of tissue paper.

Juliette had made sure that they arrived at eight-thirty, a good fifteen minutes before the school's official opening time. She took Freddie straight to his classroom, curtly informing Mrs Booth that Craig Barker had been bullying Freddie and that she had an appointment to see the head. This last point wasn't actually true, but Juliette reckoned that if she couldn't talk her way in to see Mrs Gyngell

247

then she should pack journalism in right now and go and work behind a bar.

When she popped her head round Mrs Gyngell's office, the head was poring over a pile of papers.

'Could I have a word?' said Juliette firmly. The tone of her voice made it clear that she wasn't prepared to take 'no' for an answer.

Mrs Gyngell glanced anxiously at her watch.

'I've only got ten minutes so as long as you make it quick,' she said.

'I'll try,' said Juliette, sitting down opposite the head teacher. 'But it's a very serious matter. I found out yesterday that Craig Barker has been bullying my son. Hitting him, punching, calling him names. And it's been going on for some time. You're probably aware that Mrs Booth has been concerned about Freddie for a while. He's been quiet and withdrawn in class and that simply isn't like Freddie at all. I wondered whether it was because he misses his dad. But Freddie broke down yesterday and told me all about what's been happening at school. I can't believe that none of you picked it up.'

'I see,' said Mrs Gyngell. She took off her glasses and rubbed her eyes wearily. 'And you're quite sure that Freddie is telling the truth?'

Juliette steeled herself not to lose her temper. Her flying off the handle wasn't going to help Freddie.

'Quite sure,' she said firmly. 'Freddie doesn't lie about anything.'

'I see,' said Mrs Gyngell again. 'Could you possibly leave it with me?'

Juliette stared at Mrs Gyngell.

'No, I'm afraid I can't. I need to know what you're going to do about it. *I need to know now.*'

'All right,' said Mrs Gyngell, leaning back in her chair. 'Well, like all schools, we have an anti-bullying policy and we shall of course put this into operation straight away. As you know, Craig's mother is a member of our staff, and naturally I shall pass on your concerns to her. But can I just mention a couple of things off the record?'

Juliette nodded.

'Perhaps I shouldn't say this but Mrs Barker is under a lot of strain at the moment. You probably don't know it but she's a single parent, with four children to support. Her teenage daughter has just had a baby and Craig is struggling with his school work.'

'I know all that,' said Juliette in a quiet voice. 'But just because his family has problems doesn't mean that he's entitled to bully other children and get away with it. Does it?'

'Of course it doesn't, Mrs Ward,' said Mrs Gyngell. 'And I can assure you that the school will be treating this matter with the seriousness it deserves. Why don't you come and see me again in a week's time?'

Before Juliette left for work, she looked in on Freddie once more. Much to her relief, he was busy helping Mrs Booth put out paper and paints ready for the first lesson.

'You will keep an eye on him, won't you?' she said, ruffling Freddie's hair. Today of all days, she hated him leaving him.

'I won't let him out of my sight,' said Mrs Booth. 'Don't worry. Well, I know you will. But you can count on that.'

As Juliette drove the ten or so miles into Bowater, she couldn't stop worrying about him. Was her job, especially now she was being paid six grand less than before, really worth it? Her career had always been hugely important to her, but for the first time in her life, she wasn't sure it *was*.

* * *

Stubby was overjoyed to see her back at the *Eagle*.

'I'd been wondering where you'd got to,' beamed the portly security guard. 'Thought you'd abandoned us for better things.'

'Would I do that, Stubby?' smiled Juliette. 'Course I wouldn't. How are things here, anyway? Missed much, have I?'

Stubby's genial face clouded over.

'Nothing good, that's for sure,' he mumbled. 'They've been cutting back all over the place. Two reporters went last week and Cara Bell got the old heave-ho last night. I'll be next for the chop, I should think.'

Juliette was stunned. Why on earth had Geoff Lake booted Cara out? Cara couldn't earn more than about nine thousand a year at the most – she'd put money on it. Sacking her was hardly going to solve the *Eagle*'s problems.

Wandering into the newsroom, Juliette detected a distinct change in the atmosphere. Everyone had their heads down and even George Anderson, the features sub, didn't bother to shout out his usual cheery hello.

Without even stopping to think what she was doing, Juliette marched straight up to Alex Davis's desk.

'Why did you get rid of Cara?' she demanded.

Alex looked up from the factory-farming feature he was reading on screen and glared at Juliette.

'I don't see that it's any of your business,' he said curtly. 'And in any case it wasn't my decision. It was the editor's.'

'Huh. And you're telling me that he didn't ask your opinion? Pull the other one.'

Alex's face visibly blanched. He'd been on the *Eagle* for more than ten years now and most people were scared stiff of him. No one had ever dared speak to him like this before.

'Yes, you're right,' he spat, his face white with anger. 'Geoff *did* ask my opinion. He asked me who we could afford to lose and do you know who I said? I told him there was no contest – he should get rid of you. Double quick. For God's sake, you've been nothing but trouble since you got here. Always arriving late and going early. Hanging around with that Denim Heart man. And bringing your personal problems into the office too. The rest of us have been slogging our guts out right through Christmas and the New Year. And what do you do? You go whining to the editor and he gives you two weeks off.'

Juliette listened to Alex's tirade with interest. She'd always suspected that he resented the way she'd been foisted on him from above. But up until now she hadn't known for sure. This morning, however, the gloves were off and Alex had indicated the true extent of his loathing.

'I'm bloody good at my job and you know it,' she said, her voice surprisingly cool in the circumstances. 'The *Eagle* might be in trouble but filling the paper with boring features about WI meetings and flower shows isn't going to bring the readers flocking back. You don't like me because you see me as a threat. We both know that I could do your job a hundred times better than you do. Now, if you don't mind, I've got some calls to make.'

Before doing anything else, Juliette rang Cara to sympathise about what had happened. Cara, true to form, was still in bed, but her mum insisted on waking her.

'Hi Juliette,' croaked Cara. 'Sorry if my voice sounds a bit dodgy but I had a hell of a leaving do in the pub last night. Didn't get to bed till three.'

'You should have rung me,' said Juliette. 'I've only just heard what those bastards have done to you.'

To her surprise, Cara burst out laughing.

'Oh, don't worry about it,' she chuckled. 'I've known

for months that the *Eagle* wasn't me. All those sideways glances at my clothes and sharp intakes of breath about my features ideas. No, I was just too idle to get off my ass and do anything about it before. But now I am. Doing something about it, I mean. The *Eagle*'s given me a month's redundancy money and I'm off travelling next week. First stop: Khatmandu. What do you think?'

'Good for you,' said Juliette. She was genuinely sorry that Cara was going. She'd livened up the *Eagle* no end – it would be a dull place without her. 'Just make sure you send me a postcard.'

Next Juliette turned her attention to her long list of e-mails. Her heart jolted as she scrolled through them. Apart from a couple of messages from friends and a few press releases, they all came from the same address – timdawner@denimheart.com.

She opened the most recent one, dated the day before, and scanned through the contents.

'Juliette, please call me. I've got a story for you. Tim.'

Juliette deleted it without hesitating – and all the earlier ones too. Tim Dawner was undeniably gorgeous but she had too many other complications in her life to think about him right now. There was Freddie being bullied at school, Joe tipping up when he felt like it. No, she didn't have time to dwell on what she wanted. It came a long way down the priority list.

There was also a mountain of mail waiting for her. Most of it consisted of letters from readers inquiring about a batty astrologer she'd interviewed before Christmas but at the bottom of the pile she found a large brown parcel post-marked Bowater. Intrigued, she tore it open to find a stylish red nylon make-up bag filled with beauty products from Denim Heart and a card saying 'Call me'. Juliette was tempted to chuck the bag in the bin but it was so beautiful she couldn't bear to waste it.

She stared at it for a moment, then marched across the newsroom and handed it to one of the young copytakers. It was only fair. The rest of the staff got loads of freebies and no one ever gave the copytakers anything.

'Wow,' said the copytaker, hardly able to believe her eyes.

'Late Christmas present,' Juliette murmured.

Juliette spent the next couple of hours trying to dredge up some of her own stories. Bloody hell, she told herself. She was an ex-features editor – she didn't need to rely on a no-mark like Alex Davis to drip-feed her stories.

But Alex, clearly seething at her earlier outburst, soon got his own back. Emerging from the morning news conference with Geoff Lake at eleven, he casually dropped a boring-looking press release on her desk as he passed.

'We need a feature on this for tomorrow,' he said. 'It's an editor's special. He's particularly keen on it.'

And I'm the King of China, thought Juliette as she scanned through the press release. No one in their right mind could possibly be keen on a feature about the ins and outs of the Lake District's new waste strategy. But she'd show him. She'd show bloody Alex Davis how good she was. It didn't matter whether it was wheelie bins or an exclusive interview with Liz Hurley – she could write nine hundred words of scintillating copy on anything at all. No problem.

Juliette was putting the last fascinating touches to her wheelie bin piece when her direct line flashed.

'Jules?' said a familiar voice. 'It's Tim. I've *got* to talk to you.'

'Can I call you back?' said Juliette. 'It's not a good time. I'm writing for the edition.'

This wasn't strictly true – Juliette had no idea whether this piece would ever make the paper – but Tim didn't argue with it.

'OK,' he said reluctantly. 'But you will, won't you? I'm on my mobile. Have you got the number?'

'Sure,' said Juliette.

She had every intention of ringing him back later on. But everything flew out of her head when the *Eagle* suddenly got wind of a major news story breaking on its patch. A tipster rang in to say that a light aircraft with two people on board had taken off from Carlisle in thick fog and crashed on moorland the other side of Hillthwaite. The *Eagle* immediately despatched two reporters to the scene and a third to Bowater General, while the rest of the office set to work making calls to the police, fire, ambulance service, Civil Aviation Authority – anyone they could think of who might know something.

As a rule the *Eagle* published two editions a day – the deadline was nine-thirty for the first and noon for the second. It was lunchtime by the time the news desk got the tip-off about the plane crash, but realising the magnitude of the story, Geoff Lake swiftly decided to publish a rare third edition.

'It'll cost us a fortune to bring out an extra edition but we can't wait till tomorrow to publish this,' he was heard telling Ray Henry, the news editor. 'Try and get some eyewitness accounts for me, won't you?'

A couple of the reporters were busy working their way through the telephone directories – ringing everyone in Newdale, Wath End, all the surrounding villages, to ask if they'd seen anything.

Suddenly a flash of inspiration hit Juliette. She knew exactly who to ring. She bashed the side of her head with her hand. Of course. She couldn't think why she hadn't thought of them the instant she'd heard about the crash. Dawn and Morton Lewis. They lived at Hillthwaite for goodness sake – their farm couldn't be far away.

Dawn's phone rang repeatedly.

'Come on, Dawn. Get your arse in gear. Come on,' muttered Juliette. She was on the verge of putting the receiver down and suggesting to Ray that she drive out to the farm when an anxious-sounding voice came on the line.

'Hello?'

'Dawn?' said Juliette, the urgency showing in her voice. 'Is that you?'

'Yes,' mumbled Dawn. 'It's Dawn speaking.'

'Are you all right. Is Morton all right?'

'Course we are,' said Dawn, a fraction more forcefully. 'Who *is* this?'

'It's Juliette. Juliette Ward from the *Eagle*. Have you heard about the plane coming down near Hillthwaite?'

'I'm not sure.'

Juliette dug her fingers into the palms of her hands to make herself stay calm. Losing it with Dawn wasn't going to help, but really . . . The woman either knew about the crash or she didn't.

'Is Morton there?' asked Juliette. Perhaps she'd get more sense out of him.

'He's outside, seeing to the cows.'

'Could you possibly go and get him for me?' said Juliette. '*Please*?'

'All right,' mumbled Dawn again. 'I'll try.'

It seemed an age before anything happened. Once again Juliette wondered if it would be better to jump in the car and drive up there. But then again, if she did that, she'd definitely miss today's special edition.

Eventually she heard rustling near the phone and the murmur of voices.

'Hello,' said Morton in his distinctive northern accent.

'Morton?'

'Aye,' said Morton. 'What do you want?'

'It's Juliette from the *Eagle*. I came up to see Dawn a

255

couple of times when you had Amy staying with you. But this time I'm ringing about the plane that's crashed up there. Did you see anything? Anything at all?'

'Course I did,' said Morton as if it was the stupidest question he'd ever heard. 'I was right there, wasn't I? Terrible it was, too.'

'What do you mean, you were right there?' Juliette crossed her fingers, hoping that he meant what it sounded like.

'One of the cows was poorly and I was out having a look at her – about dinner-time it was. The fog had come down like pea soup and suddenly I heard this engine noise above my head. I couldn't think what the heck it was. It got louder and louder and then there was this almighty bang. I thought that the whole world was coming to an end.'

'What did you do?' prompted Juliette gently.

'I ran for it, of course,' said Morton. 'What d'you think I did?'

'Ran away, you mean?'

'You what?' said Morton. 'Course I didn't run away, lass. What d'you take me for? A flaming coward?'

'So where did you run?' asked Juliette. She knew it was uncharitable of her to even think it but prising information out of Morton was like getting blood out of a stone. Seconds later, however, she felt guilty.

'I ran to help the people inside the plane, of course,' said Morton. 'It was difficult. I'm not saying it wasn't because when I got to it the plane was upside down. I could smell petrol and I was scared it was going to go up in flames any minute. I was lucky though, because the door of the plane had got ripped off in the crash. So first I managed to pull one chap clear and then I leaned in and grabbed hold of the other one.'

'What sort of state were they in?' said Juliette, all the time scribbling furiously in her notebook.

'Not too good,' said Morton. 'They were both covered in blood and the second one kept moaning that his legs were hurting. I think he must have broken them when the plane hit the ground. On impact like. I dragged the pair of them well clear and it's lucky I did because it was only a few seconds after that that the whole aircraft burst into flames. It was like putting a match to gas. I should think you could see it from Newdale. It was terrible to see. Truly it was.'

'What happened next?'

'I didn't know what to do,' said Morton. 'I didn't want to leave them like that but I had to get help. I had to. I ran back to the farm and dialled 999. Then I went back and sat with the pair of them. Before I knew it the ambulance was arriving and the medical people took over.'

'Did they say anything to you?' asked Juliette.

Morton thought for a moment.

'Well they asked if I was all right. Said I must have had a shock and did I want to come with them. But I couldn't leave the cattle, could I? So they left me to it.'

Juliette glanced at the clock on the newsroom wall. She had just under ten minutes to write up Morton Lewis's dramatic story.

'You know what this means, don't you, Morton?' she said quickly.

'What?' said Morton.

'That you're a hero. One of our reporters is down at the hospital and the last condition check on the two men said that they were "poorly but stable". So you saved their lives, Morton. You're a hero.'

Morton Lewis snorted down the telephone.

'Don't be soft, lass. I just did what anyone would have done, didn't I? Don't tell me any different.'

Chapter Twenty-seven

Joe stared at himself in the mirror. The man gazing back at him looked as if he'd just spent a fortnight in the Bahamas, lucky chap.

Joe had been stuck at Primetime TV's distinctly unglamorous studios in Docklands all day, plastered with two coats of bright orange make-up and an alarming amount of eyeliner. He looked unnaturally healthy for someone whose alarm went off at four am most mornings and who didn't get to see a lot of daylight.

Taken all round, today's audition had gone pretty well. It had been his second shot at presenting *Joking Apart* – in front of a live audience too – and as far as he knew he hadn't made any major cock-ups. Most important of all, the audience had seemed to like him. Well, they'd given him a rousing round of applause when he walked on, and laughed at nearly all his jokes.

Please let Primetime make its mind up soon, he thought. Professionally speaking he could take it or leave it. But there was no doubt that the *Joking Apart* money would be useful. And Freddie would be over the moon if his dad got a job on TV.

Sylvie, the make-up artist who'd slapped all the orange foundation on in the first place, now set to work with a huge wedge of cotton wool to get it off. He couldn't help wincing as she pummelled his skin this way and that.

'I don't know, you men make such a fuss about all this,' she chuckled. 'How did it go, anyway?'

'Fine, I think. I wish they'd bloody let me know one way or the other though.'

'You'll get it,' she said, giving his arm a comforting squeeze. 'I'm positive you will.'

Joe reckoned Sylvie must have been psychic – either that or she was thick as thieves with the producer – because when he arrived back in Battersea, Willy came flying out of the kitchen and began smacking him round the face.

'Hey, watch it,' muttered Joe. 'My poor face has taken enough of a pounding for one day, thanks.'

But Willy refused to let up.

'You did it, man. You did it.'

Joe looked nonplussed. He'd been up since dawn and was dying for some kip.

'*Joking Apart*,' shouted Willy. 'You've got it. They've just rung and asked me to pass on the message. They want you back in the studio on Friday to shoot the first show.'

'You're not kidding me, are you Will?' said Joe suspiciously. 'It has been known.'

Willy's face fell.

'Course not,' he said. 'We're mates aren't we? I wouldn't kid you on something important.'

A huge grin spread over Joe's face.

'So what are we waiting for?' he yelled. 'We need to get celebrating.'

Joe was so cock-a-hoop at his triumph that it never crossed his mind to ring Juliette and Freddie. One beer turned into six and even after Willy left to present his nightly show, Joe carried on drinking by himself.

He suffered for it the next morning though. He had a humdinger of a hangover and woke to find that he'd slept through both his alarm clocks. He only came to when Steve, the Radio Wave cabbie, rang the doorbell so persistently at four-thirty am that he woke Willy up.

'What the hell do you think you're playing at, man?' bellowed Willy from down the corridor. He was livid. 'Get your arse out of that bed and bugger off to work. I've only had three hours' sleep.'

Opening his eyes, Joe couldn't even work out where he was, let alone figure why someone was yelling at him. He grabbed the nearest alarm clock and, realising what time it was, shot out of bed.

Steve, the driver, thought the whole thing was bloody hilarious. All the way to Radio Wave, he kept chuckling about Joe oversleeping.

'You should have seen your face when you opened the door, mate,' he roared. 'Looked like you'd seen a ghost.'

Joe gave a false sort of laugh. Steve would have fallen about even more if he'd known that underneath his coat he was still wearing his pyjamas.

In fact Joe went on to tell the whole story on the breakfast show, leaving out the rip-roaring drunk bit and Willy going apeshit. That was the great thing about live radio. Nothing was ever wasted, no matter how embarrassing it was.

By the seven-thirty news break, Joe was starting to feel better. He knocked back two cappuccinos in quick succession and flicked through the morning papers, look-ing, as usual, for funny snippets from the tabloids to use during the show. This morning, however, the first thing he spotted was a small item at the bottom of the *Chronicle*'s diary page.

Radio Wave DJ Joe Ward's fortunes are on the up, he read. *The popular breakfast presenter has just scooped a new job as host of* Joking Apart, *Primetime TV's new game show.*

Tongues are wagging, too, about Joe's close friendship with radio producer Annie Smith. His journalist wife Juliette and son Freddie recently moved out of the family home. But Joe obviously isn't pining. He was recently spotted canoodling with the delectable Annie at a charity bash at the Savoy . . .

Joe's stomach lurched as he skimmed through the piece. He felt sick. He wouldn't have given a damn if the whole thing had been the figment of some hack's over-developed imagination. He would have just laughed it off. But the trouble was that it wasn't all lies. Was it?

Juliette was reading the papers at the kitchen table while Freddie watched *Blue Peter* before school. She still found it amazing that even though they lived in the middle of nowhere, the papers plopped through the letterbox like clockwork soon after seven am. She glanced at the *Telegraph* first, pleased to see that they'd followed up her story on the plane crash at Hillthwaite.

The *Eagle* had ended up using Morton's dramatic account of the crash as its special edition splash the day before. 'FARMER HERO SAVES PLANE CRASH TWO,' had been the headline. Much to Alex Davis's fury, Geoff Lake had been so delighted with it that he'd rushed over to congratulate Juliette personally.

'It's good to have you back,' he said, patting her on the shoulder. 'I wish we had a few more people capable of thinking on their feet.'

Still feeling pleased with herself, Juliette glanced at the front page of the *Daily News*, then flicked over on to page three. Her blood ran cold when she saw the story dominating the page.

'BACK TOGETHER – AND BUSINESS IS BOOMING,' shrieked the headline. Underneath was a huge picture of Tim Dawner looking satisfied with himself and a piece by Graham Burton claiming that his split with Helen had been a complete misunderstanding.

> '. . . we realised how much we need each other,' said Tim.
> 'We're a team and we've put all this behind us . . . We're spending some time together at our flat in London . . .'

Juliette closed the paper quickly. She couldn't face reading any more. The whole thing made her feel ill. It served her right for being so bloody smug about yesterday's splash – when all the time she'd been missing a scoop right under her nose.

Worse than that, she'd assumed that the reason Tim had kept phoning and e-mailing was because it was *her* he was interested in. She couldn't have got it more wrong. He'd wanted to tell her that he and Helen were back together again. She felt sick.

'*Blue Peter*'s finished, Mummy,' said Freddie, wandering into the kitchen.

Juliette didn't answer at first. She was miles away, racking her brains over what to do about Tim.

'What did you say, sweetheart?' she said.

'That my programme's finished.'

'We'd better be getting off to school then, hadn't we?' said Juliette. 'Have you cleaned your teeth?'

'Whoops,' giggled Freddie, scampering off upstairs.

Juliette groaned. Her son was pretty good for six, she thought, pretty independent. He always washed and got himself dressed. And recently he'd even started getting his own breakfast. She always knew when he had because there was a trail of cereal from the cupboard to the table and milk slopped all over the floor.

Glancing at the picture of Tim Dawner again though, she was at her wit's end. She couldn't just leave it – the *Eagle* would insist on following it up somehow. So how could she top the *Daily News* story?

She tried ringing Tim on his mobile. There was no answer. Then she rang his direct line at work and his home but she only got the answerphone each time.

On the spur of the moment, she made a decision. The only way to better the *Daily News* would be to get the first exclusive talk with Tim and Helen together. She was going to have to put her private feelings to one side, swallow her pride and tackle the two of them together. In person.

'Freddie,' she yelled up the stairs.

'I'm coming,' shouted Freddie, appearing on the landing with toothpaste smeared all down his jumper.

Oh well, thought Juliette. You couldn't have everything.

'School was better yesterday, wasn't it?' she said as he thundered down the stairs and jumped the last three to the ground.

'Much better,' said Freddie. 'Mrs Booth was really nice to me. And she let me be milk monitor. I told you that, didn't I? I had to give everyone their milk at playtime.'

'Mmmm,' murmured Juliette. 'And how about Craig?'

'I told you, Mummy.'

'Well, tell me again.'

'He left me alone,' said Freddie. 'D'you think he might be nice to me always now?'

'I hope so,' said Juliette. Then, seeing Freddie look anxious, swiftly added: 'Silly me – of course he will. He'll have me to contend with if he isn't.'

Inside however, she was still thinking about the Tim Dawner story, still wondering how to play it.

'I'm going to do something very naughty today,' she told Freddie suddenly.

Freddie glanced at her, immediately interested.

'I thought grown-ups were never naughty,' he said.

'Well, not exactly naughty,' said Juliette. 'But I've got to go to London today – and I want you to come with me.'

Freddie's eyes lit up. Then a worried expression appeared on his face.

'But what about school? When I didn't want to go to school before you said I had to. You told me the Prime Minister says so.'

Juliette crouched down to Freddie's level and looked him straight in the eye.

'He does,' she said. 'But it won't matter if you miss a day. Just this once. I'll ring Mrs Gyngell and tell her you won't be at school today.'

'And she won't be cross?' said Freddie.

'No, sweetheart, she won't be cross.'

Only with me, thought Juliette.

Sixty minutes later, Juliette and Freddie were boarding the nine-thirty train from Bowater to Euston. The first cheap fare train of the day, it was jam-packed with passengers – but Juliette managed to find two seats near the buffet car.

'Sweetheart,' she whispered to Freddie, who was staring out of the window in fascination. *He hadn't been on a train for ages.*

'What?' said Freddie impatiently.

'Can you just be quiet for a few minutes while I ring the office?'

'Yep,' said Freddie, sounding just like Joe.

Punching Alex Davis's direct line number into her mobile, Juliette gritted her teeth. This was the call she'd been dreading.

To her relief, however, it was Wendy, the features secretary, who answered.

'Hi Juliette,' she said. 'Everyone's having problems this morning. Where are you?'

'Er, is Alex there?' said Juliette. 'I need a word.'

'He's going to be late in. Said he was poorly in the night and was off to see the doctor.'

Juliette snorted, then tried to conceal the snort with a cough. She liked Wendy, she was a good egg, but she didn't know how far she could trust her. But Alex poorly indeed. The whole newsroom knew exactly what the matter with Alex was. You only had to look at his ruddy face and thickening paunch – not to mention his lousy temper – to know. He was an alcoholic, that was his problem.

'I see,' said Juliette. 'Well, when he *does* get in, could you tell him that I'll be in London all day? I think I mentioned it to him before but Channel Four's holding a press conference for *Lakeside Lives*. You know, the new soap that's going to be set up here? I'm doing a piece for later in the week.'

'I can't see it on the features list.'

'Oh, Alex must have forgotten,' said Juliette, knowing full well that Alex had done nothing of the sort.

'He does seem a bit distracted at the moment,' said Wendy. 'But don't worry, I'll remind him. And you'll be on your mobile if he needs you, won't you?'

'Of course I will,' said Juliette. 'And I'll be back in tomorrow.'

Ending the call, Juliette carefully switched her mobile off and stuffed it back in her bag.

'Now, sweetheart,' she said, turning to Freddie. 'How about a game of noughts and crosses? Are you going to be noughts or shall I?'

*   *   *

At the end of the breakfast show, Joe tried repeatedly to ring Juliette. Without success. The features desk told him she was out of the office all day, and for some unaccountable reason her mobile was switched off.

Damn it. He'd wanted to warn her about the *Daily News* piece before she spotted it herself.

Morton Lewis was enjoying his momentary taste of fame. It was fair to say that life had been pretty bleak in the Lewis household over the past couple of years or so. They'd faced one disaster after another – the BSE scare, foot-and-mouth, Dawn's miscarriage, Amy's decision to return home, the constant grind of making a Lakeland farm pay for itself. So it was nice to be made a fuss of for a change.

Thanks to its remote position, Hillthwaite Farm had few visitors during the winter months. No one wanted to risk that hill unless they had to. But the place had gone mad over the last twenty-four hours. Immediately after Juliette Ward's call, a photographer from the *Eagle* had come haring up in his car to take a picture of Morton for the paper's final edition. There had been a trail of reporters and photographers up to the farm for the rest of the afternoon and evening. And then to cap it all, a TV crew from Lakeland TV had pitched up at five to interview him. The report had been the lead item on the evening bulletin.

The only person who hadn't appreciated all the fuss, however, was Dawn. Morton had hoped that his role in the drama would lift her spirits, make her proud of him. But it didn't. The reporter from Lakeland TV was desperate to include Dawn in the piece too, get her to give hubby a hug and a kiss, but Dawn had refused pointblank. Even when Morton tried to cajole her into it. So while he'd sat in the parlour reliving the crash and the part he'd played in the rescue, she'd retreated up to bed again with a cup of tea and the latest *Woman's Own* for company.

Once the report had gone out on air, the telephone didn't stop ringing. Morton took call after call from people he knew – and even some he didn't – all wanting to compliment him on his heroism.

'Give over,' he said to most of them. 'It was nothing. Anyone would have done the same.'

Norma, Dawn's mum, was one of the first to call. She'd been up at Hillthwaite the night before to deliver some food and collect some washing. She couldn't believe that twenty-four hours later her son-in-law's face was plastered all over her television screen and he was being feted as a hero.

'I bet it's been a real tonic for our Dawn,' she told Morton. 'When something like this happens on your own doorstep, it brings you to your senses. Makes you see how fortunate we all are.'

At the mention of Dawn, Morton's spirits plummeted.

'I'm afraid that's where you're wrong, Norma,' murmured Morton, rubbing his brow. 'If anything, she seems worse. She wouldn't talk to any of the reporters, wouldn't say one word to the telly people. I'm at my wit's end with her.'

At the other end of the line, warning bells had begun to ring in Norma's head. For the first time in two months Morton, usually the sweetest and most patient of men, sounded exasperated.

'I tell you what, Morton,' said Norma quickly. 'When I've finished my shift at school tomorrow I'll get Ritchie to run me up in the car. The pair of you can't struggle on like this. We've got to do something. It's high time Dawn saw the doctor.'

Chapter Twenty-eight

It was early afternoon by the time Juliette and Freddie arrived in London. When they got off the train Freddie physically clung to Juliette, his eyes popping at how noisy and busy it was compared to Newdale. Then, spotting a burger joint on the other side of the station concourse, he pleaded to go there.

'Please Mummy,' he implored, pulling on her sleeve.

Glancing down at his eager face, Juliette gave in. What the hell. She was going to be in enough trouble when she got back to the *Eagle* anyway. What difference would one junior-sized portion of chicken nuggets and chips make in the great scheme of things?

Freddie fell on his lunch box of goodies like a man who hadn't eaten for a month. Where once he would have been quite blasé about the garish plastic toy that came free with it, now he was overcome with gratitude.

Juliette smiled at him. Six months ago a trip to a burger bar had been nothing special. But for a child who lived in the back of beyond, it seemed like the most exciting thing on earth.

'I hate to say this, sweetheart,' she reminded him once he'd bolted down his chips and nuggets. 'It's going to be very boring for you but I've got to get on with some work now.'

Freddie looked totally bewildered as she took hold

of his hand firmly and led him down the tube station escalator. They'd used the tube all the time when they lived in London but now Freddie was more used to biking around New Bank in the fresh air. The furthest he'd travelled in recent months was a trip to the dentist's the other side of Bowater.

By the time they emerged from the Underground at Notting Hill Gate, Freddie had started to get whiny.

'I want to go home,' he grumbled as they turned left into a terrace of elegant white stucco houses.

'Oh don't go all grumpy on me, Freddie,' said Juliette impatiently. 'Let me find the right house and then we'll have another treat at teatime.'

'What sort of treat?' said Freddie in a bolshy sort of voice.

'I'll tell you later,' said Juliette. 'Now come on, your eyes are better than mine. Can you help find number twelve?'

Freddie spotted it in no time. He raced on ahead and galloped up the wide stone steps to the front door.

'There are lots of buttons, Mummy? Shall I press one?'

Juliette glanced in her contacts book again. Tim had given her a comprehensive list of his and Helen's addresses and telephone numbers ages ago. She just hoped that this address was the right one.

'Flat four, it says here,' said Juliette. 'Can you press the button?'

Juliette stared at the name next to the button Freddie was pressing. It said Brown, not Dawner. She didn't know whether that was significant or not. But for the first time since reading the *Daily News* piece about the reconciliation, Juliette wondered if the story was one hundred per cent accurate. Graham Burton wasn't exactly the most reliable hack on the block and if Tim and Helen really were back together, it seemed odd that they weren't up in Bowater sorting the business out. And besides, Tim had repeatedly said that he hated London, avoided it like the plague. Surely if he was in the middle of some romantic idyll with Helen, London would be the last place he'd choose?

With this myriad of thoughts whizzing through her head, Juliette felt in a complete muddle. It didn't help either that Freddie kept tugging on her jacket, imploring her to go.

'Stop it, Freddie, for goodness sake,' she snapped. 'Just a couple more minutes and then we can. I promise you.'

Juliette pressed the buzzers of the four other flats in the house in turn. There was no answer from any of them. She was on the point of giving up and going when a basement window was heaved up and a young woman's face peered out.

'Are you looking for someone?' she shouted.

'Yes,' said Juliette, peering down. 'I'm trying to find Tim and Helen. From flat four. Have you seen them recently?'

The woman looked puzzled.

'I've never heard of anyone called Tim. I know Helen a bit but she hasn't been here for weeks. I work from home so I tend to know who's around.'

'D'you know where she is?' asked Juliette.

'No. 'Fraid not.'

'Can I give you my card? I'd be really grateful if you could give it to Helen when she gets back. Tell her I'd love to have a chat with her. She'll know what it's about.'

'I'm pretty sure she lives up north a lot of the time,' said the woman. 'She certainly keeps herself pretty much to herself when she's here. Nice woman, though. I like her.'

Juliette's heart plummeted with disappointment. She'd been pinning her hopes on finding Tim and Helen. And the fact that Helen Brown was 'a nice woman' was the last thing she wanted to hear. More to the point, where the bloody hell had she and lover boy got to?

Downcast and uncertain what to do next, Juliette took Freddie to the stylish-looking café on the corner of the street. Freddie wasn't that impressed but for Juliette it felt like coming home. She ordered a double latte with skimmed milk – she was a big fan of Giovanni's in Bowater but it wasn't quite up to this – and a *pain au chocolat* for both of them. To hell with the calories, she thought, taking a huge bite.

It was three-thirty by this time and Juliette had given up all pretence of doing any work. She'd fully intended to carry on the charade with Alex by popping in to the Channel Four offices in Charlotte Street and picking up a press pack about *Lakeside Lives*. But now she couldn't be bothered. Alex was going to go crazy with her whatever she did, so there didn't seem to be much point.

'What are we going to do next?' asked Freddie, looking across at her.

Juliette smiled back at him lovingly. What was she thinking of, bringing a six-year-old on a wild goose chase like this?

'I don't know. What would you like to do?'

Freddie didn't hesitate.

'Go and see Daddy,' he yelled with excitement. 'Can we, Mummy? Can we? Please say we can.'

Juliette nearly choked on her *pain au chocolat*. It wasn't that she didn't want to see Joe. No, it was more that in her haste to go racing after Tim and Helen, the possibility of fitting in a visit to Joe had never entered her head.

'I'm not sure, sweetheart. Daddy's terribly busy. I don't even know what he's doing today.'

'Please,' beseeched Freddie, his brown eyes as big as saucers.

Gazing at her son, Juliette couldn't refuse him. And anyway, just because her own relationship with Joe was like riding the Big Dipper didn't mean that Freddie had to miss out.

'All right,' said Juliette. 'I'll give you the phone and you can ring him.'

Joe was still suffering from the after effects of his marathon drinking session when his mobile rang. He'd tried everything – Paracetamol, gallons of water, even hair of the dog – all to no avail. He felt as if a steel band had been tied round his head and pulled tight. Desperate to get rid of the monumental hangover, he'd gone home, crawled into bed and tried to get some sleep.

Even this was difficult though, because Anne, Willy's ravishingly pretty new cleaning lady, had turned up and started vacuuming the place from top to bottom. Anne was a media studies student who did a bit of cleaning on the side to supplement her meagre grant. She was gorgeous, but Joe felt sorely tempted to stuff four hours money into her hand and send her off home. He didn't dare though. Willy would be livid.

The trill of the mobile phone sounded like a pneumatic drill inside his head. He reached out and grabbed it from the bedside table, knocking over his glass of water in the process.

'Hello,' he groaned.

'Daddy. Is that you? You sound funny.'

Joe sat bolt upright. He must be even more drunk than he realised. Freddie was the last person he'd expected to hear from. Why was he ringing in the middle of the day?

'Freddie? What's happened, sweetheart? Are you all right?'

'I'm very well, Daddy. And I'm in London. With Mummy.'

Joe's head was spinning with the effort of having to talk. He lay back down on the bed.

'Why?' he asked. 'Why aren't you at school?'

'Mummy said I didn't have to go today,' chirped Freddie merrily. 'So can we come round and see you?'

'What, now?'

'Yes. Right now. Mummy said that if you were there we could come and see you. Before we get back on the train again, I mean.'

'I'd love it,' said Joe. 'I'd love it more than anything else in the whole world.'

It only seemed like ten seconds later when the doorbell rang. Joe was still lying comatose in bed. He'd meant to get up but he hadn't had the strength to drag himself out of bed. His throat was impossibly dry and he couldn't stop shivering.

'I'll get it,' shouted Anne.

'It's all right,' croaked Joe. 'I know who . . .'

But it was too late. Anne had already gone to the door.

'Who are you?' said Juliette, glancing at the pretty dark-haired girl in T-shirt and jeans who'd answered the doorbell.

'Anne. Who are you?'

At that moment, Joe emerged into the hall, wearing nothing but a towel tied round his waist. His face was flushed, his hair rumpled and he looked – Juliette knew that look of old – as if he was up to no good. It was perfectly obvious what had been going on.

'I didn't expect you to get here so quickly,' he mumbled.

273

'I can see that,' said Juliette curtly.

The pair of them stared at each other for a couple of seconds. Then Freddie decided he couldn't wait a second longer to see his dad. He burst through the door and hurled himself into his father's arms.

'Daddy,' he shrieked with excitement.

'Sweetheart,' said Joe, kissing him over and over again. 'I can't believe you're here. What d'you want to do?'

'Go to the park,' cried Freddie. 'There's one over the road, isn't there? We saw it when we got out of the taxi.'

'Have we got time?' asked Joe, looking at his wife.

Juliette nodded.

'I should think so. Just. But maybe Freddie and me should go across first. Give you time to get dressed. You were obviously in the middle of something pretty important.'

Joe stared at her glassy-eyed. He didn't have a clue what the hell she was insinuating.

'Fine. I'll catch you up.'

As she and Freddie wandered through the iron gates and into Battersea Park, Juliette's mind was working overtime. It was true that after their brief rapproachement a couple of weeks ago at Christmas she and Joe had been getting on worse than ever. But she'd never thought for one minute that he'd go and find someone else. Tears welled up in her eyes. How could he do this to her? To Freddie? After everything they'd been through.

By the time Joe joined them, carrying a football under his arm and still with that sheepish look on his face, she felt too miserable to talk to him.

'Why don't you two have a kick-about on the grass?' she said quickly. 'I'll go and sit over there with the papers.'

Juliette found a park bench and took a hefty pile

of newspapers out of her bag. The only stories she'd managed to read earlier on were the accounts of the plane crash and the one about Tim and Helen. She hadn't even got a chance to look at the papers on the train because Freddie had wanted her to play games and she hadn't had the heart to refuse him.

Half-watching Joe and Freddie playing football and half-skimming through the papers, she turned to the *Daily News* diary. God, it was still full of the same old rubbish, stories about minor soap stars and friends of the editor. Suddenly her eye caught the name Joe Ward. She read on, aghast at what she was reading.

She'd managed to hold herself together at the sight of Joe and Anne together in the flat. Well, just about. But now the tears began to flow freely. No wonder Joe had looked so ill at ease when she and Freddie pitched up on the doorstep out of the blue. Annie Smith had been in the bloody flat. With him.

After half an hour in the brisk January air, Juliette was shivering with cold. Taking out her make-up bag, she tried to repair the damage to her face. She couldn't have a scene in front of Freddie and she certainly didn't want him to notice that she was upset.

'Come on, Freddie. It's time we were off. If we walk over Albert Bridge, I'm sure we'll be able to get a cab.'

Joe stared at Juliette. She looked agitated, he thought. As if she'd been crying.

'Don't be silly Jules,' he said. *'I'll* run you to the station.'

'No,' said Juliette. 'It's more fun getting a black cab. Freddie likes the fold-up seats. Don't you sweetheart? We'll be perfectly all right.'

If Joe hadn't been feeling so groggy, he would have insisted on taking them. But in his still-inebriated state, the thought of snuggling back into his soft, warm bed was a lot more appealing than battling through London's rush hour traffic. Especially when Jules was treating him as if he had the plague.

'If you're sure,' he said.

'Quite sure,' said Juliette, her voice making it clear she wasn't going to brook any arguing.

Freddie hurtled into Joe's arms once more.

'Are you coming up at the weekend, Daddy? You are, aren't you?'

'Of course I am, sweetheart,' murmured Joe. 'But it might be very late when I arrive because I'm starting a new quiz show on the telly. It's pretty exciting, isn't it? I'll tell you all about it at Saturday breakfast.'

The fact that Joe hadn't mentioned a word to her about doing a TV series only served to heighten Juliette's suspicion about his new life. In the old days he would have discussed *everything* with her. But now he'd clearly found someone else with whom he preferred to share his innermost thoughts.

Chapter Twenty-nine

Norma was meticulous about serving each child at Newdale Primary exactly the right amount of lunch, even down to the last garden pea. But she was so distracted today that she was slopping spaghetti bolognaise all over the place. She'd spilled tomato sauce down her pristine white overall and completely forgotten that a couple of the girls in Class Four were vegetarians.

By one pm however, she'd cleared up the mess, done all the washing up and her shift was over, thank goodness. She tore out of school and up to the gate where Ritchie had agreed to meet her.

Except that he wasn't there. Norma plonked her bag down and stood on the pavement, fuming. It was just typical of her layabout son not to turn up.

'I'm not asking you to take me up to our Dawn's,' she'd informed him last night. 'I'm telling you. You do little enough for your own family as it is. Your poor father would be turning in his grave if he could see the mess you've made of everything. For pity's sake, you aren't a young lad any more. You're twenty-four. It's time you started making a life for yourself, doing a bit of hard graft for a change. I thought I'd die of shame when you went inside. But the one thing, the one thing that consoled me was that it was bound to make you see the error of your ways. But has it? Has it heck.'

Norma was well aware that words like these were water off a duck's back as far as Ritchie was concerned. Both of them knew that if it wasn't for the fact that Norma did all his washing, cooked him a hot meal every night and gave him constant hand-outs, he'd have moved out to live with his mates in Bowater long ago. So last night he'd just stood there as usual – listening to her ranting and raving and not taking a blind bit of notice.

Now she replayed the words in her head all over again. Sometimes she thought that if she could just find the courage, the best thing – for Ritchie's sake as well as her own – would be to chuck him out of the house. Leave him to fend for himself for a change. But she simply couldn't bring herself to do it. When all was said and done, he was her son, her only son.

At that moment it began to rain. Norma put the hood of her anorak up and consulted her watch once more. She'd give him another ten minutes. If he hadn't turned up by then, she'd just have to go back into school and ring poor old Morton. At least he could be relied on to do what he said.

Norma was on the point of giving up when she heard the unmistakable sound of Ritchie's clapped-out old Escort roaring down the road. The car was in dire need of a new exhaust. Ritchie claimed that a pal of his was going to fix it on the cheap but it never seemed to happen. Norma was terrified he was going to be stopped by the police one day. She doubted whether the Escort had even passed its MOT though Ritchie swore on his life that it had.

'Told you I'd turn up, Ma, didn't I?' grinned Ritchie as Norma climbed into the passenger seat. He looked pale, she thought, and there was a funny smell in the car – a bit like incense or something – but Norma banished this from her mind. It was Dawn she was most worried about right now.

By the time Ritchie's car spun into the yard at Hill-thwaite, Norma's heart was beating like the clappers. She avoided being driven by him as a rule. He rarely took any notice of the speed limit and instead of slowing down at bends, revved up even more.

'Just promise me one thing, son,' said Norma as she stumbled out of the car. 'Don't drive like that with our Dawn, will you? Her nerves are in tatters as it is. I want her to be calm when she sees the doctor. Not all hyped up.'

Ritchie shrugged his shoulders dismissively.

'OK Ma,' he said. 'You go and get her and I'll wait for you here.'

Dawn was still in her dressing gown when Norma walked in.

'Get dressed love, there's a good girl,' said Norma gently. 'We haven't got long. The appointment's in half an hour.'

'It's a waste of time,' mumbled Dawn, stomping up the stairs like a grumpy child. 'There's nothing wrong with me.'

'We'll let the doctor be the judge of that,' said Norma. '*I* think you look a bit peaky but let's just see what he says.'

Dawn never did anything in a hurry these days. It was ten minutes before she emerged from her bedroom in her habitual baggy tracksuit and trainers. She hadn't even bothered to brush her hair.

On the way down to Bowater in the car, Ritchie took no notice of his mother's request to drive carefully. He'd either forgotten it altogether or enjoyed seeing the two women's panic-stricken faces as he took the bends at death-defying speed. The only up side of this was that they arrived at the doctor's surgery with a few seconds to spare.

'Drop us outside, will you, love?' said Norma, gripping on to the seat for dear life. 'And then if you could meet us in reception in an hour's time?'

'Oh, do I have to, Ma?' grumbled Ritchie. 'I'm supposed to be meeting a mate.'

'Well, your mate will just have to wait, won't he? Come on, Dawn. I'm coming in with you whether you like it or not.'

Looking back, Norma couldn't think how on earth she'd let it happen. She and Dawn made their way into the packed surgery and reported to the receptionist. Norma picked up a dog-eared copy of *Take a Break* and settled down to wait till they were called. Dawn sat next to her, staring vacantly into space. A few minutes later, however, she announced that she needed the toilet and would be back in a second.

Norma was deeply engrossed in a triumph over tragedy feature about a woman whose husband had run off with her best friend when she suddenly heard the receptionist call out the name 'Dawn Lewis'.

She looked around. Where on earth had Dawn had got to?

'Dawn Lewis,' called the receptionist again, a little more briskly this time. 'Can Dawn Lewis please go to Dr Carter's room immediately?'

Norma put her magazine down regretfully and went in search of her daughter. There was no sign of her, neither in the Ladies nor anywhere else. Dawn had simply vanished into thin air.

By this time Norma was getting increasingly anxious. Up until today, Dawn hadn't ventured out of the house for weeks. Where could she have gone?

Spotting a phone box on the corner of the street, Norma

decided to call Morton. It was possible that Dawn hadn't been able to face seeing the doctor and had rung and asked Morton to collect her in town.

'Morton? Our Dawn's disappeared. One minute she was sitting alongside me in the surgery and the next she was gone. She hasn't rung, has she?'

Norma feared she was clutching at straws, and she was right.

'No,' said Morton. 'But she's a bit funny about doctors at the best of times. She could have gone for a breath of fresh air or something. Look, you stay where you are and I'll be straight down. We'll go and search for her together.'

Dawn crept along the passageway that ran behind the row of terraced houses, counting till she got to number thirteen. She pushed open the gate, thankful that it wasn't locked and, taking a quick furtive look behind her, hurried into the back yard. There was nothing there, apart from a battered old skateboard and a row of greying babygros and muslin cloths hanging on the washing line.

She peered through the kitchen window. A large tin of Cow & Gate baby milk, a couple of empty bottles and a dummy had been left on the side. There was no sign of a baby.

Dawn gingerly turned the back door handle. She knew that the Barkers, like most of their neighbours, generally kept their houses unlocked during the day. The handle squeaked slightly as she touched it. She paused for a moment before opening the door, just in case someone had heard it.

Once inside, the house seemed strangely quiet. Tip-toeing down the familiar hallway, Dawn saw that the sitting room door was slightly ajar. Her heart beating, she peeped inside and smiled. There, at last, was what she was looking for.

Amy gradually came to and stretched out her arms and legs. She'd never done this before, not since she and Billie arrived home from hospital two months ago, but she had just had the most blissful sleep. For once in her life she'd left the ironing in a heap on the side and put off making tea for the rest of the family till later. Then, when Billie dropped off in her pram downstairs, Amy had slunk up to her bedroom to lie down.

Wondering what time it was, she gazed up at the clock on the bedroom wall. When she realised that it was almost three-thirty, she scrambled out of bed. Three-thirty. She should be down at the school gate by now, waiting for Craig to come out. She laughed to herself as she rushed down the stairs. Billie was usually like clockwork in the afternoons – but today she'd slept for a good three hours, far more than her usual two. Oh well. They'd both been exhausted. It would do them the world of good.

'Come on sleepyhead,' called Amy as she pushed open the sitting room door and looked in.

Her whole body froze. The sitting room was empty. Billie's pram had gone.

For a couple of seconds Amy thought she must be mistaken. Perhaps she'd left Billie's pram in the kitchen or something. She'd never put it there before but she'd been so tired today she could have done anything. Amy ran down the hall and into the kitchen.

There was no pram. And no Billie either.

The teenager let out a long howl of anguish. Running out into Langdale Avenue, she kept screaming and screaming. 'My baby,' she shrieked. 'My baby. My baby's gone. Someone's taken my baby.'

Amy had no idea how long it was before a few of the neighbours heard her screams and came rushing out of their houses.

'Amy,' said old Mrs Grainger, the kind-hearted pensioner who lived next door. 'Amy dear. Whatever's the matter? You're screaming fit to wake the dead.'

At the mention of the word 'dead' Amy's cries became even more hysterical than before.

Mrs Grainger was at a loss as to what to do.

'Where's your mum?' she said. 'Where's Carol? Is she out at work?'

Amy was in such a state of shock, however, that she couldn't think straight.

'I don't know,' she yelled. 'I don't know.'

Finally Mrs Grainger grabbed Amy's hand and ushered her back inside number thirteen.

'Now you sit there while I ring the police,' she said firmly. 'They'll be able to sort all this out.'

Although there had once been a bobby on the beat in Newdale, he'd been pensioned off years ago. Now all calls were routed straight through to the police station at Bowater. So it was half an hour before two police officers arrived at the house. An irate Mrs Gyngell turned up just before them, leading an embarrassed-looking Craig firmly by the hand and walking straight into the house.

'I thought you were supposed to be meeting him, Amy,' said Mrs Gyngell sternly. 'Your mum told me you'd be there every afternoon at three-thirty.'

'I'm sorry, I'm sorry,' said Amy, bursting into tears all over again.

Like most seven-year-old boys, Craig couldn't stand yucky crying and stuff so he immediately bolted upstairs to watch children's telly in his mum's bedroom.

Realising for the first time the state Amy was in, Mrs Gyngell's tone changed.

'Whatever's the matter, Amy?' asked Mrs Gyngell, crouching down to the teenager's level. She'd known Amy since the day she'd started in Newdale's reception class, nearly ten years earlier.

Amy tried to get the words out but she couldn't. Mrs Grainger was in the middle of trying to explain what had happened when the police arrived, followed seconds later by Carol Barker.

'What the bloody hell's going on?' shouted Carol. 'What are you lot doing in my house? Is someone going to tell me, or what?'

Norma and Morton had spent two hours walking round and round Bowater and drawn a complete blank. They'd kept ringing Hillthwaite Farm, but there was no answer.

At their wits' end, they finally decided to drive back to Hillthwaite – just in case Dawn had gone home and was sitting there, ignoring the telephone. They both knew she was perfectly capable of it.

'I'm worried, Norma,' confided Morton as they made their way to the car.

Norma glanced at her son-in-law. His chubby face was usually open and wreathed in smiles. But now he looked as if he was about to burst into tears. She linked her arm through his in an effort to comfort him.

'I know,' she said in a soothing voice. 'I don't think either of us realised quite how ill Dawn is. There I was, bulldozing her into seeing the doctor. She must have panicked, thought we were plotting behind her back or something.'

Lost in his own thoughts, Morton didn't appear to be listening.

'She hasn't been right since she lost the baby,' he murmured. 'Not since she had the miscarriage. A baby. That's all she ever wanted. It cut her up so bad when she lost it. I'm not much good with words but I kept telling her that it didn't matter, that we'd have a baby one day . . . All in good time. But she wouldn't listen to me. She never listens to me any more. I keep trying. Every day I try. But I can't get through to her. She won't listen.'

It was five-thirty now and the two police officers, a man and a woman, were gently trying to coax as much information as possible out of Amy.

'Where's Billie?' cried Amy. 'Why aren't you out looking for her? None of this matters. I just want my Billie back. She's so little and look, it's dark outside now. She's only wearing a nappy and a babygro – there's no warmth in them, is there? And she'll be hungry. She'll need feeding. How will they know what to feed her?'

'What colour is her babygro?' asked the woman police officer, gently. 'And what kind of nappy has she got on?'

'White,' shouted Amy. 'And her nappy's from the supermarket. But what does any of that matter? You should be out looking for her, we all should . . .'

Amy was curled in a ball on the floor, with her head buried in her lap. Her mum knelt on one side of her, Mrs Gyngell on the other.

'Amy,' said Mrs Gyngell, her voice kind but firm. 'The police are trying to help you. They know what they're doing. They've got people out searching the whole area but if you can tell them anything – anything, no matter how unimportant you might think it is, then you'll be helping Billie. You know that, don't you?'

Step by step, the police officers took Amy through everything that had happened so far in Billie's short life. Her daily routine, her sleeping and feeding times, even where Amy took her out for walks in her pram.

'And what about Billie's father?' asked WPC Jackie Sharp, the woman police officer. 'Can you give us his name? Does he see Billie on a regular basis?'

Amy's face clouded over in an instant.

'Does he, Amy?' prompted Jackie Sharp.

'No,' said Amy quickly. 'No, he doesn't.'

'What's his name, Amy?' said Brian Lloyd, the male police officer.

Amy stared at them stony-faced.

'Come on, Amy, you've got to tell us. You've got to. It might well help Billie.'

Carol had remained silent for most of the interview, but now she gripped hold of Amy's hand and touched the side of her cheek.

'Amy,' she said in a softer tone than Amy had heard for a long time. 'Look, all you care about is getting Billie back. Is that right?'

'Right,' said Amy, her tears starting to flow again.

'Well, then. What does it matter who Billie's dad is? I don't care who he is – just tell them, will you? Please? For Billie's sake.'

Chapter Thirty

Sitting on the northbound train, Freddie's head slowly sank on to Juliette's shoulder.

What a bloody awful day it had been, thought Juliette. She'd dragged Freddie halfway across the country, failed miserably in her crazy mission to find Tim and Helen and Alex Davis was going to go up the bloody wall with her when she got back to the office . . .

But all this paled into insignificance compared to her discovery that Joe was having an affair. Juliette still couldn't believe it. She and Joe had been married for getting on for eight years, for God's sake. She couldn't exactly play the innocent herself, she admitted that. There'd been that moment of madness with Tim Dawner just before Christmas. She'd so nearly ended up in bed with him. But the difference between her and Joe was that she'd drawn back from the brink. And he so obviously hadn't.

If Juliette hadn't had Freddie in tow, she would have had things out with Joe on the spot. She and Joe had always had a feisty relationship, never believed in holding anything back. But for some reason, even though Juliette had been tempted to cross-question Joe on what exactly he thought he was playing at, when it came to the crunch, she couldn't. She just couldn't. Freddie adored his dad, worshipped the ground he walked on.

It wouldn't have been fair on him. Having things out with Joe would have to wait till the weekend, till they were on their own.

The train was just pulling out of Manchester Piccadilly when Juliette's mobile rang.

'Hello,' she said without thinking.

'Where the bloody hell do you think you've been?' yelled Alex Davis.

'Er, London, of course,' blurted out Juliette, cursing herself for not switching her phone off again after Freddie's call to Joe.

'Why?' demanded Alex.

'Didn't Wendy tell you?' replied Juliette, trying her best to sound both charming and convincing. 'I've been to a press conference for *Lakeside Lives*.'

'Good stuff, was it?' inquired Alex in a menacing voice. 'Will it make a spread?'

'Mmmm, it was OK. I mean, not brilliant but I'm sure it'll make . . .'

There was a long silence at the other end of the line.

'Cut the bullshit, will you?' shouted Alex. His voice was so deafening that she momentarily had to move the mobile away from her ear. 'And if you're going to lie through your teeth, make a better job of it next time, will you? The *Lakeside Lives* team has been filming in Bowater all day. I spoke to them myself and for some strange reason none of them knew anything about this press conference in London. Not even the producer. Odd, isn't it?'

'Very odd,' murmured Juliette. 'But perhaps . . .'

At this point, Alex exploded.

'You're sailing pretty close to the wind on this one,' he hissed. 'So at least have the decency to appreciate that you've been rumbled. Come on, own up. Did you just fancy a day's shopping? Hmmm?'

This time it was Juliette's turn to go off the deep end.

288

'No I bloody didn't fancy a day's shopping,' she yelled. 'As a matter of fact, I *was* working. Just not on the story I said I was.'

'Oh yes?' said Alex, his voice heavy with sarcasm. 'And what story *were* you working on then?'

'I was trying to track down Helen Brown and Tim Dawner,' she said reluctantly.

'And did you succeed?'

'No,' conceded Juliette, her voice heavy with reluctance. 'I doorstepped their flat in Notting Hill but they weren't there. No one had seen either of them.'

'Tell me something,' said Alex.

'What?'

'Is this the way you operated on the *Daily News*? I mean, you were features editor, weren't you? So when one of your feature writers had a hunch about something, you just let them take off without telling you, did you?'

'Of course not.'

'Well, isn't that exactly what you've been doing on the *Eagle*? You read some fanciful story in the *Daily News* and hare off down to London without a by your leave to anyone. You'd probably call it using your initiative but in my book it's lack of bloody professionalism. If it happens again, girl, you're fired.'

'I'm sorry . . .' began Juliette, but Alex interrupted her.

'And for your information, the whole *Eagle* knows perfectly well where Tim Dawner is. He's been at the Denim Heart factory all bloody day. The tabloids are on his tail but he's refused to come out of his office. Put that in your bloody pipe and smoke it, will you?'

'Who was that, Mummy?' asked Freddie drowsily when she'd switched her phone off.

'Oh, only the *Eagle*,' said Juliette, trying to sound as bright as possible.

'Were they cross with you?'

'Don't be silly, sweetheart,' said Juliette. 'What makes you think that?'

'I could hear someone shouting at you,' mumbled Freddie.

Juliette stroked the top of Freddie's hair. It felt as soft as silk.

'It's just the way my boss talks,' she said. 'He's got a really loud, *booming* voice.'

Freddie laughed and closed his eyes once more.

'He sounds like a silly man,' he said.

'Yes, he is,' murmured Juliette. She couldn't agree more. 'He's a very silly man.'

Joe was back in bed. He'd tried to get to sleep but he couldn't. Even though he felt dreadful, his mind was still spinning like a bloody Catherine Wheel. The more he tried to relax, tell himself that he had tomorrow's show to think about – not to mention the first *Joking Apart* show – the more wide awake he seemed. He'd tried watching the telly, tried doing the most boring things he could think of, like polishing his shoes and ironing a shirt for tomorrow, but still sleep eluded him.

The problem was Juliette. Juliette and her bloody moods. It had been great to see Freddie today, it really had, but as for Juliette . . . She'd been so cold, so distant – anyone would think they were strangers. What the bloody hell was wrong with the woman?

By the time Juliette and Freddie stumbled bleary-eyed off the train at Bowater it was getting on for eleven o'clock. Freddie was so shattered that he could scarcely put one foot in front of the other and Juliette didn't feel much better.

'Come on, sweetheart,' urged Juliette. 'It isn't far to the car now.'

'Can you carry me?' pleaded Freddie.

Juliette glanced at him. He weighed a ton, but she was damn well going to try. She slung her bag over her shoulder, then crouched to the ground and told Freddie to climb on her back.

'Not far now,' she grimaced under her son's weight. 'You'll be snuggled up in bed in no time.'

There was no answer from behind. Turning her head awkwardly to look at him, she smiled. Freddie was fast asleep on her back.

Chapter Thirty-one

'It's Ritchie,' whispered Amy in a voice so quiet that no one in the room could be sure they'd heard it properly.

'Who?' said Jackie Sharp, the woman police officer.

'Ritchie,' said Amy, a little more forcefully this time. 'He's Billie's dad.'

Carol racked her brains in puzzlement. She couldn't think of anyone called Ritchie. Unless . . . No, surely not . . . It couldn't be . . . He was a good ten years older than her daughter.

'Ritchie who?' prompted Jackie Sharp.

'Ritchie Gray,' whispered Amy again.

'The bloody bastard,' growled Carol, her face white with anger. 'Wait till I get my hands on him. Amy's just a kid. I'll bloody kill him . . .'

It was Mrs Gyngell who leaned forward and laid a restraining hand on Carol's forearm.

'Not now, Carol,' she murmured. 'The only thing we've got to concentrate on at the moment is getting the baby back.'

Knowing that the head teacher was right, Carol nodded wordlessly. But inside, she still felt murderous. Amy had been thirteen when she got pregnant. Bloody Ritchie Gray was in his mid-twenties. Not only that, but he couldn't have been out of jail for more than a few weeks, maybe less, when it happened.

The name Ritchie Gray had clearly struck a chord with the police too. Withdrawing to the hallway, they quickly conferred before returning to the sitting room.

'Where does Ritchie live, Amy?'

'5 Top Row, Wath End,' interjected Carol before Amy had a chance to answer. 'He's a complete waste of space, but you probably know that already, don't you? He's not exactly an unknown quantity where the police are concerned. Lives with his mum, Norma Gray. She's – well, she was – a friend of mine. She's the cook at Newdale School.'

Once again, Brian Lloyd, the male police officer, retreated into the hall. They could hear him giving Ritchie's current details over the phone.

'Does Ritchie see Billie at all, Amy?' asked Jackie Sharp.

'No,' mumbled Amy, not looking up.

'Has he ever had *any* contact with her?'

'No.'

'But he knew you were pregnant?'

'Yes,' said Amy, her voice cracking.

'And how did he react when he found out?'

Carol squeezed Amy's hand comfortingly.

'Come on, love. You've got to tell the lady.'

'He went mad with me,' cried Amy. 'He said he didn't know why he'd gone with me that time. That he must have been desperate when he came out of jail. He said he didn't care what I did with the baby. But if I went and had it, he said he'd never have anything to do with it . . . Or me . . .'

'Has anything happened recently to change his mind?' asked Jackie Sharp.

'No, I don't think so,' mumbled Amy. 'Why? You don't think it's Ritchie who took Billie, do you?'

'I don't know,' said Jackie, her voice sounding grim.

'It's impossible to say at this stage. But we'll soon know about it if he has. We've got police officers on their way round there right now.'

Amy staggered to her feet. She was wearing a creased mini skirt and hooded fleece and her long pale legs were bare. She looked like a vulnerable foal trying to find its feet.

'Can we go too?' she asked plaintively. 'If Billie's there I want to see her. *I need to see her.*'

Jackie Sharp sighed to herself. A seasoned police officer who specialised in domestic issues, she was used to dealing with complex family cases. But this one was distressing in the extreme. Amy Barker was only fourteen when all was said and done – an under-age kid who'd been seduced by a much older man. Not only that, but it turned out he was a family friend who'd just done time for beating up a couple of teenagers. Poor kid. She'd got pregnant, had the baby and, from what she'd heard this afternoon, had been coping pretty well in the circumstances. And now someone had walked in and stolen her little daughter. It was tragic. Tragic for both of them.

'I'm sorry, Amy,' she said soothingly. 'It's best if we wait here. It really is. They'll ring the instant they've got any news.'

Amy collapsed sobbing into Carol's arms. She couldn't bear it. She simply couldn't bear it.

Dawn hummed softly to herself. She'd never felt so happy in her entire life.

Baby Katherine was sleeping peacefully on the sofa. Dawn had draped a couple of blankets over her tiny form and dimmed the lights. She herself sat on the floor, gazing at the baby in wonder. Then she took hold of Katherine's tiny hand and stroked each of her fingers in turn, marvelling at how perfect they were. She still couldn't quite believe that the baby who was rightfully hers was here at last.

Dawn had known that Katherine would settle without any problem. There was no question about it. The baby hadn't stirred on the walk back to Wath End. It was a good mile or so from Newdale and yet she'd slept soundly all the way. It was only when Dawn wheeled the pram up Norma's garden path and unlocked the front door that she'd looked down and realised that baby Katherine was staring gravely back at her with eyes as blue as blue.

The minute they'd got into the house, Dawn had lifted Katherine out of her pram and cuddled her tight. Dawn closed her eyes, overcome with the sensation of having a baby in her arms at last. She'd been waiting for this moment for years – and now it had come.

Dawn had no idea how long she stood in the hallway holding the baby to her chest. She didn't move until Katherine began to wail piteously – and it occurred to her that she must be hungry.

Laying Katherine carefully back in the pram, Dawn wheeled her down the hallway and into the small kitchen at the rear of Norma's cottage. Then she boiled the kettle and using the baby milk she'd grabbed from the Barkers' house, made up a bottle. Katherine was crying hard now but Dawn didn't panic. She simply put the bottle in a jug to cool, took the baby out of the pram once more and began rocking her back and forth. She knew instinctively what to do.

'Sssh, sssh,' she soothed. 'You're all right. Your milk will be ready soon. It won't be long.'

Dawn tested the temperature of the milk on the back of her wrist, just like she'd always done for the newborn lambs whose mothers rejected them. When she was satisfied that it wasn't too hot, she took baby Katherine back into Norma's cosy sitting room and began to feed her. The baby sucked at the teat with surprising force, draining it within ten minutes. When she'd finished, Dawn lifted her up to wind her and reluctant to put her down, even for a second, began cradling her in her arms once more.

Observing this touching scene from the road outside, the two police officers had to steel themselves to act. Neither of them had known quite what to expect on this one – that hard-faced yobbo Ritchie Gray and some of his mates perhaps. But not this sweet-faced woman cuddling a baby – a baby who looked exceptionally contented and well cared for.

'Come on, lad,' grimaced the elder of the pair. A father of two himself, he hated cases involving babies and young children. 'Christ knows if that baby's Billie Barker, but we'd better go and find out. Maybe you ought to go round the back, Chris, just in case she tries to make a run for it. It's unlikely, I know, but you can't be too sure.'

At the sound of hammering on the door, Dawn nearly shot out of her chair with fright. She must have conveyed her sense of fear to the baby, because the little girl started bawling fit to burst her lungs.

Dawn froze with fear, uncertain what to do. Someone wanted her baby – this was the first thought speeding through her muddled mind. Someone wanted to take her baby from her. Wide-eyed with terror, she jumped up from the chair and disappeared along the narrow hallway to the back door. Wrenching it open, ready to flee into the cold night air, she gasped in terror as she instantly came face to face with a policeman in uniform.

She turned and ran to the front door, only to confront another one. Trapped, like a fox cornered by a pack of hounds, she screamed and screamed. Her cries were so loud that – as one of the police officers told his wife later – they could probably be heard in Bowater.

'Now come on love,' said the policeman at the front door, stepping towards her. 'Try and calm down. You're going to upset the baby with all that screaming. There's no need to be frightened. We don't want to hurt you. We're here to help you, that's all.'

Clutching the baby tight, Dawn couldn't take any of this in.

'Why . . . what are you doing here?' she mumbled incoherently. 'What do you want with me? With us? We haven't done anything wrong . . . Neither of us have . . .'

'Let's go and sit down, shall we?' said the first police-man in a kindly voice.

He took Dawn by the arm and led her back into the sitting room. Glancing down the passageway, he couldn't help noting the distinctive old-fashioned pram in the kitchen and the garish changing bag with nappies spilling out of it, dumped by the door.

'What do you want?' repeated Dawn, still holding the baby close.

'A young baby by the name of Billie Barker has gone missing from her home in Newdale,' the older policeman said. 'And we have reason to believe . . .'

A look of complete bewilderment crossed Dawn's face. Then she began to laugh.

'Oh, but you've made a mistake,' she said, her face pink with relief. 'My baby's called Katherine. And she lives here. Here in Wath End. Not in Newdale at all.'

'Right, let's start from the beginning,' said the older officer, the one doing all the talking. His colleague remained by the door, just in case the woman tried to make another run for it. 'You are . . . ?'

Dawn's mind went blank. She wasn't sure who she was anymore.

The older officer tried again.

'Now then, what's your name?'

'Dawn,' said Dawn monosyllabically.

'Dawn who?'

'Dawn Lewis.'

'And how old is the baby?'

Dawn tried to work it out.

'Um, about three months. Give or take a day or two.'

'When was she born?'

'November,' said Dawn, sounding a little uncertain.

'When exactly in November?'

'November the tenth,' said Dawn. She was guessing wildly now.

The police officer scratched his head. None of this added up.

'Where was she born?'

More confident on this one, Dawn answered straight away.

'Bowater General. In the maternity unit there. I was in the ward with bright yellow walls. Like custard they were.'

'And you're sure of that?'

'Course I'm sure,' said Dawn. She gazed lovingly at the top of the baby's downy head.

'Can anyone help vouch for what you're saying?' asked the officer.

'My husband can,' said Dawn.

'And where's he?'

'At home, of course.'

'But I thought this was your home.'

'No. We live up at Hillthw . . .'

Dawn stopped in mid-sentence, suddenly aware of what she'd just said.

The older police officer nodded quickly to his colleague, who then disappeared out into the hall.

'Can I hold the baby for a bit?' said the officer left in the room. 'Have a cuddle like? They're so gorgeous when they're this age, aren't they? Both my nippers have grown up into sulky teenagers now.'

Dawn shook her head.

'Katherine doesn't like strangers,' she said, her voice just a little uncertain.

Sensing her confusion, the policeman got up and walked over to her.

'Come on, just a little cuddle,' he said, holding his arms out. 'I'm very good with babies.'

Dawn gave him a muddled sort of smile and reluctantly handed the baby to him.

'You will be careful, won't you?' she whispered.

'Of course I will,' said the policeman. Then, holding the baby with the expertise borne of years of experience, he got up abruptly and strode to the door.

'Chris?' he shouted. 'Have you radioed through?'

'Yes, guv. They're on their way now.'

A feeling of panic was starting to grow inside Dawn's brain. She tried to get to her feet but her legs felt so wobbly that she couldn't manage it and fell back against the armchair.

'Katherine,' she cried, her voice choking with grief. 'Katherine. Give my baby back . . . What are you doing . . . Where are you taking . . .'

It was at this moment that Norma and Morton burst through the front door. They rushed into the sitting room, alarm written all over their faces. After tramping round the streets of Bowater for two hours they'd sped back to Hillthwaite only to find the farm locked and in darkness. Even the stoical Morton had put his head in his hands and wept.

'What are we going to do, Norma?' he'd wailed. 'She could be anywhere. She could have walked under a car the state she's in. I'll never forgive myself if anything's happened to her. I should have done something. I should have . . .'

Completely at a loss as to what to do, Norma had wrapped her arms round her son-in-law. Morton wasn't normally one for physical contact but for once he didn't move away.

'Come on Morton, will you stop blaming yourself?' soothed Norma. 'We've both got to be strong for Dawn now, haven't we? Remember how she supported me when I got done for shoplifting? And how she's always been there for you through thick and thin?'

Morton nodded slowly.

'Well then. Now it's Dawn who needs *our* help, isn't it?'

'So what shall we do?' said Morton. He sounded like a helpless child.

'Right,' Norma had said, trying to work things through as she went along. 'We'll drive down to Wath End first. See if she's at mine. She keeps the key in her purse so it's more than likely she'll have gone there. But if she's not, then I think . . . Well, I think that we should call the police.'

At this, Morton had given a small sob. But then catching Norma's steely gaze, he'd managed to pull himself together. Norma was right. Dawn was the one they had to concentrate on now.

All the way down to Wath End in the car Norma had been dreading what they might find. Visions of Dawn lying on the floor with her wrists slashed and a packet of pills next to her kept flooding through her mind. If only she'd acted before, she kept thinking. She'd known how much Dawn minded about losing the baby. And she'd known how desperate she'd been to care for Amy's baby. If only she'd done something at the time. If only . . . Oh it was ridiculous thinking like this. They were nearly there now.

As Morton turned the corner into Norma's lane, his heart nearly stopped. Parked outside the tiny cottage was a small white car with a blue flashing light on top. It was a police car.

Neither of them uttered a word. Morton braked sharply and jumped out without even bothering to take the key out of the ignition. Norma followed close on his heels.

Stumbling into Norma's sitting room, Morton stopped in his tracks. Dawn was collapsed on the floor, sobbing her heart out, while a policeman with a small baby in his arms looked on.

'What the bloody hell's going on?' bellowed Morton. He dropped down on to his knees to help Dawn but she pushed him away. Pushed him away with surprising force.

'Give me back my baby,' she screamed at him. 'Tell him to give me back my baby.'

'Dawn?' mumbled Morton, unable to comprehend what was happening. 'What baby? What's wrong, love? What's wrong?'

Dawn stared back at him blindly. Once there had been nothing but love in her eyes when she looked at him. But now there wasn't a flicker of recognition.

Chapter Thirty-two

Carol Barker awoke in a cold sweat. She'd just had the most horribly vivid dream. She could hardly bear to think of it now because it had been so terrifying. She'd dreamed that they'd all been watching telly in the sitting room and someone had crept upstairs and snatched baby Billie from her cot.

Glancing at the illuminated clock face beside the bed, she groaned. It was only five-fifteen. She turned over and tried to drift off to sleep again. No matter how hard she tried, however, the image in her head just wouldn't go away. In the end she stumbled out of bed, taking care not to trip over Craig's empty mattress, and, her heart beating wildly, crossed the landing to check that her small grandchild was all right.

Peering round the door of Amy's tiny box room, she breathed a sigh of relief. The street lamp on the pavement outside had bathed the room in a pool of orange light and Carol could see that Amy was sleeping peacefully. And there beside her, in the little white cot that Sheila Frost, the community midwife, had given them, was baby Billie. She was shifting about in her sleep and making little sucking noises. It wouldn't be long before she woke up.

Carol was on the point of creeping out again when Amy murmured something.

Carol turned to look at her daughter and saw that Amy's eyes were wide open.

'What did you say, love?' asked Carol, tiptoeing back and kneeling by the side of the bed.

'Just thanks,' mumbled Amy. 'Thanks for helping and everything. You know.'

Carol kissed her softly on the forehead.

'Don't be soft, love,' she said. 'That's what mums are for. I know I go off my rocker with you all sometimes but I don't mean it. Not really. Now come on, you had a hell of a day yesterday. Try and get some sleep while you can. Billie will be wanting feeding soon, won't she?'

Amy smiled and snuggled beneath her duvet. She was sound asleep again within seconds.

Once again Carol tried to doze off herself but her brain was spinning like a hamster wheel. Finally, when the clock downstairs chimed six, she gave up and padded downstairs in her nightie and slippers.

She made herself a cup of strong, sweet tea and slumped on to a kitchen chair. She was tempted to go back to bed and switch on breakfast TV. A good dose of showbiz froth was exactly what she needed to blot out the awful events of the night before – but somehow she couldn't settle to anything.

Carol sighed heavily. She never ever wanted to go through another night like last night. She'd had some tough times in her life, there was no doubt about that – John abandoning her with four young children to bring up on her own, Amy announcing she was pregnant at thirteen, Craig constantly getting into trouble at school. But all of it, the whole lot, was nothing compared to the agony of last night.

It had been well after nine before they'd been given any news. She and Amy had sat staring at the carpet for hour after hour, fearing the worst. Wayne and Sarah had come in at five-thirty and as for poor Craig – she'd forgotten about him altogether till he'd stumbled down from her room at six, declaring that he was starving hungry.

It was funny, thought Carol as she sipped her tea now, because she and Vicky Gyngell had never seen eye to eye in the past. To put it bluntly, she'd always thought the head teacher was a right stuck-up cow. Not only that, but the woman had been forever on at her, accusing her of cutting corners, not cleaning the floor in the school hall properly, failing to listen to Craig's reading. But Mrs Gyngell had bloody well turned up trumps last night, that was for sure. She'd disappeared into the kitchen and made Craig – and everyone else for that matter, the police too – tea and sandwiches. Amy had refused to eat or drink any of it but when Mrs Gyngell told her it was important she had something to keep herself going, she'd listened and at least tried to force a bit down.

And then, when it got to eight and poor Craig was beside himself with tiredness, Mrs Gyngell had jumped up and announced that she was taking him back to her house for the night. Craig had admittedly looked appalled, but Mrs Gyngell had got round him by promising to make him some of her special cocoa and introduce him to her cats.

After that, it had been a matter of waiting. Just her, Amy, Sarah and Wayne – and the two police officers. Amy had kept bursting into tears and wailing that she was never going to see Billie again. Carol had done her best to comfort her but what could she say? What could she say when the only thing Amy wanted to hear was that Billie was safe? And that was the one question that none of them could answer.

Finally, at nine, Jackie Sharp's mobile had rung. They'd all stared at the policewoman – willing the call to be something hopeful, terrified that it might be the news they most dreaded.

Jackie had quickly left the room so they couldn't hear what she was saying. Amy burst into tears again and began chewing her nails, which were already bitten to the quick. Carol put her arm around her and Wayne and Sarah stared helplessly at one another. Brian Lloyd, Jackie's male colleague, paced the room several times before joining Jackie in the hall.

It was ten minutes before the pair of them returned. They both looked serious.

Jackie had crouched on the floor at Amy and Carol's feet and begun to talk to them.

'There is some news,' she said softly.

A glimmer of hope flared in Amy's eyes and then – as it dawned on her that the news might be bad – died away as quickly as it had come.

'Have you found Billie?' she said urgently.

Jackie took hold of Amy's hand and squeezed it.

'I want you to be very brave, Amy. It's hard, I know, but you must try. Now listen, some of my colleagues have found a baby. A little girl matching the description of your Billie . . .'

'She's not . . .' began Carol. But seeing the panic-stricken look on Amy's face, she broke off what she was saying.

'The baby's fine,' said Jackie firmly. 'Absolutely fine. But she's been taken to Bowater General. Just so that the doctors can check her over. It's standard procedure in cases like this.'

'Can I see her?' cried Amy, jumping to her feet. 'Can we go? Can we go right now? I've got to see her. I've got to.'

Jackie gripped on to Amy's hand.

'Amy,' she said, her eyes boring into the teenager's.

'You've got to remember that there is a chance that the baby might not be Billie. I know you want it to be her and we think it is, but please . . . please don't get your hopes up. When you see her, just stay calm and tell us whether the baby is Billie or not. Do you understand?'

Even now, thinking about it in the cold light of day, Carol could remember nothing about the journey to Bowater General. Jackie had driven her and Amy straight there in the car, while her colleague Brian stayed behind at the house with Wayne and Sarah.

There had been no messing about when they got there. They'd been directed straight up to the paediatric department and ushered into a small, private room. The baby was lying on a bed wearing just a nappy. Two doctors and a nurse were bending over her, with a middle-aged policeman looking on. Amy ignored all of them. Rushing over to the bed, she'd gazed down at the baby and unable to believe her eyes, burst into tears once more.

'Billie,' she cried, picking up her daughter and smothering her with kisses. 'It's Billie. It's really my Billie. Mum, can you see?'

Carol smiled to herself now. There had hardly been a dry eye in the house. Maybe she'd been imagining it but even the police officer had looked slightly emotional.

'So you're sure that this is Billie, your daughter?' Jackie Sharp had said, clearing her throat. ·

'Of course I'm sure,' beamed Amy, cuddling Billie as though she'd never let her go. 'Of course this is my Billie. Can you tell them, Mum?'

Carol had scarcely been able to get the words out through her tears but eventually she'd manage to nod and confirm that yes, the baby was indeed her granddaughter.

It had been another three hours before the police and the doctors had let them go home. Billie, it turned out, was none the worse for her ordeal. Indeed, now she'd been fed and changed and reunited with her mother, she was smiling and looking around – the life and soul of the party.

No one had told them anything much about what had happened. Jackie had murmured something about 'ongoing inquiries' and mentioned that they had 'a couple of people to interview' but that was all.

Sitting in her kitchen now, Carol wasn't sure how she felt about whoever it was who'd snatched Billie. Half of her was simply relieved to have her granddaughter back safe and sound, while the other half wanted to kill whoever had done such a wicked thing.

Thinking it over, it seemed impossible that Ritchie Gray could have had anything to do with any of this. He was a waste of space all right, but what on earth would he want with a baby? He'd as good as told Amy 'to get rid of it'. No, it was highly unlikely that he was the one who'd taken Billie.

At that moment the phone rang. Carol quickly ran into the hall to answer it. She didn't want Amy and Billie to wake up before they were good and ready – after last night they needed all the sleep they could get.

'Hello,' she said, trying to keep her voice down.

'Carol, is that you?'

'Yes. Who's that? Norma?'

There was a sob at the other end of the line.

'Yes,' wept Norma. 'It's me. You probably don't want to talk to me but I had to ring you. I haven't been able to sleep all night for worrying. I'm so sorry about what happened. I'm so, so sorry.'

'What the blazes are you on about?' snapped Carol. Norma sounded as if she'd gone off her trolley.

'The baby,' said Norma. 'I'm talking about the baby. I'm just so sorry. I don't know what came over . . .'

Carol stood there, transfixed. She couldn't believe she was hearing this.

'You mean it was . . .'

'Yes,' murmured Norma softly. 'But she's ill, Carol. She didn't know what she was doing.'

'Hang on a minute,' said Carol. 'Let me get this straight. Who are you talking about? *Who's ill?*'

'Dawn, of course,' sobbed Norma, breaking down all over again. 'Me and Morton, neither of us realised how ill she is. It goes back to that miscarriage of hers. And then when Amy came to stay with her . . . Dawn thought that Amy was going to let her have the baby, bring it up like. Her poor brain was so mixed up that she somehow managed to convince herself that Amy's baby was hers . . .'

Carol felt a wave of anger sweep over her.

'So you're telling me that she crept into our house and stole Billie,' she muttered. 'Has she any idea what she put Amy through last night? She's fourteen, Norma. Only fourteen. I thought she was going to go mad with the pain of it all. What is it about you and your bloody family? First Ritchie goes and gets her bloody pregnant. And now this.'

'What are you talking about?' whispered Norma, shocked by what Carol had just said. 'About Ritchie being the father. Are you sure?'

'What?' said Carol. 'You mean to tell me you didn't know?'

'No,' murmured Norma. 'Well, it did strike me a couple of times that Billie looks a bit like Ritchie did at that age, but I thought I must be imagining things. Oh Carol, I'm so sorry. About all of it. Truly I am.'

'But how could Dawn do it?' asked Carol. She couldn't rest till she knew. 'How could she do it?'

'She did it because she was ill,' said Norma quietly. 'I don't understand either. But she's very, very ill.'

'Where is she now?'

'In hospital,' said Norma. Her voice was so faint that Carol could hardly hear what she was saying. 'They've taken her to a special place near Carlisle. Morton's there with her now. But she's very confused, can't remember anything about taking the baby. It looks as though she'll be there for months.'

Carol was silent for a moment.

'What a mess,' she said finally. 'What a bloody, bloody mess.'

Chapter Thirty-three

'Don't forget to tell Mrs Booth that you had a tummy-ache yesterday, will you?' said Juliette. 'And that's why you had the day off school.'

Freddie stopped munching his strawberry jam toast and gazed at his mum.

'But I didn't,' he said, puzzled. 'I didn't have a tummy-ache.'

A wave of guilt swept over Juliette. Here she was, encouraging a six-year-old to lie – just because she didn't want to get into trouble herself. It was pathetic.

'No, you're right,' she said, after thinking about it for a few seconds. 'You didn't have a tummy-ache. I had to go to London for the day and I thought it would be fun to take you too. But it was very educational going on the tube and walking around Battersea Park, wasn't it?'

'What does educational mean?' asked Freddie, stuffing the rest of his toast into his mouth.

'It's something that teaches you a lot,' said Juliette. 'Like walking around Battersea Park taught you a lot about nature, didn't it?'

'Did it?' said Freddie, clearly not at all convinced.

'Yes,' said Juliette in a firm voice. 'Now come on, we'd better dash or we'll be late.'

Freddie didn't move. He was mulling something over in his mind.

'But going to that burger bar was very educational, Mummy,' he said finally. 'Because it taught me an awful lot about chicken nuggets and hamburgers and things.'

Juliette rolled her eyes. She should have known better than to start this conversation.

When they got to school, however, Mrs Gyngell didn't seem to be that bothered about Freddie missing school the day before.

'I shall put it down in our records as an unauthorised absence,' she said briskly. 'It's not something we approve of at Newdale but I'll overlook it just this once. Make sure it doesn't happen again.'

Juliette stared at the head teacher. She'd been expecting a five-minute lecture at the very least. But Mrs Gyngell, come to think of it, didn't look quite her usual efficient self today. She had huge dark rings around her eyes and seemed a little distracted. She was also only wearing one dangly earring rather than the usual pair, and her hair was all over the place.

'Are you feeling all right?' asked Juliette, concerned.

'Of course I'm all right,' said Mrs Gyngell briskly. 'A little tired perhaps, but that comes with the job.'

In truth, Mrs Gyngell *was* feeling a bit jaded round the edges. But her exhaustion owed less to her heavy workload and more to the demands of looking after Craig Barker for the past twelve hours. The little boy had barely slept a wink. He'd been up and down like a yo-yo all night, asking for biscuits, sweets, a hot water bottle and yet more cocoa. Mrs Gyngell felt so weary that she couldn't imagine how she was going to get through the day.

Craig, however, had seemed as merry as a grig. Despite his lack of sleep, he'd been up at dawn watching *Rugrats* on the TV. Mrs Gyngell didn't approve of this at all – her own children, now grown-up, had never been allowed to watch television before school – but she'd been too shattered to have an argument about it. Carol had rung at seven to say that baby Billie had been found safe and sound but Craig couldn't tear himself away from the telly for a single second to talk to her.

Juliette's next ordeal was facing Alex Davis. She was dreading the prospect. Grovelling to Mrs Gyngell hadn't been *too* painful. But she couldn't imagine Alex being quite such a pussy-cat.

'Wotcha Jules,' shouted Stubby cheerily as she strode through the revolving doors of the *Eagle*.

'Morning,' said Juliette with a smile. 'Hey, Stubby. I was away all day yesterday. Did I miss anything? I'm relying on you. You're my only source of gossip now Cara's gone.'

'Just the usual,' sighed Stubby, adjusting his cap. 'Geoff Lake had a couple of suits to see him and Alex Davis wasn't exactly the life and soul of the party . . .'

'So what's new?' murmured Juliette.

'Giving you a hard time, is he?' said Stubby.

'Too right he is,' said Juliette with feeling.

Stubby glanced at her for a second.

'He's not all bad, you know,' he said out of the blue.

'Isn't he?'

'No,' said Stubby. 'You might find it hard to believe but underneath that gruff manner there's a heart of gold.'

'Really?' said Juliette. 'But you're absolutely right. I do find it hard to believe. No, not hard exactly. More like impossible.'

Juliette's negative opinion of her boss was borne out the instant she set foot in the newsroom.

'Juliette Ward,' bellowed Alex from the other side of the editorial floor. 'Come here at once.'

It was just like being at school, thought Juliette with a grimace. No doubt Alex was going to give her an ear bashing and threaten her with detention.

Her fears were proved right when Alex proceeded to castigate her in front of the whole newsroom for her 'laziness, lack of professionalism and downright dishonesty'. Most of the other hacks kept their heads down during this tirade, though Juliette was certain that they were secretly loving every minute of it.

'I'm sorry,' she said, trying to look contrite. 'It won't happen again.'

'You're absolutely right it won't happen again,' yelled Alex, jabbing his finger in the air. 'Because I won't let it happen again. If you step out of line one more time I'll have you fired. I've said it before but I mean it this time. And now you can go and do the police calls for the news desk. They're short-staffed today.'

Juliette shrugged her shoulders and made her way to her seat. To tell the truth, she couldn't care less what she did at the *Eagle* any more. If ringing round the emergency services to check if they had any news stories for the paper was Alex's idea of a punishment then it was fine by her.

She spent the next half-hour painstakingly making her way down the list of police, ambulance and fire stations in the Bowater area. The best she'd managed to come up with so far was a chip pan fire in Burndale.

She'd left Bowater police till last, figuring that they were the most likely source of a decent story. She was absolutely determined to find something good – if only to spite Alex bloody Davis.

'Have you got anything for us?' she asked the desk sergeant.

'Couple of burglaries,' he said. 'You interested?'

'Yes please,' said Juliette. He sounded like he was selling her a kilo of Granny Smiths.

She took down all the details and thanked him profusely.

'Anything else you can think of?' she asked.

'There might be,' he said. 'Can you hang on a sec? I'll just have to check.'

Juliette doodled in her notebook for a couple of minutes while the chap conferred with a colleague.

'You still there?' he asked when he got back to the phone.

'Yep,' said Juliette. 'I'm not going anywhere.'

'Right. Now, this is a bit of a sensitive one but we had a baby snatch in Newdale last night. That any good to you?'

Juliette had to restrain herself from sounding too keen.

'Yep,' she said. 'Have you got the details?'

'A two-month-old baby was taken from her home in Langdale Avenue in Newdale at approximately two forty-five yesterday afternoon. Thanks to painstaking detective work by police the child was recovered from a house in Wath End at around nine pm. She was taken to Bowater General where she was found to be unharmed and in good physical condition. She is now back with her mother.'

Juliette tried to contain her excitement as her pen flew across her notebook. Despite the officer's stilted police jargon, she knew a good story when she found one. And this sounded like a corker.

'Has anyone been charged?' she asked.

'No,' said the police officer. 'And speaking off the record I'm not sure they will be. It seems that the woman who took the baby is mentally ill. She's a friend of the family and although they are very upset I think that both they and the police are inclined to let things be.'

'How about some names?' said Juliette.

314

'Sorry. I can't give you any at this stage. But Newdale isn't a very big place, is it?'

Instead of informing Alex Davis about the baby snatch, Juliette opted to tell Ray Henry, the news editor. It was a news story after all, so she was just following office protocol. But she couldn't wait to see Alex Davis's face when he realised that putting her on the police calls this morning had given her a cracking story.

It was only when Juliette and one of the *Eagle* photographers arrived in Langdale Avenue half an hour later that it struck her that the snatched baby could well be Billie Barker.

Larry May, the photographer, marched straight up to the first house in the terrace, ready to knock on the door.

'Hang on a minute, Larry,' said Juliette. 'I've got a feeling that it's number thirteen. I know the family who lives there. Let's try them first.'

The instant Carol opened the door, Juliette knew that her instincts had been right. Carol looked tired and drawn, as if she'd been up all night worrying. And even though it was gone ten-thirty she was still wearing her nightie.

'Oh,' said Carol dully. 'It's you. I should have known it wouldn't be long before you lot turned up like a bad penny.'

For a few seconds, Juliette forgot that she was there to do a job. The thought of someone creeping into this house and stealing Amy's baby was simply too shocking for words. She couldn't shake it from her mind.

'I'm so sorry, Carol,' she said. 'I've only just heard what happened. Are Billie and Amy OK?'

'I think so,' said Carol wearily. 'I wouldn't go so far as to say that they're none the worse for their ordeal but they seem all right. Billie's sleeping and Amy's in the kitchen having some breakfast, poor lamb. I could hardly persuade her to leave the baby and come downstairs.'

'Look,' said Juliette, trying to find the right words. 'You know that I work for the *Eagle*, don't you? Now, if you don't want anything in the paper, just say the word and we'll go.'

There was a sharp intake of breath from Larry May, who was standing behind her. You had to give it to Juliette, he thought. She certainly didn't believe in taking the conventional approach. Most reporters would have put their foot in the door and kept on talking till the woman allowed them in.

'Give us a moment, will you?' said Carol. 'I can't agree to anything without asking Amy first. But if she's happy to talk to you then that's fine by me.'

'You're stark raving bonkers,' hissed Larry after Carol had shut the door. 'She'll never say yes now you've given her time to think about it. She'll refuse to answer the door next time we ring.'

Juliette glared at him.

'Just trust me on this one, will you?' she said. 'I know them and if they won't talk to me they won't talk to anyone. Amy's a nice kid. She'll see me. I'm positive she will.'

Larry, like most snappers of Juliette's acquaintance, was a natural pessimist. He didn't look at all convinced.

'It's bloody cold, isn't it,' he said, blowing on his fingers. 'They'd better not keep us waiting out here for too long. I'm due at the football later on.'

Juliette stamped her feet on the pavement. She wished she'd worn something warmer.

'Give it another couple of minutes and Carol will invite us in for a brew,' she said, trying to sound confident. 'I bet you.'

316

'How much?'

'A pint?' said Juliette.

'You're on,' said Larry, slapping her on the hand.

In fact Carol kept them waiting for another ten minutes. But sure enough the door finally opened and Carol, who'd managed to throw on an old tracksuit, gave Juliette a thumbs-up sign.

Juliette and Larry followed Carol along the dingy passageway and into the kitchen, where Amy was sitting at a tatty Formica table. She was wearing a pair of faded flowery pyjamas that made her look even younger than fourteen. Looking up from the bowl of cornflakes she was eating, she gave Juliette a shy smile.

'It was nice of you to come,' she said. 'You promised you would.'

'And here I am,' said Juliette. She wanted to give Amy a huge hug but she hung back, anxious not to overwhelm her. 'But you do know that this isn't a social call, don't you, Amy? The *Eagle* is very keen to do a story about you and Billie. About Billie being snatched, I mean.'

'OK,' mumbled Amy, continuing to spoon cereal into her mouth.

'I can't think of anything worse than someone stealing your baby,' murmured Juliette.

'It was awful,' said Amy in a quiet voice. 'I was so scared I'd never see her again. I couldn't have coped with that. I never want to let her out of my sight.'

Up until now Juliette had remained standing, while Larry hovered awkwardly by the door.

'Why don't you both sit down?' said Carol, pulling out a couple of chairs.

'Thanks,' said Juliette. She put her notebook on the table and stared at Amy. 'What I want you to do, Amy, is to tell me in your own words exactly what happened. Right from the very beginning. From the moment when

317

Billie fell asleep in her pram to the moment the police arrived. Can you do that for me?'

Amy, as Juliette well knew, was a girl of few words. But once she started talking about the snatch, she couldn't stop. Her horror at discovering her precious baby was missing spilled out so fast that Juliette, scribbling it all down in shorthand, was hard pressed to keep up.

Once Juliette was satisfied she'd got Amy's account straight, she turned to the question of who had taken Billie.

'Dawn,' whispered Amy, ignoring the warning look Carol shot at her. 'It was Dawn. How could she do it? How could she do it when we were so close? She was so kind to me all the time I was pregnant. I can't believe she could do something like this. Mum says she wanted a baby, so she took mine. But how could she do that?'

Juliette's jaw dropped at this revelation. Poor Dawn, she thought. Poor, poor Dawn. It had been pretty obvious how desperate she was for a baby of her own – her strange behaviour in the maternity ward bore testament to that. But to steal Amy's baby . . . She couldn't get her head round it. No one could, she was sure.

Amy wiped her nose, trying to stave off the tears.

'She's ill, love,' said Carol, putting her arm round her daughter. 'I'm bloody livid with her myself, you know I am. I'll never ever forgive her. But we've got to remember that she's ill and she needs help.'

'I s'pose,' said Amy. 'Is it all right if I go and check on Billie now?'

'Course it is, love,' said Carol. 'Off you go.'

Once Amy had trailed upstairs, Larry brought up the subject of pictures.

'What's in it for Amy?' asked Carol, sounding more like her usual hard-nosed self.

'We'd be prepared to pay her five hundred pounds,'

said Juliette quickly before Larry could jump in and start muttering about picture desk budgets and stuff. She was well aware that the *Eagle* didn't usually pay for pictures but this story was different. And for God's sake, the sum was peanuts to the *Eagle* – they'd recoup it in no time syndicating the photograph to other papers.

Carol's face brightened. That kind of money would make a huge difference. The three of them – she, Wayne and Sarah – worked their bloody socks off but it was still hard making ends meet. Life, especially now they had another mouth to feed, was tough in Langdale Avenue.

'Sounds fair enough,' she said. 'D'you want to do them now then?'

The moment Juliette saw Amy sitting on her bed cradling Billie in her arms, she knew the pictures were going to be sensational. Amy had put on a plain white T-shirt and jeans and, at Juliette's behest, pulled her shoulder-length hair back from her face. Looking at her, laughing and beaming at Billie, the love for her baby daughter shimmering in her eyes, Juliette felt a lump in her throat. It was heartbreaking to think about Dawn, about her longing for a child of her own, but for Amy and Billie perhaps this was going to be a new beginning.

Chapter Thirty-four

It was after six by the time Juliette collected Freddie from Fi Nicholson's house that night. Luckily, no one minded. Freddie was engrossed in building a giant wooden railway track with Lizzie and Molly while Fi had put her easel up and was sketching the three of them.

'The perfect domestic scene,' murmured Juliette as she crept into Fi's kitchen.

'Don't you believe it,' chuckled Fi. 'You should have seen us half an hour ago. Lizzie and Molly were tearing each other's hair out and I'd just dropped a bag of self-raising flour all over the floor. In fact Freddie was the only calm one. Isn't that right, Freddie?'

Freddie gave her a toothy grin and bent over his train track again. Juliette went over and ruffled his hair.

'Come on, sweetheart,' she said. 'It's time we were off.'

'Ohhh,' protested the children in unison.

'Can Freddie stay the night?' said Lizzie brightly. 'He could sleep in me and Molly's room. It would be so cool. Loads of other people at school have sleepovers.'

'Oh I don't think so,' said Juliette, gathering up Freddie's coat and lunch box. 'Your poor mum puts up with us quite enough as it is. And I've got a pretty good idea what sleepovers are like – staying up late and midnight feasts under the covers.'

Fi glanced at Juliette. Her friend looked as immaculate as ever, in narrow black trousers and a short scarlet jacket, but her pale, washed-out face gave the game away. She was clearly knackered.

'He's very welcome to stay, you know,' said Fi. 'He's no trouble and the girls would love it.'

'Please, please say I can,' yelled Freddie, grabbing her by the waist. '*Please*. I promise I'll be good.'

Juliette was torn in two. Fi did so much for them as it was – she didn't want to impose on her any more than she already did.

'Are you sure, Fi?' she said. 'Haven't you got enough to cope with without having Freddie to look after as well?'

'Quite sure,' said Fi firmly. 'And if he gets homesick then either me or Dai can pop him straight back, can't we? You're only a few doors away.'

Knowing she was well and truly beaten, Juliette rushed back home to collect Freddie's pyjamas, toothbrush and Growler, his favourite teddy. She handed them to Fi, then wrapped her arms round Freddie.

'I'll miss you, sweetheart,' she told him. 'See you in the morning.'

Wandering barefoot into her bright yellow kitchen, Juliette couldn't settle to anything. It was weird, she reflected. A couple of hours ago, she would have given anything to go home and put her feet up in front of the telly by herself. She'd felt so emotionally drained by the baby snatch story that all she'd wanted to do was go home and sleep for twenty-four hours on the trot. But now that Freddie was staying the night at Fi's and she didn't have to make his tea or read him a bedtime story she felt like a lost soul. She kept drifting aimlessly round the house. She'd lit the fire, and poured herself a glass of white wine, though it sat untouched on the table. It was stupid, she knew it was, but she couldn't even be bothered to clear the breakfast things up or sort out her clothes for the next day.

She was on the point of giving up and going to bed when the doorbell rang.

Convinced that it must be Fi or Dai bringing a homesick Freddie back, she rushed to answer it.

'How come you're back so soon . . .'

Her words died in her throat as she realised that it wasn't Freddie at all. It was Tim Dawner.

'Hello stranger,' he said softly.

Her heart almost missed a beat at the sight of him but she sternly told herself not to be so ridiculous.

'What the hell are you doing here?' she said briskly.

'I thought you'd be pleased to see me,' he murmured.

Juliette couldn't think of anything to say. Tim looked as divine as ever, in a pair of beige chinos and a stylish black polo neck. His hair was slightly longer than when she'd last seen him and he hadn't shaved for a day or so, but it suited him somehow.

'What's the matter, Jules? Aren't you even going to ask me in? You don't seem very friendly.'

Juliette hesitated. She hadn't felt very charitable towards Tim since the piece in the *Daily News* announcing that he and Helen were back together again.

'I'm not feeling very friendly,' she muttered.

A pained look crossed Tim's face.

'But that's terrible. Why not?'

Suddenly Juliette relented. Old Mr Spratton next door, and some of the other neighbours too, would have a field day if they saw Tim Dawner hanging around on her doorstep at this time of night.

'Oh, all right,' she said reluctantly. 'You'd better come in.'

Juliette felt so irritated with him that instead of taking

him into the sitting room, with its soft lighting and blazing open fire, she showed him straight to her tip of a kitchen.

'You'll have to ignore the mess,' she said, waving her hand vaguely at the cereal-encrusted bowls and half-drunk mugs of tea. 'Just take me as you find me.'

'I can't think of anything I'd like more,' said Tim. He moved alarmingly close.

'Er, why don't you sit over there?' suggested Juliette hurriedly. 'Glass of wine?'

'Great,' said Tim. 'But come on, Jules, what's the matter? I thought we were friends. Why are you giving me the cold shoulder all of a sudden?'

'D'you really mean to tell me you don't know?'

Tim stared at her with an astonished expression on his face.

'Don't be silly – I wouldn't be asking you if I knew, would I?' he said.

Juliette wasn't convinced he was telling the truth. She felt a bit like a small bird being played with by a cat.

'I saw the piece about you in the *Daily News*,' she said finally.

'Oh yes?' said Tim, giving nothing away. 'Which piece was that?'

It was the innocent-looking smile on Tim's face that did it. Juliette finally saw red. The events of the last couple of days – the trip to London, the discovery of Joe's infidelity, the baby-snatch – had used up all her reserves of energy. She simply didn't feel in the mood for playing games she didn't understand.

'Oh for God's sake, Tim. You know bloody well what I'm talking about. The story in the *News* about you and Helen being back together. All that lovey-dovey stuff about *"we realised how much we needed each other . . ."* All

323

that crap. It made me bloody sick. I wanted to throw up when I saw it.'

Tim stared at her for an uncomfortable thirty seconds or so. Juliette held his gaze as long as she could but in the end she had to look away.

'Why did it make you bloody sick, Jules?' he whispered softly, catching hold of her hand.

Juliette wrenched it away and glared at him.

'Because I was the one you were supposed to be giving stories to,' she blurted out, aware that she sounded like a spoilt child. 'If anything happened at Denim Heart, I'd thought you'd tell me about it first.'

'I tried to ring you,' said Tim. 'And what about all those e-mails I sent you?'

'But none of them mentioned anything about Helen being back on the scene.'

'You're kidding yourself, Jules,' said Tim, 'and you know it.'

Just the very sound of his voice, the way he said 'Jules' made her go weak at the knees.

'I am not kidding myself.'

'I think you are.'

'I am not,' insisted Juliette.

'Shall I tell you what I think?' said Tim.

'You're obviously going to anyway.'

'Yes, I suppose I am,' admitted Tim. 'I think that you're jealous.'

Juliette snorted with derision.

'In your dreams,' she muttered.

Tim, however, didn't appear to be listening.

'I've been having a bloody horrendous time, Jules,' he murmured. 'The business is in a mess. The bank has got its men in suits trawling through everything they can lay their hands on. And Christ knows where Helen's got to . . .'

324

'But I thought that you and Helen . . .'

'Well, you thought wrong,' snapped Tim. 'Didn't it cross your mind to wonder why the *News* didn't use a picture of us cooing to each other like a couple of lovebirds?'

'Well yes,' said Juliette slowly. 'But I just assumed you refused to let them take one. People do, you know.'

'Maybe,' said Tim. 'But not this person, Jules. No, I'm afraid I told a bit of a whopper to the *Daily News*. I'm not particularly proud of it but that's exactly what I did.'

'But why?' exclaimed Juliette, aghast. She still quite couldn't grasp what Tim was on about.

'I was desperate. I had to do something. The business was going pear-shaped – I had to restore everyone's confidence in it. Maybe it was a crazy thing to do but I figured that if I got the *Daily News* to run a story saying that me and Helen were a team again, that we were sorting the business out together . . . Well, I thought that it would help matters. And actually, I think it's worked. The orders have come flooding in over the past couple of days. And our suppliers are back on board too. Mind you, I hadn't bargained for all the tabloids pursuing me all round the houses to follow the story up. The office has been completely mad over the last couple of days.'

'But . . . but . . . what did Helen say about all this?' Juliette was so astounded that she could hardly get her words out. 'Didn't she mind?'

Tim shrugged his shoulders.

'Haven't a clue,' he said. 'I still haven't heard a word from her. Not since she walked out. Well, nothing apart from that hysterical call at Christmas. Not that I care any more.'

Juliette was still trying to take all this in.

'I . . . I don't know what to say,' she mumbled.

Tim caught hold of her hand again and this time she didn't snatch it away.

'Don't say anything,' he whispered. 'You must know how I feel about you by now. It's you I want to be with, Jules. Not Helen. No one else. I never thought I'd feel this way about anyone . . . Please tell me you feel the same way.'

Juliette's head was spinning. First at Tim's cool announcement that his reconciliation with Helen had been a complete fabrication. And now at this extraordinary declaration.

She leaned back in her chair and took a series of deep breaths. She was attracted to Tim, there was no doubt about it, but she felt in such a muddle. She was married, for God's sake, married with a small son. What the hell was she playing at even looking at another man? As her thoughts turned to Joe, however, she suddenly remembered their meeting the day before. It was quite obvious that he'd slept with that girl Anne – there'd been no mistaking his dishevelled appearance and flushed, guilt-stricken face. He'd let her down, and yet there he'd been, bold as brass, trying to pretend that everything between the two of them was absolutely fine and dandy.

One thing was crystal clear to her though. Joe didn't want her any more, whereas Tim seemed to need her desperately.

'Come on, Jules,' sighed Tim. He was still holding her hand tight between his own. 'Put me out of my misery. Tell me you feel the same way.'

Juliette looked at him across the table.

'I . . . I'm not sure,' she began. 'Everything's such a mess. I don't really know what I think.'

Tim got up from his chair and walked round the table to her. He pulled her to her feet and, without giving her a chance to say no, took her in his arms and kissed her passionately. For a few seconds, Juliette stood there like a block of ice, determined not to respond. Then slowly her resolve ebbed away and she found that she was kissing him back.

'I want you so badly, Jules,' he moaned.

His fingers crept beneath her T-shirt and began to caress her breasts. Juliette groaned with pleasure.

'Don't stop,' she murmured. 'That feels . . .'

'Can we go upstairs?' Tim whispered. 'And I won't stop, I promise you . . .'

Juliette took hold of Tim's hand and led him up to her bedroom. She hadn't set foot in it since first thing that morning and the place was as chaotic as the rest of the house. There were clothes strewn all over the floor, a cup of milk and one of Freddie's Thomas the Tank jigsaws, half-finished on the bedside table.

Later on, she wondered what on earth had come over her. How had she come to be standing in her own bedroom – surrounded by the paraphernalia of family life – in the arms of a man she barely knew, still less trusted? It could have been the sight of Freddie's jigsaw or Joe's old coat hanging on the back of the door but she suddenly dropped Tim's hand like a hot brick and shook her head.

'I'm sorry, Tim,' she said, 'but I can't. I just can't. Not here. Not where me and Joe . . . I'm sorry. It's too soon. I'm not ready.'

She could have sworn that an expression of irritation swept across Tim's face. But seconds later, he was all sweetness and light.

'No, it's my fault, darling,' he said, taking her in his arms once more. 'I should have been more sensitive. Will you promise me one thing though?'

Juliette looked at him questioningly.

'Let's get right away from all this. From the *Eagle* and Denim Heart and everything else. I know a fantastic country hotel up on the Mull of Kintyre. If I book a room there at the weekend, will you come with me?'

'But it's Friday tomorrow,' protested Juliette. 'I can't possibly get away at such short notice. And Joe's coming up. He'd wonder what was going on if I announced I was off to Scotland for a couple of days.'

'Next weekend then?' suggested Tim.

Juliette was starting to feel hemmed in.

'I'll think about it,' she said, trying to keep her voice as casual and light as possible. Then, seeing the despondent look on his face, she quickly added, 'I mean, I might be able to. I just need to see how I'm fixed, with Freddie and work and stuff.'

And Joe, she thought. One way or another, she was going to have to ask him the truth about Anne. And soon.

Chapter Thirty-five

Juliette slept appallingly that night. Images of Joe and Anne entwined in bed together kept floating through her head. And then just when she'd got them out of her mind, up popped Tim Dawner, threatening that if she didn't spend the weekend with him he'd tell Joe about 'us'. She'd protested over and over again that there wasn't any 'us', but he refused to listen.

It was a huge relief when the alarm went off at seven. She couldn't wait to go and collect Freddie. But even this didn't turn out quite as she'd hoped. When she arrived at Fi Nicholson's house, he pleaded to be allowed to go to school in Fi's car, with Lizzie and Molly.

'All right,' she agreed, half-pleased that he liked Fi's girls so much, half-disappointed that he didn't appear to have missed her at all. 'I'll see you this afternoon then.'

Work wasn't much better either. She'd been looking forward to seeing her baby-snatch story splashed across the front page, with her byline in full technicolour glory. She couldn't believe her eyes when the first edition of the paper appeared.

'STOLEN' shrieked the Eagle headline, while the strap-line underneath ran; 'I thought she was my friend but she snatched my baby.'

Yes, Geoff Lake had splashed the story all right, but it was Larry May's photograph of Amy and Billie that took up the whole of page one, together with *his* picture byline. Juliette's interview was all over pages two and three, admittedly, but it wasn't quite the same as having it on the front.

'Cracking story,' muttered Alex Davis as he strolled past with a carton of coffee from the office machine.

Juliette did a double-take. Was she imagining things or had her boss just paid her a compliment? She must be more tired than she'd realised. He couldn't possibly have said anything nice.

Glancing after him, it crossed her mind that Alex looked worse than ever today. He'd never been a snappy dresser, that was for sure, but today his appearance was shambolic. He looked as if he'd slept in that stained old tweed jacket of his. And as for his trousers – you'd probably catch something if you went too close.

The day seemed endless. Apart from Geoff Lake coming over to congratulate her on her story, Juliette spent the entire morning and afternoon poring over a couple of tedious council reports about noise pollution. That, and referring calls from the national papers about the Amy and Billie photograph to the picture desk.

At five pm she filed her council stuff to Alex and began putting her coat on. Thank God it was nearly the weekend.

When her direct line flashed, she was inclined to ignore it. She was desperate to get straight off home. But old habits died hard. There was always the possibility that it might be something earth shattering.

'Hello,' she said.

'Is that Juliette Ward?'

The voice was female, well spoken and unfamiliar to Juliette. It was probably someone from the pro-hunting lobby – or someone who wanted to rant and rave about teenage mums. She'd had a couple of those already today. She wished she hadn't been stupid enough to answer the phone.

'Yep,' she said in a weary voice. 'Who is it?'

The woman hesitated for a few seconds.

'It's Helen Brown,' she said finally. 'You've been running a lot of stories about Denim Heart. I think it's high time we met, don't you?'

Stunned by this announcement, Juliette started stuttering.

'Y-y-yes, I think we should,' she said.

'Are you free this evening?' said Helen. 'I need to put you straight on a few things.'

'Where?' Juliette asked quickly.

'Do you know the Peacock Hotel?' said Helen. 'It's a small bed and breakfast place on the far side of Lake Bowater. I'll be there at six-thirty.'

'But how do I . . .'

The question on the tip of Juliette's tongue was how could she be sure that the caller really *was* Helen Brown, and not some hoaxer pulling a fast one. But it was too late. Helen – or the woman who claimed to be Helen – had put the phone down.

Juliette instantly dialled 1471, only to find that the caller had withheld their number. To hell with it, she thought, she'd just have to go along to the Peacock Hotel and find out for herself. She'd been trying to track Helen Brown down for so long; she couldn't possibly ignore the call.

On the spur of the moment, Juliette decided to tell Alex what had happened. She'd never believed in taking stupid risks – especially with Freddie to think of – and she'd be crazy to turn up to this meeting without telling someone at the *Eagle* where she was going. The woman could turn out to be a raving lunatic.

'I'll come with you,' murmured Alex. He didn't bother

to look up from the press release he was reading.

Juliette nearly fell over backwards. Alex Davis virtually never left the office. By all accounts he hadn't been out on a job since he'd started at the *Eagle* donkey's years ago.

'Are you sure?' she said.

'I wouldn't have said so if I wasn't, would I?' grunted Alex. 'We'll leave in twenty minutes. That should give us plenty of time.'

'Do you want to drive or shall I?'

'You drive,' said Alex gruffly.

Before she did anything else, Juliette rang Fi to ask yet another favour.

'Something really, really important's come up at work,' she said. 'Could you face hanging on to Freddie till nine or ten?'

'Of course I don't mind,' said Fi. 'You know that. In fact he can stay the night again if you want. He's still got all his stuff here.'

'Oh Fi, that's so kind, but I'll come and collect him tonight. I really missed him last night. And Joe's coming home this weekend too.'

Juliette was overcome with guilt when she put down the phone. Why did life always have to be so complicated? Perhaps she was naïve but she'd thought that moving north would change everything. She'd been confident that living up here would mean she could work *and* have loads more time for Freddie. The best of both worlds, in other words. But the *Eagle* was proving to be every bit as demanding an employer as the *Daily News*. Not only that, but her four-day week still hadn't materialised either. It was pretty obvious she couldn't carry on like this much longer.

Alex was strangely silent on the drive to the Peacock. When Juliette glanced at him his eyes were closed and he was snoring.

Juliette felt increasingly nervous as they neared the far side of the lake. Her heart was thumping so loudly that she was amazed it didn't wake Alex. Bloody hell, she was about to meet Tim's partner, the woman he'd done nothing but slag off for months.

Much to her surprise, the Peacock turned out to be a complete dive. Tim had told her constantly that Helen was a woman of expensive tastes – and her flat in Notting Hill had certainly borne his claim out. It was dark by the time they drew up outside the Peacock, admittedly, but she'd been expecting it to be a pretty guesthouse with roses round the door and breathtaking views over Lake Bowater. In reality it was a scruffy establishment a couple of streets away from the lake.

Alex awoke with a start as Juliette switched off the engine. He took one look at the Peacock and frowned.

'Are you sure this is the right place?' he muttered.

'I think so,' said Juliette. 'Doesn't look much cop though, does it?'

'Certainly doesn't. Come on, then. Let's go and find out what Helen Brown's got to say for herself.'

'How shall we play it?' asked Juliette. It was ridiculous, she knew, but she'd be quite happy to take a back seat and let Alex take over the interview.

Alex stared at her.

'What do you mean?'

'Well, there are two of us. Do you want to ask the questions, or shall I? Or shall we both chip in?'

'You're the interviewer,' said Alex. 'You do it.'

'Can I ask you something?' said Juliette.

'Fire away.'

Juliette hesitated for a moment. She wasn't quite sure how to phrase this.

'What made you come with me tonight? Is it to check up on me? Check that I'm doing what I say I'm doing.

333

Or is it because you think that I've become too closely involved with Denim Heart?'

'Haven't you?' said Alex dryly. 'Become too closely involved, I mean.'

'Of course not,' said Juliette. She was well aware that she sounded defensive.

'There's been talk in the office about you and Tim Dawner,' said Alex.

Juliette opened her mouth to protest but Alex cut in again before she had a chance.

'Look Juliette. What you get up to in your private life is neither here nor there as far as I'm concerned. As long as it doesn't interfere with your work. So it's totally up to you what you do with Tim Dawner – or anyone else for that matter – outside office hours. But, and this is a big but, you've got to remain objective at work. I'm not teaching my grandmother to suck eggs – you know it as well as I do. Personally, the more I hear about Mr Dawner, the more I'm inclined to think he's an out and out shit, but I'm not going to let that cloud my judgement either.'

Juliette flushed. She knew Alex had a point but that didn't make it any more comfortable to listen to.

'Right,' she said quietly. 'I'll bear it in mind.'

'And while we're on the subject of your work, can I say something else?'

Juliette nodded her assent.

'I seem to have spent the past four months, or however long it is that you've been with us, bawling you out for something or other. And perhaps I've been a little unfair. But that's not to say that I haven't got the highest regard for your work. Certainly, when I saw that splash of yours today . . . well, no one else on the *Eagle* could have dug up that story . . .'

Stunned by this praise from a man who had done

nothing but castigate her for months on end, Juliette was speechless.

'Right, now I've got that off my chest, shall we go in?' said Alex.

The woman in reception directed them to a down-at-heel sitting room with harsh megawatt lighting and an ornate bar in the corner. The room was empty, apart from a glamorous blonde woman and an elderly gentleman sitting on a sofa in the large bay window.

The blonde looked up from the sheaf of papers she was reading when Juliette and Alex came in.

'Juliette Ward?' she asked.

'Yes. Are you Helen?'

'Yes – and this is Michael Johns, my solicitor. The way things stand, I thought he should be here.'

'Right. And this is Alex Davis, the *Eagle*'s features editor.'

Juliette didn't mean to be rude but she couldn't help staring at Helen. After hearing so much about this woman, it was extraordinary to meet her in the flesh. Helen was wearing an elegant black trouser suit and a long string of pearls round her neck, but she looked much older than Juliette had imagined. She'd assumed that Helen was about thirty-seven – Tim had told her she was a couple of years or so older than him. But meeting her in the flesh, noticing the fine lines around her eyes, Juliette reckoned she looked nearer forty-five.

'You said on the phone that you wanted to put me straight on a few things,' said Juliette.

'Yes, I did, didn't I?' said Helen. 'The thing is that I've been away for a couple of months. In South Africa. And I had no idea that people at home were quite so interested in me until I spoke to a friend of mine on Christmas Eve. She told me that Tim had been making all sorts of wild accusations about me. Wicked accusations, all of them untrue. At first I couldn't cope with coming back to face the music. But after a bit I thought – bugger it, I'm going to make sure Tim Dawner gets what's coming to him. He's done his best to destroy my good reputation – but he's not going to get away with it. No way.'

'South Africa?' questioned Juliette. 'But Tim told me you were in the Caribbean. I've been trying to track you down there for weeks.'

'Did he now?' murmured Helen. 'That's strange because I quite distinctly remember telling him that I was going to Cape Town. In fact I gave him my number there. *And* I rang him on Christmas Eve.'

Juliette was dumbfounded by this revelation, though she tried not to show it.

'Maybe we'd better start at the beginning?' she said. 'When you and Tim launched Denim Heart?'

Juliette and Alex both listened attentively as Helen described the early days of the business.

'We moved up here because we wanted to launch a mail-order business of our own. It seemed the ideal place. Overheads – everything from wages to rents – were so much cheaper here. I hit on the idea of selling make-up and beauty products because there was so little choice outside London. And it really took off. Especially with the Internet and everything. It took off in a big way.'

Juliette stopped scribbling in her notebook for a second. Once again, Helen's version didn't tally with Tim's at all. Tim had always claimed that Denim Heart had been his idea, his concept. Yet here was Helen saying she was the brains behind it.

'How did you divide up your roles in the business?' asked Juliette. 'I mean, who did what?'

'That's what wore me down in the end,' said Helen with a heavy sigh. 'It wasn't too bad when we started out. I managed the business and Tim took control of the financial side. But it became more and more apparent that he simply wasn't up to the job. The Denim Heart accounts got increasingly chaotic. And instead of admitting that he couldn't cope, Tim just kept lying about it. Typical of him.'

'Be careful what you say,' murmured Michael Johns, Helen's solicitor.

'I'm sorry,' said Helen. 'But truly, if it hadn't been for my hard slog Denim Heart would have gone out of business long ago. The trouble with Tim is that he wouldn't know the truth if it hit him in the face. I suppose I turned a blind eye to it for years because I was in love with him. Well, I thought I was. He didn't give a damn about me. But in the end I couldn't pretend any longer. And even then he was completely pig-headed. He wouldn't listen to a word I said. It had become clear to everyone, the whole workforce, that he was making a pig's ear of everything but he still wouldn't let me take charge and sort it.'

'So what did you do?' asked Juliette.

'I bailed out. I told Tim that I'd had enough and I needed a break. Looking back, it was a cowardly thing to do. I admit that. But I simply couldn't bear to stand by and watch the company I'd worked my guts out for being destroyed. And all by Tim's arrogant incompetence.'

'What are your plans now?' asked Juliette.

Helen groaned and put her head in her hands.

'Well, I'm not going to sit around while Tim goes about making false and completely libellous accusations against me, that's for sure,' she said finally. 'I mean, what would *you* do if someone made up a tissue of lies about you? It's very upsetting. I still can't believe that after all the years we spent together he actually had the brass neck to claim that I'd defrauded my own company.'

337

'And had you?' asked Juliette. She felt uncomfortable asking Helen this outright but she had to.

'Of course not,' said Helen. 'Unlike Tim, I'm straight. What you see is what you get. Can't you understand that he's made up this cock and bull story to cover up his own ineptitude? Or has he blinded *you* with his charm too?'

Juliette didn't answer. Helen was closer to the truth than she probably realised.

'But what about the flat in Notting Hill?' said Juliette quickly. 'Tim told me you used Denim Heart money to buy it. He said it cost £320,000.'

This last question seemed to upset Helen more than anything.

'That's a wicked thing to say – and Tim knows it,' she muttered. 'My parents bought me that flat when I was twenty-one. I was going to sell it a couple of years ago so I got it valued. The estate agent said it was worth around £320,000. But in the end I changed my mind. No way did Denim Heart have anything to do with it.'

'But I thought your parents were dead,' said Juliette slowly.

'What?' said Helen, aghast. 'Did Tim tell you that?'

'Yes.'

'Well they're not,' said Helen, wiping her eyes with a tissue. 'My parents were very fond of him at one time. That is so wicked. I don't know how he can live with himself saying things like that.'

A sick feeling came over Juliette as she listened to all this. God, she'd always thought she was so clever. So astute. She'd believed that no interviewee would ever pull the wool over her eyes. Yet ever since she'd first met Tim Dawner she'd swallowed everything he'd told her. Swallowed everything hook, line and sinker.

And what was worse, she'd compromised herself, her job and her newspaper by getting personally involved with him. Helen Brown was absolutely right. She *had* been blinded by Tim Dawner's charm.

Chapter Thirty-six

When the first edition of the *Eagle* dropped midway through Monday morning, Juliette felt sick with nerves. She'd spent most of Saturday night writing up the interview with Helen – and she still hadn't been happy with it when she filed it to the copytaker late on Sunday. The whole story was a legal minefield for a start, what with Helen making wild, unsubstantiated accusations against Tim and threatening to sue him. Not only that, but Juliette was apprehensive that having swallowed everything Tim had told her, she was now in danger of falling into exactly the same trap with Helen.

It hadn't helped either that Joe had gone and bloody let her down again. Freddie had been chattering nineteen to the dozen about his dad arriving when she picked him up from Fi's on Friday night. And then the instant they set foot through the door, Joe had rung to say that rehearsals for *Joking Apart* had over-run and he was going to have to film all through the weekend.

'But Freddie is going to be in pieces,' Juliette had told him. His absence meant she'd have to put off tackling him about Anne. And it wasn't exactly going to help her write up the interview with Helen either. She'd been relying on Joe to look after Freddie while she worked.

'I'm so, so sorry, sweetheart,' Joe kept saying. 'Can

you tell Freddie that I'll make it up to him a million times. The show's just got a few teething troubles, that's all. Once we get everything sorted we won't have hiccups like this. The producer swears everything will be fine.'

Freddie had been so upset that Juliette ended up taking him to an indoor play centre on the Saturday to make up. But despite this, he'd still been whiny and difficult for most of the weekend.

Back in the office on Monday morning, she had the added problem of feeling like death. Freddie had crept into her bed during the night complaining that he had a headache and his tummy hurt. She'd given him some medicine and they'd both managed to get a bit of sleep. But while Freddie had woken up bright, chirpy and pretty much back to his normal self, Juliette had thrown up twice before leaving the house. She'd been so convinced she was going to be sick again on the way to work that she'd stuffed the washing-up bowl in the car – just in case.

'You look appalling,' Alex had muttered when she dragged herself into the office soon after nine.

Juliette had glared at him. Clever clogs remarks from Alex Davis were all she needed right now.

'Look who's talking,' she'd mumbled. 'My God, if I didn't know better I'd have sworn you'd been sleeping in those clothes for a fortnight.'

She'd known immediately that she'd hit a raw nerve. Alex was brilliant at handing out insults, but he couldn't handle being on the receiving end. His whole face had fallen at Juliette's jibe and for one awful moment she'd thought he was about to burst into tears. Stubby's words from last week suddenly drifted through her mind. 'He's not all bad,' the kind-hearted security guard had said. 'Underneath that gruff manner there's a heart of gold.'

'I'm sorry, Alex,' she said quickly. 'Don't take any notice of me. I feel like something the cat dragged in today. I'm sure I'll snap out of it.'

Juliette had retreated to her desk and tried to keep out of Alex's line of vision for the next couple of hours.

It was eleven-twenty by the time Striker, the youngest and spottiest messenger on the *Eagle*, slapped a copy of the first edition on to her desk.

'Thanks Striker,' she murmured, and as usual, Striker blushed bright red and scuttled off.

Juliette gazed at the front page. Geoff Lake had splashed with the latest unemployment figures for the region – boring – but at least he'd used her story about Helen as the second lead on the front page. And her in-depth interview was on the centre spread.

'*BACK FOR GOOD*' ran the headline. '*Helen vows to save ailing Denim Heart.*'

Juliette started to skim through her piece. She didn't get very far. The words were swimming in front of her eyes. She couldn't face reading another word about Denim Heart.

'Juliette?' said a concerned voice behind her. 'Are you all right?'

Juliette lifted her head to see two Alex Davises standing beside her. She must be hallucinating.

'You look terribly pale,' he said. 'I thought you were going to faint.'

'I'm sorry,' Juliette moaned. 'I think I must have caught some bug off Freddie. There's loads going round.'

'Come on,' said Alex bossily. He picked her bag off the floor and plonked it on the desk.

'What are you doing?' mumbled Juliette.

'I'm sending you home,' said Alex. 'There's nothing much doing at the moment – I'll get one of the snappers to drive you home.'

'But . . .' began Juliette, then stopped, too feeble to argue.

'But nothing,' said Alex. 'Anyway, for once you haven't got the strength to tell me where to go. You're going home. Come on. No arguments.'

By noon, Juliette had collapsed into bed. One of the photographers had dropped her off at the cottage and she'd just about summoned up the energy to crawl upstairs. If she could get a bit of rest before Freddie came home from school then she'd be OK.

Sure enough, Juliette awoke three hours later feeling much more like her usual self. She rang Fi and told her what had happened.

'I'm absolutely fine now,' she said. 'Do you think you could possibly drop Freddie straight back this afternoon? It would be nice to have a bit of extra time with him.'

'Let's see how you are first,' said Fi firmly. 'If you suddenly have a relapse then I'm taking him to our house for tea.'

Juliette gingerly made her way downstairs again. The mere thought of eating or drinking anything first thing had made her feel sick – but now her mouth was absolutely parched.

She was standing in the kitchen in her dressing gown when the doorbell rang. She frowned. Who the hell could that be? She only knew a handful of people round here – and they'd all expect her to be at work.

She padded down the hall in bare feet and opened the door. When she saw the tall figure of Tim Dawner standing in front of her, she stepped back a foot or two. He was the last person on earth she wanted to talk to right now.

'It's not a good time, Tim,' she said nervously, pulling her flimsy dressing gown more tightly round her. 'Can we leave it for another day?'

Tim's face looked thunderous. She'd never seen anyone look so angry.

'No, we bloody well can't,' he said, barging straight past her and into the hall.

'I'm not up to this,' she said in a feeble voice. 'I'm really not. I'm not feeling very well. The office sent me home . . .'

'I know,' he said bluntly. 'They told me. But you're wasting your time. You may have conned those idiots you work with but you certainly can't con me. That little girl lost act of yours doesn't fool me for a second.'

He stared at her, his eyes black and accusing. Then suddenly, he completely lost control and pushed her up against the wall.

Terrified, Juliette struggled to get his arms off her shoulders. If she'd been feeling stronger, she might have stood a chance. But in her current fragile state, he was immovable.

'You bloody bitch,' he spat. 'You bloody, bloody bitch.'

The whole of Juliette's body felt like concrete. She was so frightened she couldn't get her head round what was going on.

'I'm sorry, Tim, but I don't understand what you're talking about . . .'

'And so you bloody should be sorry,' he hissed. 'You sneak off to meet Helen behind my back and you don't even have the guts to tell me. After all that we've meant to each other . . . you go and do this to me . . . you double-crossing bitch . . . How can you believe her lies? How can you print them?'

Thinking as quickly as her addled brain would allow, Juliette decided that maybe if she let him rant and rave for a bit, he'd get it out of his system and go. But he didn't. He kept on and on at her for ten minutes or more, saying repeatedly that he'd thought he

344

could trust her and how could she go behind his back like this.

'Helen's mad,' he shouted. 'She's stark raving mad. Surely you can see that? She pushed off and left me in the lurch and now she can't bear the fact that I'm managing fine without her. I thought you loved me, Jules. I thought we had a future together. But it's pretty obvious that you were just stringing me along, isn't it? You went to bed with me because you wanted to get a better story out of me. You're nothing but a whore.'

Tim's onslaught had become so vicious by this stage that Juliette was beginning to feel really frightened.

'But we didn't go to bed together, Tim,' she muttered. 'You know we didn't . . .'

'You're nothing but a fucking prick-teaser, aren't you Jules?' he said, his voice growing more menacing by the second. 'And you know what happens to them, don't you?'

Juliette's heart was racing with fear now. She couldn't believe that she'd ever trusted this man. That she'd ever been taken in by him. She'd been so dazzled by his charm, so bewitched by his good looks, that she'd never peered below the surface and seen him for what he really was. A lonely, inadequate loser.

'Tim,' she said softly. She knew from her experience of interviewing victims of crime that it was crucial to stay as calm and composed as possible. 'Look. I'm sure we can sort this out. I've got a bottle of wine in the sitting room. Why don't I go and pour us both a glass and then we can talk about this? I didn't mean to upset you. Really I didn't.'

'You're not going anywhere, Jules,' said Tim. He grabbed her hand and squeezed it hard, making her wince with pain.

'What do you want me to do then?'

Tim smiled menacingly at her.

'You just said that we didn't go to bed together, didn't you Jules?' he murmured.

'No, we didn't . . .'

'Well then,' said Tim. 'I think it's high time we made up for it, don't you?'

Once again, Juliette struggled to free herself from his grip.

'You love your little games, don't you Jules . . . Well, let's just . . .'

Out of the blue, the doorbell rang. Juliette froze. She could hear Freddie on the other side of the door, chattering merrily to Fi about something he wanted to watch on TV.

Please, please don't go away, she willed. Please Fi. Do something.

The doorbell rang again and this time Juliette had the presence of mind to scream. Instantly Tim clamped his hand over her mouth and dragged her into the kitchen. Juliette heard Fi flip the letterbox open and shout 'Juliette. Are you all right?'

Tim still had his hand pressed over her mouth so she couldn't make a sound. They stood there for five minutes or so, with Fi shouting 'Juliette' over and over again. Finally she gave up and Juliette heard the click of the garden gate as they disappeared down the lane.

'If you think your friends are going to help you, then think again,' smirked Tim. 'Now then, I think it's time for bed, don't you?'

Holding her arms tight behind her, Tim forced her upstairs. Upstairs to the room where a week earlier she'd so nearly made love with him. Juliette closed her eyes. How could she have been so stupid?

Tim pushed her roughly down on to the bed and fell on top of her. Then noticing the telephone on the bedside table, he got up and wrenched it out of its socket.

'No one's going to disturb us now, Jules,' he murmured as he began to rip off her dressing gown and nightie.

Tears began to course down Juliette's cheeks but Tim didn't take any notice.

'Admit you want me,' he said in a sinister-sounding tone. 'Come on Jules. Admit it.'

'I . . . I want you . . .' whispered Juliette, the tears flowing faster and faster.

'That's good,' said Tim. 'That's very good. Say it again.'

Juliette was about to do as he said when she heard the sound of a car screeching to a halt outside. This was followed by the thundering of feet up the garden path.

'Police,' shouted a male voice through the letter-box. 'If you don't open this door in ten seconds we're coming in.'

Tim panicked.

'I'll barricade the door . . .' he muttered to Juliette. 'Stop them getting in.'

'There isn't time,' cried Juliette, her voice hysterical. 'Look. If you run down to the kitchen you can escape out of the back door.'

Tim stared at Juliette, unable to decide. She just wanted him as far away from her as possible. Finally though, he charged down the stairs and made a run for it.

Seconds later, Juliette heard police smash the front door in and dash through the house.

'I'm in here,' she moaned, before bursting into tears all over again.

For hours afterwards, Juliette couldn't stop shaking. To her dismay, the police insisted on taking her down to

Bowater police station – they said she had to undergo medical tests *and* make a full statement. All Juliette wanted was to sit and cuddle Freddie but she realised that they had a job to do.

'Have you found Tim Dawner yet?' she asked Detective Inspector Colin Black at around six pm.

'No, but don't worry,' he said, his voice grim. 'It's only a matter of time till we get him. In fact I should think that that paper of yours will be able to help track him down.'

Juliette hit her forehead with the back of her hand. In all the confusion it hadn't even occurred to her to ring Alex Davis.

'Can I give them a call?' she said quickly.

'Course you can,' said DI Black, passing her the phone on his desk. 'Use this.'

True to form, Alex was still at his desk.

'My God, that's terrible, Juliette,' he muttered, his concern clear. 'Are you sure you're all right?'

'Well, I am now,' said Juliette. 'But I thought you of all people would be saying "I told you so". You always reckoned that Tim Dawner was a complete bastard.'

'Maybe,' said Alex. 'But I'm just relieved you're all right. He could have killed you.'

Juliette was all too aware of this herself, but she didn't want to think about it.

'You'll do a piece, though, won't you?' she said. 'Because he's still on the run ... It might help the police catch him.'

Alex fell silent for a moment.

'You will, won't you?' said Juliette urgently.

'What? Oh yes, of course we will. No, I was just thinking about something else. Would you be up to writing a first person piece, Juliette? About what happened, I mean.'

348

Juliette swallowed hard.

'What? Now?'

''Fraid so. If we're going to run it, it'll have to be tomorrow.'

Juliette's first person piece about the attack was one of the hardest things she'd ever written. It was fine relating other people's stories but telling your own – especially when it showed what a gullible fool you'd been – was another matter entirely.

Juliette wrote the piece in laborious longhand, sitting at the DI's desk. It took her forty-five minutes and when she'd finished she read it aloud to herself.

I've been a journalist for more than ten years, she'd written. *I've covered murder trials, been on drugs raids and trekked through a Kenyan game reserve. But I've never been as scared as I was in my own home yesterday afternoon . . .*

Juliette read on to the end. Then, before she could change her mind, she picked up the phone and filed the piece to the *Eagle's* evening copytaker.

Chapter Thirty-seven

After his hectic few days filming *Joking Apart*, Joe was feeling jaded. It was six thirty-five am now and the Radio Wave breakfast show had been on air for more than half an hour. Only another one hundred and forty-five minutes to go.

Joe yawned and stretched his arms in the air. Steps were singing their latest anodyne hit – they were due to finish in fifty-three seconds. What was he going to drone on about next?

Stuck for ideas, he pulled the pile of Tuesday morning's papers towards him and began to sort through them. All of a sudden, his heart began to pound. Jules's face was plastered all over the front of the *Chronicle*. And the *Daily News*. Oh my God, and the *Express*. What the hell was going on?

Without even thinking about it, Joe swiftly pressed a few buttons on the computerised play-out system. He needed to ensure that the instant the Steps track finished, the George Michael one would start and when that was through, then U2 would launch into their latest release. That should just about give him time to try and find out what had happened to Jules.

With mounting alarm, Joe turned first to the *Daily News*.

The boss of a high profile beauty business is being hunted by police following an attack on a former Daily News *journalist,* ran the story.

Tim Dawner, the whizz-kid managing director of the Cumbrian-based mail-order cosmetics company Denim Heart, allegedly forced his way into the home of writer Juliette Ward yesterday afternoon. Juliette, thirty, managed to raise the alarm but she suffered bruising and shock in the attack. By the time police arrived at Juliette's house in the picturesque Lake District village of Newdale, thirty-five-year-old Tim Dawner had managed to escape . . .

Tim Dawner, thought Joe. The name definitely rang a bell . . .

At that moment Annie Smith charged into the studio.

'What do you think you are doing?' she yelled at him. 'We've got enough to fit in before the seven o'clock news without you playing three tracks on the trot. You're supposed to be announcing the results of our "What's That Sound" competition – or had you forgotten . . . ?'

Joe glared at Annie. They still hadn't managed to resume the easy-going relationship they'd had a few months ago.

'Fuck the "What's That Sound" competition,' he shouted back. 'I've just discovered that Jules has been attacked. I've got to find out what's going on.'

Annie's face went pale.

'Oh my God,' she said. 'Is she all right? And what about your little boy?'

'I don't know,' grunted Joe. He flung his headphones down on the desk. 'But if you could give me a few minutes. Please?'

First he dialled Jules's number in Newdale, praying

that she'd pick the phone up. Within five rings, however, the answerphone switched on.

'Hello. This is Juliette Ward. I'm sorry but I can't take your call right now. If you'd like to leave your name and number . . .'

Next he tried Jules's mobile. There was an answerphone message on that too.

Joe slammed the phone down and put his head in his hands. He was becoming increasingly fearful. Where on earth were Jules and Freddie?

In fact, Juliette and Freddie were safely tucked up in bed at Fi's house. The police had sent a carpenter round to the cottage to repair Juliette's front door but she hadn't been able to face going back home. Not yet. Not so soon. And especially not with Tim Dawner still on the loose. God only knows what he was capable of in his current state.

So once again, Fi had come to the rescue.

'You can stay for as long as you like,' she'd told Juliette, giving her a huge hug.

'But there's hardly enough room for all of you as it is,' said Juliette, thinking guiltily of Fi's three-bedroom cottage, a mirror image of her own.

'Oh, we'll be fine,' Fi had said airily. 'Lily can go on a camp bed in Lizzie and Molly's room – she won't mind. And you and Freddie can have Lily's room. It won't exactly be the Ritz, but we'll manage.'

'I can't thank you enough,' said Juliette. She didn't think she'd ever met anyone as kind-hearted as Fi.

It was after nine by the time Joe managed to track Juliette down to Fi's house. He'd somehow managed to stumble through the breakfast show, making telephone calls in between bursts of music and bumbling chit-chat. He was well aware that he'd probably just given the worst performance of his entire radio career but quite honestly he didn't give a damn.

He'd kept ringing Jules's direct line at the *Eagle* – rung it over and over again. Finally, at nine, Jules's boss had snatched it up.

'Yes?' said Alex Davis in a grumpy voice.

'It's Joe Ward – Juliette Ward's husband. I'm trying to track her down.'

After what had happened the day before, Alex was immediately suspicious.

'When's her birthday?' he demanded.

'June the twelfth,' said Joe. 'Look, it really is me, you know. Joe Ward.'

'What's your boy called then?'

'Freddie,' said Joe. 'Look, please tell me where she is? I'm going out of my mind here.'

'She told me she was staying with a friend of hers,' said Alex Davis. 'Fi Nicholson? Does that name ring any bells? If you wait a second, I'll find the number for you. I'm sure I wrote it down somewhere.'

As soon as Joe had the number, he rang Fi.

'Are Jules and Freddie all right?' he yelled as soon as Fi picked up the phone. He was so panic-stricken that he didn't have time for niceties like 'how are you?' or 'could I possibly speak to Jules?'

'They're both fine,' said Fi, her voice calm. 'I've just dropped Freddie off at school with my daughters – we thought it was best to try and keep things as normal as possible. And Juliette's gone back to bed.'

'Why?' said Joe. 'Isn't she feeling well?'

'It's probably the shock of it all but she keeps saying she feels sick. I'm sure it'll wear off. My husband's a GP so we'll take good care of her, I promise. And the *Eagle*'s given her the rest of the week off – that should help.'

'I should bloody well think so too,' grunted Joe. 'If it

353

hadn't been for them she would never have got involved with this Dawner guy. He sounds like a madman.'

Fi didn't say anything. Juliette hadn't confided in her but Fi suspected that she and Tim Dawner had been closer than she'd let on. She'd seen that flashy car of his outside Juliette's cottage late at night a couple of times.

'When are you coming up?' asked Fi. 'Juliette could do with a bit of support right now. Freddie too.'

'I . . . I'm not sure,' mumbled Joe. 'Getting time off my radio programme isn't a problem but I'm in the middle of shooting this new game show. We've got to film four shows this week so I might not be able to get up till Friday . . .'

'That's a bit of a shame,' murmured Fi.

'Can you explain to Jules?' said Joe. 'Tell her I'll ring her later. And that . . . oh, it doesn't matter.'

Joe had been on the point of asking Fi to tell Juliette that he loved her. But at the last minute he felt embarrassed. And anyway, he was pretty sure that it wasn't reciprocated.

Helen Brown was sitting in Tim Dawner's office at Denim Heart reading the *Eagle*. She'd always coveted this vast room, with its breathtaking views across the fells, but the instant they'd launched the company Tim had commandeered it for himself. *She'd* been assigned to a windowless box room next to the factory floor.

She'd read Juliette's first-hand account with horror – and yes, a certain amount of sympathy. She too had had her suspicions about the nature of Juliette's relationship with Tim – but she couldn't help feeling sorry for the woman. She knew from experience what Tim could be like when he lost his temper. He'd never hurt her, that was true, but his rages could be terrifying. They seemed to erupt out of nowhere, over the tiniest thing.

Whatever happened, Helen knew that Tim was firmly out of the picture at Denim Heart now. The police were bound to track him down eventually and charge him with assault. Not only that, but by the time the bank had finished trawling through Denim Heart's deplorable accounts he would probably be done for fraud too.

Helen sighed heavily. She was astute enough to recognise that Denim Heart didn't stand a hope in hell of surviving. The receivers would be moving in any day now – and they'd strip it bare of all its assets. She had to accept that. No, the most she could hope for was that one day she'd be able to start all over again. On her own. The end of Denim Heart, the end of all that she'd worked for, was heartbreaking. The only thing she could do was look to the future. And maybe – without bloody Tim throwing his weight around and making a hash of things – just maybe she might be in with a chance next time round.

Chapter Thirty-eight

By Friday, Juliette decided she was well enough to go back to work. She still felt dire in the mornings, but she was going to die of boredom if she didn't get off her backside and do something soon. And she was sure Fi must be getting fed up of her drooping around the house all day.

When Juliette arrived at the *Eagle* after dropping Freddie and Fi's two younger daughters off at school, she was stunned by the welcome awaiting her. The minute Stubby spotted her walking into reception, he rushed over and planted a huge smacker on her cheek.

'What on earth's that for?' grinned Juliette.

'Because you are a superstar,' beamed Stubby. 'And because we've all missed you.'

He then proceeded to kiss her on the other cheek.

'And that one's for not grassing up Alex Davis,' he whispered in her ear.

Juliette looked puzzled.

'You what?' she said. 'What are you on about, Stubby?'

'Alex told me that he was sure you'd guessed about his little trouble and all that. He said that you could have gone spreading it around everywhere. But you didn't. That's sweet of you, love. You could have landed him – and me, come to think of it – in big, big trouble if you had. I would definitely have been for the chop. No doubt about it.'

Juliette stared at him in utter incomprehension.

'Stubby, I really don't have a clue what you're on about,' she said.

The diminutive security guard winked at her.

'Right Jules,' he said. 'If that's the way you want to play it, we'll say no more about it.'

Shaking her head in confusion, Juliette stepped into the lift and pressed the button for the first floor.

When the lift doors slid open at the newsroom, she couldn't believe her eyes.

There, draped across the entire editorial department, was a huge banner with the words 'Welcome Back Juliette' emblazoned on it.

Juliette gulped.

'I d-don't know what to say,' she stuttered.

'Don't say anything then,' said Geoff Lake, the editor, plonking a massive bouquet into her arms. 'But on behalf of everyone at the *Eagle*, we want to say – well, that we're very glad to have you back. Very glad indeed.'

Embarrassed by all this fuss – and incredibly touched – Juliette wiped a tear from her eye. She didn't know what was the matter with her; she seemed to get emotional about everything these days.

'Thank you,' she said. 'Thank you so much.'

'Right,' said Geoff. 'Now we've got the speeches out of the way, I want you all back to work. You'll be pleased to know that circulation was up a fraction last month – so let's make sure it goes up even more this month.'

When Juliette sat down at her desk, she realised that Alex Davis was standing right behind her.

'Don't worry, I won't overload you too much today,' he said. 'Could you just . . . ?'

'Alex?' said Juliette suddenly.

'What?'

'Can I ask you something? It's been puzzling me for a while. And I know that I'll burst if I don't ask you. The trouble is that it's a bit confidential.'

'Fire away,' said Alex.

'It's Stubby,' said Juliette. 'When I arrived this morning he kept on thanking me for not blabbing my mouth off about "your little trouble". That's what he called it anyway.'

Alex's face turned ashen.

'Oh, I'm sorry,' said Juliette, noticing his discomfiture. 'I didn't mean to speak out of turn.'

Alex stood there for a few moments, not saying anything.

'Oh, it's all right. I know I can trust you. I can, can't I?'

'Of course,' nodded Juliette.

'You've probably heard that my marriage has broken up. Well, Isabel – my wife, I mean – is living in our house. With our two daughters. We've got a huge mortgage on the place so we're trying to sell it. But I didn't know where to go. I couldn't afford a place of my own. Not yet, anyway. So for a few weeks I kipped in the office. Stubby turned a blind eye and I managed somehow. There's a shower upstairs and I've been taking my clothes to the laundry down the road. But, it's funny . . . I thought that you'd guessed all this.'

'No,' said Juliette. 'Well, I know I was rude about your jacket once – but I had no idea. You should have said. It I'd known you didn't have anywhere to go, you could have come and stayed at my house.'

'Oh it's all right now,' murmured Alex. 'One of the subs has offered me a room – so I've moved in there for the time being. In fact I can't believe I was so stupid for so long. It's probably why I felt so lousy all the time. I never got a decent night's sleep and I know that I took it out on people here. Especially you.'

'I'm glad you've sorted things out,' muttered Juliette.

'Me too,' said Alex. 'Now, can I give you a weather feature to do? It shouldn't be too tricky. We don't need it till next week so there's no pressure.'

After her few days off, Juliette quite enjoyed the novelty of getting her teeth into a story for a change. She spent half an hour interviewing the *Eagle's* amateur meteorology expert and had just put the phone down when it immediately rang again.

'Mrs Ward?' said a female voice.

'Speaking,' murmured Juliette, scanning through the last paragraph on her computer screen.

'Oh thank goodness. I've been trying to get through to you for ages. It's Mrs Bailey. From Newdale School. I'm sorry to bother you at work but it's Freddie. He's had a bit of an accident. He fell off a bench in the playground and he's split his head open. I don't think it's too serious but Mrs Gyngell has taken him to Bowater General. To the casualty department.'

The blood drained from Juliette's face. Forget what Tim Dawner had done. This was her worst nightmare – something terrible had happened to Freddie.

Without even thinking, Juliette got up and rushed out of the office. She had only one thought in her head – and that was to get to Freddie as soon as possible. Nothing in the world mattered except getting to Freddie.

She charged through reception – Stubby tried to waylay her but she took no notice – and ran into the street. It was best to go on foot, she thought, breaking into a run. Bowater General was only a few streets away from the *Eagle* at the most.

When she got to the hospital, she dashed up the

front steps and, without stopping to ask for directions, followed the red signs to the Accident and Emergency Department. All the time she kept muttering 'please let Freddie be all right, please let Freddie be all right' like a mantra to herself.

By the time she got to Casualty she was so out of breath that she could hardly speak.

'Freddie Ward,' she spluttered to the first nurse that she saw.

'And you are . . . ?'

'Juliette Ward,' mumbled Juliette. 'His mum. Where is he? I need to see him.'

'He's in the third cubicle on the right,' said the nurse. 'The paediatrician's just been looking at him. And so's his . . .'

Without waiting to listen to the rest of what the nurse was saying, Juliette ran down the corridor and into the cubicle that the nurse had pointed out. She opened the curtain and slipped in.

To her astonishment, Freddie was sitting up in bed, with a huge crepe bandage round his head and a broad grin on his face. And sitting next to him, holding his hand, was . . . Joe.

'Oh sweetheart,' she said, flinging her arms round her small son. 'Are you all right? I was so worried . . .'

'I'm all right,' smiled Freddie, who seemed as happy as a sandboy. 'The doctor said I could go home. And guess what? He glued my head back together.'

'What do you mean?' asked Juliette, not understanding a word of this.

'He told me I had a nasty cut but he could make it better with some special glue,' beamed Freddie. 'And do you know what?'

'What?' said Juliette.

'He said that I was the bravest boy he'd ever known.

And look, he gave me a special certificate. Didn't he, Daddy?'

Up until this moment, Juliette had barely even acknowledged Joe. But now she glanced over Freddie's head and gave him a quick smile.

'How come you got here so fast?' she asked, mystified as to how her husband had arrived before her. She hadn't expected him to get to Newdale till tonight.

'I got off early,' he said quietly. 'The school rang me on my mobile on my way up. They'd been trying to get hold of you but your phone was constantly engaged. Anyway, I'd just come off the motorway so I headed straight for the hospital. Mrs Gyngell and Freddie had only just got here themselves.'

'How long are you staying this time?' asked Juliette in a curt voice.

'That's what I need to talk to you both about,' murmured Joe.

Juliette stared at him, fearing the worst. Was Joe on the point of telling her the very thing she most dreaded hearing? The thing she'd been dreading since she'd spotted the diary piece about him and Annie Smith?

'What?' she whispered.

'I've jacked it in,' he grinned.

Juliette's head was spinning. What was Joe talking about? What had he jacked in?

'What do you mean?'

'Radio Wave,' he beamed. 'I've jacked in Radio Wave.'

Juliette still couldn't make head or tail of what Joe was on about.

'But you love it there,' she said. 'You always said that doing the breakfast show was your big chance and you had to go for it.'

'Yes, well that's what I did,' said Joe. 'I went for it. And I think I made a pretty good job of it too. But I've

361

been doing a lot of thinking over the past few days and I've come to the conclusion that . . .'

He hesitated and gazed lovingly at Freddie.

'What?' demanded Freddie.

Joe ruffled his hair.

'That I can't stand being away from you, Freddo,' he said. 'I've missed you so much over the past few months and I can't stand it. I can't stand it any more.'

'So what are you saying, Joe?' said Juliette. 'Can you explain all this in plain English?'

'I'm saying that I handed in my notice after the breakfast show,' said Joe. 'I'm far too old for Radio Wave anyway. The kids who listen to it are into rap and body piercing. They don't want an old codger like me droning on about the Sex Pistols and Johnnie Rotten.'

'But where . . . where are you going to work?' asked Juliette.

'I've got *Joking Apart*,' said Joe. 'It's going to pay pretty well – and I'll only have to be away for two days a week at the most. And you never know, maybe I can pick up some radio work round here too.'

Freddie threw his arms round his dad.

'So we're all going to live together again,' he shrieked excitedly.

'Yes son, we are,' smiled Joe. 'We are, aren't we Jules?'

Juliette nodded wordlessly. Joe's bombshell had taken her by surprise – that was for sure. But it was quite obvious that his momentous decision to join them up north had nothing to do with her. He'd made that clear. He was coming up here because he missed Freddie. He'd said nothing whatsoever about missing her.

Chapter Thirty-nine

Freddie insisted he wanted Joe to drive him home from the hospital. Juliette felt hurt at the way he instantly chose his dad – though at least it meant she could pop back to the *Eagle* and explain why she'd dashed out so dramatically. Afterwards, anxious to spoil Freddie after his ordeal, she stopped off to buy all his favourite things – chicken nuggets, chocolate milkshake and strawberry jelly. She was on the point of buying a bottle of champagne for Joe too, but thought better of the idea and put it back on the shelf.

By the time she arrived in Newdale, Joe and Freddie were immersed in a game of Frustration. The pair of them were so absorbed that they barely said anything when she walked in laden with carrier bags. Juliette shrugged and went into the kitchen to start preparing Freddie's tea. She felt like the invisible woman.

When the chicken nuggets and chips were ready, Juliette put her head round the sitting room door.

'Do you think you could give Freddie his tea, Joe?' she asked. 'I've got to finish something for work.'

'Course,' said Joe. He didn't bother to glance up from the Frustration board.

'If it's not too much trouble,' she murmured under her breath.

Juliette disappeared upstairs to her bedroom. She

didn't have a piece to finish at all but she wasn't going to sit downstairs like a spare part. As she sat down on the bed however, she was overcome with nausea all over again. She lay down on her back, praying that it would go away soon. Feeling like this was the last thing she needed right now.

Five minutes later, Joe appeared at the door with a cup of tea in his hand.

'I've brought you this,' he said sheepishly.

'Thanks. Can you put it on the table?'

Joe did as she asked and came and sat down on the bed next to her. He put his hand on her forehead.

'Are you all right?' he said, his voice full of concern. 'You look dreadfully pale.'

'Oh, I'll be fine,' she murmured. Just the smell of the tea made her feel sick.

'Do you want me to go then?'

Part of Juliette wanted to cry out 'No, no. Please stay. I need you. I need you more than I've ever needed you'. But her fierce sense of pride – that, and the certainty that he'd been having an affair with someone else – stopped her.

'Yes. I'll come down later.'

But by the time Juliette woke up, the house was eerily quiet. Glancing at the alarm clock beside her, she saw that it was nearly midnight. She must have been asleep for five or six hours. She crept out of bed and – still wearing the now very crumpled shirt and trousers she'd been wearing all day – put her head round Freddie's door. Freddie was fast asleep on the top bunk and there, sleeping on the bottom bunk, was Joe. He could barely fit into it. His legs stuck out at the bottom and he hardly had room to turn.

Juliette gulped back a tear. Joe was obviously so repelled by her these days that he'd rather sleep in Freddie's room than with her.

She tiptoed down into the kitchen to get a glass of water. When she switched the light on, she saw that Joe had left her a note.

'The police rang,' he'd scrawled. 'Tim Dawner's been arrested near the Mull of Kintyre. They said they'll probably charge him in the morning.'

A shiver of fear ran through Juliette's body as she read this. She slumped on to a chair. The Mull of Kintyre. She bet they'd picked him up at the country hotel he'd talked about taking her to. What an idiot she'd been. It hadn't crossed her mind to mention the place to the police.

Juliette lay her head on the table and wept. She couldn't have made more of a mess of everything if she'd tried. Joe moving up here was the first good thing that had happened in ages – but he'd made it quite clear that he was only doing it because he missed Freddie.

Juliette was sobbing so hard now that she didn't hear Joe come into the room.

'Sweetheart,' he whispered. 'Jules, what's the matter? Is it my note? Is it that bastard Tim Dawner who's upset you? I'll kill him.'

Joe knelt by her side and took hold of her hand. It felt strong and reassuring. But she would have given anything for him to take her in his arms instead.

'Yes,' wept Juliette. 'I mean no. Oh, I don't know.'

'My God, you must be ill,' smiled Joe. He smoothed her fringe back tenderly. 'I've never known you so lost for words before. Come on, tell me what's the matter.'

'Why did you go and sleep in Freddie's room?' she cried accusingly.

Joe looked surprised at this.

'What? That's not the reason you're so upset, is it? But that's ridiculous, Jules. I decided to sleep in there because you were feeling so ill and I didn't want to disturb you. And anyway, I didn't think you'd mind.

You've made it pretty clear you can't stand the sight of me over the last few weeks.'

Juliette stared at Joe in incomprehension.

'But . . . but that's not true.'

'Isn't it? All I remember is that man Dawner ringing on Christmas Day and then you going all frosty on me.'

'But it was you being frosty to me,' said Juliette. 'And when I saw the piece in the *Daily News* about you having an affair with Annie Smith it all fell into place.'

Joe groaned at the very thought of the spiteful *Daily News* piece. He was surprised, though, that Juliette hadn't mentioned it before.

'Are you telling me you believe everything you read in the *News* diary?'

'No, of course I don't. They get loads of stuff wrong.'

'Well then. Did it ever occur to you that the diary piece was a load of garbage?'

'Maybe,' admitted Juliette. 'But Annie was with you at Willy's flat that day. I saw her with my own eyes. And it was pretty obvious that something had been going on. You were only wearing a towel. And you'd just got out of bed. When me and Freddie arrived, I mean.'

This time it was Joe's turn to look mystified. He thought back to the afternoon Juliette and Freddie had turned up at the flat. Suddenly everything fell into place.

'But sweetheart, that was *Anne*. She's Willy's new cleaning lady. She was at the flat doing – guess what? – the cleaning. You've got completely the wrong end of the stick. There's nothing going on between me and Anne. And Annie Smith is – I mean she was – my producer at Radio Wave.'

'So did something happen between you and this Annie Smith?' asked Juliette.

Joe hesitated. For a split second he was tempted to lie through his teeth, pretend that the *News* had got it all wrong and there had never been anything whatsoever between him and Annie.

'Well no,' he said slowly. 'It didn't. But I admit it could have. We were close for a bit and there was a moment when we could have got closer. But we didn't, Jules. I swear to you we didn't. I couldn't go through with it. It's you I love. You know that.'

'Do I?' mumbled Juliette.

Joe took her face in his hands and gazed at her intently.

'Bloody hell. You should do by now. Why do you think I'm coming home if it's not because I love you?'

'Because you love Freddie,' said Juliette.

'Yes of course I love Freddie. You know I adore him. But I love you too, Jules. I always have. Surely you know that I'm coming home because I want to live with *both* of you?'

'But everything's gone so wrong between us recently. You'd never have looked at Annie Smith in a million years if things had been fine with us. And I'd never have looked at Tim . . .'

Juliette clapped her hands to her mouth, aware of what she'd just said.

'I mean, nothing happened – but it nearly did,' she muttered. 'I was so lonely without you. You seemed so preoccupied with your new life and your exciting new friends and your game show . . .'

It was a few moments before Joe replied. Juliette was terrified she'd ruined everything. She wished she'd never mentioned Tim Dawner's name.

'Do you know what I think?' he said.

'What?'

'I think all these problems date back to one thing – the day we stopped talking to each other. You were convinced that I had far more thrilling things on my mind than you and Freddie. Weren't you? And I truly thought that you didn't want me any more . . .'

'That just wasn't true,' protested Juliette. 'But I suppose I wanted everything. I wanted you and Freddie and a career and a life away from grotty old South London and . . .'

She stopped, reluctant to go on.

'And what else?' prompted Joe.

'. . . Another baby,' she whispered.

Joe looked stunned by this last disclosure.

'But sweetheart, you never said. Why didn't you say so before? I thought you didn't want any more children.'

Juliette looked straight at Joe.

'Well I do.'

'Then we will,' said Joe. 'I'd love another baby too. And Freddie would adore a little brother or sister.'

Juliette's face lit up at Joe's last remark.

'Do you really mean that?'

'Of course I do. I'd love it. I'd absolutely love it. There's nothing I'd love more. We can start trying straight away . . .'

'Well actually,' began Juliette. She wasn't sure how to broach this. 'You know how terrible I've been feeling for the last few days?'

'Mmmm,' said Joe. 'Poor darling. I'm sure you'll feel better soon. We could start trying then, couldn't we? What do you think?'

'We won't have to,' said Juliette. 'I'm pregnant already. About six weeks.'

Joe stared at her, a look of utter astonishment on his face.

'What?' he cried. This was the last thing he'd been expecting. 'Have you done a test? Are you sure?'

Juliette nodded.

'But that's fan-bloody-tastic,' he yelled. 'Why on earth

didn't you tell me before? I can't believe you didn't tell me.'

'I only found out myself a couple of days ago. And I didn't know whether you'd be pleased or not.'

'That, sweetheart, is only the most brilliant news I've had in six years. It's the most brilliant news since we discovered that Freddie was on the way. Do you remember how you felt? You couldn't take it in at all. You had to do about a hundred pregnancy tests before you believed it was true. I had to look at so many blue lines my eyes started to go funny.'

Juliette smiled at this memory. Joe was absolutely right. She'd wanted Freddie so much that she'd done test after test – unable to take in the momentous news.

'You look shattered, sweetheart,' said Joe. 'Come on. It's time you went back to bed. You've got to start taking better care of yourself. You need your sleep even more now.'

Juliette wrapped her arms around him and nuzzled her face in his neck.

'I'll go back to bed – but on one condition,' she murmured.

'What's that?'

'That you come with me. I don't want you sleeping in Freddie's bloody bunk bed any more . . .'

'Sweetheart,' said Joe, rubbing his aching back. 'I thought you'd never ask . . .'

Epilogue

Juliette couldn't take her eyes off the small chestnut-haired figure standing on the stage. Dressed in long white robes, the little boy was narrating the Christmas story. His voice was confident and clear, with just a hint of a Cumbrian accent.

'Aren't you proud, Joe?' whispered Juliette when Freddie reached the end of his speech. 'He's a natural, isn't he? Half the shepherds got their words wrong. *And* one of the three kings. But Freddie was word perfect all the way through.'

Joe smiled and squeezed her hand.

'I'm really proud,' he murmured. 'But you'd better sssh or you'll wake Junior down there. And if she starts bawling you'll never hear the last of it from Freddie.'

Instinctively Juliette and Joe both glanced down at the angelic bundle dozing in the car seat at their feet. Lucy Rose Ward was ten weeks old now, a gorgeous little girl with chubby cheeks, blue eyes and a few tufts of white-blonde hair.

Freddie had been highly sceptical about his parents bringing his new sister to the school nativity play.

'But she'll cry, Mummy,' he'd protested. 'It'll be so embarrassing.'

'You don't need to worry, sweetheart,' Juliette had soothed, giving him a hug. 'If she makes so much as a squeak I'll take her straight out, I promise you.'

In the event though, as if sensing her brother's anxiety, baby Lucy was as good as gold. She didn't stir till the nativity play ended and the children were taking their bows. Once Mrs Gyngell had thanked the parents for coming, Freddie jumped down off the stage and ran to greet Juliette and Joe.

'You were fantastic, sweetheart,' said Joe, picking Freddie up in his arms. 'We're so proud of you we could burst. So's Lucy. Look, she's smiling at you.'

Freddie glanced at his little sister. He *quite* liked her, he supposed. Well, she wasn't *that* exciting, but she was quite sweet. He just wished she wouldn't cry for her milk so loudly in the middle of the night and wake him up. And as for her nappies – yuk, they were gross.

Seeing this myriad of emotions cross Freddie's face, Juliette and Joe grinned at each other. Considering that Freddie had been an only child for seven years till Lucy's arrival, he was coping with his younger sibling pretty well.

Juliette couldn't believe the transformation in her son over the past twelve months. A year ago, he'd been utterly miserable at Newdale. She'd feared he'd never settle in. But now he was the life and soul of the place. He had loads of friends, was a whizz at computers and was completely obsessed with mountain bikes. He and Craig Barker still didn't see eye to eye but at least Craig didn't pick on him any more.

'Is this your new baby?' said a voice behind them.

Juliette whirled round to see Norma Gray smiling shyly at her.

'Norma,' she said, giving her a huge beam. 'Yes. This is Lucy. She's getting on for three months.'

'She's beautiful,' sighed Norma. 'I'm so pleased for you both. I wanted to pop round when I heard but I didn't like to. Not after everything that's happened . . . you know . . .'

Norma's voice trailed away sadly. Without thinking Juliette put her arm around her. She'd been feeling guilty about Norma for months. The woman had virtually gone into hibernation after Dawn snatched Amy's baby. And then she'd had to cope with the shame of Ritchie going to jail again, for having sex with an under-age girl. Norma had carried on working at Newdale, that was true, but she always scuttled off home afterwards, eager to avoid prying eyes.

'How . . . how's Dawn getting on?' said Juliette, steeling herself to ask.

Juliette half-expected the shutters to come down, but Norma's face brightened.

'Oh, she's much better, thank you. She came out of the clinic a few months back and she . . . she seems more like her old self every day. Morton's been such a support, of course. He's stuck by her through everything – he's a dear man. She's lucky to have him. I think she realises that.'

'I'm glad,' said Juliette softly. 'They've had a terrible time. They both deserve a bit of happiness.'

'There's something else too,' said Norma suddenly. 'I haven't told anyone but . . .'

Norma broke off what she was saying, unsure whether to go on.

'You can trust me,' said Juliette. 'I won't mention it, whatever it is . . .'

'It's Dawn,' muttered Norma. 'She's expecting. After all this time, she's expecting.'

Norma's eyes filled with tears of relief. When Dawn had confided in her a couple of months back that she thought she was pregnant Norma had been doubtful. She'd felt guilty for even thinking it but she'd fretted that it might be a figment of Dawn's imagination.

But then she'd accompanied Dawn to see the doctor in Bowater and with her own ears heard him confirm that her daughter was indeed pregnant.

So fingers crossed, Dawn and Morton were going to be parents at last.

As everyone filed out of the school hall, Joe hand in hand with Freddie, Juliette carrying Lucy, Joe caught Juliette's eye.

'Happy?' he mouthed at her.

Juliette reflected for a moment. She and Joe still had their moments – but didn't everyone? Joe's second series of *Joking Apart* had just ended and he feared there might not be another. And while she was loving every minute of her maternity leave, she dreaded the thought of leaving Lucy and Freddie and returning to the *Eagle*.

But deep down, yes, Juliette *was* happy. All that really mattered to her were Joe, Freddie and Lucy. And if they were all right, then everything was.

'Blissful,' beamed Juliette. 'And if Lucy sleeps for six hours on the trot like she did last night then everything will be just perfect.'

Moving On

Emma Lee-Potter

There's a first time for everything . . .

Kate and Laura Hollingberry are sisters. But whilst they have a close relationship, they couldn't be more different. While Laura is happy to get an undemanding little job to pass the time until she finds Mr Right, Kate wants more out of life than just a suitable husband.

Kate wants a career too. Determined to make her own way in life and not rely on her tycoon father's money or influence, she's taken a position at a local newspaper far away from home. But it's her first job, her first bid for independence, and anything can happen . . .

Praise for *Moving On*:

'A fresh, contemporary women's read' *Publishing News*

Praise for *Hard Copy*:

'pacy exposé . . . tightly written, with snappy dialogue' *Daily Mail*

'fast and furious' *The Mirror*

'An authentic witty insight into life behind the headlines' *Books Magazine*

Would I Lie To You?

Francesca Clementis

Lauren Connor doesn't usually tell lies. She's really only trying to make conversation when she meets Chris Fallon at her best-friend Stella's party. But somewhere between running out of small talk and agreeing to a date, she ends up telling a few inconsequential lies to make herself seem more likeable. Now Lauren's going to have to deal with the fall-out from her fabrications . . .

If that wasn't enough, she's about to get caught in the cross-fire from her well-intentioned friends and relatives. But could it be that Lauren isn't the only one telling lies . . . ?

From the bestselling author of *Big Girls Don't Cry* and *Mad About The Girls*, *Would I Lie To You?* is a warm, witty and intelligent comedy of errors about love, life and deception.

Praise for the novels of Francesca Clementis:

'A tangle of lies and lives worthy of *Cold Feet* . . . perceptive and funny' *Mirror*

'BOOK OF THE WEEK . . . a refreshingly funny portrayal of the realities of relationships' *Sunday Mirror*

'Read this . . . Hysterical!' *Now*

'Top read' *Company*

'. . . wickedly funny – we can't wait for her next' *Sunday Post*